THE
CORSET

THE
CORSET

LAURA PURCELL

RAVEN BOOKS
LONDON · OXFORD · NEW YORK · NEW DELHI · SYDNEY

Raven Books
Bloomsbury Publishing Plc
50 Bedford Square, London, WC1B 3DP, UK

BLOOMSBURY, RAVEN BOOKS and the Raven Books logo are trademarks of
Bloomsbury Publishing Plc

First published in Great Britain 2018

ISBN: HB: 978-1-4088-8961-9; TPB: 978-1-4088-8960-2; EBOOK: 978-1-4088-8959-6

2 4 6 8 10 9 7 5 3 1

Typeset by Integra Software Services Pvt. Ltd.
Printed and bound in Great Britain by CPI Group (UK) Ltd, Croydon CR0 4YY

MIX
Paper from
responsible sources
FSC® C020056
FSC
www.fsc.org

To find out more about our authors and books visit www.bloomsbury.com and sign
up for our newsletters

For Steph

Oh, Men, with Sisters dear!
Oh, Men, with Mothers and Wives!
It is not linen you're wearing out,
But human creatures' lives!
Stitch – stitch – stitch,
In poverty, hunger and dirt,
Sewing at once, with a double thread,
A Shroud as well as a Shirt.

But why do I talk of Death?
That Phantom of grisly bone,
I hardly fear its terrible shape,
It seems so like my own –

From 'The Song of the Shirt',
Thomas Hood (1799–1845)

I

Dorothea

My sainted mother taught me the seven acts of corporeal mercy: to feed the hungry; refresh the thirsty; clothe the naked; shelter the traveller; comfort the sick; visit those imprisoned; and bury the dead. Most of these we undertook together, while she lived. Then Papa and I buried her, so that was another one checked off the list.

A single merciful act eluded me: visiting those imprisoned. A lady in my position has ample opportunity to feed and clothe, but who can she call upon in gaol? Which of her genteel acquaintances is ever incarcerated?

I mentioned the difficulty to my father once, at breakfast. My words hung in the air with the steam from our tea; hot, uncomfortable. I can still see Papa's grey eyes narrow over the pages of his newspaper.

'Charity is not a competition, Dorothea. These "acts of mercy" – you do not need to perform them all.'

'But, sir, Mama said—'

'You know your mother was a ...' He looked down at his paper, searching for the word. 'She had odd notions about religion. You must not take what she said to heart.'

We were silent a moment, feeling her absence in the empty chair at the end of the table.

'Mama was a Papist,' I told my toast as I buttered it. 'I am not ashamed of that.'

Had I sworn before him, he could not have flushed a brighter hue. His cheeks went puce.

'You are not scampering around prisons,' he barked. 'Never mind your mother – I am your *father*. And I say you are a Protestant. That is my final word on it.'

But Papa never really has the final word.

When I came of age, I inherited my own money from Mama to spend as I pleased. Papa could do nothing when I decided to lay it out in improvements for prisons.

Prison, along with Mama's Catholicism, was attractive to me because it was forbidden, because it was danger-ous. I sat on women's prison boards, set up committees to help the poor wretches in Newgate and purchased pamphlets on Elizabeth Fry.

I cannot say these actions made me a darling of soci-ety, but I acquired friends enough for my liking: charitable spinsters, rectors' wives. Far worthier people than the fash-ionable young ladies Papa wished for me to associate with.

'How do you expect to find a husband,' he said, 'when you are always off on these squalid sallies to gaol?'

'I am fair and I have an ample dowry from Mama,' I retorted. 'If any man is fool enough to be put off by a few charitable enterprises, he does not deserve me.'

So I won my way, as I always do.

Two years ago the Oakgate Charitable Women's Society began a project to dismantle the old, sinking hulk that passed for a penitentiary in these parts and build a new prison. That was my chance. When the women's wing was complete, the Society ruled it would be beneficial for lady visitors to call upon the inmates and improve them with edifying conversation. Naturally, I volunteered.

In my visits, I have seen many wretches. Desperate, friendless, craving comfort. But I have never met a crim-inal quite like her.

I was feeding Wilkie, my pet canary, this morning when the note from Matron arrived, informing me we *had another one*. I knew she meant the worst of all criminals: a taker of human lives. My blood began to hum. I ordered the carriage and dashed for my hat and gloves.

Anticipation dried my mouth as I rumbled along in the carriage towards the prison. One never knows what to expect with a murderer. When I was young, I used to imagine they all had compelling reasons to commit their deeds: a stolen lover; vengeance for a parent; betrayal; blackmail. This is a fallacy. Murder can have the strangest, most mundane of motives – or sometimes none at all.

I remember Mrs Blackwood, who maintained that she 'never drowned those poor dear children, it was *them* that came and did it, *they* were always killing and *they* always made her watch'. Then there was Miss Davies, who told me she 'bore no malice to the young black, never did mind his kind, but alas it was necessary for him to die, a sacrifice had to be made'. Most chilling of all, I think, was Mrs Wren. Yes, she had killed her husband. Did he beat her? No. Visit other women? Oh no, never. Had he in fact done anything to merit his death? Certainly, the brute – he had criticised her cooking. Not in general, no, just the once. It was enough. What wife would *not* kill him, she wanted to know.

Phrenology is the only answer to the behavioural patterns of these women. They are born with the propensity to kill. It is all there, mapped out on the cranium. If precautions are not taken, or the wrong organs become inflamed, they give way to vice. Our society is at fault in neglecting this essential science. Had we measured the heads of these females whilst they were young, we might have averted their crime by careful instruction and conditioning. Alas, I fear the cerebral malformation has now progressed too far. And if we cannot change their characters, what hope for their souls?

New Oakgate Prison reared up from the horizon, its stone shining white as redemption. Scaffolding covered the unfinished male wing, but within it I discerned the contours and the gaps where the windows would eventually gleam. On the women's side, we have them shaped like portholes, giving the place the feel of a great steam paddler. Saplings ring the high, iron fences. One day they shall grow and cover the exercise yard in green shade. It looks like a hopeful place, a place where perhaps all is not lost.

The porters opened the gates, which did not whine or clank but glided easily on their fresh hinges. As I climbed out of the carriage and arranged my skirts, another porter met me and marked my name off in his ledger. Then came one of our warders to guide me through the limewashed corridors I know by heart, straight to the office of our principal matron.

She was sitting at her desk. When I entered she rose with a clink, drawing my eyes to the leather belt about her waist and the keys suspended from it. They did not look like instruments of incarceration. They were polished, shining with the same spanking newness of the gaol. Her office smelt fresh, of wood and lime.

'Miss Truelove. How prompt you are.' She offered me a curtsey and another metallic jingle.

'But of course, Matron. I am all eagerness to meet our new inmate.'

Her face moved into an expression – I am not sure what it was, but it was certainly not a smile.

Matron is one of those unreadable women who fade so easily into the mechanics of an institution: age indeterminate; features regular and without distinction; voice monotonous. Even her skull remains concealed beneath a starched cap, showing no discernible bumps. If I was forced to reach a conclusion, I would say she does not like me – but of course she offers no evidence, nothing tangible for me to base this on.

'I must urge you to observe caution, Miss Truelove. This one is dangerous.'

A thrill chased up my spine. 'Murder, I think you said?'

'Yes indeed.'

'Was it dreadfully grisly?'

'No.' Her mouth tightened, but her voice did not change. 'Devious. She killed her own mistress. Slowly, by degrees.'

Not an act of passion, then. I yearned to ask how she committed the deed, but I reined in my curiosity. Matron is not like me; she does not question motives and hope for change. It is enough for her to ensure the women are fed and clothed – she does not appear to believe the prisoners possess souls.

'A maid, I presume? What age is she?'

'That is the worst of all. She is but sixteen years old.'

A child!

I had never met a child murderer. This would enhance my work greatly – to assess the tender skull and see if the criminal organs had already grown to their full extent.

'Her name?' I asked.

'Ruth Butterham.'

I appreciated that plosive surname: it seemed to strike the air like a fist.

'Perhaps you will take me to her cell?'

Matron obeyed in silence.

Our footsteps crunched on the sanded floors, stopping finally outside a barrier of iron. Such a large door,

I thought, to keep a child in. The enamel plaque swung blank – Ruth had not been there long enough to have her name and sentence inscribed.

Matron creaked open the iron observation flap on the door. Holding my breath, I leant forwards and peeked through.

I shall never forget that first sight of her. She sat on the side of her bed, fully dressed, with a spiral of tarred rope on her lap. Her head was bent, her shoulders stooped, so I could not make out her height, but it seemed to me she was no more than the average size. Wiry black hair fell about her temples. The staff crop it short, to the chin. This helps keep the prisoners free of vermin and gives them the look of a penitent. Yet somehow the operation had the opposite effect on Ruth Butterham – she appeared to have *more* hair than an innocent woman, for it frizzed and expanded into a dark aureole around her head. I could not glimpse the criminal organs of the skull beneath. Perhaps the centre of Murder above the ear was engorged, but I would have to feel with my hands.

I did not despair of her letting me perform such an experiment. The picture she presented was one of tranquillity. Her hands moved smoothly as she picked at clumps of oakum. Certainly, the arms were muscular, but not in a menacing way, the definition of the biceps being a natural occurrence in those who work for their bread.

'You want to talk to her, I suppose. We've been short on murderers, since the hangman took Smith.' Matron did not wait for my response before she clanked her keys and let us in.

The girl glanced up as I entered. Dark eyes, framed by stubby lashes, tracked my movements. Her hands stopped their motion. The rope fell slack. I swallowed, feeling every tendon in my throat. How could she bear to hold the thing, knowing her life might end with such a rope around her neck?

'Butterham, this is Miss Truelove,' said Matron. She gave a sniff that might have been disapproval. 'Come to visit you.'

I sat down on the one chair provided in the cell. Its legs were uneven; I had to adjust my skirts.

Ruth looked me full in the face. Not impertinent, precisely, but curious. I must confess to a twinge of disappointment. She was a plain creature, almost masculine, with a strong jaw and eyes set too far apart in her head. The nose was curiously flat. *Flat nose, flat mind*, they say. But then I have noted that murderous thoughts seldom trouble the pretty and the fashionable.

'I don't know you,' she said.

'Not yet.' I tried a smile – it felt rather foolish. She did not speak with a child's voice. Hers sounded tired, harsh. Something in its depths caused the hair on my neck to prick up. 'I come to visit all of the women. Especially those with no kin.'

'Well, you can suit yourself, I suppose, a rich woman like you.'

She began to pick at the rope again. As her hands moved, her eyes drifted over the mug, trencher and Bible neatly laid on the windowsill. I noted how deft she was, how continually handling the oakum had stained her nails and the creases in her fingers black. 'Perhaps I do have the liberty to come and go as I please. But I do not attend for my own amusement. I come for you. To offer some comfort.'

'Hmm.'

She did not believe a word of it. Perhaps there has been no kindness in her short life.

'I'll stand outside,' said Matron. 'The observation hatch is open. No funny business, Butterham.'

Ruth did not deign to reply.

The door clanged shut, and I was alone with the child murderer.

Strange to say, I have never called upon a prisoner who had more self-possession. Grown women like Jenny Hill have sobbed on my shoulder, or begged me for mercy. Not she. This was no weeping girl, no child in need of mothering. The more she picked at the rope, the more it seemed to resemble a pile of human hair in her lap.

She killed her slowly, by degrees.

I shook myself. I must not leap to conclusions: not all silences are sinister. After all, the crown of her head looked enlarged beneath that fuzzy hair – it might be that her organ for Dignity was overgrown. Or that she had never known the meaning of the word *comfort*. How could I expect her to turn her thoughts upwards and repent if she had been starved of sympathy? She needed to learn what it was to have a friend. She needed *me*.

I cleared my throat. 'Matron calls you Butterham. It is the way of the staff here, I believe. But I should like to address you by your Christian name. You do not object to my calling you Ruth?'

She shrugged. The muscles on her shoulders pulled at her serge gown. 'If you like.'

'Do you know why you are here, Ruth?'

'I'm a murderess.' No pride in the title – little shame, either. I waited, sure of more to follow. But she just went on impassively picking, with none of that torrid explanation or madness I have come to expect.

It chilled me.

'And who was it that you killed?'

Her brow clouded. She fluttered her short lashes. 'Oh, I suppose – a great many people, miss.'

I was not prepared for that. Were there others the police had not discovered?

The blasted rope dust irritated my eyes, making it hard to think. Perhaps Ruth did not know the exact allegations against her? We have had instances where the enormity of a prisoner's deed wipes their mind of the incident. Had she suppressed the memory of killing her mistress? Did she merely parrot the keepers when she told me she was incarcerated for murder? I decided to tread cautiously.

'Indeed? And are you sorry for what you have done?'

Two yellow teeth worried her bottom lip. 'Yes. Well, I mean, it depends, miss.'

'Upon?' I could not prevent the note of incredulity that crept into that word. 'Are there qualifications for remorse?'

'Some I never meant to kill. The first, they were an accident.' Her voice hitched, the first crack in her facade. 'Then there were others … I tried to stop. I tried to stop it, but it was too late.' A sigh. 'I'm sorry for those ones. But … '

'Yes?'

'There were a few …' That strong chin jutted out, took possession of the face once more. 'A few I hated.'

My tongue itched to call Matron back. If what Ruth said was true, there were more murders the police should be made aware of. Yet to 'peach' on her, as the prisoners say, so early in our acquaintance would ruin any chance of gaining her trust. I would never get my fingers on that scalp and prove what she truly was.

'So … you do not regret killing the people you disliked?' I reproached.

Her dark eyes pinned me. 'What do you think?'

She unnerved me, yet I had a small glimmer of hope. Her expressions of hate were reassuring in their way; proof that she had acted in passion and was not a cold-blooded killer, as I had first apprehended.

Her fingers worked of their own accord while she watched me: scratching, tearing. Skilful, in a frightening way.

'I wonder they have employed you thus,' I said at last. 'Picking is a dirty business. Would you not prefer to make shirts or knit stockings? I am sure if I spoke a word to Matron, she would let you into the sewing room.'

A quirk at the corner of her mouth. Not a grin, exactly, but bordering on it. 'Oh, Matron wants me in the sewing room all right. Had to fight her tooth and nail to stay in here. Don't you think it's rum? They lock me in this place, search everyone who enters in case they slip me something. Then, casual as you like, Matron tells me to go to the sewing room!'

'Why should she not? Do you not find sewing a wholesome, industrious occupation?'

For an instant, her face lit up with humour. 'Oh, miss!'

'What is it? I do not understand you.'

'It's in the sewing room that I'm most dangerous!'

Perhaps she was a trifle mad, after all. I decided I would leave off telling Matron about the other murders until I was quite sure they had taken place. It would be mortifying to be fooled by the ravings of a delusional prisoner and have Matron snickering behind my back.

'Sewing is not dangerous. There is a small risk, I grant you, with needles and pins but they are careful. They always have an attendant to supervise. You cannot really hurt someone with a needle, Ruth.'

She cocked her dark head. I felt gooseflesh, skittering over my skin.

'Can't I?'

2

Ruth

If I'd been born a boy, it never would have happened. I never would have picked up a needle, never known the power I possessed, and my life would've gone down some other path. I might have been able to make my way in the world, to defend my mother. But instead I shared the fate of all girls who are poor of pocket: I was tied to my work, like a needle tethered by thread.

You can live your life through a piece of sewing; that's what people don't realise. You can ply your needle with any emotion in the human heart and the thread will absorb it. You can sew with tenderness, you can stitch yourself from panic to calm, you can sew with hate. Sewing in a fury never got me anything except tangled skeins and botched seams, but you can do it. Better to wait for hate. A slow, measured hate. No one can tell it's there, simmering in your fingertips, except for you and the needle.

People say hate is a wasted emotion, a destructive force you can do nothing useful with. They're wrong. I've gripped rage, I've wielded it like a weapon. But look at your face, miss. You've never hated one of your fellow creatures, have you?

It takes someone special to make you feel it for the first time. A person you would love, if they'd only let you. But their scorn shrivels you up, like a crape gown in the rain. They show you an image of yourself, and it's weak and loathsome, even to your own eyes. Yes, it takes someone with a peculiar talent for cruelty to make you hate them like that.

Someone like Rosalind Oldacre.

She was a doll of a girl. Long, blonde curls. When she walked, it was with poise, a maturity far beyond the rest of us. Of course the teachers adored her. I could tell you about many things she did to me, that year when I was twelve, at Mrs Howlett's finishing school. But there was only one that really mattered.

It happened on an afternoon in early autumn, when the days began to close in. The school bell rang and we all poured out into crisp, cool air. Already the moon bobbed above waves of grey cloud. Braziers burnt in the square. I scurried across the cobbles, watching the other girls peel off into the side streets.

Going home ought to be the best part of the day, but for me it was a time of heightened awareness, where every sound and sudden movement made me jump. It was the time I needed to run.

There was a passageway opposite the school, at the other end of the square. If I could make it through that quickly, I'd be safe for the rest of the evening.

Sometimes I was fast enough.

Not that day.

That day Rosalind was already there, lurking in the shadows that filled the passage. I stumbled to a halt beside a brazier as I caught sight of her. A bonnet concealed her blonde curls. Beneath it her expression was stiff.

'Butterham.' I'd always liked my name before, but now it sounded shameful, inappropriate on her rosehip lips.

Other girls trailed at her heels, their faces turned into a confusion of shades and hollows by the flames in the brazier.

'Let me pass,' I begged.

'You're poor, Butterham. You were made to take orders, not give them to your betters.' The dusk heightened her looks but it was a terrible beauty, a frightful one.

'Let me pass!'

'I do not see how I am stopping you.'

Her slender frame didn't fill the passageway. I might slip past her, but there were others behind, their eyes shining in the gloaming like rodents' do. A gauntlet of girls. Dare I run it?

I launched myself forwards and tried to shove through but Rosalind caught me, her fingers sharp at my waist. 'Not fast enough, not strong enough! I would not employ you. How ever will you earn your bread?'

Girls massed around me, penned me in. Something hit my nose and pain fizzed to the back of my throat.

Rosalind was right: I wasn't strong, then. I couldn't push my gabbling words through my lips, let alone break free from her grip.

Hands scuffed at my bodice. Material ripped. 'You are not a lady, you shouldn't be wearing these clothes! You belong in the gutter, Butterham. You're a rat, a beast!'

They hooted. Cold air rushed inside my smock as they exposed my corset, my shift.

'Look at this,' Rosalind laughed to a girl behind her. 'Tight lacing. She's trying to be fashionable! You'll never get a good silhouette, Butterham. Not with these corset bones.' Her fingers nipped at my waist, tight, tight. 'Cheap. What are they, cane? Goose-quill?'

I screwed up my courage and spat in her face.

All at once, she dropped me. My cheek hit the cobbles with a crack. Before I could gather my wits, her black, pointed boot flew towards me. Pain exploded in my ribs.

'You see? They are really very weak supports.' The girls gathered about her, each a malicious shadow. Row upon row of dark feet. 'Cane bones are useless in a corset. How long will it take for them to break?'

It took longer than you'd think.

The streets were winding down for the evening by the time I dragged myself up and back towards home. Gone were the milkmaids and the fruit mongers; in their place lay orange peel and heaps of manure. No running boys, no clattering wheels. Only the sellers of second-hand clothes shambled by, and the pie man – I couldn't see him but I smelt him, rich and meaty through the coal smoke.

The refuse of market day lay on the cobbles and I, the refuse of all things, walked over it. Hateful, unwanted. My feet pattered across puddles, around horse dung, and every step was agony. A cold, fearful sweat had coated me from head to foot, leaving salt crystals to rub raw beneath my shift.

I had a cloak – too short for me, but still service-able – which I used to cover my bodice. I didn't want Ma to see the footprints and the rips. Even so, I couldn't conceal my limp. I couldn't control the sharp intake of breath every time a snapped corset bone poked into my skin. As for my bonnet, I dragged it behind me on its broken ties.

If I didn't get inside the house and upstairs without being seen, I'd have to tell my parents everything. That would be more painful than another beating.

Our house was modest, hunching in a terrace of identical siblings near the river. Three rooms up, two down,
and an ash privy behind. Many had it worse. When I
pushed open the battered, unvarnished door and stepped
inside, the air was clean, if chill. Ma sat in the window,
syphoning the last rays of the sun.

My ma was always marooned in a sea of material:
cheap linen, cambric, wads of muslin. Sometimes I
fancied it sucked the colour from her, leaving another
grey streak in the black hair, another cloud in the blue
eyes.

I crept towards the stairs.

She didn't hear me come in. Her focus on the eye of
her needle was complete. I watched her lick the thread
and slot it through the tiny hole in one smooth motion.

My foot creaked on the bottom step.

Ma jumped. 'Ruth?' Rising stiffly to her feet, she
stared across the white expanse of cotton separating us.
'Whatever happened to your bonnet?'

Was it too late to run? I took another step up, but she
was already fussing about the linen, pushing aside piles
to make her way over to me.

'Nothing, nothing happened,' I said hurriedly.

'It doesn't look like nothing! Your bonnet is crushed!
I told you to mind it, we cannot afford another.'

Why did she care about the bonnet? It was *I* who
needed sewing together.

She grabbed the hem of my cloak, pulling me back
towards her. 'How could you be so careless? I have
nothing to replace the ties, let alone the *time* … You'll
just have to wear it like that and look foolish. Perhaps
then you'll learn to keep things nice.'

It was too much. On top of all the pain, Ma scolding!
My eyes began to prick and sting, as if I'd taken every

pin from Ma's cushion and rammed them through my
pupils. 'I'll never have nice things. Never!'

'What do you mean, Ruth? This was the best—'

'No!' I yelled. 'Everything I wear, everything about
me – it's ugly!'

A beat.

'Ugly!' A mother's indignant horror, high-pitched. But
I was too quick for her – I saw. I saw the second before
her expression changed. It was in her eyes, red-rimmed
and bloodshot: shame. She had known, all along. 'What
put a wicked thought like that inside your head?'

My tears came gushing out. I cried, in those days.

'Oh, Ruth!' She took me into her arms. Those infer-
nal corset bones scratched against my bruises like claws.
That, and her familiar scent of linen and faded rose petals
made me cry even harder. 'Forgive me. I didn't think …
Was it the other girls? Did they do this?'

Of course, it never would have happened to Ma:
petite, elegant Ma. I'd failed her. Failed her with my eyes
too far apart, my blunt chin.

I sobbed.

'My poor darling.' She took out her handkerchief, the
one with the monogram in the corner, the only one left
from the old days, and dabbed at my face. 'You sit down
and cry it out. I'll fetch you some supper.' She stroked
my hair behind my ears. 'Don't worry, my Ruth, I'll fix
your bonnet. We'll find a way.'

She sat me in the chair with the shiny seams and a
moth-eaten antimacassar: the best chair in the house.
Not that it was comfortable to me, sitting bruised in a
broken corset. Placing the handkerchief on my lap, she
disappeared into the kitchen.

Pots rattled. Trying to steady my breath, I picked up
the handkerchief and ran my fingers over the monogram.

Old, friendly stitches, worn and loose. *J T.* Jemima Trussell. The Ma of the past, before she met Pa, before her fingers turned scaly. I closed my eyes, rubbing the letters, praying somehow they'd transform me into that young lady.

'I can stitch the rim up good as new,' she called from the kitchen. 'We'll have to replace the ties, but I'm sure I'll find something in my stores.' Another clatter. 'It isn't *very* squashed. If we stretch it out, the shape might come back.'

Wait until she saw the state of my gown beneath the cloak. Even kind Ma would struggle to cast a fair shade upon *that*.

She reappeared with a heel of bread and a wedge of cheese sweating on a plate. She held a cup in the other hand. 'Tea. It will make you feel better.'

'We can't afford it,' I replied instantly.

'Just this once.' She coaxed the handkerchief out from between my fingers and replaced it with the hot cup. Warmth bit into my palm but it was a good pain, satisfying.

We didn't drink quality tea as you'd do it, miss. The grocers cheat you if they think they can: dye the leaves, bulk them up with wheat. Still, it was a treat for me.

'Do you know,' Ma said, sitting down by my side, 'that I am to blame? I made Pa send you to a school where the girls are … better off. Young ladies, like I once was. I should have realised they would tease you.' Her lips pursed, as they did when she tackled a difficult stitch. 'I'm sorry, Ruth. But you mustn't mind them. They are silly girls and they will soon tire of it. They'll find someone else to torment.'

I took a sip of tea and closed my aching eyes. 'They hate me.'

'They don't hate you. I know how these things are, I remember my own school. Always some petty quarrel going on. Girls' allegiances shift so quickly. Wait until they see your fine needlework! Won't you be the most popular girl, then?'

I didn't answer. I just pulled my cloak closer around me.

'Now, let's see about this bonnet.'

I couldn't eat my supper. I sat staring at my plate as the light slipped from the room, queasy at the thought of food, at the thought of myself. Would they be sitting down to supper too, those cruel, conceited girls? I imagined Rosalind Oldacre at a table spread with clean linen, lit by a pair of candlesticks. She pushed her glossy, blonde curls behind her ears and cut up a salmon, taking tiny, delicate bites. If only I could hurt her, the way she'd hurt me. If only I could pick up one of those silver candlesticks and smash in the white teeth. Then she'd know what it was to have girls laugh at her, to feel the shame of her face.

'Stop it, Ma.' I set my plate down, untouched, on the floor. The cheese glowed, a miniature moon. 'You'll get behind if you work on my bonnet.'

A thought seemed to strike Ma. She smiled with a mouth full of pins. 'Maybe you can do some of the Metyard work for me.' She spat the pins out and set them on the arm of her chair. 'Would you like that?'

Shadows cloaked her, I couldn't tell if she was serious. 'What if I make a mistake?'

'You won't. I trust you.'

She rose and crossed to the other side of the room. My stomach clenched. The Metyard work! The holiest of holies, the fine fabrics that mustn't be marked. Mrs Metyard made Ma buy it all in advance from her shop. If the work was late or spoiled, she paid a fine.

'Look at this. A piece of fancy embroidery if ever we had it. Gloves for a bride.' She laid the shot silk down on my lap reverently, as if it were a sleeping child. White warp, blue weft. A sheen ran down the shaft of the thumb. Beautiful. The wearer would have moonbeams at her fingertips. Ma had begun to embroider a pattern of orange blossom and myrtle in silver thread on the left hand. 'I made up that pattern myself, can you see? All you need to do is copy it.'

I swallowed. My mouth was dry. I wanted to smash and destroy but here was another path for the storm raging inside me: to create.

'Let me wash my hands,' I croaked.

Never before had she let me touch the Metyard work. I knew she was taking a risk, trusting me with something important, just to make me feel better. If I refused or made a mistake, I wouldn't get another chance.

Going upstairs, I took off the cloak and winched myself out of my ruined clothes. With a great deal of pain and cursing, I managed to change into a fresh shift and gown – a long-sleeved, high-necked one that hid my bruises. When I returned to Ma, she'd lit a tallow candle.

'Silk can be slippery to work with, Ruth. The silver thread is coarse; it sticks if you're not careful.'

'I'll be careful.'

I gathered the gloves into my hands, ready to embroider. Just one touch and I could feel the denier, sense the holes I'd make. We knew each other, those gloves and I.

Smoke from the candle stung my eyes, already sore from weeping. The silver thread glittered fiercely in the flame. I squinted until all I could see was the tip of my needle. And then my hands moved by themselves.

Tears pooled in my eyes as I worked. My mind went over the events of the day, bringing them up in a reflux: every taunt, every kick, every tug to my hair.

I thought of the bride who would wear these gloves: an image in white with a man ready to swear eternal devotion to her. I'd never have that. I'd sew gloves and perhaps people would hanker after them, but they'd never want *me*. I'd stand in a haberdasher's with cold money in my hand, while beautiful women put on my gloves and danced out of the shop into their lives.

There were only three things I desired for my future: a face I wasn't ashamed of; a husband to love me; the ability to make and wear gorgeous clothes. It didn't seem a lot to ask. But already, at only twelve years of age, I was learning those things would never be. *Could* never be. So what was I to do with my life?

'Ruth!'

I jumped, pricking myself. Instinctively I snatched my injured finger away, caring more for the material than my skin.

'Sit back from the candle, it spits. You'll mark the silk.' Ma came over and lifted the gloves clear of the flame. She examined them, her eyes darting up and down before growing still.

'Have I done it wrong?' I fretted. 'I'm sorry, I can unpick it and—'

'Ruth,' she said.

'Please forgive me, Ma, I—'

'Ruth, how did you do this?'

Her eyes didn't move from the gloves. My needle dangled from the untied thread, winking in and out of existence in the candlelight.

Shaking the cramp out of my hand, I hunched over in the chair, expecting a scolding. Why had I let my thoughts run away with me? I should have focused on the task, I should have been careful.

'Where did you see this?'

For the first time in over an hour, I studied the silver shapes I'd sewn. Blinked. I hadn't copied Ma's pattern, but improved it. Butterflies hovered over the orange blossom. The myrtle now had berries as well as flowers and buds. Something I'd rendered in the turn of the leaves, the long stamens, made them look real. The left glove, where Ma had started the pattern, would need going over. Beside mine, her embroidery looked plain.

'Did you see this design in a shop window coming home from school?'

I faltered. Perhaps I had. I *hoped* I had. Surely I couldn't sew such a thing without even looking? 'Yes,' I stuttered. 'I ... saw it in a shop.'

Finally, she tore her eyes away from the gloves. They shone, losing their usual worn, bloodshot look. 'But this is brilliant, Ruth, quite brilliant! I *told* you that you were equal to it. Come, let's go and show Pa.'

Hoisting me up by the shoulder, she marched me from the room. I sighed. Always this attempt to involve Pa in our women's business. He didn't live in our world; his was a land of colours and brushstrokes. Sometimes I thought he could see no further than the edge of his canvas.

At one point in time, Ma said, he did rather well with his portraits. Fashionable ladies admired the spark he cast in his sitters' eyes, and his attention to the finest detail of dress.

He didn't get commissions now.

That's why Ma took in piecework and flowering from Mrs Metyard: to keep us afloat. Pa always used that term, *afloat*. And it seemed to me Pa *did* float – he kept his head above the water and painted his pictures. Beneath was Ma, kicking through dirt and reeds.

We knocked on his door and waited for his laconic 'Enter' before going in. Light hit us in a blast; not for Pa the stinking, smoking tallow candles, but a glass-covered oil lamp.

Stacks of canvases leant against the walls. A full-length spaniel in oils faced us, watching me with doleful eyes. I picked my way across paint-spotted floorboards. Behind the easel in the centre of the room stood my father: a handsome, dishevelled man in shirtsleeves and a leather apron. His waistcoat was always buff-coloured, his cravat always loose.

He peered around the side of his canvas. 'Ah! Come to say goodnight, have we? I thought you'd be long abed.' His moustache grew uniformly, but not the hair on his head. It was from him I inherited my fuzzy, unmanageable locks. Pa's corkscrewed to the level of his chin. Even in the days we could afford pomade, it always sprang free from the grease.

'Ruth wanted to show you something.' Ma used the forced, jovial tone reserved for speaking about me. 'She has been working hard this evening.'

Miserably, I accepted the gloves from Ma and shuffled to Pa's side. I held them aloft, careful to keep them away from his slick, dangerous brush.

'Oh, you did that, did you? Capital. Very pretty.' His gaze flicked back to his painting. I could see now that it was a city at night, the gas lights reflected in the river. 'I like the … the butterflies.'

Ma cleared her throat. 'It's as fine work as I've ever seen, let alone for a girl her age.'

'And only – how long – at finishing school?'

Ma nudged my shoulder. It hurt, but I said nothing.

'Actually, Ruth has been having some trouble at school today.'

I felt my cheeks flush. That was private, for Ma and me. I didn't want Pa to know.

'Trouble?' he asked absently. 'What sort of trouble?'

'Some girls have been filling her head with wicked lies and upsetting her. Teasing her about her appearance. I expect their clothes are rather finer than the ones we can afford.'

'Now look here, my girl.' He pointed his brush at me. I hunched over the gloves, holding them protectively against my chest. 'Those stuffed-up chits don't know what they're talking about. You have fine qualities, qualities those girls will never acquire.'

'Like a good heart,' Ma put in.

I didn't have that either, but Ma wasn't to know.

'Make them see *you*, Ruth. Your worth. This talent you have with your needle, it is an art. And your true self is in that art, do you see?' He gestured at the gloves again, alarming me with a spray of black dots. I stepped back hastily; they splattered on the floorboards by my feet. 'You are the butterflies, the flowers. Inside you possess everything the other girls lack. When they see that, they will *have* to admire you.'

I let him talk, but his words ran against the tide of everything I knew. At school, this wasn't what happened. If a girl saw another with a quality she lacked, she tore her limb from limb.

'See, Ruth? Those girls talk a lot of rot. Come tomorrow they'll forget all about it. Kiss Pa and then it's time for your bed. I'm sure you'll sleep better now.'

I handed her the gloves and went to him. He took me in his arms, paint-freckled and smelling of whisky. His brown eyes ranged over me, and I think it finally dawned on him that his hair was my hair, his chin was my chin – that he'd inflicted this misery upon me. Features handsome on a man are not so on a woman. It does a girl no good to be the spit of her father.

'Look,' he whispered, 'I keep my gun locked in the desk. If those jades give my girl any more trouble, you let me know, eh? Won't I go after them?' He winked at me.

For the first time that night, I smiled.

3

Dorothea

When I exited the prison, I made it my business to acquaint myself with the particulars of Ruth Butterham's case.

Tilda, my maid, was in the carriage where I had left her, huddled under her shawls. 'Can we go home now, miss?' she asked as I climbed in.

'Soon. I have ordered Graymarsh to stop in town.'

'Oh no, miss.'

I flashed her my best smile. 'Spring is coming on. I have a great fancy to see the botanical gardens – do not you?'

Tilda knew as well as I that our immediate port of call would not be the botanical gardens. First we pulled up in a cobbled street where the smog was tinted a deep shade of brandy. Close by, a police lamp spread a spectral blue glow.

'I hate going in there,' Tilda grumbled. 'Full of drunkards and villains, it is.'

'It shall only be for a moment.'

She pulled her many wraps up around her shoulders. 'Look at that pea-soup! How will I even find the door?'

'The blue lamp will be your guardian angel,' I teased, but she did not find it amusing. She shot me a very saucy look indeed before she jumped out and trotted, cursing, into the brown mist.

Poor Tilda cannot help it, of course – it is the shape of her head. When standing behind her, I have noticed a decided protrusion on the right at the baseline of the crown. Self-Esteem, Self-Love, all the selfish sentiments. She was not formed to wait upon others.

After ten minutes, she huffed back into the carriage. Soot clung to her hair.

'Well?'

She made a show of settling herself into the seat, blowing on her hands and drawing the hot brick near to her feet before she met my eye.

'The botanical gardens,' she said at last. 'Half an hour.'

I drew out my watch and marked the time. 'Excellent. Drive on, Graymarsh.'

Buds adorned the trees growing at the edge of the park where we stopped, close to the black iron railings. Everything was fresh and dewy here, with none of the town smog. Yellow crocuses pushed their heads above the soil. I let down the window to inhale. Greenery. Life.

'I'll get a cold in my head,' Tilda warned.

'Well, Tilda, I am sure you will make the most of it.'

Young ladies were venturing out again, although they made straight for the temperate house. It would be a few weeks yet before nursemaids came with their delicate charges bundled in blankets. I longed to take a turn myself, latched on to David's arm ... But that could not be. Not yet.

As a distant clock struck the hour, he appeared at the end of the road: a tall shape, made even taller by his hat, walking with hands joined behind his back. The sky became brighter, the air a little more fresh.

Each arrival of his brings with it a an echo of our first meeting. The relief I felt to see that figure, running full pelt after the hateful beast who had snatched my reticule. I believe I loved him from that very moment; loved him all the more when he returned my belongings. My precious miniature of Mama was safe inside the bag and it felt as if – I know this is fanciful – he had returned a part of her to me.

I pinched my cheeks. 'Tilda, my bonnet. Straighten my bonnet.'

By the time she had finished, David was nearly upon us. I heard his boots tap on the pavement and, a moment later, he appeared at the window.

'I don't have long,' was the first thing he said.

The poor soul looked done-up: shadowed eyes, dishevelled whiskers and hair that stuck out beneath his hat. I felt rather ashamed of my own leisurely morning.

'You are ever gallant, Constable,' I teased. 'Fortunately, we do not require much of your time.'

'It's been busy,' he explained, fiddling with the buttons on his blue coat. 'I only just managed to get out. I'm not meant to be on patrol until this evening.'

'Pardon me for disturbing you. It is only that I met a new prisoner today, a girl by the name of—'

'Ruth Butterham.' Unbuttoning his coat, he removed a parcel and thrust it through the window. 'Already made the copies, didn't I? Knew you'd be down here the minute they nabbed her.'

I beamed. The parcel felt warm, delicious, and I hugged it to my chest. It carried his scent: wool and cedar wood. 'You really are a dear heart.'

He shook his head, but he could not hide the glow upon his face. 'I can't keep doing this, Dotty. Sneaking down to the archives, copying things out, coming to see you. They'll catch me.'

'Not you. You are too smart for them.'

'They're the *police*.' He jerked his coat up over his shoulders and refastened the buttons. 'They were made for catching people. I know it's hard for you to understand, living as you do, but when you work for your bread, Dotty, you need to keep your wits about you.'

While his eyes were cast down, I took the opportunity to admire him.

This is what a real man does: puts himself at the front of the action, works hard to make the world a better place. Were I born of the stronger sex, I like to think that I would do the same. And yet I know my father, who sits on his rounded behind all day smoking and reading newspapers, would have the gall to sneer at David.

'It is the last one,' I promised.

'You always say that.'

I laughed. 'Well, what do you want me to say?'

He cast a glance at Tilda, who pretended to be intent upon her knitting. I could see she was not concentrating – she had dropped three stitches.

'You know what; I want you to set a date.'

A corkscrew in my chest. 'You know I shall. Only, not yet.'

What it cost me to see his dear brow darken, the disappointment dulling his eyes. 'It's been a year. What is there to stop us now? I could get permission from work to marry. Jones did so, only last week. And I know your father won't like it, but he can't prevent you, you're of age.'

Tilda's needles clacked.

'Yet it would still make a terrible noise in society. I fear even your colleagues would frown upon it. It would be necessary to move away from here, my dearest, and how can we do so without saving first?'

'I think you're wrong. We could stay in Oakgate. It does a fellow credit to set up his own home with a wife. My superiors take the head of a household seriously, sometimes advance them. They already pay me a pound a week, and with your own money ...'

'I have money,' I explained, 'but only for my life-time. There is such a formality in the legal papers ... If I die before Papa, my income reverts to him, not my dependants.'

'What of that?' He glanced behind his shoulder to check no one was near. 'Why should you die before your father?'

I was obliged to avert my eyes and watch Tilda's needles. 'Wives do die, more frequently than spinsters. It is an occupational hazard.'

Tilda lost another stitch.

Comprehension dawned and, with it, a blush. 'Yes. Of course. I didn't consider that,' David mumbled. 'But who knows if God would even bless us with children?'

'We must be prepared. I must save against such an outcome to ensure you and any family would be provided for. It is because I lost my own poor mother that I worry so. You do understand?'

He nodded, slowly. What a perfectly shaped head his is, beneath the stovepipe police-hat! Everything in proportion: the subjective and the objective. You do not come across a specimen like that every day. Especially not combined with a handsome face and an open heart. I cannot afford to lose him. I will never see his like again.

'I understand, but ...' He heaved a sigh. 'It is diffi-cult to wait so long. To keep putting off my mother, when she says I should walk out with a friend's daughter. Sometimes I fear you are playing with me, Dotty. Dangling me.'

This cut me.

What a small modicum of patience the male sex possess! Soldiers and sailors have required their women-folk to wait eternities for them, yet when the shoe is on the other foot, they chafe.

'I worry, too,' I replied with a tremor in my voice. 'I worry that you will grow weary. That it will prove too complicated in the end, to marry a lady of my station, and you will make another selection.'

He did not deny the possibility, but pressed my hand, briefly, before pushing away from the window. 'I must be getting back.' Damp air rushed inside – already the carriage felt colder. 'People will notice me standing here.'

'I will call upon you soon,' I promised.

He touched his hat to me, nodded at Tilda. 'Soon,' he repeated.

Then he was gone.

———

I have locked myself in my room under the pretence of writing letters. Papa would not approve of my reading material. Certainly, it is a frightful perusal. After the horrid detail of the coroner's report, I have been forced to lie down and recover.

The victim – the sole victim, as far as the police are concerned – was a young woman whom Ruth had known for years. A pretty thing, married, not yet a mother. The body was in a dreadfully emaciated state, yet the insides were undamaged, as if supernaturally preserved.

Ruth held a trusted position in the household, I have learnt, even nursing the dying woman in her illness, all the while nursing a secret in her bosom, a black serpent twisting around her vital organs. Servants do kill their masters, of course. I see it often in the newspaper and eye Tilda askance for the next few days. But this ... It seems so calculated. Day after day, the consistency of intent, to murder by hairbreadths. Somehow it would have been more comforting if Ruth had simply stabbed her mistress through the heart.

What troubles me most, I admit, is the memory of Mama wasting away slowly, though from quite another cause. I recognise the descriptions of thinning hair, downy fuzz on the body. A cruel death. And to think someone might have brought it about on purpose ... A mere child!

Why?

I would like to console myself with the idea that Ruth is innocent – that her mistress suffered from a disease similar to my mother's. But there is her own confession, copied out before me. Her words at the prison. The very air around her, prickling with something dark.

My canary, Wilkie, begins to chirp. I prop myself up on one elbow and watch him flutter. His cage is far prettier than Ruth Butterham's.

What will she be doing now? Brooding? Her deadly fingers worrying at the oakum?

I wonder if a girl like that can really be saved. God says *yes*. Even my mother, who died in a similar way to her victim, would have said *yes*. It is my duty to try and lead Ruth to repentance. And more than that. I have a phrenological theory of my own she can assist with.

Ever since the pamphlets began to be mass-produced and the middle classes took to studying the crania, the moralists have become ticklish. They think our discoveries take away the notion of personal responsibility.

For instance, if a person is born with protrusions all through the Torrid Zone, are they not a villain from the cradle? How can we then be justified in punishing them for something they cannot help?

But I wish to plait my faith together with this science. *I* believe the infant skull grows to reflect the soul as it forms, shaped by every decision. If we can detect vice in a timely manner and point the child down another path, the shape of the head, as well as the texture of the spirit, may change.

Should I be able to reform Ruth and prove this, my mind would rest much easier. I could even write to Mr Combe at the Edinburgh Phrenological Society with my findings. Imagine Papa's face then, seeing the studies he has derided endorsed by a learned man!

I recall the incredulous murmur Ruth made when I told her I did not visit the prison for my own amusement. She was right to doubt me. My motives are not *entirely* selfless.

'Well,' I say to Wilkie. 'If I should find a sort of fascination in the lives of these people, if I should derive excitement from rubbing shoulders with depravity, where is the harm in that? It is no less beneficial to *them*.'

He watches me, his eyes shiny like wet pebbles, and begins to sing.

Lifting myself from the bed, I go to my dressing table and tidy my hair. 'I *shall* continue visiting Ruth Butterham,' I tell the girl in the mirror. I might find Ruth distasteful, and the memories of Mama's death hard to bear, but there is fruit to be reaped. I can bring her to salvation, and she can … give me her skull.

'Do not look at me like that,' I scold Wilkie's hopping reflection as I fasten the combs above my ears. 'If I can prove this theory, think how many lives would be saved!'

The gong sounds for dinner. A deep tremble runs through the house. I sit for a moment, feeling the vibrations beneath my skin. Wilkie scuttles to the sandpaper at the bottom of his cage, his feathers puffed out.

He is afraid.

4

Ruth

I didn't talk to Ma about school after that. She was already weary, crumpled like an old bedsheet. I didn't want her to rip. So I hid my torn dress and broken corset, and never told her about the bruises. I trotted off every morning in my battered bonnet and slunk home in the evening, choking on my sense of grievance. When I came in, she looked up, misty-eyed from her work, and asked how my day had been.

I lied.

I only told the truth to the gloves.

I liked to work on the gloves. To feel the cool silk in my hands; to jab a needle through resistant threads.

But one evening, a few weeks later, when we were sewing in the dusk, Ma took them gently from my lap. Even without the sunlight to shine on it, the silver thread gleamed like tears. 'These are a work of art, Ruth. Tie off that thread, and I will take them along to Mrs Metyard's when I go tomorrow. The bride will call for them soon.'

I yearned to snatch them back. Only the delicate nature of the material stopped me. They were *mine*. My work, my labour. I hated the idea of another woman touching them. 'They're not ready yet.'

'Yes they are, they're perfect.' There was a warmth, a pride in her voice I had never heard before. 'I cannot wait to see the look on Mrs Metyard's face when I show them to her. She should give me an extra shilling, in fairness, for work like that.'

I'd never set eyes on Mrs Metyard, but I imagined a showy, middle-aged woman with a squint. How I yearned to fling the money back in her face. Take the gloves, use them to conceal my own calloused fingers and broken nails. Become someone else.

But as Ma laid the gloves back on my lap, I saw how hopeless it was. A girl like me, in her mended and stained gowns, could never wear gloves of this quality. It was as Rosalind Oldacre said: I wasn't a lady. To them, I would always be little more than a beast. I could never have what I wanted.

Ma perched on the edge of the comfortable chair, hands clasped. Lines of worry pleated her forehead. 'You have … enjoyed working on the gloves?' she asked tentatively.

I gathered them closer to me. 'Yes.'

'So you would not object to helping me with more embroidery?'

Could there be another project as beautiful? I closed my eyes, dreamt of heavy felted wool, shimmering taffeta, a rainbow spread of cotton. A girl could lose herself in colours like that. 'No.'

'That's good. Because I thought perhaps you might learn the work alongside me. As a kind of apprentice. Only there would be some … changes.' Her voice caught, like a knotted thread. 'You would have to stop attending school, for instance.'

My eyes flew open. The room looked very cold, very black after my visions of sumptuous fabric. 'Why?'

'To focus on the task, to …' she began, but even Ma couldn't brazen this through. Exhaling, she raised a hand to her forehead. 'If I am honest, it is because we need you to earn a wage. Full time. We cannot afford to keep paying out for school. I'm so sorry, Ruth. I wanted you to have opportunities, to be able to pick your path in life. But if you sit and sew with me during the days, I can teach you what I learnt when I was your age. I did French, you know, and some history. I will not let you grow up ignorant.'

I ought to be relieved to leave school and the teasing girls behind. I *was*. But it was all so sudden. 'Why did you send me to school in the first place, if you knew you couldn't pay for it?'

'I thought we could, but … '

'Something has changed.'

Dark as it was, she refused to meet my gaze. 'Yes. It's a thing I never expected to happen, not after so long.'

'What?' I demanded.

'It's a baby, Ruth. I'm going to have another baby.'

———

A baby. Wasn't that just my luck? A snivelling, shrieking baby to torment my leisure hours. Not that I had those, over the next few months. Every waking minute was spent sewing items of tiny clothing. I never thought I would miss school, but I did. Far from being a release, my needlework was now a horror. I resented that baby to its backbone before it was even born.

Sewing for the baby wasn't like the Metyard work; there was no creativity to it. Whatever I made, no matter how fine, I knew it would be drooled and urinated on.

I learnt, during those long and weary hours, that I could slip a needle under the skin on the pad of my thumb without making it bleed. It was like a roasting jack with my thumb as the pig. You couldn't see where I ended and the needle began. Ma said it was a disgusting trick and it made her go dizzy. But I kept doing it.

My thirteenth birthday came and went with the multicoloured rain of Bonfire Night. Pa bought me a firework and set it off because I loved the smell of their smoke. It was the only bright patch on my horizon. Afterwards, the weather cycled through various shades of gloom. I sat in the window like Ma, my back stiff, watching the same leaves blown up and down the street like old rags.

Sometimes, below the howl of the wind, I thought I heard another noise. A laboured creak. It woke me at night, nagged at me throughout the day. Neither Ma nor Pa mentioned it. But when I closed my eyes and listened close, I knew I recognised the sound. It was the groan my corset had made, when Rosalind Oldacre's feet snapped its bones.

Ma might take me out of school and distract me with chores, but I hadn't forgotten.

I would never forget.

———

One day, I was working on a blanket for the baby, alone downstairs, when Ma lurched into the house with a box and a parcel wrapped in brown paper. I thought expectant mothers were supposed to bloom but she was puffy and bloated, more of a frog than a flower.

'Phew! The material seems to get heavier each time.' She let me take the box and put it by the window while she watched, stretching out her back. Beads of rain stood on her cape. 'Thank you, Ruth.'

I bent and opened up the lid. A coarse and itchy perfume rose to meet me. Piles of hard-wearing cambric and buckram for lining garments – no wonder the box was heavy.

Ma discarded her bonnet and half-fell into the comfortable chair, her head lolling against the antimacassar.

What was this wretched baby: a leech, a parasite? Sewing long hours had drained Ma's colour, but *this* – she looked positively cadaverous. I knelt down beside her and unlaced her boots.

'Did the butcher's boy come while I was out?' she asked.

'No. He still hasn't been. That's a fortnight now.'

I was looking at her feet, but I *felt* her expression in the slow release of her sigh. 'Oh. Oh dear. We must be behind on our bill.'

'Then we should pay it. Didn't you get any extra money for the gloves I embroidered?'

'Oh, Ruth,' she said sadly. 'I should have done. It was excellent work. The bride was delighted. But you don't know Mrs Metyard.'

It was lucky I had to turn away to put Ma's boots aside. She didn't see the sudden spasm in my face, the anger I could not conceal. My gloves. Still mine, but adorning someone else.

'Actually, I heard some rather strange news today about that bride. Miss Kate – that's Mrs Metyard's daughter – happened to be friendly with one of the Lindsay servants, so I thought I would ask if she knew how the wedding went off.' Ma tilted her head. 'Well, what do you think? The bride didn't stop crying, the whole day of her marriage!'

'I suppose she was so *mighty* happy,' I growled.

'No, that's just it! She'd seemed very happy before, choosing her dress material and having it fitted. But on the wedding morning she looked in the glass and burst

into tears. Poor thing, she kept sobbing and saying how
ugly she was, how she ruined the nice clothes! Can you
imagine? She wept fit to break her heart all through
the service. Heaven only knows what her husband
thought!'

There was a dark glee in picturing it: a rich lady, finely
dressed, feeling the same dismay that consumed me while
I sat embroidering her gloves. A throb of connection
through the stitches. 'How ungrateful. Fancy whining
when there are real spinsters and ugly old maids. She has
no right to feel that way.'

Ma's cheeks sagged. She looked unlike herself –
vulnerable, raw. 'Everyone is entitled to a feeling, Ruth,
even if they are not at liberty to act upon it. Perhaps she
could not esteem the man she was marrying. Perhaps she
had no choice in the matter.'

I turned away and picked up my blanket again. It was
essentially finished but I made a fuss of tying up the
threads, knotting them like a garrotte and biting them
short. I was no simpleton; I'd realised long before now
that Ma only married my father to escape the match her
family had arranged. But was it really the right choice?
A rich wife had diamonds and satin to keep her warm
when her husband's affection cooled. Ma had nothing
but drudgery. She deserved much more. It made me
furious.

'Careful, Ruth. Why aren't you using your scissors?'

'I've nearly finished anyway. I suppose you'll want
caps next.'

'Well, and won't you like that? You were complaining
that the work was too plain. At least you can add some
pretty detail to a cap.'

Could I? Lace was too costly. All the trims my imagination conjured up were far beyond my reach. I could do

some white-work, I supposed, but it didn't appease my ambition.

'Ma,' I said suddenly, 'what will we do when the baby comes?'

'What do you mean?'

'What will we *do*? Will we send for a physician?'

'Oh.' She closed her eyelids and leant back in the chair. 'No. We could never afford that. Mrs Simmons and Mrs Winter said they will come and help.'

Mrs Simmons and Mrs Winter from church were kind women – nice enough to share a pew with. But could they deliver a child? No one had told me about the birth process. I knew there was blood involved. Something about hot water. Our church friends seemed too dignified to take part in an operation like that.

I unpicked the scrap of white thread hooked around the eye of my needle and let it float to the floor. Then I slotted the needle carefully back in my cloth book.

'Don't you think Pa might stretch to it? If we ask him? He sold that picture of the dog last week.'

'No, no, don't be silly.' She still had her eyes closed. That was deliberate. Lines of tension around her temples showed she was concealing something behind the lids. 'A second child is always easier.'

'Aren't you afraid?'

'No!'

I stared at her, wishing my gaze could pierce through her eyelids. 'Truly?'

'I managed with you. I have no concerns at all.'

The false brightness of her voice made me sick to my stomach. Mumbling an excuse, I stood and went upstairs.

Ma's housekeeping chatelaine lay splayed on her bed. Rust had devoured all but a few of the keys. Softly, I pushed them round the ring until I came to the one I sought: Pa's studio.

I liked to be in the studio alone because I wasn't meant to be, because I wanted to see the pictures Pa called his *true self*. And because of the gun.

I unlocked the drawer and eased it open, slowly revealing the barrel, with relish. Bullets, powder and ramrods lay behind. I wasn't interested in them. I picked up the pistol itself, enjoying its cool weight in my hands. Then I propped it on my lap and studied the little hammers, the sidelocks, the silver-mounted leaves on its tortoise-shell handle. Beautiful. Not a cheap banger. A good piece; something Ma's own father might have possessed in the old days.

I thought Pa should sell it to help Ma with her baby. Yet when I raised the sight to my face, I understood why he didn't. There was solace in the pistol. Solid, heavy. That odour it gave off, metallic and corrupt.

I liked to know it was there, waiting for me. I liked to close the drawer and hear the bullets roll.

5

Dorothea

Today my carriage passed through the gates just as a Black Maria trundled to a halt in front of the prison. I reached to put down the window and tell Graymarsh to slow his pace, but he anticipated me. Our horses broke their trot and settled into a walk.

Police transportation is seldom pretty. Beneath the ecstatic blue of the morning sky, the Black Maria and its dark pair of horses looked positively funereal. I noted gouges on the body of the coach and great scratches that might have been made with fingernails. I attempted to imagine a violence as rabid as that: a force that cannot be contained.

Staff had gathered on the steps of the prison. Not merely the matrons but burly men with very little neck. This one was a fighter.

Policemen unbolted the doors. David would not be out on such an errand, yet still I searched for his whiskers amongst the blue-coated men as they pulled a faceless, shapeless mass from the vehicle. It stumbled, unsteady on its legs. Only the ripped skirt dragging on the gravel suggested it was female.

Little by little, she unfolded. A wild tangle of hair, grey with dirt, and a sharp face. I did not like the eyes.

I knew she would lunge and she did, just as the prison bell tolled. It was futile. Masses of policemen and hordes

of staff were prepared to restrain her flailing limbs. She
could not seriously have expected to escape. Perhaps
she just wanted to claw and inflict injury while she still
could? Her shrieks and curses joined with the bell in a
terrible evensong.

'I think I shall leave off visiting that prisoner,' I told
Tilda. 'At least for the present.'

By contrast, Ruth Butterham's cell seemed a haven
of peace when Matron shuffled me inside. Jaundiced
light fell through the circular window of yellow glass
and wire, touching the top of Ruth's unkempt head. I
narrowed my eyes, hoping to discern the lineaments of
the skull, but her hair was impenetrable.

The prisoner tilted her chin up as I entered, and I saw
with relief that she was not picking that awful oakum. A
Bible lay spread on her lap. Her hands, though stained,
were motionless.

'Good morning, Ruth. How pleased I am to see you
so employed.'

'Oh, it's you, miss.' She did not speak with much
enthusiasm.

'Yes. I told you I would come.'

Matron clanged the door shut. I felt it with my body. She
did not say anything this time about keeping a watch on
us. I pushed down my sense of foreboding and took a seat.

Ruth's dark eyes studied me. Up and down, pausing at
my cuffs, my hem and my waist. Her mother had been a
seamstress, of course – she would be noting every detail
of my dress.

'Tell me what you have read today, Ruth.'

Ruth sighed and closed the Bible softly. 'People are
always asking me that. They think, because I did bad
things, that I never read the Bible or went to church. But
I always did.'

'Well, perhaps you have never really understood the Gospel? It may not have been explained to you properly.'

Her brow furrowed. It made her eyes look even farther apart. 'Maybe it hasn't. But I know enough. I think people know when a thing is wrong, but they do it anyway. They do it because they want to.'

I shifted on my chair. 'But if that were true, Ruth, if we all acted on our baser instincts, we should all be in prison.'

'Why, miss!' A smile crept up her cheek. 'You don't mean to say that you have bad thoughts, too?'

Sauce and impudence! A blush hit my face like scalding water. I checked over my shoulder to see if Matron was hovering at the hatch. It was shut. 'No one is perfect, Ruth. For myself, I belong to the Roman Catholic Church. If I am ashamed of any thought, I confess it to the priest and ask him to absolve me.'

'I gave my confession to the bluebottles, but I don't think *they'll* let me off, do you?'

'But that is not the same. Surely you see? You only signed a paper saying you had killed your mistress. You did not explain what was in your heart at the time.' She turned her head away; a typical, childish gesture. 'And then when you spoke to me the other day, you mentioned others. People you had killed by accident. What about them? Were you in earnest, or was that an invention?'

She did not answer. Closing the Bible, she held it in one hand, drumming her fingertips upon the cover. Raw. Black-tipped. What had those fingers done?

'You could tell me.' My voice came out strained. 'You have started to talk about your life at home with your family. Why not confide in me further? You might find it a purgative, Ruth.'

'Ah! So you're a gossip, are you? That makes sense.'

'I am not a gossip!' I flared. Too loud. Matron's steps echoed in the corridor, coming our way.

Ruth closed her eyes. Her lips compressed. 'You want a story. Something you can tell your friends over tea. Well, I've had enough of people talking behind my back.'

'People will talk, whatever happens. There will be newspaper accounts … Maybe even ballads. Only you can reveal the truth.'

She smiled. Not a pleasant smile. It chilled me. 'Happen I will tell you, miss. But don't pretend it's for me. It's about you.'

Before I could respond, the door screeched open. Matron banged in, her keys tinkling like rain. 'Everything all right, Miss Truelove?'

I stood. To my mortification, one of my legs trembled beneath my skirts. I did not like to appear discomposed before Matron.

'Yes, thank you, Matron. Everything is in order. I was just moving on to visit Jenny Hill.' I looked at Ruth. Usually I would extend a hand for her to shake, but I blanched at the idea of those fingers upon my gloves. Instead, I nodded. 'I will come again next week, Ruth. We can talk at greater length.'

She stuck out her chin. 'You won't like it, miss.'

I fear that perhaps she is right.

6

Ruth

Pins and needles ran up my legs. I scooted round on my knees, trying to draw the chalk line straight on the bolt of calico.

'You need to start the pattern closer to the edge,' Ma called from the window. 'Otherwise you'll waste material.'

I nodded, but I didn't obey her.

'We have been using rather a lot of material, recently.'

'I'm sorry, Ma. This is new to me.'

Ma rubbed the bridge of her nose, then returned to the stocking she was seaming. 'I understand that, dear. I would bend to do it myself, if I could, but …'

'I know. The baby's too big.'

Always the baby. At least this time, it was doing me a favour.

You might think it was a shabby trick, making waste on purpose. But if Mrs Metyard and her customers could dress in silk and lace, I reckoned I was entitled to a scrap of calico from her stores. Calico was the perfect lining.

I finished my marks and dusted off my hands. 'There.'

'Good. Could you cut it out?'

Reaching for the fabric scissors, my hand brushed something smooth. I turned my head.

It was a scrap of peach sateen, entwined seductively around the scissors. My fingertips began to tingle.

Such a soft, sweet colour. Warming. A rose opening on a spring day. I wanted to touch it, wanted to *be* it. Cautiously, I picked up the scissors and the sateen together, holding them close to my apron.

'The light is poor today,' Ma sighed. 'Your father will be having a hard time of it in the studio. It is so important for him to render the shadows correctly.'

Carefully, carefully, I slipped the material into my apron. I felt a bit brighter, a little more beautiful, just having it about my person.

'Can you see to cut, Ruth?'

Only my scissors answered with their sharp *snip*.

'A bit wider than that, darling, for the seams.'

'Yes, Ma.'

Seams be damned. What I had in mind was more important.

Cutting out panels was long and laborious work, especially in the gloom. The scissors grew heavy; their metal handles bit into the skin around my fingers. I fought to see the chalk lines through tired eyes. My pupils felt drier than parchment, sprinkled with sand.

'I thought I had some rushlights down here, but the box is empty.' Ma frowned, looking across the room. 'And do you know what became of our matches? I couldn't find them in the kitchen.'

'No. Should I run out and get some more?' I offered.

'Well, perhaps you should. You are struggling to cut that.'

Ma laid down her stocking and rummaged for a coin. Pocket after pocket turned out empty. Of a sudden, she stopped and clutched her stomach.

'Ma? What is it?'

She didn't heed me. She was listening to something, deep inside.

'Ma?'

She shook herself. 'All is well. It's the baby, wriggling. Go upstairs and put on your bonnet, dear. I will find some money by the time you come down.'

It was just what I wanted to hear.

Pa was in his studio. I listened cautiously as I mounted the last few steps, afraid he might come out. There was a clink and a sigh from within. Then silence. I darted into my room, shut and locked the door behind me.

The loose floorboard was beneath my bed, hidden by the chamber pot. Dust made me sneeze as I scrabbled about and hooked my finger under the slat. There, glinting in the hole, was my hoard.

Ma's matchbox and a handful of rushlights lay in a nest of pilfered material. Fabric layered upon fabric: soft and smooth; silky and rough; a kaleidoscope of colour. My greedy hands caressed it all. It was a hotchpotch, a harlequin's wardrobe, but it was mine.

The mission was simple: remake the corset. Remake myself.

Every night I worked in secret and every night the garment became a little more real. This corset was taking a different shape to the last one. There were fewer gussets, shorter straps. It wrapped serpentine around my torso. Tight.

My busk was ruined. Nothing in my stash would serve for bones, but I found I didn't need them. I could fortify the corset with cording: hessian, twill and buckram. Its strength would be mine. My labour, my stitches, my blood.

I laid the sateen in place and let down the floorboard. As I climbed to my feet, I remembered Rosalind

Oldacre's face that night. Once again I heard the snap of cane bones and the crack of my own shattered pride. *How long will it take for them to break?*

Not this time.

I vowed, there and then, to create something as strong as my rage. I would make more than a corset, more than a garment. I'd sew something that no power on earth could break.

7

Dorothea

We are entertaining guests for my twenty-fifth birthday! I expect I should be grateful to Papa for throwing
such a lavish affair, with musicians hired especially for
the occasion, but in all honesty, when a lady reaches
a certain age, she prefers not to draw attention to the
fact. I do not wish to mix with half of the wealthy
families he deems it proper to invite, and I cannot flatter myself they would care a straw for my company,
were I not set to inherit a fortune upon my father's
death. Besides all this, it falls to my lot to write the
invitations and organise the necessary provisions of
food and alcohol. On the whole, it is a troublesome
undertaking.

This morning, I was sitting at my cherrywood desk
writing directions for Tilda to take to the confectioner –
although our cook is proficient in his way, he could
never create the ornate meringues and towering jellies
called for – when there was a tap at the door.

Wilkie chirruped as I answered, 'Enter.'

Papa walked in, still wearing his smoking jacket.
'Forgive me, my dear. Do I interrupt you?'

'You do, sir, but it is a pleasant interruption. I have
had as much blancmange and spun sugar as I can take.'

He smiled at the detritus on my desk. 'Why, Dorothea, I am charmed to find you employed in this way! You say it is tiresome, but I would so *rather* your head be full of desserts than …' A stiff nod in the direction of my shelves, groaning with books and porcelain phrenology busts. He does not know about the real skull, hidden inside my desk. 'It is much more agreeable. More *becoming*.'

My shoulders tensed. After nearly twenty-five years, I am well aware that Papa's views on female propriety are not my own. He has an acute sense of embarrassment, a fastidious need to obey social strictures as if they were Gospel. You would imagine the world were one enormous pair of eyes scrutinising his every movement. No amount of cajoling, explanation or reasonable argument on my part will change his mind. I must simply divert him down a different path.

'Oh Papa,' I rolled my eyes drolly. 'Do not be such an old bear! Grump, grump, grump.'

Thankfully, he threw back his head and laughed. He was in a good mood. 'Will you be able to civilise me in time for the party, do you think?'

'I *had* hoped to. But look at this!' I flicked my fingers at his sleeve. 'A smoky old jacket in the company of ladies! I should have thought you would know better.'

'I beg your pardon, Dora.'

'Dotty,' I corrected.

The name snuffed the light from his eyes. 'You know I cannot call you that. I called your mother Dotty.'

I began to shuffle the papers on my desk. A stitch of memory opened: Mama, propped up in a bed of cushions, wheezing at me, her face the colour of tallow. Even then, she was still beautiful. I never experienced the dread children often conceive for sick relations. There was not a single moment when I feared her. But

Papa did. I can feel it in the shift of air, whenever I mention her name. I can hear it in his silence.

Papa cleared his throat. 'I forgot to ask if you have ordered Cabinet Pudding.'

'Have you acquired a sudden taste for it, sir?'

'You know that I have not. It is Mrs Pearce's favourite.'

Of course I knew she was attending – I wrote the invitation with my own hand. All the same, it made me cross to have her spectre raised in my room: her pencilled eyebrows and lantern jaw jutting straight at me. *Enthralling*, they call her. I see no beauty – only arrogance.

'And heaven forfend that Mrs Pearce should be disappointed,' I breathed, addressing my menus. 'Particularly on *my* birthday.'

'That is not worthy of you, Dora. I know you do not like the idea of me marrying again, but your mother *has* been gone—'

'She will not make you a good wife,' I warned. 'For all her acclaim in society. There is a decided *dent* right where Conjugality should sit, and I never saw smaller domestic propensities.'

He went on as if I had not spoken. '—a good many years, now. You do not consider that you will soon be married, yourself, and I shall be left quite alone.'

Alone. I let the word ring for a moment. Ruth Butterham in her cell; Mama on her sickbed – that was the true meaning of alone. What Papa meant was he would have no one to play the piano while he read his newspaper.

Wilkie scuttled across his sandpaper, claws scratching.

'*I* will soon be married? Pray tell me to whom, for this is the first I have heard of it. Has a gentleman applied to you, Papa?'

'No, of course not.' Irritation in his voice. 'But you must choose a suitor. Leave it any longer and you will be a confirmed old maid. I could not bear the shame of that.' A pause. 'As a matter of fact, there is someone I would like you to meet.'

Panic leapt. Another one. With every year that passes, it is harder to turn them aside. Members of Parliament; estate owners; even an earl, once. Not one of them can stand beside my David: the scourge of pickpockets, the upholder of justice. Someone truly good and useful. I have never felt a flicker of attraction for anyone save him. But if Papa ever suspects my attachment …

'Oh? Do go on.'

'Sir Thomas Biggleswade is the name,' he said. 'A fine model of a man, excellent hunter. He has local connections and owns a place down in Gloucestershire.'

My smile felt like it had been carved into my face with a knife, but I held on to it. 'Gloucestershire. Heavens, what a distance! How far I should be from my charitable work.'

'Pish! Aren't there prisons that need reforming in Gloucestershire?'

'Well, I expect there are.'

A thought seemed to strike him, and his expression hardened. 'But look here, Dora, you're not to mention any of your prison folly at the party. Especially to Sir Thomas.'

'He does not approve of charity, sir?'

'I am in earnest. I will not have you spouting on about criminals, or science, or any other topics a young lady should be ignorant upon. I have had to face down enough foolish tittle-tattle in my time. I won't have it said that I cannot keep my own daughter in check.'

I bit my lip. When did he suppose he ever had me *in check*? 'Dear Papa, no one would say such a thing.

Surely there is nothing remarkable in a gentleman giving his only child an education?'

'There *was* nothing remarkable in the education I gave you. It is these books you buy and these – these *heads*.' Colour rose in his cheeks. 'I remember last Christmas. I assure you, everyone recalls the incident. We have yet to live it down. Mrs Pearce was not impressed. We must consider ourselves fortunate that she is kind enough to overlook your behaviour and continues to show you such attentions.'

As if it were my fault that the young men, after imbibing alcohol, asked me to read their scalps! I was being amenable. Certainly, it was no *pleasure* for me to run my hands through their bear-greased locks.

'I am sorry, Papa. It was only meant in jest.'

He regarded me intently. Muscles twitched beneath the stubble on his jaw, fighting one another. I pouted and gave my most contrite expression, but it seemed as though he saw two ladies before him: one he loved dearly; the other he feared.

'You do not know, Dorothea …' he began. He raised a hand to stroke his moustache. 'You were very young, when your mother died. You would not recall how … strange she became towards the end.'

I recall everything: every line of her face, every word that she spoke. She was never strange to me.

'The … ah, religious mania. You have to understand how it was, back then.' He perched on the edge of my desk. 'The Catholic Emancipation Bill was still years away. When she suddenly converted, like that … It was the end of good society for us.'

I turned my eyes to the menus, for I could not conceal the scorn in my face. He spoke as if Mama should prefer good society to the sanctity of her own soul!

'Looking back, I think it was the onset of the illness. Her behaviour … I do not like to tell you this, Dora. Perhaps it was not her fault, but she embarrassed me. In public. There was *gossip*.'

A protective flare in my chest. I wrestled it down, determined to reply with composure. 'As you say, sir, it was a long time ago. You cannot doubt your position in society today. Nobody thinks the less of you for having a – what shall we say? – *eccentric* daughter?'

When his voice came, it was iron hard. 'You do yourself no favours. What you call eccentricity, others will call bad blood. They will call you your mother's daughter.'

'What else would I be?' He hesitated. I could read his thoughts, and for a moment I lost my control. 'No! I do not care if she does accept you – I will never, *never* be the daughter of Mrs Pearce!'

'That is sufficient, Dorothea!' He surged to his feet, shaking my desk. A paper fluttered to the floor. 'I mean it. You will behave at this party. You will be biddable, you will be feminine and you will talk to Sir Thomas about reasonable, everyday topics. Am I understood?'

'Yes, Papa. Only—'

His index finger pointed within an inch of my nose. 'And whatever happens, whatever people say to you, there will be absolutely no talk of *heads*.'

'But Papa, what if—'

'You will behave!' he roared, marching from the room and slamming the door behind him, to poor Wilkie's considerable fright.

Temper, temper. One of the seven deadly sins. Not that Papa would ever mind that.

I was angry too; my heart thudding hard against my ribs, my tongue itching to upbraid him. But of course

I took the time to compose myself and be reasonable about it.

Now I am calmer, I reach into the bottom drawer and retrieve my secret skull. Smooth bone against my hands. A light thing, really, without all the flesh. I place its forehead on my own. The pressure, the cool touch, seems to ease my pounding nerves.

Dark, cavernous holes gape where the eyes once were. Inside lies a white-grey cave. The thoughts and fears that echoed there are gone. No tumult, no strife remains, only bone. How trivial our mortal cares are, when all is said and done.

Recovering from his little scare, Wilkie flutters back up to his perch and tries a wary chirp.

'I know, dear boy. He does not understand me.' I place the skull back in its drawer and retrieve my second treasure. Time has softened the folds in the paper and erased most of the print. In the corner are two pale splashes – I suppose she must have spilt tea upon it as she read. I trace the stains with my fingertips, longing for her.

This was the first thing I found in Mama's bundle of papers when I was tasked with sorting through them upon her death. Tied with a ribbon, it encased the letters from her friends and the silhouette sketches. It is a pamphlet on phrenology.

If only Mama were here to help me defend the science I have learnt for her sake. We might study the guests at the party together. I should dearly like to compare findings with her.

I should like to know if she looked at Papa's skull, and saw the things that I see.

8

Ruth

It was around midnight. A sickle moon hung in the sky above the deserted street outside. Its rays weren't white or silvery but a sickly, phlegmy yellow.

I sat on the cold floor by the window, leaning in close to my rushlight. It stank of fat. I feared it would spit on to my work, but I had little choice. I needed to see.

My corset lay, stretching its wings over my lap, waiting for me to put the blood into its veins: the cords that would hold my body in place. It might cost *me* blood, I knew, to thread cords as unyielding as the ones I'd planned.

So be it.

Flattening the twine, I threaded it through the eye of a thick, blunt tapestry needle. Between the lining and the outer layer were the narrow channels I'd sewn and must fill. Gleaming fibres of peach sateen parted to make way for the very tip of the needle. I began to tug.

It was like extracting a tooth. Slowly, slowly, the needle inched down its shaft. I pulled as hard as I could, working the material along the tail of twine. Only the tiniest movement rewarded each haul. My wrists shrieked with pain. Somehow I knew that was part of the magic; that if it didn't cost me agony, it would be worth nothing. I bit my lip and kept on pulling. *Strong, strong.*

After an hour, blood started to trickle from my cracked fingertips and stain my work. I wanted to give in, to cry. But that was what I always did. That was how I lost my corset in the first place. I couldn't be that girl any more.

Strong. I pictured the twine as a noose around Rosalind Oldacre's neck. I pulled tight. Tighter.

Then I heard the scream.

I flinched, coming back to the cold, bare reality of my room. It wasn't Rosalind crying out, not even the Rosalind of my dream. This was deeper, primal.

I threw my sewing on to the bed, snatched up my rushlight and looked out of the window. Only fog wandered, ghostly, in the street.

The cry soared again. It had come from inside my house.

Shivering, I inched open my door and peered out on to the small landing. A light burnt beneath the door in my parents' room. I heard Pa's voice, low and urgent. Ma didn't respond.

My heart beat up in my temples. It couldn't be …

Ma screamed again.

I darted across the landing, barrelling into the room. 'Ma!'

Pa stood at the foot of the bed, facing away from me. His damp nightshirt clung to the backs of his knees. For a foolish moment, I thought he'd made water in the bed. But he was speaking to Ma and there was no shame, no apology in his words, only fear.

'What do I do? Jemima, tell me what to do.'

I couldn't see Ma.

'Please, Pa, what's happened?'

He turned. The candle flame juddered. In a flash I saw it wasn't urine sticking his nightshirt to his legs – it was fluid streaked with blood.

'It's coming? The baby?'

'Yes, it's coming all right.'

I ran to the bed but instantly recoiled. A smell, animal and sharp, was all over Ma, all over the sheets with that yellow-red liquid.

'It's too soon,' she panted at me. 'It's too soon.'

Pa began to pull on his trousers. 'I'll run for – for – who was it?'

'No, it's the middle of the night!'

'They must have known that might happen when they agreed to come! Mrs Simmons, wasn't it?'

Ma gritted her teeth and winced before respond-ing. 'Mrs Simmons is in Dorset with her daughter. She thought we had weeks yet—'

'The other one. The tall lady.'

'Mrs Winter.'

'Where does she live? No, never mind, I recall. Here, here.' He thrust the candle into my trembling hand.

I couldn't keep up with their conversation. Pa began to change his shirt but I kept my eyes on Ma, horrified. She looked grotesque, indecent, a thing that shouldn't be seen. Each time she groaned her swollen breasts wobbled beneath her nightgown.

'You'll be a good girl and look after Ma,' Pa said. It wasn't a question. 'I shan't be long.'

He ran a hand through his chaotic hair and then he was gone.

A choir started up inside my head.

'Don't be – don't be scared, Ruth,' Ma gasped. Her words only made me more afraid. She looked ghastly as she said them. 'We'll get through it, you and I. We did before. Only … it wasn't this bad with you, Ruth. It was slower. There were big gaps between the pains but now – oh!'

Screwing up all my courage, I forced my legs forwards and went over to her. I knelt on the floorboards and took her perspiring hand in my own. Her grip was like a vice.

I had no words of comfort to reassure her. All I could do was stare dumbly, watching her pant. She didn't talk to me. All the air she sucked into her lungs was blown straight out again, as if she were trying to puff the pain away. Time stretched to twice its normal length. I tired of holding the candle so I threw it into the grate, where it caught a pile of cinder and simmered.

By the time Pa hurtled back into the room I couldn't feel my hand. Ma's fingers had drained the blood from it. But that paled to nothing when he said, 'She can't come.'

'What?' It was me, not Ma, who cried out.

'Her girl has the measles. She can't leave her and she can't come here, it would be too dangerous for the baby.'

'But she has to come.'

Pa and I regarded each other for a long time – longer than we ever had before. He looked younger than I remembered; young and terrified.

'It's all right,' he said, crossing the floor and kicking off his shoes. 'Jemmy, it's all right. We can do this. We didn't need anyone for Ruth, did we?'

She must have recognised the tone – it was the same artificial, cheerful one they used on me. But she didn't respond. She seemed cut off from us now, submerged under waves of pain.

'I'm going to check you.' Pa's throat bobbed as he swallowed. 'I'm going to see if it's on its way out.'

He threw the sheets off her legs and pulled up her stained nightgown. I caught a glimpse of angry, purple flesh straining over a misshapen lump.

I tried to jerk away, but she wouldn't release my hand.

'It's the head,' Pa declared, as if that awful sight pleased him. 'Baby's the right way around, at least.' Then he must have seen how pale I was, how deadly sick. 'I'm sorry about all this, Ruth. Perhaps it's not quite the thing for a girl your age but ... I'm going to need your help.'

'Send for the doctor,' I begged him. 'If the baby's early, something might go wrong.'

'I can't. I wish I could.'

'You must! I'll go first thing in the morning and pawn everything I own, I promise. Just save Ma!'

'I can't, Ruth. Old Dr Barber saw me in a tussle with the wine merchant last week. He'll never give me credit, he knows I'm no good for it.'

'I don't know what to do.'

He waved a hand at me. 'Go, quickly, and boil some water. Then see what you can find for your mother to drink. Heat wine if there's any left. I might have a drop of whisky.'

'I can't go.'

We both looked down at my hand, blue in Ma's grasp. She wasn't screaming now. Her lips moved but they didn't form words, it was all gibberish.

'I'll take over,' Pa said and struggled to wrench me free.

I stumbled out of the room without looking back. My knees wouldn't stop shaking. Not trusting myself on the stairs, I turned into my own room, fell into a pile beside my bed and threw up in the chamber pot.

I felt a bit steadier, after that. I hurriedly dressed in the gown I'd discarded that evening and drew a shawl over my shoulders.

Nothing was real: not the deserted, black room downstairs, nor the sleeping street. *I* wasn't real, walking to the pump with my creaking bucket. I worked the lever. It gurgled and groaned at me as if awaking from a slumber. I carried the bucket back, intensely aware of the sound of my footsteps. Sloshing water, I staggered into the house and heaved my bucket through to the kitchen.

It was no quick task to re-lay the range, light it and bring the water to the boil. I was glad of it. Far better to be occupied than dwell upon my thoughts. I tried not to imagine what was occurring upstairs, and to block out any noise with the crackle of the fire. The cupboards didn't hold any wine but I found Pa's whisky. A quarter of the bottle was left. I decided to take it all.

My legs shook even harder on the way upstairs. My shoulders quivered too – not from cold, but from fear of what I'd find.

It was worse than I expected: Ma on all fours in the middle of the floor lowing like an animal at market. Tangled hair covered her face but I caught a disgusting flash of her rear end, matted with blood.

Pa snatched the bottle from my hand. He pulled out the cork with his teeth and took a swig before pressing it to Ma's lips. She tried to drink, but spluttered. I set the hot water down on the floor.

'Don't just stand there,' Pa cried. 'Get some linen, change the bed. And find something to wash your mother.'

Ma howled.

He patted her back, looking tentatively round to her parted legs. His face puckered. 'Ruth, how long were you gone?'

'I don't know. An hour?'

'More than that, I think. And the baby is no further along.'

I wept as I changed the bed. No one observed me. I thought I'd feel better after a cry but my head ached. Perhaps that was when I started to realise how futile tears really are.

Dawn inched up the horizon. It didn't bring light, only turned the sky from black to grey. Everything in the room had a washed-out, sickly look.

Ma had stopped her frightful cow impression. That was no comfort. Instead she grew listless and dreamy. We had no trouble putting her back in the freshly made bed; she flopped on to it like a rag doll, her face chalky against the pillow. I put a hand to her forehead – it was burning.

Pa was beside himself. 'She's getting weak. Much more of this and she won't even have the strength to push the baby out.'

I opened the window for air. Black-suited clerks dashed by our house, heading off to their employment. The river folk went the other way.

Pa leapt up. 'It's no good. I have to cut her.'

'*Cut* her!'

'Look, look.' He gestured. Reluctantly, I peeked again at that scrap of head and Ma's stretched, tortured flesh. 'She can't open wide enough. The only way to get the baby out is to cut her.'

I clenched my thighs together. 'You can't!'

'I must.'

'She'll bleed to death.'

He put both his damp hands on my shoulders. 'Ruth,' he said, more serious than I'd ever heard him. 'Ruth, you need to be very brave. After I cut her and pull the baby out, you will have to stitch her up.'

Only his grasp on my shoulders held me upright. 'Stitch her *skin*? Down *there*!'

'Yes. It's the only way.'

'I can't. Pa, please, I can't—'

'You have to. If we don't act now, both Ma and the baby will die.'

I hated him. I hated Ma; the gory wreck she'd become.

Pa went to his studio for a penknife and I returned to my bedroom. My needle holder looked abhorrent now, a cloth book perforated with lines of torture. I selected my thickest, sharpest tool and picked up a reel of cotton, saliva filling my mouth, urging me to throw up at the very thought of what I must do.

Could I do it? My eyes were so heavy, my hands shook from lack of sleep. I'd never felt less able to complete a task in my life. And this was worse than the Metyard work. A mistake didn't mean a fine, it meant – I didn't know. I didn't *want* to know.

Pa and I returned to Ma and stood either side of the bed. We looked like people about to commit a terrible crime. The light in the room wasn't strong, but still it glinted on the edge of the knife.

'We must make them clean,' Pa said. 'Heat it in the fire then plunge it into the whisky.'

I watched him and copied his actions. My needle flashed, molten for a moment, before it sizzled and steamed in Pa's whisky. It smelt sharp, heady.

'Right.' He pushed his shirtsleeves farther up his arms. They were trembling. 'Let me show you what I'm going to do.'

Together, we bent over Ma. She lay supine, uncomprehending as he lifted her nightgown and rolled it up as far as her breasts. Against her vivid flesh, the half-moon of the baby's scalp glowed.

'Here.' His quivering finger drew lines above and below the protrusion. 'The top first, then the bottom. I'll reach in and pull the baby out. The moment I move away, you must start to stitch. There will be a quantity of blood. The afterbirth may come out while you're working. Don't worry about that.'

I had no conception what an afterbirth was, but I didn't want to ask.

'What if you nick the baby's head?'

He paled, as if that hadn't occurred to him. 'I won't.'

I glanced at the folds of skin, the fat veins throbbing between them. Suppose he caught one? What would we do?

My needle retained heat from the fire. I pinched it between my fingers until they hummed.

'Ready?'

I didn't see Pa's expression as he braced himself. Every nerve was concentrated in the tip of his knife, hovering over the baby's squashed head. For a moment it seemed absurd that we'd even thought of such a thing. He wasn't *really* going to cut that taut skin. But then his wrist flicked and it was all too real.

Ma screamed.

Blood pulsed out and splashed on the knife. Crimson, brighter than I imagined. Another flick, another scream. I was glad Ma cried so loud – it covered the sickening sound of her tearing flesh.

Pa threw the bloody knife across the room and placed a hand either side of the baby's head. It was slippery with gore. I couldn't comprehend what I was seeing. A series of images flashed before my eyes: blood trickling over Pa's wedding ring; skin yielding; shapes slithering and rushing. Before I knew it, Pa was dashing past me with a grisly bundle in his arms shouting, 'Now, Ruth! Now!'

How I managed to move forward and touch her I'll never know. Her stench, hot blood lubricating my hands.

Don't look, I told myself. *Do not see.*

There was so much fluid. My fingers struggled to grip Ma's slick skin and pinch it together. I took a breath. Pierced flesh with my needle.

It was thick and unyielding, ten times worse than cording. The thread felt horribly weighted as I dragged it through her.

Do not see.

Rather than tidying her, my stitches puckered the torn skin, made it angry.

When something else hot and damp began to emerge, I knew it must be the afterbirth Pa spoke of.

I didn't see. I willed myself blind, brought down the shutters. My hands moved mechanically, as they'd done over the silk gloves. *Blind, blind*. Behind me Pa moved frantically, rubbing at something.

The needle was strong, the needle got through. It powered through skin, through that horrifying friction.

A harsh cry jerked me from my work. Objects bounded back into focus: my hands, red and shining; Ma criss-crossed with stitches, her skin fierce and raw but joined together. I'd done the impossible.

Pa stood opposite, tears running down his face. 'She's alive! She wasn't breathing but I managed to—'

The baby squalled again and cut him off.

She. A girl. I craned my neck for a better look.

My sister was a scrunched, red hunk like meat. Mucus coated her cheeks. She blinked her glazed eyes at me and opened her mouth in a wail.

I didn't hate her now. I didn't hate her a bit.

9
Ruth

It wasn't the banshee wail of my nightmares. Instead, a whimpering snuffle awoke me and sent me tottering, bleary-eyed, across the room towards the crib.

Although Ma had said I wouldn't need to do anything for the baby, she was indisposed from loss of blood. She slept deeply through the long, sagging nights. Lucky her! I had the crib in my room and was up every four hours or so, trying to fill a wet, dribbling mouth with spoons full of pap. And even when I wasn't mushing brown bread with water to feed her, my ears detected the baby's every sound, her every breath. When rest came, it was as thin as a reed and easily snapped.

In the grey light of dawn, I bent over the crib and blinked down at the little girl Pa had named Naomi. She'd emerged from the womb completely bald. Her head looked wrong, cold. I placed my palm over her scalp and she snuggled against it. She didn't want food, only company.

It gave me an odd sensation in my chest to see her lying there. Her face was my face. Her features were smaller, of course, but she had the same nose, the same blunt chin. Pity came in a deluge and I lifted her from the crib to clamp against my chest. Hadn't I always wanted someone to understand me and love me for what I truly was? Maybe Naomi was that person. My ally, at long last.

'You need a cap,' I told her. 'Come on.'

Even at that hour, Pa was in his studio. I heard glass chink and knew that, somehow, he'd got hold of more whisky. It helped him to paint, he said, but I knew why he really drank. It was the same reason I woke, night after night, covered in sweat.

Ma's stitches were obvious, yet there were other wounds inflicted that evening – wounds no eye could see. Mine cut deep.

Be blind. Those were the words I repeated while I stitched Ma up, and at the time I thought they'd worked. But part of me *had* seen, part of me retained every detail.

I clutched the baby tighter and descended the stairs.

'No lace or white-work, I'm afraid,' I whispered to her. 'Just a simple cap.'

Even that felt beyond my ability.

I settled Naomi on her back, in the seat of the comfortable chair, and took Ma's usual place by the window. All the material looked dishwater grey. I dug through it, trying to find the lawn-cotton shapes I'd cut for a cap days before. I'd left them unsewn, expecting the baby to come later. I'd thought, as people always do, that I had time.

'Here we are. This won't take long.'

Naomi turned her head to the side and watched me with her wide, dark gaze. The whites of her eyes shone through the dawn light.

I settled down and began to sew. In and out, in and out. White thread. White lawn. Up and down, the needle dipping. White against white.

Red.

I blinked. A trick of the poor light. There was nothing red on the fabric.

Naomi whimpered.

I shook myself and tried again.

In and out. I managed another three stitches before my hand began to quake. *Blood, so much blood.*

The motion of sewing awoke something terrible. It came back to me in vivid flashes I couldn't control: Ma, screaming; flesh, squelching.

In and out. All I could think of was blood. Yet my hands moved with a language they knew instinctively.

Naomi started to cry.

———

I'd lied to my sister. It took me a great deal of time to make her plain cap. My mind was a loose seam, threatening to unravel. For long moments I was forced to put the work down and stare, fixedly, at the stitches until they resumed their proper shape.

At blessed intervals, the wash of red that filled my vision receded. I thought of Pa's gun; imagined pressing the cool metal to my temple, what a relief it would feel.

It was during one of these reveries that I heard movement on the stairs. My nerves jolted into life; I turned and saw Ma, stumbling round the newel post. She was a wreck. Sunken cheeks and lips like flaking pastry.

'Why are you up and about?' I whispered. 'You should be resting.'

'Ruth, I need your help.' Her voice was so low, it might have emerged from the crypt.

'What is it, Ma? Are you ill?'

'No, I'm behind on the Metyard work. Hopelessly behind.' She shivered in her nightgown.

'How can you think of work?' I slid a look at Naomi, checking that our voices hadn't disturbed her. She slept on, clutching the blanket I'd made against her downy cheek and crushing its corner between her lips. 'Look at you, Ma. You're barely fit to stand.'

Her body must've heard the truth in my words, for it sagged against the banisters. All the same, she shook her head. 'I'll be fit for even less if we can't afford bread and coal. I must work.'

Making a final knot, I snipped off my thread and held up Naomi's cap. The shape of my fingers showed through the thin material.

'Will you help me, Ruth? Please? I hate to ask, I know it will be a hard stint. But I'll never make the orders on time, not even working through the night.'

In the days before Naomi's birth, I'd yearned to tackle the Metyard work. Now, the prospect sounded as daunting as riding a horse. All those hours, all those horrific flashes of red, just to make this flimsy cap in my hands. How would I cope with helping Ma?

Instead of answering, I crept over to Naomi's side and raised her soft skull. Her eyelids flickered as I smoothed the cap on.

'There. Much better.'

The moment I tied the ribbon beneath her chin, Naomi's eyes burst open. They met mine, wide with shock.

It took me in a wave: slaughterhouse red, rust and salt; the perfume of blood. The images were back, the smell was back. I choked on acid in my throat.

'Ruth? Are you going to help?'

'In a moment, in a moment!' I snapped.

Barely able to see through the visions, I pulled Naomi to my chest. Her feeble heart beat back against mine. Somehow it seemed if I could just hold on to her warmth, just listen to her whistling breath, I might make it through.

'What are you doing? Ruth? Come back!'

I dashed up the stairs, holding Naomi tight, and went into our room.

Gradually, the nightmare passed and my sight returned. I found myself sat on the edge of the bed with Naomi sprawled on my lap. She was still staring at me, wide-eyed.

What a fate for that poor child! An ill-favoured face, a house of want, a father distracted. She didn't even have a proper mother; only a sort of half-nurse cobbled together from Ma and me. I extracted the blanket from her grip. How plain it looked. Drab, workaday, not good enough for her. I needed to fix that.

Tucking Naomi into the crib, I covered her with my old shawl instead.

Ma was waiting for me downstairs. Could I really work at her side? Being near her might bring the flashes of panic hurtling back. How would I endure it? Where would I find the strength? I could think of only one place.

Shaking with anticipation, I took the bundle out from beneath my bed and unwrapped its folds of calico. There, protected and untouched, lay my creation: brown jean patched with duck cotton, peach sateen and buff, firm-woven twill. I'd flossed the cording channels with a plum colour. Here and there, its hue was echoed in smears of blood from my overworked fingers.

It wasn't an elegant garment. Mrs Metyard would have snorted at it. Even now, in the first flush of my pride, I saw its flaws. The body was too short, I hadn't allowed for the shrinkage of the material when the boning cords were added. But *I* had done it.

I fastened the corset over my shift, felt the cording push my body into a new shape. My gown went over the top. Only I knew it was there now, holding me close. My talisman, my secret.

I found Ma by the window, rubbing her eye with the heel of her hand. She blinked in rapid succession before picking up her needle. She couldn't thread it. I watched her try twice, three times. On every attempt the cotton shot wide of the eye.

'I'll do that for you.' I took it from her, licked the thread and pushed it through in one go.

'Thank you.' Ma tried to laugh it off. 'I have fallen out of practice in such a short time!'

I sat down in the comfortable chair, strangely erect in posture. Without a corset I'd slumped over like a slattern, but now I felt different, poised. My chair was near the back of the room and put a fair distance between me and Ma. That would help me to concentrate. I didn't really need the window for light. Spring light, such as it was in the town, didn't help much. Ma once told me that spring in the countryside was clear and sweet, but to me spring was the fetid stench that wafted from the warming river, and the glare that bounced off wet cobbles.

'Can you start on the quilted petticoat?' Ma said. 'That's the most pressing.'

Taking a deep breath, I began to sew.

Perhaps it was the comfort of my corset, or the urgency of the work, but I didn't suffer as much this time. The flashes of red, of skin, were shorter and further apart. I paced myself, ignoring Ma, ignoring everything.

For a while, there was escape.

Shortly before dusk, Ma stood and lit a tallow candle. She said nothing but I saw her brows flex, troubled. She didn't usually resort to candles until well after dark.

While she trimmed the wick, I took the opportunity to snatch some silver thread for Naomi's blanket. My embellishment could only be small – Ma mustn't spot it in the crib and realise I'd taken Mrs Metyard's things.

With my best stab stitch, I worked a tiny silver angel in the bottom right corner. It caught the candlelight with the faintest shimmer. I smiled to myself.

'It's no good.' Ma slammed down her work and made me jump. 'It's too dark. Don't you find it too dark, Ruth?'

I glanced around the room. Sepia light radiated from the candle. Outside, the sun trembled on the edge of the horizon. 'It is ... a little dark, I suppose.'

'I can't see my stitches. I can barely see at all.'

'Why don't we go upstairs? Pa's oil lamp will be brighter.'

She hesitated. I waited, my needle poised, curious to see what she'd do.

'The paint will ruin the clothes.'

'Not if we sit at the back, and lay a blanket over the floorboards.'

'I think we will have to,' she said quietly. 'I'll never get the orders done otherwise. I'm sure Pa won't mind.'

We gathered up our work baskets and I blew out the tallow candle, leaving its smoke lingering behind us. Usually I'd trail Ma up the stairs, but she bumped and shambled, forcing me to go first.

There was something uncanny about the way she moved – like a creature risen from the grave. Deciding not to wait for her, I tripped up to the landing and entered the studio.

I hadn't been there since before Naomi's birth. The room wore an air of dejection. New stains splashed the walls. The stack of canvases had grown and tottered to the side. I noticed a broken pen left to drip upon the desk, and beside it—

The penknife. The very penknife. I saw it flash, heard it slice.

What sort of man was Pa? Trimming goose-quill with the blade he'd used to … My legs gave way.

'Whoa there!' Pa gripped my shoulders. I managed to keep my feet, but Pa's hold wasn't entirely steady. Alcohol fumes rose from him like spirits at a séance. 'Are you ill?'

'The knife,' I whispered.

He looked over to the desk. His hair was wilder than usual. 'I'm just … writing a letter.' His voice was strained. Something that lay on that desk disturbed him, although it didn't appear to be the knife.

'Take it away, please, Pa.'

Checking I was firm on my feet, he staggered over to the desk and placed the knife, pen, and a bundle of paper in the pocket of his leather apron. His fingers shook.

Ma crept into the studio behind us. 'James? Pardon us, love. I wondered if we might work by the light of your lamp? I cannot stitch downstairs. It grows very dark.'

He regarded her blankly. He could see, as well as I, that it was hardly dark enough to light candles and lamps yet. 'Well … yes. Yes, I suppose. But make sure you don't touch anything.'

Ma gripped at the doorjamb. 'No, of course not. We will just spread a sheet in the corner. Forgive me, I don't mean to intrude upon your work but—'

'It is no intrusion,' he said, too quickly. 'I have done for the evening. I will … I'll go and sit with Naomi.'

So eager was he to get away that he pushed past Ma. His footsteps sounded on the landing, but didn't cross to

my room where Naomi slept. Instead, they trod down
the stairs, to the kitchen, and there was another clink of
glass.

'How is it we can still afford whisky?' I asked.

Ma's expression became guarded. 'I believe he has
switched to gin.'

I carefully laid the blanket myself, making sure all the
paint and canvases were safely out of reach. Ma sat in
Pa's chair, while I took the floor. We worked without
speaking much. Ma needed to concentrate on her back-
stitch; I on my breathing.

In and out. In and out. Each exhalation pushed my
ribs against the corset. I breathed deeper on purpose,
feeling comfortably encased. Even when the dreaded
flashes came it was there, anchoring me.

Dawn had seeped through the skylight before I looked
up again. My hands and feet were numb and I had a pain
in my side. Awkwardly, I twisted on to my knees. Ma
still sat by the lamp. Its flame didn't reflect in her eyes.
They appeared dull, more solid than liquid.

'Are you done, Ma?'

'Almost.'

It was a lie. Her pile of folded, finished work was
much thinner than mine. I saw her stitches, skewed and
clumsy. 'I could take another—'

'You get on to bed.'

When I stood, fatigue hit me. All at once I felt the
exhaustion of my nights making the corset, my disturbed
dreams and my hours rocking Naomi to sleep. Half-
drunk with weariness, I picked up Naomi's blanket and
blundered back to my room.

Rubies glimmered in the ashes of my fire. By their red
glow I saw Pa stooped over the crib, a glass bottle in one
hand. Gin, not milk.

It galled me to see him there, breathing liquor over the baby. Part of me still hated him for what he'd made me do to Ma, and his behaviour during her indisposition had hardly redeemed him. Who fetched the milk now, ran out for hot pies, burnt their arms and blistered their hands trying to do the laundry alone? Not Pa.

'Does she smell? Does her clout need changing?'

He leapt at my voice. I meant for that to happen.

'No. She's been good as gold all night. Hasn't woken at all.'

That was odd. I'd expected to hear Naomi scream-ing out for Ma's milk while we worked, if not the bread pap. But she slept so deeply, it felt cruel to disturb her. Instead, I arranged the blanket over her little body. Pa caught sight of the angel I'd embroidered and smiled. At least, I think he meant to smile, but it came out as a grimace.

'She *is* an angel, isn't she? And I've failed her. Utterly failed her.'

Looking back, I wish I'd said a kind word. Contradicted him. But I was tired and peeved. I wanted him gone.

'Do you remember how hard I worked to revive her, Ruth? We both thought she was dead, but I rubbed her and slapped her and forced her back to life.' He took a swig from the bottle. 'I shouldn't have done it. I should've left her be.'

I didn't remember him reviving Naomi, I was too busy floundering in my own mother's blood. 'You're drunk,' I snapped. 'Stop saying shameful things and leave the baby to sleep.'

He turned to face me. The movement sent him giddy and he grabbed the crib with one hand. I expected to see anger in his eyes – I'd never chided him before – yet they gazed right through me, to some hidden hell only Pa could see.

'It's a copy,' he said.

'What are you talking about?'

'The painting of the dog. I copied it. I didn't think the artist would ever find out.'

In some degree, I knew he was telling me momentous news, but my mind was too woolly to process it.

'Are you … in trouble, Pa?'

He held up the bottle, as if that were an answer. Then he patted me on the head and left the room.

I was almost too tired to undress. I didn't bother to tie my hair up in rags, but simply pulled off my gown and stockings and left them in a heap on the floor. My fingers strayed to the hooks at the front of my corset, ready to release them and feel my torso slowly inflate.

I couldn't loosen it. The metal bit into my fingertips as I pulled and dug in with my nails. Still I couldn't unfasten the hooks from the eyes.

'Hang it.'

I collapsed on my bed, half-dressed as I was, and fell asleep.

10

Ruth

The smell: beef on the turn, dead flesh. I retched and bucked away. No use – the odour thickened until I could taste it. Rancid.

Where was it coming from? I couldn't see; there was nothing before my eyes but suffocating black.

A squelch. Gingerly, I flexed the fingers of my left hand. They moved slowly, weighted with a thick, sticky liquid.

Drips. Scarlet splashed, vivid against the black. Another spot. Another. Faster.

Scarlet melded to red, then claret. Purple mixed in, blending gradually like colour on Pa's palette. Only this wasn't paint. Not with this warmth and density. It was another liquid, a liquid I knew.

It was in my ears, up my nose, running from my lips. Hot, sharp. Drowning me.

A knock fell on the front door. I jerked awake, spluttering. My room solidified around me, the same chips in the floorboards and blackened paper peeling from the walls. No blood stained my sheets. The liquid I'd sensed was only sweat, beading above my top lip and sticking my hair to the back of my neck.

Naomi woke up, too. She screamed in a guttural way she'd never done before. The noise seemed to pierce through my skull.

Another knock on the door.

Floorboards thumped as Pa went downstairs – either to answer it or escape through the kitchen. I didn't hear which. I was too busy peeling myself from the damp sheets and trying to pacify Naomi.

It wasn't her baby face I saw in the crib but a malefic thing, full of rage. She must be starving – that was the only explanation. She'd gone all night and most of the morning without milk or pap. I swept her up, sniffing her bottom as I did so.

Naomi hadn't passed a motion in her clout, but she smelt wrong. Her buttercream scent had soured. Veins stood out in her forehead as she bawled. Her nostrils bubbled; I wiped them with the corner of the blanket and brought away foul-smelling slime.

Ma was still asleep. Juggling Naomi into one arm, I poked her awake.

'She needs milk.'

'Hmmm?'

'Naomi. You need to feed her.'

'Oh.' Scarcely opening her eyes, Ma fumbled at the neck of her nightgown. I handed the baby over and turned my face away.

Naomi snuffled, a pig at its trough.

'She's ravenous, poor soul,' said Ma. 'I don't think I am producing enough milk for her. Are you still giving her the pap?'

'Yes, but she eats less and less of it. Is there a way you can make more milk, Ma?'

'Only by eating good food. Drinking wine.'

By doing all the things we could no longer afford to do. I thought for a moment. 'Can't you take in more work from Mrs Metyard? I'll do it. Then maybe I can buy some proper food for you, not just baked potatoes off stalls.'

Before Ma could answer, Naomi spluttered and coughed.

It was no ordinary cough: deep-throated, more like a bark from a hound. I twisted around to look.

Something was wrong. Naomi *looked* wrong. Instinctively, my hands reached out and I transferred her to my left shoulder, where I administered three sharp taps to her back. Milky vomit trickled down my sleeve.

'Is she all right?' said Ma.

'I think it just got stuck in her throat.' I lifted Naomi off my shoulder and stared into her face. Her glassy eyes met mine. Then she coughed again.

I needed to change my shift, so I handed her back and left Ma vainly shushing her while I returned to my room.

Even by the light of day, I couldn't unfasten my corset. The hooks felt solid, as though they'd rusted into the metal eyes. Contorting myself, I loosened the laces and spent painful minutes half-strangled by my shift as I tugged my arms out of their sleeves. Now the corset was against my skin: breathing with me, moving with me.

Naomi's cries swelled. They held all the static charge of a thunderstorm, massing at my temples.

As soon as I was dressed, I went back for Naomi. She cried less when I held her, but she didn't stop coughing. More of that dark brown slime crusted her little nostrils.

Ma touched her forehead. 'She must have a cold. Feel how warm she is.'

'I'll run for the doctor.'

She caught my arm. 'Easy, Ruth. It's only a cold. You had plenty of them when you were a baby.'

'What can I do for her?'

'Not much. We'll give her some Godfrey's Cordial and keep her warm – that's right, tuck the blanket up

under her chin. If she isn't better by tomorrow, we'll
purge her with rhubarb and castor oil.'

But she wasn't better by the next day. She was worse;
feverish and fretful. Ma's rhubarb and castor oil moved
her bowels, but she didn't suffer any less. After I juggled
her into a fresh clout and wiped her eyes, nose and
mouth, I stood back to inspect her.

It was bad. At first I thought she was hunching up her
shoulders, but on closer examination I saw she had a bull
neck, swollen to twice its usual size. The inside of her
mouth looked grey. On the surface of the skin around
her throat I saw small circles, like pressure points. There
was an unpleasant movement in my chest. 'Can you
breathe, Naomi?'

She barked at me.

I gave her some more cordial, three drops on to her
tongue. It smelt like treacle and sassafras. Naomi took
it, uncomplaining, from my treacherous hands, trusting
me to make her better.

Neither of us realised what those hands had already
done.

———

She stopped crying. All she wanted to do was sleep. Ma
thought it heralded an improvement, but that brassy
cough remained, waking me throughout the night.

Sewing was impossible. Every time I picked up a
needle my stomach soured with worry. Ma tackled
the Metyard work alone, squinting by the light of Pa's
oil lamp. Every few hours, I ferried Naomi to her for
another attempt at nursing.

'She won't suck,' Ma told me. 'It's getting worse every
day.'

I looked into Naomi's wizened face with its dilated pupils and willed her to drink. All she did was cough.

Tears gathered in Ma's eyes. 'She's thin, Ruth. I don't know what to do.'

My heart stumbled. I knew, as all children do, that when an adult cries all hope is lost.

'We must send for the doctor,' I said. That was all I said, in those days, when I still held faith in medicine, in natural philosophy.

'Run for Mrs Simmons. Her husband was a physician, God rest him. She'll know what to do.'

I sped there and back like the hounds of hell were at my heels. Mrs Simmons came willingly. She was a good woman; matronly in a plump, lace-collar fashion.

We ran straight to Pa's studio. Mrs Simmons removed her glove and pressed her fingertips to Naomi's damp forehead. Then she looked in her mouth. 'God help us.'

Ma gripped Mrs Simmons's arm. 'Do you know what it is?'

'Yes. I've seen it before.'

Silence.

I asked the question Ma couldn't. 'What is it, Mrs Simmons?'

She hesitated.

'What?'

'I'm so sorry, my dears. It's … it's the strangling angel.'

Ma screamed.

'The … *what*?'

Mrs Simmons placed a hand on my shoulder. It felt unbearably heavy. 'The strangling angel has visited your sister.'

It couldn't be possible. Could it?

I tore out of the studio, almost knocking Pa back down the stairs. 'What is it?' he cried. 'Ruth, what's happened?'

Ignoring him, I darted into my room and slammed the door behind me. I made it as far as the crib before my knees buckled. Naomi's blanket lay on the bottom, its silver angel winking. I took it in my shaking hands. Then I began to rip.

The fabric gave way like water. Faster, faster. Seams unravelled. White shreds flew into the air. My nails tore but I couldn't stop until every last piece was obliterated. I had to unpick every stitch.

'Ruth!' My mother's voice.

Panting, I looked down and saw what I'd done. The crib was a rat's nest of frayed cotton and snapped threads. There was no silver, no trace of the angel.

'Ruth, come quick!'

I thought destroying the blanket would cure her. But as I entered the studio, I saw the desk cleared and Naomi laid upon it, the adults gathered around her. Her lips were dark. Between them her tongue protruded, shockingly pink.

'I'm sorry, Naomi, I'm so sorry.' Apologies tumbled from my mouth. 'I never meant ...'

Naomi's eyes rolled back. White filled the space beneath her lashes. There was a prolonged, rattling wheeze. Then she went still.

Ma's sob ripped through the house. The adults moved around me, crying, praying, trying to restore life, but they fell into the background.

All I could see was the side of Naomi's neck, the marks resembling fingerprints. They changed colour, became bloodless and grey. Trembling, I stretched out my hand.

My fingertips fitted exactly.

11

Dorothea

Spring is in full force! I do so love this season with its gentle, lemon light and the sense that all the world is awakening from a bad dream. The winter slush is gone, and it is too early for summer dust. One can actually walk, actually breathe.

Pink blossom rains down as Tilda and I stroll through the botanical gardens towards our usual bench. No snowdrops or crocuses line the paths, but a host of daffodils, as Mr Wordsworth would have it, sway in the breeze. Deftly, I reach down and pluck a bloom from the grass. Its petals resemble butter.

'You're not meant to do that, miss,' Tilda tuts.

'Oh, hush. It is not for me.'

I am thinking of my poor women, locked away from the soft pastel colours of nature and the trill of the birds. They have an exercise yard, certainly, but it will be a number of years before the saplings planted around the walls peek their heads over the top. For now it is eternal winter.

Tilda and I sit down on the white iron bench. The sun has failed utterly to warm it; cold bars press through my skirts against my thighs.

'It won't be good for you, miss,' Tilda says, with her usual expression of doom. 'It's not warm enough to sit out for long periods, yet.'

She is correct – now I have stopped moving, I do feel a chill in the air. The sun, though bright, is weak and watery. But you cannot give in to Tilda, so I simply reply, 'Bosh.'

A nursemaid and three different spaniels pass us by the time David finally arrives, short of breath. He does not wear his uniform on a Sunday – although I understand that, in London, some unfortunate policemen must.

'Constable Hodges. What a pleasant surprise.'

He wears a dun-coloured suit, the waistcoat checked through with lines of green and red. It freshens his face. Without the tall police-hat he appears shorter, less stern.

'Miss Truelove!' He raises a brown bowler, gifting me with a brief glimpse of the hair beneath; not oiled and greased like so many of our young men, but natural with a light wave. The colour is unremarkable – I would liken it to the coat of a hedge mouse – yet it suits his complexion. 'Fancy a young lady like you sitting about on a damp spring day! I wonder your maid doesn't scold you for it.'

Tilda looks very much as if she might scold *him*.

'Oh, the scolds have been plentiful, sir. You have missed them, I am afraid.' I smile up at him. Sunlight touches his cheek and he looks quite heavenly standing there, beneath the blossom. I do not mind these little charades that have become indispensable to our meetings: the affected surprise and fictions concocted to place us at the scene together. It grants me time to simply look and feel how superior he is to other men. Of all those prominent in my life, he is the only one I can truly esteem. That is of the utmost importance in a husband. I know only too well how it smarts to be under the dominion of a man I cannot fully respect.

'Have I? Well, I hope you'll grant me the liberty of scolding along with her. Look at that sky!' It does appear to be turning; the pale blue colour has bled out, leaving a remnant like milk. 'At least allow me to escort you to the temperate house. What would I do if you caught cold? Your father should never forgive me.'

Tilda sniffs and I swallow a chuckle. A cold is the very least thing Papa has to forgive.

With my hand placed lightly upon David's arm, we walk side by side to the great glass structure at the centre of the botanical gardens, Tilda trailing at our heels. Dirt from the path marks the hem of my new printed-cotton dress. Petals settle in the brim of David's hat. We do not mind a jot. All that matters are his muscles, hot and tight beneath my palm, and the way our steps match, left and right, left and right, the same stride, a pair born in time with one another.

Were I now to glimpse that vagrant, the one who took off with my reticule, I would bless him. Without his crime, my love and I should never have met.

Magnolia buds tremble on the trees flanking the approach to the temperate house. With a few more days of sun, I wager they will blow. The purple tulips in the parterre are still pursed and tight-lipped – they shall take more coaxing, yet. Behind the parterre gleams the house itself, shaped like the upturned hull of a ship. Wood and copper do not hold it together; the materials are lighter: panes of glass and white iron. What with the clouded windows, one could almost fancy it a ghost ship.

David opens the door with his free arm. Steam rushes out to touch me, warmer than flesh.

Inside, all lies green and enchanted. Palms tower up to the iron arches of the ceiling. I smell them, moist and wonderfully fresh. Shorter specimens squat in clay pots, these darker in colour with a strange, chipped sort of trunk that puts me in mind of a pineapple.

About half a dozen couples dawdle in our jungle: some sweethearts with a chaperone, others ladies conversing with friends. None of my acquaintance. I note with pleasure that not one amongst the walkers regards our entrance with any interest. This is our world, apart from society, a place warm and secret.

We take the path to the right, where the broad leaves of what I believe is a banana plant brush over our shoulders as we walk. Once or twice, I detect a short exhalation of breath at my back; I can only imagine the vegetation flipped off me, straight into Tilda's face.

'How are you keeping?' David asks me. 'It feels an age since I saw you last.'

'It *has* been an age. And not the Golden Age, either.'

Concern in his deep blue eyes. 'Trouble?'

'Not trouble precisely. Only … vexations. I have been to the prison but rarely, and I do not progress in my studies at all.'

'Really? I thought the girl, that Butterham, would keep you occupied for months.'

Months? Lord, I believe I would need years to untangle her soul to my satisfaction. When I think of Ruth, my mind is as knotted and thick as that tarred rope I found her picking, the very first day. 'She does interest me, without a doubt. But I had hoped to meet with a child a little less … mad.'

He laughs. 'You did? Dotty, I don't think a person *can* commit a crime like hers, without being a trifle mad.'

'I had not thought of that. Perhaps you are right. But I have mapped the heads of such prisoners before. Mrs Smith, Mrs Wren … I expected, after reading your papers, the opportunity to measure the skull of someone truly ... evil. Evil in its infant state.'

David blows out his breath. 'Well, I would say it is a blessing that you didn't find it.'

'Not so! Imagine if we could devise a system to detect, scientifically, without a doubt, all evil propensities in the young. What steps we might take, what work you might be saved.'

He muses on this. Somewhere in the depths of the temperate house, moisture drips. 'You know me, Dotty, I'm not a man of natural philosophy. I don't like the idea of our character being written in our skulls. Somehow, it takes away the notion that we might have a choice.' He clears his throat. 'But tell me, what *do* you find in the Butterham girl, if not evil? Is she truly mad?'

Perhaps *mad* is unfair. 'Hopelessly ignorant,' I amend. 'Do you know, she told me that she killed her sister with the strangling angel?'

He blinks. 'You mean diphtheria?'

'Yes! A well-known disease. Plenty of babies succumb to it. But Ruth's neighbour called it by the common parlance of "the strangling angel" and the foolish girl thinks – she truly believes – that she *summoned* this angel to kill her sister.'

I see him trying not to smile. 'Oh dear. Whatever did she summon it with? Magic words?'

'A needle and thread.'

This time he cannot help it, he really does grin. 'Good lord. Maybe you'll be moving her to Bedlam, after all.'

'If I am not institutionalised first, myself! This week has sent me half-distracted with flower orders and matching napery. We are entertaining, you see, for my birthday.' His mouth tightens. 'Oh my dearest, do not look cross. You know I shall not enjoy it, not a straw, without you there.'

'You wouldn't want me in your drawing room,' he says quietly. 'Amongst all that lot. I'd look ridiculous.'

'Ridiculous! On the contrary, you would make *them* appear foolish, with all their silly bow ties and silk trousers. You would expose the whole affair as the inane frippery it really is. You know that I avoid society wherever I can.'

A half-hearted incline of the head. Of course he does not like to picture me there, herded about amongst eligible gentlemen, with my father pulling their strings like so many marionettes. *I* do not like to picture it, particularly the famed Sir Thomas Biggleswade. I have an intuition that this particular tick will be hard to shake off.

'Still … Won't it be nice, for you, to have a party, Dotty?'

'I daresay I could glean *some* enjoyment, were it not for a certain woman who has received an invitation.'

'Mrs Pearce.' David's voice is so full of sympathy, it is like an embrace.

'I could not avoid it. Papa *will* have her there.'

'My poor Dotty.' He pauses for a moment, running his fingers along the leaves of a plant. 'Why not …' I stop walking too, and look him in the face. 'Why not leave it behind? After all these years being mistress in that house, you couldn't bear to make way for another woman. I know it. Not even if your father picked a paragon of virtue.'

'I expect not.'

'Well, then! Let him marry who he likes, and good luck to him. We can be far away, in a home of our own, before they even read the banns. Never mind the money. We'll get by.'

Noble soul! He is everything that I wish I could be. No doubt he would be able to do it: forget and forgive all that has passed. But to think of that awful woman as mistress in my mother's house raises feelings so bitter and unchristian that I am sure they would sour our lives, wherever we might turn.

'I think, my dearest, that is precisely what he wishes: to move me out of my home and put his paramour in my place.' I catch Tilda's beady eye, hovering between green spines. 'Should they have children, I would be cut out of my inheritance on his side.'

'And so? What is that, to us?'

'Little, I suppose. But how would Mama rest easy?' A cloud of steam drifts up into the leaf canopy. My imagination paints it as her spirit, wandering, lost. 'It is her house. Papa's fortune is primarily her money. Imagine it all settled on Mrs Pearce and her spawn!'

'Your mother would want *you* to be happy, Dotty.' I gaze into his earnest young face, beaded with sweat in the heat, and realise he will never have troubles like mine. Such a clear-cut, worthy skull. Whereas my own ... 'I think your mother would ask you, as I often do, what exactly it is you are waiting for.'

I take a breath to speak, but I cannot put the answer into words. In short, I am waiting for a miracle. To find a way to marry the man of my own choice without forgoing all the comforts of the station I was born to. To remain at once David's wife and Mama's daughter. It does not seem just that I must decide between my love and my birthright.

'You are correct,' I admit. 'The time is approaching. I should set a date ...'

Tilda steps abruptly out from behind the plant. Her cheeks are flush, though not in a pleasant way. She looks like a rhubarb.

'Pardon me, miss. I think it's time you were getting home.'

12

Ruth

The house descended into a sepulchre. Curtains shut out the light, clocks were stopped at the minute of Naomi's last wheezing breath. I couldn't cry. I was too numb for that. My heart didn't seem to beat at all.

Now, at night, the flashes came with greater intensity. Not just the blood of Naomi's birth but the awful struggle of her death. I saw her choked face. Sometimes it was mine. Sometimes my fingers were around her neck and I was sobbing, begging for someone to stop me. But if I cried out in my sleep, my parents didn't come with reassurance. Their own sorrow absorbed them as they sat up to keep watch with the corpse, and I was left alone to stare at the empty crib. Only the corset embraced me. Refused to let me go.

There was no money saved against a funeral. We feared Naomi would end up in the common pit until Mrs Simmons set up a subscription to bury her in the churchyard. 'I'm so ashamed,' Pa kept saying, 'I can't even bury my own daughter,' as if that were the hallmark of every good parent.

On the day of Naomi's funeral, the callous sun shone with all its might. Ma tottered out of the house on Pa's arm, wearing a weeping veil that brushed her hips as she walked. Every step cost her effort. For me it was different. I stood beside my parents, ready to walk to the church, and my mind was cold.

The little handcart trundled out, bearing poor Naomi bound up in her shroud, the wheels maliciously cheerful on the cobbles.

We followed behind. Summer was upon us, bringing with it the river stink and another smell from Naomi's cart: ripe and low, like rotting meat.

I roasted in my one good gown, which I'd dyed black for mourning. Beneath it, my corset squeezed, trapping its own layer of heat. I deserved to swelter. But poor Naomi didn't deserve that pauper's burial, her corpse bumping over cobbles as dust curled up from the wheels of the cart. If only the charitable subscription had stretched as far as a coffin! But death is an expensive business, miss, as I'm sure you know.

Under a sky of hard, glazed blue, we entered the churchyard. Posturing angels and death's heads loomed over us, half-devoured by lichen. The place was a mess of bracken, moss and nettles. We approached a rectangular grave, fresh cut and pitifully small, like a privy pit.

It wasn't that long ago we'd gathered in the chapel for her christening. Now the minister looked pained, his voice husky as he said, 'I know that my Redeemer liveth, and that He shall stand at the latter day upon the earth. And though after my skin worms destroy this body, yet in my flesh shall I see God.'

Ma remained frozen until she heard the hollow pat of Naomi's body meeting the soil. Then she folded in half. Pa held her, his sobs drowning her own, and I wanted to be anywhere, with anyone, rather than there in that horrendous tableau.

The vicar intoned his ancient words. He spoke of God's kindness to children. Now, I thought. Now someone will look at me and realise what I've done. They'll hear my heart pounding.

But no one did. God didn't strike me down. Soil tumbled upon Naomi, even a clump from my own hand, and still nothing happened. The vicar blessed me, just like the rest, and sent me home to love and serve the Lord.

Our house looked tired and grey when we came in from outside: a place buried in silt. Shadows crept out from under the chairs, spreading across the floor towards the kitchen. There, flies droned over my abandoned tubs of lye and dirty clouts.

There would be plates to clean, as well as the laundry. I hadn't been able to keep up with it all. After Naomi's death, my first menses had arrived – the mark of Cain, I thought – leaving me with even more to wash. Odours of sweet blood, dirt and grease mingled together; our home was marinating in the scent of death.

Ma was no help – her eyes were worse than ever. I watched her grope her way across the room to collapse in the comfortable chair.

Pa went straight to the box where I'd packed up Naomi's things. He looked smaller, somehow, hunched over her binder, barracoats and shirts. Every item he turned over in his hands drained him, took something else from his face. Soon I would be able to fold him up and pack him away too, there was so little substance to him.

At last he settled on the plain cap I'd made, still waxy from her scalp. He tucked it under his waistcoat, next to his heart, and shut the box.

How quiet the house was. No baby crying, no clocks ticking; only the buzz of flies, on and on, the lullaby of decay.

Pa lifted his morose eyes to me, but I had nothing to offer. He wet his lips. 'I … I don't know how to occupy myself, now.'

'You could paint, couldn't you? Or do you not do that, any longer?' We both flinched from the venom in Ma's voice. I'd never heard her speak like that – but then I'd never seen her look like that either: ugly, her pretty features contorted by grief.

'Jemima, how can I possibly set my mind to work? Our little girl—'

'We still have a daughter,' she snapped. 'One I would very much like to keep alive, if it's not inconvenient to you.'

The atmosphere had shifted, quick as a blink, from despair to rage. Pa glared at her, his chest rising and falling beneath his black waistcoat.

'So that's your conclusion, is it? You've decided Naomi's death was my fault?'

'Don't say her name!' Ma screeched. 'Don't you dare say her name.'

Silent accusations ate their rapacious way through the air. I longed to tell Ma and Pa the truth, to stop them hurting each other, but my lips refused to part.

'There's no guarantee that a physician would have been able to save her,' Pa said at last. 'You heard Mrs Simmons talk about her husband. He saw many children who—'

'She would have had a chance,' Ma cut him off. 'Naomi wouldn't have been so weak and sickly if we could afford to feed her properly, to keep the place warm. God above! When I think of her skinny little arms! It would have been kinder to put her in the workhouse!'

'Well, perhaps I would have been able to paint superior pictures if my studio wasn't full of women's frippery.'

'I had to sew up there.'

'Nonsense.'

'I did, I had no choice.'

'What utter rot. Why on earth would you need to invade the only place I can create with all your—'

'Because I can't see!' she roared. 'I can't see to work, even in your precious studio. You've made me rough it out down here in the dark for too long and now my eyes have gone. They're *gone*, James.'

An awful pause.

'What do you mean?' His voice was blank, disbelieving.

'I can't work. Not any more.' Tears leaked from her dead eyes. 'I'm done. You will have to support the family alone.'

Something sank in my stomach, a leaf settling on the bottom of a pond. Deep down, I'd known. I'd known it for weeks.

Pa stormed to the kitchen and threw open the cupboards. Glass knocked against wood and a cork popped.

'Oh, that's right!' Ma called bitterly. 'Have something to drink. That will help, won't it? No money for Naomi, but always enough for gin.'

He slammed back into the room with a bottle. Ma lunged towards him. Flailing, she caught hold of the gin and grappled with him. For a moment they wrestled, veins standing out in their necks, but then the bottle slipped and shot from Pa's hands to shatter against the wall. The scent of gin bloomed, judgemental.

'Damn you, woman! I wish I'd left you where I found you, rotting in the countryside.'

'So do I!'

He flung himself away from her and thudded up the stairs. I heard him banging in his studio, throwing objects around.

Ma burst into sobs.

A good daughter would have comforted her. Or she might have gone to her father and calmed him down. But I slunk into the kitchen with the flies, where I belonged, and closed the door behind me.

Mechanically, I began to wring out the linen with my hands. The cold water I'd used to soak it was now green-brown, the colour of gangrene. Two or three flies had drowned and floated on the surface.

It was good to have a task, even a disagreeable one. Good to see that my body could move while my mind veered out of control. I poured the used water out in the soakaway at the back of the house, and as I watched it slop I thought how strange it was, that Naomi was dead and I was still cleaning up her mess. The spirit went but the filth lingered; the waste of things remained.

I set pans of water heating on the range and searched the cupboards for our washing jelly. Nothing but mice and their droppings. Pa had swung one of the cupboard doors off its top hinge.

He'd seen the angel on the blanket. Why didn't he mention it to me? Blame me? Perhaps he didn't believe that small piece of embroidery could summon the strangling angel. I could scarcely credit it myself.

Wisps of steam began to curl from the pans.

But it must be true. For there was that lady, wasn't there, the one I embroidered the gloves for? Somehow I'd passed my sadness on to her. And then I'd made a corset so strong, I couldn't take it off.

My thoughts, my stitches. An unbreakable link between the two.

Gently, the water started to bubble.

I'd have to take great care in future, for with Ma's eyesight failing, all the Metyard work would fall to me ...

I dropped the wooden beater. *Ma.* I'd sewn her too, hadn't I? They were my stitches in her flesh, but when I sewed them I wasn't thinking of strength. I was thinking ...

Do not see. Be blind.

And now she was.

The kettle whistled. I was only dimly aware of it. I stared, transfixed, at the empty cupboard, as the enormity of what I'd done began to dawn.

It couldn't be a coincidence. Not with Naomi as well. Somehow, a part of me had bled into those stitches. The darkest, bitterest part.

Steam filled the kitchen. I wiped my brow as my insides churned. What else had I sewn? Hundreds of things, countless items, each with its own poison. I couldn't separate them in my mind. I didn't remember making them.

Only one garment flashed before my eyes: Naomi's cap, set against a backdrop of red. I recalled the horror as I laboured over it, the waves of blood. Hideous images I could only stop by remembering the gun—

The gun.

I hurtled to the door and threw it open. Steam swept across the threshold with me. Ma gasped.

'Ruth, what in the name of—'

Even as she spoke, the pistol cracked. It rang through the house, rang through my soul.

'Pa!'

I ran up the stairs, hoping against hope, knowing I was too late. Smoke snaked out of the studio door, filling my mouth with an astringent taste. Gunpowder.

God knew I'd seen enough horror. I should have turned back. But instead I trembled forwards, on to the threshold, and sank to my knees before Pa's last masterpiece.

He hadn't put the gun to his temple, as I'd thought. It went through his mouth. Where his head hung forward, I could make out the shattered remains of his skull and his hair, my hair, matted with blood.

Red washed up the wall, over his easel, over the portrait of Ma, painted all those years ago when they first met. It dripped, with gobbets of something awful, on to the pile of Mrs Metyard's work.

And there at the centre of it all, falling from his waist-coat: a flash of material, clean amidst the carnage. A plain cap, worked with innocent white stitches.

My stitches.

13

Dorothea

Now, I know the young are inclined to be fanciful. I am not *so* far past the age of sixteen that I do not recall my own freaks and vagaries. But even bearing that in mind, it strikes me that Ruth Butterham's tale is veering too forcefully into the realms of imagination.

I have visited other prisoners who allege impossible things, yet Ruth does not seem to be of apiece with those who talk of demons and visitors from beyond the planet, only to be transported to secure hospitals. On some topics she is collected, thoughtful even. Had her education been what it ought, she might be an able inter-locutor. But her monomania about these stitches ...

I can only suppose the girl lost sight of her reason amidst the chaos that, she claims, blighted her early years. Grief is a violent emotion, a sort of acid that eats away at the best parts of us. The bereaved are in agony, yearning for someone to blame, and if they cannot find a culprit, they turn their fury upon them-selves. Hence Ruth, buffeted by disaster after disaster, sought to give her suffering a meaning by attributing it to a supernatural power. Well, that is my theory, at any rate.

Today I decided to take a holiday from the wearisome demands of planning my party and journey into town, to research the matter further. I reasoned that if I could establish some details about Ruth's family, I might gain a better understanding of her character and how truthful she has been with me. In relation to the sister, Naomi Butterham, I did not hold out hope of finding more than the mere facts of the unfortunate child's birth and death, but I thought the father, James Butterham, might yield more interesting information.

I was right.

James Butterham, it transpires, was an aristocratic by-blow!

I pieced the clues together myself. Newspapers cannot always be explicit, and I do not have a great deal more from the archives than journalistic nods and winks. However, with the help of an assiduous little archivist, I found enough to establish that a certain Lord M— caused a stir locally by dismissing an octogenarian gatekeeper who had served his family loyally for threescore years, and lifting a stable hand into the vacant place. This groom, or whatever he was, took immediate possession of the gatehouse along with his 'widowed' sister. No one in the locality recalled the woman's late husband – a curious circumstance, given the swelling belly that denoted he had been dead for less than nine months. Stranger still, when her son James was finally born, he resembled no one so much as the owner of the estate himself.

Imagine the scandal! There was a Lady M— with her own children besides. A miserable existence it must have been for her, living with a rival at the end of the drive, glimpsing the proof of her husband's infidelity each time she came in or went out! The son was never formally acknowledged, however, and his education befitted his expectations in life. There was no question of him growing up alongside his legitimate siblings.

From there, James Butterham would have dropped out of notice had he not taken to the business of portrait painting. Society could not resist commissioning such a youth and sneaking a look at him. Added to which, Butterham possessed some talent. Perhaps he would have made his way after all, were it not for the heiress Miss Jemima Trussell.

The elopement of these two young, ill-matched persons blazed across the old society magazines. No doubt they exaggerated when they said the shock of it fairly killed Lord M—, but it is true that he died very soon afterwards. As for Miss Trussell, she had breached contract with a most eligible match arranged by her family. She was cut off without a penny.

Part of me had hoped to find a happy ending for the young lovers. Notoriety is by no means a death sentence in the world of art; I thought perhaps patrons would be caught by the glamour and excitement of the pair. Alas, Lord M—, Mr Trussell and the young lady's intended were all darlings of the world, not to be offended. The Butterhams sank, and they sank fast.

So much for love conquering all! This is a lesson for me to heed, when I am tempted to run away with my David. We must be prepared, we must do things properly.

The next newspaper entry to mention James Butterham was bleak indeed: a coroner's jury finding the verdict of self-murder at the age of thirty-six. It is not incredible that a man, on the day of his daughter's funeral, harassed by money troubles and quarrelling with his wife, should put a gun to his head. Do not mistake me – it is a sin against God and his remaining family alike – but is the motive not comprehensible?

The jury declared Butterham sane at the time of suicide, which ruled his property forfeit. For another family this might have been a calamity, but the deceased's estate was eaten up by debt, to the extent that an artist planning to sue Butterham for breach of copyright gave up there and then. Bailiffs took possession of all.

A charitable subscription had saved Naomi's body from disgrace, but that could not be the case here. Not with a suicide. According to custom, James Butterham's remains were toppled into an unmarked grave on the north side of the church – the Devil's side – under the cover of night. There were no mourners, and he received no service of burial.

Although I am back in my own room with Wilkie trilling, and I have scrubbed the newspaper print from my fingers, I cannot stop thinking about the history I have read. I begin to wonder if it is true that a child pays for their father's sins. Lord M— fell, then James suffered, and now Ruth ...

I tidy my hair back into its combs and strive for rationality. Ruth's silly fancies must be taking a stronger hold on me than I thought. But sad as they were, my discoveries are a *positive* thing; they do not paint Ruth as either a liar or a madwoman. She has simply told herself a story to deal with the grief she cannot face.

I expect we can all understand that.

I apply a dab of salve to my lips, watching my reflection in the mirror. I am not content with the image I see.

I must return to Ruth. Conscience upbraids me with neglecting my other women: Liz Carter, who I am teaching to read, and Jenny Hill who requires constant encouragement. But they will be incarcerated for many years yet; I shall always have them to call upon. Not so with Ruth.

Now we approach the meat of her history, the time when she met her victim for the first time. This is the story I particularly wish to hear.

My heart skips along. My eyes look brighter, and I know I will appear to far more advantage in prison, listening to Ruth, than I will at my own birthday party.

Perhaps Papa is right to be concerned about that.

14

Ruth

They say that vinegar gets out bloodstains. Vinegar and cold water, that will do it. But there's a variety of blood that comes from deep within, and this can't be erased. Scrubbing until your arms ache, scarlet frothing from the brush – still it remains.

So it was with the matter that fell upon Mrs Metyard's work. Ma and I lugged the bundles of cloth between us, trying not to slip on the oyster shells and dung littering the streets. It was full summer then, swarming with flies. Thick, white dust rose in clouds from the horses' hooves to whiten the railings and whatever patches of grass had survived the heat. No use now, trying to shield our material from smuts. All was marbled in brown and yellow where the blood had dried, and I'd tried to wash it. It didn't look like my father's life force, staining those clothes. It looked like the contents of a chamber pot.

You'll call me heartless for thinking such thoughts. Maybe I was: a cavity yawned in my ribs, where once I'd felt a heart beat back. We'd lost everything. Everyone. And as I stumbled down that road, calling out to Ma to avoid potholes and carts, I didn't see that there was any future for us.

Mrs Metyard was our last creditor. Her claim was the only reason we'd been allowed to keep the ruined materials from the bailiffs. After we dealt with her, we would be cast adrift. No home to return to, no friends who wanted to associate with us after this disgrace.

'Can't we go and live with your parents, Ma?' I whined. 'I know they didn't like Pa, but surely now ...'

'No,' she replied stiffly. 'I wrote many times after you were born, seeking reconciliation. Only one answer to all those letters! And the language they used, about your father ... That I never can forgive.' Her lip quivered, and when she spoke again her voice was rough. 'Though perhaps they were right. They saw more clearly than I. For he has deserted us, hasn't he? Left us all alone, like the scoundrel they called him. How *could* he?'

'He wasn't himself, Ma. It wasn't Pa who pulled that trigger.'

'Then who did, Ruth? Tell me that.' Her milky eyes glared at me, demanding, even without their focus. 'Who else ruined our family?'

It was me.

Little by little, the streets grew wider. Cobbles gave way to granite setts underfoot. Although the flavour of sweating horses lingered, there weren't so many carts and wagons on the road. Here, I pulled Ma from the paths of omnibuses, with their brightly painted advertisements, and smart hansom cabs. Vendors didn't sell oysters in this part of town, or pickled whelks. It was coffee and gingerbread. Even the pedestrians that stared as we straggled past were of a higher class: colourful, fine-napped dresses adorned the ladies while gentlemen swung gold watch-chains.

I bent my head down, trying to hide beneath the rim of my battered bonnet. No wonder Rosalind Oldacre had laughed at me. This was her world. They might be her lapdogs, trotting across the road in front of a harried lady's maid.

'Is this Cross Street?' Ma asked me.

'Yes.'

'Then it's up ahead. Just a bit farther, on the left.'

Metyard's stood at the end of a row of shops, next to a barber's. It sprawled larger and taller than its competitors, more like a genteel residence than a place of commerce. I saw its wooden sign, hanging limp in the heat, and beneath – diamonds. Not real diamonds, of course, but panes of clear glass sparkling in the sun. Despite the dust, Metyard's bow windows were immaculate, displaying a tableau of headless figures. Silk flowers overflowed from birdcages hung between the models. A red gingham blanket and a picnic basket were spread on the false floor.

It was only when we drew near that I began to make out the fine detail on the gowns. I thought nothing would bring me joy, after all that had passed, but as I gazed upon the scalloped flounces and guipure lace in that window, it felt as if I'd never lived before. Such colour! An evening gown, off the shoulders, in pink watered tabby with a gloss like ice. Bishop sleeves on a cerulean carriage dress. Then the mint-green pelisse-robe with a series of silver ribbon knots that fastened it at the side. Nankeen gloves, dimity shawls. I yearned to touch, to possess, with an intensity that made my eyes water.

'Round the back, Ruth.'

Not for us the wide, swept stone steps that led up between the bow windows. We turned to the side and pushed through a wooden gate that creaked on its hinges. This gave access to a plot of miserable ground fenced in by walls and stacks of chimneys. A crippled tree hunched in a square of mud. Six or seven feet in front of it was an iron disc set in the earth, with a ring to pull it open.

'What do they keep underground?' I asked Ma. 'Under that hatch, there?'

It was pointless for Ma to look where I gestured, but she frowned and thought for a moment. 'You must mean the coal hole. Mrs Metyard doesn't want the boys and their sacks coming on to the premises. Too much dust threatening the fabric.'

The rest of the ground was paved over. There was a pump, but it was burnt so orange with rust that I doubted it would work.

For the customers, Metyard's was arrayed like a paradise, but here on the underbelly, where the tradespeople entered, there was no glamour. We hadn't paid for it.

My forehead was drenched with perspiration from the walk. Sweat had leaked through my glove and stained the bundle of material with an imprint of my hand. It hardly mattered, now.

'Let me talk, Ruth,' Ma said. 'Whatever you do, don't interrupt.' Her arms were shaking. Her clouded eyes widened, dominating her face.

'Why? What will you say?'

'I … I will have to ask her for terms. Permission to pay back the fines in instalments.'

'And if she refuses?'

'She cannot. Not after all that has happened. She is a widow herself, she must …'

As she trailed off, prickles of apprehension ran up my spine. Ma still wanted to believe there were people with good hearts. I knew better.

Tentatively, Ma knocked on the door. Footsteps and low voices sounded behind. I clutched at my bundle, terrified by the prospect of a fashionable female answering and sneering at me. Nothing happened. Ma knocked again. We heard a shout, followed by the quick thud of boots. The door eased open a crack, revealing a tall girl with large, wary eyes. Her skin was as black as a peppercorn.

Foolishly, I smiled. The girl didn't smile back.

'I need to speak with your mistress, dear,' Ma said. I couldn't tell whether Ma recognised the girl, or if she was just speaking in the direction of the door. 'Can you ask if Mrs Metyard will see us?'

'She's busy in the showroom.' Her voice wasn't precisely hostile, but defensive. As if we posed her some sort of threat.

'Well, can you ask all the same? We'll wait.'

The girl's nostrils flared. Not a flare of pride, as I'd seen in the young ladies at school; more like a horse snorting when it's frightened. She dithered for a moment before hanging her head. 'You'd better step in.'

Rather than opening the door wider, she simply backed away and left us to follow.

The trade door led on to a small, whitewashed room with a tile floor. It smelt like mud and boots. A large sink, such as you see in a scullery, ran along the left wall, but that was the only ornament.

I helped Ma up the step. Our guide had already turned her back to us. She wore a gown the colour of caramel. It was too short for her, and tight across the shoulders.

'Just a moment,' I pleaded. 'My mother has difficulty walking.'

Although she didn't turn or acknowledge my words, the girl slowed her step, and held the next door open. I liked her the better for it.

We entered a kind of lumber room. Brass rails lined the walls and from them hung offcuts of fabric, perhaps out of fashion now or saving for the cooler weather. Hat stands sported broken bonnets. The girl moved a wicker basket full of cotton reels off a battered old chair and I placed Ma upon it.

'Wait here,' the girl said. As she opened another door, I caught a glimpse of her right hand. Flinched. One finger was missing: the smallest.

The door slammed behind her.

It was crowded in the lumber room, but at least it was cool. Ma and I dumped our bundles on to the floor. It was a relief to be free of them, although I hadn't felt their weight as I thought I might. My arms seemed stronger, able to bear more.

'I hope Mrs Metyard won't be angry, being called from the showroom,' Ma whispered. 'I do not like to inconvenience her further. But Miss Kate can take over with the customers, can't she?'

I hardly knew how to answer, for Mrs Metyard wasn't being called from the showroom: underneath the door I could still see the feet of the girl. She was hovering there. Evidently, Mrs Metyard was not a woman to be interrupted.

Fifteen minutes passed. I amused myself by examining the offcuts, imagining what a corset I would have made if I'd had access to these materials. But Ma could only sit. She looked gradually paler, more frightened.

At last a bell tinkled to signal the customers leaving the shop. Movement sounded in the corridors. Ma clenched her hands together. I heard a sharp intake of breath, then the murmur of the girl.

A strident voice answered, 'What, in there?'

I wondered where Ma usually spoke to Mrs Metyard, but I didn't have time to ask before the door burst open and Ma scrabbled to her feet.

Mrs Metyard. If they find me innocent of my crime, and I live to be a hundred years old, I don't suppose I'll ever forget that first meeting with *her*. My dislike was instant, visceral. She had a square face marked with strong lines in the forehead and around the mouth. People would describe her features as handsome, but never pretty; they lacked the warmth necessary for beauty. Her spotted, silk gown had fashionable tight sleeves and gave her a military bearing. Later, I'd learn she acquired this stance from her dead husband, who was a captain in the army.

Outwardly, she was attractive enough for a woman in her fifties. But I think – and I know it sounds strange, coming from me – that sometimes you can just *tell* if a person is no good. You sense it as an animal does, and your hackles rise.

Ma cringed in a curtsey. 'Mrs Metyard. Forgive me for interrupting you. This is my daughter, Ruth.'

I inclined my head.

'I expected you to come,' Mrs Metyard said carelessly. 'I read about your husband in the paper.'

'Yes.'

'Shameful.' She peered down her nose, which was long, directly at me.

'I cannot make excuses for my husband,' Ma said softly. 'But as for myself …' She opened her clasped hands, gestured at the bundles on the floor. 'I have failed you, and come to apologise. There was … accidental damage to the work.'

As Mrs Metyard cast her baleful gaze upon the material, I saw how it must look through her eyes. Not just a filthy pile of cloth, but an affront to her shop and the beauty it stood for.

'That's not damage, woman; it's blood. So the brute shot himself all over your work, did he? Heaven and earth! Did his selfishness know no bounds?'

Ma crumpled.

Here it came at last: my breathless, silent fury. I glared at Mrs Metyard and thought how exquisite it would feel to knock that square head straight from its shoulders.

'I cannot—'

'It's of no matter,' Mrs Metyard cut her off. 'As you know, the work is long overdue. I had to give it out elsewhere, at great expense. But at least my orders are fulfilled. My reputation is safe – with no thanks to you.'

'Please accept my apologies, Mrs Metyard.'

It's a frightening sensation, watching your mother regress to a girl. I'd never seen her so meek. When Ma was young, she'd been Miss Jemima Trussell and ordered gowns from women like Mrs Metyard on credit. How far she'd sunk.

'I do accept them. Now kindly pay what you owe and take your leave. I hardly need say that our business relationship is at an end. Even if I could trust you to deliver the work on time …' Waving a contemptuous hand at our bundles, she added, 'You purchased this material from me, so keep it. I have no use for anything in this state. *You* might.'

'The – the payment,' Ma said, to her feet. 'I cannot, at present, pay it all.'

'No? How much of it *can* you pay, Butterham?'

'None of it. Not at the moment.'

'Oh dear.' Never had I heard those two words spoken with less warmth. 'How unfortunate. I suppose I must notify the proper authorities.'

'No!' Ma started forward, stumbling on her skirts. 'Please. I will find work and pay you back, Mrs Metyard, every penny. Only give me a little time, that's all I ask.'

'You, find work? Don't delude yourself. Your eyes have gone, Butterham, and your sewing is sloppy. Do not think I have failed to notice. I was merely too kind to speak out. But we should have come to this pass in the end, even if your husband had possessed the decency to stay alive.'

'I will find something!' Ma flailed for Mrs Metyard's hand. The dressmaker shrank back with distaste. 'I'll pay you something, I swear, even if it is only a little. But if you send me to the debtors' prison, your money is gone forever.'

Debtors' prison. Of course, that was what made Ma so afraid. The lumber room seemed to shrink around me, swathes of material pressing close, close.

'The money is already gone, Butterham. I know that to my sorrow. Come, I am not unreasonable. In other circumstances, I might have let you sew here until you had paid off your debt. But I cannot put out work like yours, even on undergarments. You see that, don't you?'

I considered *see* a cruel choice of word.

For a moment, it looked as if Ma would break, but suddenly her brow cleared and she said, 'Ruth.'

'What, *her*? Can the girl sew?'

'Oh yes! She can sew better than anyone; she flowered the gloves for the Lindsay bride. She could sew for me.'

I stared at Ma, horrified. It was like one of those nightmares where you're powerless; I could only shake my head and croak, 'No.'

'Hmm. And she is ... how old?'

'She'll be fourteen this November.'

Neither of them looked at me. I might as well have been a hat stand in the corner. Only the black girl shot timid glances in my direction, but she wouldn't meet my eyes.

Mrs Metyard sighed. 'Well, Butterham. It puts me out. I won't lie to you – it's wretchedly inconvenient on my part. But I *could*, out of the goodness of my heart, turn you a favour.' Ma held her breath. 'I've been considering another apprentice. Usually they would pay *me* for the chance but … Say I add the fee on, to what you owe? The child works here, wages withheld, until her earnings pay the debt?'

A single word wrestled its way out of my mouth. 'Ma!'

She ignored me. Her decision had been made, swift as a blade cutting through cotton. 'But Ruth could live here. Eat here. She'd be safe and warm?'

'Bed and board would of course be deducted from the wages, before they settle your score. Undoubtedly, it will take a long time for her to repay. But your daughter won't starve.'

'Then you must do it, Ruth.' At last, Ma turned her glassy eyes my way. 'At least then I'll know that you are well.'

I gripped her hands so tight that the very bones shifted. 'No. You can't …' Excuses crowded to the tip of my tongue. I wanted to tell her that the thought of staying with Mrs Metyard was worse than the prospect of living on the streets; that I'd lost everyone dear and couldn't lose my ma, too. But then I thought of the alternative.

For we wouldn't be on the streets, would we? This bitch would have us locked away. I imagined Ma, slowly wasting in a dank cell. She had no money to bribe guards or buy food. She would be penned in squalor, an unprotected female. God only knew what horrors she would endure before death finally took her.

'Don't fret about me, Ruth. I will manage by myself.' Even now, a lie. The bright, false tone she'd used throughout my childhood resurfaced. 'I will write to you when I find a lodging.'

Write? She couldn't see to write, even supposing she could afford pen and paper!

'It is the only way, you know,' Mrs Metyard said. She raised a hand to inspect her nails. A signal that she was bored of us, of our sordid little lives. 'If you don't, your mother will face gaol.'

'For me, Ruth,' Ma pleaded. 'Do it for my sake.'

Conscience ambushed me. If my mother was blind and widowed, whose fault was that?

'It's agreed,' Ma said abruptly. 'If you give me a paper, I will sign it.'

'Good. I trust you will not forget this kindness, Butterham.'

Mrs Metyard went to the living quarters to draw up the document, but she returned with surprising speed, as if she had such a paper ready-written in her desk. I recalled what she'd said about Ma's sloppy stitches. What fools we were, not to notice before.

An embroiderer's hand is as distinctive as a scribe's. Mrs Metyard must have known there were two hands, not one, sewing over the last few months. She'd seen Ma's stitches, and mine. Knew there was a daughter at home. She'd always planned to get me.

'Come along then, witness the document,' Mrs Metyard barked at the black girl, who'd waited there, as if expecting the duty.

The girl stepped forward, held the pen awkwardly in her left hand and made a cross where her mistress pointed.

I wasn't asked for my signature. Gripping a brass rail for support, I watched the scene play out in silence.

The corset clutched at my torso, protective. I felt its dark power flare within me. Swallowed. My stitches had already taken the lives of two people. Now they would be unleashed upon the ladies of Oakgate.

I won't recount the parting from my mother. I *can't*. So much of it was blurred, unreal. Nothing could convince me she was actually leaving, repeating her ridiculous promise to write.

If I'd had time to think about it, I would have told Ma that I understood. Because I do, now. She thought she was saving me; she had no idea what was going to happen. And I would have held her a little tighter, impressed upon my memory the scent of her skin and the sound of her voice. But it's too late for regrets.

The moment Ma left, Mrs Metyard seized me by the shoulder and steered me away from the lumber room.

'Kate!' she boomed. 'Kate, where are you?'

'I'm rolling the ribbons, Mother.' The voice that answered was that of a young woman, slightly nasal. I recalled Ma mentioning *Miss Kate*, the daughter of the house.

'Turn the sign to *Closed*,' Mrs Metyard ordered.

We made our way through a corridor and up a short flight of stairs. Mrs Metyard's grip didn't let me turn my head, but I couldn't hear footsteps behind us, so the girl must have gone.

There was no dust, here. The walls were newly painted, the air warmer. It felt like emerging above ground.

We came up short against a door. With her spare hand, Mrs Metyard turned a brass knob and revealed the showroom.

I'd been enchanted looking in from the street, but that was nothing compared to what I felt staring through that doorway. The space was twice as large as my old classroom; palatial, by my standards. A carpet of cream stretched out to where three circular tables stood, covered in lace doilies. Cheval mirrors reflected the pots of feathers and boxes inlaid with satin that sat on top. The walls were painted duck-egg blue. Here and there were alcoves displaying hats or an array of gloves and scent bottles. Glass chandeliers hung from a pure-white ceiling. My eyes ran past a dressmaker's dummy, past the bolts of silk and velvet suspended in rolls upon the wall, to a glass counter on my left. It displayed ribbons, trims and buckles of all sorts. Behind it stood a young woman, winding a reel.

You won't believe me, but it made my heart lift to look at her. It was like seeing a bird fly, or the sun setting over rooftops.

A bunch of dark curls fell over either ear. The face beneath was heart-shaped, gently pointed at the chin. Her small nose tilted up towards the end. What struck me most was her complexion: spotless and even, the hue of that scrap of peach sateen I had so treasured. Her eyes gleamed like spangles sewn on a gown.

Kate wore a high-necked dress, striped black and white. Even from this distance, I could see it was laced tight, no more than twenty inches at the waist.

In that moment, we could've been anything to each other. Our relationship was a bolt of cloth spread out

wide, full of endless possibilities. The pattern hadn't
been chalked. I could have loved her. I could have taken
the scissors and cut panels of friendship, sisterhood. But
she made the first snip.

'What is that?' The sparkling eyes grabbed mine.
Their expression wasn't kind.

'Lindsay gloves. Told you I would get her cheap.'

A grunt. Not the noise I expected from a young
woman in her position. 'Starting when?'

'Now.'

'Fine.' Kate replaced her coil of red ribbon under the
glass counter. I expected the daughter to seize me, as
her mother had, but instead she pushed past me on the
threshold and turned right.

Mrs Metyard chivvied me out and shut the door to
the showroom. The corridors seemed dark, without the
light of the bow windows. 'Come on, then. What are
you about?'

We didn't mount the wide stairs, carpeted in claret,
which led up into the light. I turned and followed Kate's
black and white skirt. Instinct told me I couldn't walk
by her side. I must trail her, watching the fabric of her
gown swish and her tiny waist bob. Visually, she wasn't
hewn from the same stone as her mother, but I could tell
from the way she carried herself, the way she lifted the
hem of her skirt, that she was proud.

In this part of the house, there were no cream corridors. Paint peeled from the walls like patches of dry
skin. Kate produced a key from her pocket and opened
a door that looked like a cupboard.

Chill air reached across the threshold to touch my
ankles. An ancient moss smell, close and stale, came with
it. Peering forwards, I saw walls of rough grey stone.
Wooden stairs yawned beneath.

'Mind,' Kate said. She lifted her humbug skirts another inch and descended.

Warily, I followed, my feet creaking on the wood. The third step was half-rotten, which I suppose was what Kate meant by her warning. I wobbled but didn't fall, continuing slowly down, down into the grey depths. After my walk across town in the heat, I should've been glad to enter a space so cool and shadowy, but it was no relief at all. The skin on my arms crawled. My body knew something about that place that my mind didn't – not yet.

Damp crept through the floor. At the base of the steps, four mushrooms grew.

'This one's you,' Kate said.

Her voice drew my attention away from the mushrooms. I looked up, felt my stomach plunge when I noticed that there were straw pallets arranged against the wall. Somewhere, water dripped.

'To … sleep?'

The look she gave me could wither the leaves off a tree. Rather than answering, she kicked the pallet, second from the left. 'You share. Her on the left, you on the right.'

On the right of the pallet lay a neatly folded grey nightgown. Waiting in expectation, as if it knew that I would come.

Kate put her hands upon her hips. They were slight, like the rest of her. 'I'm in charge here. Do you understand?'

'Yes. But—'

'What?'

I fumbled. 'But what shall I do? Do I work in the showroom, or—'

'No. Not today. Today you sleep.'

I stared at her. It sounded like a gesture of kindness, yet there was nothing kind in her face. 'Sleep? But it's only four o'clock and Mrs Metyard said—'

'Never mind that, what did *I* just say?'

Resentment swelled in my chest. She wouldn't let me finish a sentence. She had to stick out her leg and trip me up at every step.

'You said ... you said that you're in charge.'

'Right. And I'm telling you to sleep.' She fixed me with a cold, hard look. 'Trust me, you're going to need it.'

————

When all's said and done, this prison cell is comfortable. It didn't scare me half as much coming here to New Oakgate Prison as it did to be locked up in that dreadful cellar.

I lay flat on the straw pallet. It might as well have been stuffed with glass. Only the reinforcement of my corset stopped it from scratching the skin on my back to pieces. Somewhere out there, another person was sleeping on my old mattress, which the bailiffs had taken. I'd whined about that mattress. Now, by comparison, it seemed like a cloud.

My new bedroom was loud, too. Muffled sounds came from above. Some were in the house, others in the street; wheels rolling, the tap of determined footsteps. A narrow strip of glass on the wall above my head admitted a leprous, diseased light. Through it I saw a flurry of movement. No one could look down and see me; only if they lay flat on the pavement, their bellies in the dust.

My treacherous mind tried to creep back into the past, but what use was that? It had gone. I'd stitched the shroud for my family's old life, and this was my punishment. A dank cellar and the snipes of Miss Kate.

It was freezing. Colder than a summer should ever be. Above my head, the sky burnt blue and pedestrians sweated in the heat. But beneath the ground, I trembled. The blood in my veins became ice. My heart rusted in its cage and somehow, amidst the stench of wet straw, I managed to fall asleep.

Only once in the night did I wake. Darkness pressed on my face like a hand. I heard shuffling feet, sighs, and then there was a real hand, beneath my shoulder, shoving me to the right.

I nearly forgot. I nearly cried out for Ma. But the pallet squeaked and sagged, and then the whole sorry day came back to me. Flashes of gowns, ribbon, Ma crying. I heard Kate's cut-glass voice. *Her on the left, you on the right.* I didn't sleep alone.

The girl sharing my bed had a scent to her – not unpleasant, but foreign, a skin I didn't know. I wondered what she'd do if I started up in the night with one of my terrible flashes of blood. From what I'd seen that day, I didn't expect any sympathy.

Gradually, the air warmed. Female breath, female snores. Half a dozen, perhaps? It was hard to tell. All nameless, faceless girls. I could think kindly of them, in the dark.

The girl beside me didn't snore. She didn't seem to move. All I heard was a gentle click, regular, repetitive, as if she was grinding her teeth in her sleep.

Carefully, I shifted my shoulders and lay as I'd begun, flat on my back. From the corner of my eye I made out her figure, lying there like an effigy: hands at her breast, gaze on the ceiling. The whites of her eyes shone.

Click, click. What was it? Her shadowy fingers moved, turning the same object again and again. Not a coin. It was white, even in the dark. Not round. I couldn't make out the shape, but I thought I recognised the substance as it flashed between her fingers quickly, deftly.

Bone.

15

Dorothea

Today, I received an early gift for the anniversary of my birth. Like Salome, I requested a head on a platter – and that head shall be Ruth Butterham's.

Despite a vexatious cold and stomach complaint that have troubled me for days, I wrapped up in furs and called at New Oakgate Prison. The exterior looked pearly and clean beneath the April sun. Inside it was a different story: the brighter light showed up every cobweb and dust mote. I will tell the committee to have the floor re-sanded, and the walls washed with lime again before the summer … but that is by the by.

When I arrived, the women were out in the yard taking their exercise and keeping Matron occupied, so I was left to the entertainment of Mrs Jenkins, a turnkey, while I waited for Ruth. This was a stroke of luck. A turnkey is always an excellent creature to pump for gossip, and there is none better than dear old Mrs Jenkins. She told me more in those fifteen minutes together than Matron has revealed in our entire acquaintance, and she did it with relish.

From Jenkins, I discovered that Ruth has consented to the visits of the prison chaplain. What hopeful news for the salvation of her soul! I flatter myself that my influence has played no small measure in bringing this about.

However, knowing girls of Ruth's age to be sensitive about the interference of their elders, I did not mention it the moment I greeted her, but allowed her to continue her recitation of her past life as usual. Her tale interests me more and more. She has introduced the infamous Metyards and I like her depiction of them exceedingly: the cruel, superior mother and the insolent daughter. How much of it is true, I cannot say at this stage. I do not know what quantity of her brain is given over to deceit.

While she spoke I watched her, eager for clues. She has what the physiognomists would call a 'tiger' face: large-mouthed, eyes far apart but slanting down towards the nose. 'Tigers' are considered domineering and revenge-ful, and this accords with what I can see of Ruth's head: it is wide, like all with a ferocious disposition.

Dark eyes and dark hair suggest power, but also coarseness. Those wiry locks that spring from her scalp reveal the texture of the feelings within: rough and uncultivated. I wonder how they would feel, under my hand. Whether they would be hard or soft, like crows' feathers.

It was only when I stood up to leave that I ventured to say, 'Ruth, I hear you have been speaking with our chaplain. How do you get along?'

She shrugged. 'All right, miss. He's not ... he's not like you.'

A warm glow in my stomach. I should be above such pettiness, I should not want the child to prefer me to a man of the cloth, yet I do. 'How do you mean, he is unlike me?'

'He doesn't listen. It's all talk. I think he says the same thing to everyone. Maybe he gets bored, with so many of us.'

'Bored? I should hope not! It is his vocation, a precious charge, not some mundane task.' I became conscious, then, of my own neglected women, those who in truth I have grown tired of now that I have Ruth. 'What is it that the chaplain says to you?'

She frowned. 'There was one thing. A thing about bitterness.'

'Yes?'

'He says ... I must let it go.'

Suddenly she looked her age. I saw what her face might be without its habitual scowl and it was vulnerable, bereft.

'Well,' I said softly, 'and do you not feel that he is right? What use is your anger, in here?'

'Sometimes you embrace anger, because ... because it's warm, when all around you turns cold.'

She sounded pitiful.

'It is an old friend,' I guessed.

'Yes.'

Our eyes met and there I was at the age of seven, robbed of my mama and alone, just like Ruth. Of course I had Papa and Tilda; I was not shut up inside a cell, but nonetheless I was alone in that house. No other had witnessed the heartbreaking scenes that waltzed round and round in my head. There was no friendly face to discuss Mama's last hours with, no bosom I could confide in. I was utterly lost. Providence saved me, I was fortunate enough to find my faith, but Ruth found ... something else. And I fear it has driven her to the limit of her wits.

'Ruth, will you allow me to do something for you? The next time that I call?'

Quick as a blink, the guard came up. 'What?'

'I would like to study your crania.'

It is better to say *crania*, I have found. People are apt to turn peculiar if you talk about their *skull*. But I mistook my audience in Ruth, for her brow furrowed as she repeated the word.

'Your head,' I explained. 'The palace of the soul. You see, there are chambers in your mind, each for a specific purpose. Some think we are born with them fully developed. But I believe each organ will grow, depending on how much you use it.'

I am not sure how to describe the look she gave me, but it was certainly not one of consent.

'What I mean,' I hurried on, blushing now, 'is that if you work with the chaplain to amend your character, I believe that the shape of your skull may change.'

'And that ... matters?'

'It matters to me.'

'Why?'

'Because if I can prove this, it will help so many others. Mothers will be able to spot the warning signs in their children and turn them down another path. Penitentiaries will know, from a simple touch, if a prisoner has truly reformed. It will mean that we are no longer bound to follow the dictates of our wilful bodies. It will mean that we can make a difference, that we can change.'

I stopped, out of breath. My voice had grown louder. Ruth was regarding me curiously with her dark eyes, and I felt a rictus of shame.

What if the other prisoners overheard, or Matron? They would think I was hysterical. Deluded. A female out of her depth, wading where only men should tread. Perhaps they would be right. Deep down, I am aware that I seek proof primarily for my own peace of mind. The benefits to mankind at large are a welcome addition – not the purpose.

But as for Ruth, she did not pronounce an opinion. She only rolled her shoulders in their sockets, making them click. 'You can measure my head if you like,' she sighed. 'They'll do it anyway, I expect.'

'They?' I echoed.

'The doctors.' She tilted her head. It looked fragile at that angle. Held on by a mere thread. 'The doctors will do it when they cut me up.'

Anatomists. I had forgotten, but Ruth was right: when they hang a murderer, the body is turned over to the surgeons for medical science. They will not baulk at the corpse of a child. In fact, they will pay more.

'Try not to dwell on such things.' I shivered, though in truth I was dissecting her in my mind's eye. I could not help it. 'I know it is difficult, but try not to imagine … that.'

She watched me. Something ignited in that dark gaze. 'But I don't need to imagine it, miss. I've been there.'

It was in her pupils as they dilated: all the blood and the horror. She has stood in the presence of death. She has peeled back the skin and found … what? Do I really want to know?

'I remember what it sounds like,' she went on, gently, like a caress. 'The cut, the saw. How it smells. You forget who I am, miss. I've seen it all before.'

Try as I might, I could not produce an answer to that.

16

Ruth

As it happened, I did need the sleep forced upon me. At the break of dawn, my companions began to stir. I awoke to see them throwing off their covers and rising to their feet.

I copied their movements, rubbing my bleary eyes. Four girls lined up in single file, ready to shuffle up the steps and through the door. Like me, they wore long-sleeved, high-necked nightgowns worked in grey linsey. One of them seemed to be the same girl in duplicate. Perhaps I was still half-asleep.

I took up the rear of the line. Directly in front of me stood the girl who had signed Mrs Metyard's document. It was she who'd shared my bed, who owned that strange object made of bone. For some reason, the knowledge made me glad.

'What's your name?' I whispered.

She didn't reply.

'Your name?'

Her answer was so quiet, spoken down and into the chest, that all I caught was the letter M.

'Mim?' I interpreted. There was no response, either to confirm or deny, so Mim she became to me from then on.

My bare feet were cold on the floor. I shivered, trying not to let my teeth chatter. The other girls didn't appear bothered by the wait or the chill; they just looked weary.

Finally the lock moaned and Kate's face appeared.

'Come on, then.'

We marched up the way I'd come yesterday: through the corridors and the lumber room. The ghost of Ma seemed to hang there with the unwanted material.

We crossed the next threshold and stopped on a tiled floor, by the off-white sink. Today, four buckets sat in it. Without being asked, Mim collected them, two in each hand, and went outside.

It promised to be another hot day. Mist and dew were already melting away from the desolate garden. Mim went to the pump and plied the lever. Despite the rust, water spluttered out.

No one spoke. Kate was moving around in the lumber room while the other girls stood with their heads down, staring at their feet. Two of them *were* the same. Lanky brown hair, low brows. Thin, pursed lips. They must be twins. The expression on their faces would have curdled milk.

The third girl was different. Older, to judge by the shape of her body. She had pale, freckled skin that looked like an egg, and cinnamon hair. I couldn't tell what she was thinking. Her countenance was a perfect blank.

Mim returned with the buckets, one at a time. Only after all the buckets were lined up did she notice that there were four of them and five of us. She hesitated, but Kate barked, 'Twins share.'

One of the twins, the taller, shoved me to the side as she made her way to stand opposite her sister. I suppose before I arrived, she'd always had a bucket of her own.

'Quickly,' Kate said.

They stripped naked. Averting my eyes, I agonised over what to do. The corset … How could I get it off? I'd look mad, wearing it next to my skin, instead of over a shift, and keeping it on to wash. Desperately, I reached beneath my nightgown and tugged at the hooks. Useless. They were clamped into the eyes, unyielding as the teeth of a bulldog.

I sponged myself as best I could, washing beneath the cover of my nightgown. You would think I'd stink to high heaven, after the days I'd been trapped inside the corset, but I didn't. Neither did the material mark with my sweat. The corset looked exactly the same as it had when I first put it on.

Kate gathered up items from a clothes-horse in the lumber room and threw them at us. The girl with the cinnamon hair moved to grab the first shift, her feet squeaking on the wet tiles. Apparently there was an order to collection, which the others knew. I assumed my clothes would come last, and they did.

We were all dressed the same: in a plain cotton shift, a single petticoat and the caramel dress I'd seen Mim wearing the day before. None of the items fitted well. Still, they had the virtue of being clean.

Kate gave one of her grunts and marched out of the lumber room. The others trooped after her, except for Mim. She stayed to empty the buckets.

Kate's dress bobbed in front, leading the way. Blue, this morning. Peacock blue. The colour of feathers, jewels and mountain waterfalls. I could taste it.

The workroom was in the attic. We didn't travel up the carpeted staircase I'd glimpsed that first day but another, rickety structure with treads that complained. They led to a space with a high ceiling. Two rectangular tables and several stools occupied the floor. Everything was spotlessly clean.

There was no fireplace and very little room to move around the stools. Waist-high cupboards lined the back wall. There were skylights, but they were high up and distant as the sun itself. No doubt too much light would fade the material we worked on. Material mattered in that world. Taffeta, paduasoy, tulle: they were the pampered monarchs. Flesh and blood came cheap.

All of the girls took a stool – these were assigned, too. Kate banged a new seat into place at the end of a table and said, 'Ruth.'

I didn't realise she knew my name. It sounded strange on her tongue.

I sat. Kate stood behind my stool. I felt the warmth of her body, caught a trace of her scent: lily of the valley.

'Slops,' she said. 'You start on slops.'

I opened my mouth to ask what she meant, but the next minute she dumped a pile of half-sewn shirts, chemises and cheap cotton day-gowns before me. Slop work, or piecework, as Ma had called it: the ready-made items requiring little skill.

Even here, they wouldn't let me touch the good stuff.

Kate unlocked a drawer beneath the table and slid it open. Needle points glittered before my eyes. Tiny bayonets. None of them safe.

One of the twins took a needle first, followed by her sister, then the freckled girl. I hung back.

'Ruth. Needle.'

A weapon. I was choosing a murder weapon.

'Take one.'

I grabbed one of the smaller needles at random and took my stool again.

I rolled the needle between my thumb and index finger. My stomach lurched. Already I felt the power buzzing in my hand. Tempting. This wasn't my own needle, yet it was alive, sentient. Capable of things I didn't want it to be.

I swallowed.

The others had already started their work. Kate stared at me, thunderous.

I had no choice but to begin.

I promise you I tried. I tried to empty my mind, to erase myself, to become nothing as I sewed.

It didn't work.

By the time Mim thudded up the stairs and sat on the stool by my side, I'd already dwelt upon how much my back hurt and wondered where Ma might be. It was a relief to stop sewing, just for a second, and hand Mim the next piece of work in the pile.

Mim and I were both on slops. The twins were improvers and the other girl, the older girl, seemed to be the Second Hand.

Of course, Kate was in charge. She worked at a separate table, drawing designs and cutting them out. She had a pair of shears, fastened to her table with a length of rope.

Nobody spoke. I only heard their breath: in and out, in time with the snip of Kate's shears. My stitches followed the rhythm.

Now and then, I dared to look up. My eyes took everything in small sips: the room, the girls. They were so remote from me, they might as well have been the women I was sewing for. Nameless, without character. Could I really see out years of my life in this place? Even if I managed to control my traitorous stitches, I would grow up without any prospects of marriage, without even the chance to make a good friend.

I shifted in my seat. My corset nipped. It was the only thing that understood, the only thing that knew me.

After about three hours, a tinny, whining sound made me jump.

'Miss Metyard,' said a voice. 'Would you be so kind as to attend in the showroom?'

Kate threw down her shears. She went to the corner and leant over what I'd thought was a pipe for gas. 'Please allow me a moment, I will be down directly,' she said into the bottom.

I stared. The voice she used to speak through the pipe was entirely different from her usual, brusque tones. And that genteel person on the other end – it couldn't be Mrs Metyard? The pipe must lead into the showroom, I supposed. Customers could hear it.

Taking off her apron, Kate brushed down her peacock-blue dress. All of the girls paused to watch her. She looked over at Mim, her jaw tight.

'Tea,' she said.

A scrape as the girls pushed back their stools and rose to their feet. Kate passed through the door with Mim in her wake. A different order, this time, for us to descend the stairs.

I still went last.

When we reached street level, Kate peeled off towards the showroom, while Mim led us workers to the kitchen. The Metyard house was like a rabbit warren; you didn't know where the next twist or turn would take you. Or at least, I didn't.

The kitchen had a range and a copper that whistled as it steamed. Like our sleeping quarters, the walls looked damp. No doubt all the laundry was hung out here to dry. There was a long, knife-marked table with benches running down either side. The twins claimed one bench immediately, and the elder girl sat opposite them.

I wavered. I would rather sit next to Mim again, but she was clanging pots around. It seemed she was the maid, as well as a slop worker. Reluctantly, I crept over and sat next to the elder girl.

She shifted to the side, ever so slightly. Making space for me, or pulling away? The twins both gave me the same look: like a mule with its ears put back. I wasn't welcome here, any more than I'd been at school.

Although the freckled girl was the eldest, and seemed to be the highest-ranking seamstress, Mim served the taller twin first. Next came her sister, then the freckled girl, then me. Last of all, Mim herself. This was the hierarchy they'd established for themselves.

It didn't surprise me: two are stronger than one. The twins had an air of insolence and self-regard. They weren't pretty, but they'd managed to develop the sneer and the languid manner of the fashionable misses at school. It must be nice, to have an ally like that. A sister who would never leave your side. I remembered Naomi, her little cheek resting on my chest.

The corset pinched.

Grateful to hide my face, I looked down at my breakfast. The liquid Kate had called 'tea' was even worse than Ma used to serve: dingy with a sort of film. Beside it sat a slice of unbuttered bread.

'Thank you, Mim,' I said.

The twins sniggered.

'We don't usually talk at meals.' It was the freckled girl next to me. She wasn't scolding, but she didn't sound kind, either. Her voice was much like her expression: blank.

'Why?'

She bit her lower lip. 'Habit, probably. From the Foundling.'

'You were at the Oakgate Foundling Hospital?'

'Yes.' A downward note. That was the end of the conversation.

I bit into my bread, mulling this over. Ma had mentioned, once or twice, that Mrs Metyard used to own a shop in London. I thought she'd take her apprentices from the city, too, not the local home for unwanted children. But Mrs Metyard sought out girls with no ties, no family. For what terrible purpose, I couldn't have known, back then.

'What are your names?'

From the exasperated way the taller twin groaned, you would have thought I'd asked her to recite an epic ballad. 'Ivy,' she hissed. Pointing to her double, 'Daisy,' and finally, 'she's Nell. Now will you shut your trap?'

'It's her first day,' Nell said quietly. 'Don't be too hard on her.'

Ivy glared.

'I bet you miss your mother,' Mim whispered to me.

It took all my self-composure not to cry. 'Yes. I do. And I expect you ... did you ever know your mother?'

Her face suddenly smoothed, as linen does when you pass a flatiron over it. 'No, but I've got something of hers. Sometimes mothers at the Oakgate Foundling Hospital leave a token with the baby, in case they come back to claim them. My mother left a bone gaming fish.'

'Not *sometimes*,' Ivy mocked, clearly eavesdropping. 'They haven't left tokens at the Foundling for decades. You get a receipt, now. Everyone knows that.'

'So your ma was stupid,' Daisy added. 'As well as a gambling whore.'

Mim slammed a plate on the table. A crack ran through it. Her hand was shaking. 'At least she cared. At least she left me something.'

'Probably by accident.' Daisy grinned. 'She meant to bet you on the faro table.'

Ivy wasn't smiling. 'You're for it now, Blackbird. You've broken a plate. Dear me. What will Mrs Metyard say? I hope no one tells her.'

'Hold your spiteful tongue!' Mim's cry sent a shiver through me. She wasn't shy and reserved after all. The same rage that lit my heart burnt within her.

It was a thread, tugging us together.

17

Dorothea

The day had to come, of course. I have reached the age of five and twenty. Mama survived but two more years before she passed from this life. What a melancholy reflection.

Despite Pa's doom-laden prophecies about my eccentricity, I seem to have retained my popularity in the neighbourhood – or at least, my money has. All day the bell has been clanging, sending maids running to and from the door to receive gifts. Wilkie was not amused. However, he was impressed with the bouquet that arrived early this morning, which I made Tilda position in a jug by his cage. He came right up to the bars and tilted his head to regard each flower.

'There's no note on this one, miss,' Tilda said knowingly.

'Why, how very odd.'

Nodding bluebells – those for 'constancy'. Yellow acacia means 'secret love'. The message of pink camellia is 'longing for you'. Oh yes, I know very well who they are from.

I wonder how my birthday celebrations should progress, were I now David's wife. Would we have the leisure or means to mark the day at all? I think I should prefer to be surrounded by policemen and their worthy ladies, rather than the guests at my ball. I feel they would be an improving influence upon me. David points me in the correct direction, just as I assist Ruth. A droll thought indeed!

I do hope David has not spent too much upon my flowers. For myself, I have been positively frugal. Papa gave me a bank note for a new gown, but I only laid out a fraction of it, saving the rest for my future with David. The dressmaker has not done badly. I have a little creation in daffodil silk, with a pointed waist and cartridge pleats in the skirts. The sleeves fall off my shoulders into five rows of lace flounces. A fabric flower sits in my corsage, matching the fresh ones Tilda shall arrange in my hair. All in all, I will not disgrace myself, although perhaps the guests will be expecting something more from a lady of my means.

I find I cannot commission clothing these days without a thought for Ruth Butterham. It discomforts me to imagine young girls sewing in cramped conditions to construct my ball gown. Naturally, I do not believe Ruth's absurd claim that she wove hate into her stitches, but still the question remains: *do* they despise me? Do those seamstresses hunch on their stools, plying their needles, full of bitterness for the lady who makes their fingers work? Perhaps the plight of distressed seamstresses is another cause I shall take up. Papa cannot complain – it is at least *related* to fashion.

He is in a fidgety mood today. It pleases him to host a party and display our house to advantage, yet I feel him glance at me as a fruit monger regards his wares: eager to sell them before they grow soft. No one wishes to be saddled with overripe goods. As a daughter well married, I could still be a credit to him, yet if I remain unwed for much longer ... I shall be an embarrassment. An encumbrance. The things Papa hates most of all.

This hurts me. I am sure Papa does not mean it, but his deflating comments lend an undercurrent of reproach to all I do. He wishes me pinned like a butterfly: beautiful to display, firmly in my place. Without life.

I find I cannot look up to him, as a daughter ought. He belittles my charity and reviles my religion. I do not think he is a bad person. Not deep down. Only, he does act like one more often than I am comfortable with.

Day after day, I look for improvement in his skull. An enlargement in his organ for Philoprogenitiveness – that is, the love of children. A decrease to the areas of Excitability, Combativeness and Destructiveness. I pray that he will change.

It has not happened this year.

Now the party is over, I may report on its success. On the whole I cannot complain. My gown was laced and my hair dressed in plenty of time. For the last few weeks, Tilda has been saving the 'rats' from my hairbrush to make false pieces. She arranged it very well, with plaits looped under my ears and extra curls cascading from the chignon at the back of my head. Once the yellow flowers were added it appeared fancy, without being absurd.

I wish I could say as much for my guests.

No sooner did I begin my descent of the staircase than I heard a high laugh tinkle from the drawing room. It shivered up my arms and made me wince. The Pearce woman, here *already*.

She was taking a glass of punch with my father before the fire: he at one end of the mantelpiece, she at the other. A charming picture, if it were any other couple.

Her thin eyebrows shot up at the sight of me and her smile became fixed. Putting the punch glass on the mantelpiece, she stepped forward with both hands extended.

'Miss Truelove. My *dear*. Many happy returns to you!'

I was forced to endure the clasp of her hands and a kiss on either cheek. A cloud of jasmine emanated from her skin and made me choke – it was as though I had bitten into a bar of soap.

'Now, let me look at you. So grown up, I declare, and more handsome every day. The image of your father.'

I scrabbled for a compliment to pay in return, but in all honesty I was hard-pushed. When Mrs Pearce first came to Oakgate, about two years ago, she was in the last stages of mourning for her late husband. She wore pale colours, as dictated by custom. Alas, since shedding all that remained of her weeds, she has evinced a penchant for hues so vivid, so *loud*, that they give me a headache. I can only fancy that Mr Pearce succumbed to some sort of apoplexy, induced by prolonged exposure to them.

'How kind you are. And your gown, Mrs Pearce, it is so very … orange. Pray tell me, what shade do they call that?'

'Pumpkin.' She patted the bodice, delighted. 'I am determined to make it quite *the thing*. No virtue in following fashions – one has to start them!'

'Hear, hear.' Papa raised his glass.

I could easily have toppled her into the fire. Goodness, that sounds unkind. Perhaps I do not mean it. Only it was so very provoking, having her there in all her tawdry glory. She has never left off the hairstyles of the last decade, and as a consequence her head takes up a disproportionate amount of space. Gigantic Apollo

knots, a cupid's arrow through the middle and everything arranged *à la chinoise*, as they used to call it.

How can Papa say *I* embarrass him in front of his
friends and their daughters, when it is Mrs Pearce who
is so avant-garde? But the fashion papers approve of her
singularity – there is the difference.

Just then the doorbell sounded and more guests
arrived. Papa insisted he would go to greet them while
we ladies had a 'chat'. That is a vulgar phrase he has
picked up from Mrs Pearce.

'Miss Truelove,' she simpered. 'Ah! How I enjoy
saying your name. So wonderfully romantic, is it not?'

From the way she threw her head up and back, towards
the centre of Self-Esteem, I knew she was picturing the
day she would take my surname for her own.

'Not,' she added, dropping to a conspiratorial whisper, 'that I would have you put off exchanging it. There
are *some* trades one is quite willing to make.' She worked
her fan. '"Lady Biggleswade", for example … that rings
ever so pleasantly in one's ear.'

For my part, I think it sounds like a character from
The Pickwick Papers, but I do not suppose 'Mrs Hodges'
is much better. Dear me. *Mrs Hodges*. Rather dull and
frumpy. I shall have to grow accustomed to it.

Thankfully, a flurry of company and the arrival of the
musicians demanded my attention. With a brief apology, I
was free from Mrs Pearce for the rest of the evening.

Dusk began to fall and the candles were lit, making
the crystal chandeliers in our ballroom sparkle. The
company was predominately female: my old classmates
from school and some of the richer ladies in the district
Papa wishes for me to associate with. Their skirts rustled
as they moved across the waxed floorboards. I spotted
my particular friends, the Misses Awning, before an urn

of roses, and thought that perhaps I might pass my time pleasantly after all. Both share my interests. Fanny is a keen reformer and Rose practises physiognomy, rather than phrenology; she believes more answers lie in the lineaments of the face than in the skull.

It had been an age since last I saw them and there was much for us to discuss. However, my liberty was short-lived. Papa interrupted an interesting conversation with Fanny Awning about the penal system by touching my arm and saying, 'Dorothea. Let me introduce you, my dear.'

I did not need three guesses to ascertain I was about to behold Sir Thomas Biggleswade.

Fanny and I both curtseyed, and I dared to peep up under my eyelashes. Sir Thomas was not the ludicrous figure I expected. He was dressed respectably but not foppishly in a cardinal-red coat with a brown velvet collar. The chocolate waistcoat underneath was plain, not extravagantly patterned as seems to be the current *mode* with young men. Unfortunately, from that angle, I could not see his head.

'Sir Thomas Biggleswade, may I introduce my daughter Dorothea Truelove? I know you have been very eager to meet her. This is her old school-fellow, Frances Awning. How pleasant to see you, Frances, dear.' Papa slid me a glance of satisfaction, as if to say *look what I have found you now*. 'I think I mentioned, Dorothea, that Sir Thomas hails from Gloucestershire?'

'Indeed you did.' This was a miserable beginning to the conversation. I could think of nothing to ask the baronet about Gloucestershire. 'And ... what brings you to Oakgate, Sir Thomas?'

'My sister. In a round-about fashion.' He stifled a yawn. 'She lives this way. A dashed reclusive widow. If I

want to see anything like life, I have to jump on my mare
and hoof it down the road.'

It was all I could do to keep my countenance.

Sir Thomas is one of those young men who mimic the
manners of their stable boys. I need not worry about
him. It is doubtful I will rouse even his interest, let alone
a serious design.

'Sir Thomas's sister,' Papa whispered, 'is Lady Morton.
Do you recall Lady Morton?'

When he mentioned it, I did see a resemblance in the
set of the delicate nose and those sloping, sleepy eyes. It
astounded me. Lady Morton was a friend of my mother's,
but I had not realised she was still alive. Certainly, she has
not set foot out of Heatherfield Manor in recent years.

'Oh! Then I do hope you will be so good as to pass on
my regards to her ladyship?'

'I might,' said Sir Thomas.

I almost liked him. He is not, after all, ill-looking. His
sandy hair is tousled in that extraordinary way you see
in fashion plates from the Prince Regent's time. At his
temple, the organ for Order is small. This denotes a slapdash man who can never find what is wanted and allows
his affairs to wallow in perpetual confusion. There was
evidence before me: his cravat was tied but loosely and
did not quite match the rest of his attire.

Papa inclined his head, as if Sir Thomas had paid us
the greatest compliment, and said, 'I am so glad to see
you acquainted at last. My dear Dorothea, the time for
supper draws near. You must go in first, naturally, as
our guest of honour. I thought Sir Thomas would be the
proper person to accompany you.'

Fanny drooped a little at my side. Poor Fanny, she
would be giddy on the arm of a man only half as rich.
If only I could gift her all of my unwelcome suitors.

'It would be an honour, undoubtedly. Only I thought *you* were to lead me in to supper, Papa.'

He laughed affectedly and patted my hand. 'Me? No, no. A beautiful creature like you does not want a fusty old man at your side. Do go in with Sir Thomas; it would please me enormously.'

'Of course. I should be delighted.'

Sir Thomas merely bowed, but I suppose that was acquiescence enough.

Every eye turned upon me as I took Sir Thomas's arm. My chest felt constricted beneath the butter-coloured silk of my bodice. Mrs Pearce whispered behind her fan to Papa. Fanny shot me an envious look and Mr Dowling, who tried to court me last year, fairly grimaced. They were all imagining it, I knew: the society wedding, Sir Thomas and I arm-in-arm, walking from the church.

He smelt of pepper and horses. Under his sleeve, the muscles were softer and less defined than David's. For a moment I contemplated how giddily self-destructive it would feel to marry him. Painful but exhilarating, like jumping from a cliff.

We led the company, two-by-two, through the ball-room into the dining room. I was pleased to see the housemaids had displayed all of our china to advantage on the sideboard. My careful directions for the food had reaped dividends. Although we called the meal 'supper', it was heartier than most dinners: jellies, pyramids of fruit, mixed nuts, pigs' trotters and marzipan all took their place. The only oversight was Mrs Pearce's Cabinet Pudding – it was nowhere to be found. What a terrible shame.

'I see you have a pineapple,' observed Sir Thomas. 'Capital.'

That proved the limit of his conversational invention. He was gallant to a degree, fetching me food and punch without needing to be prompted, but he was more of an observer than an interlocutor. Time and again, I saw his eyes drift from me to Papa. Assessing.

Mrs Pearce, predictably, had seized the opportunity to take my father's arm in to supper. She stuck to his side like a leech. An orange leech with ridiculous hair. Really, every time I see her I notice something new and deplorable about the shape of her head. A skull so wide, so round – it indicates a selfish propensity, not to mention animal desires ...

'So, Sir Thomas,' I said, twirling the stem of my glass, 'your sister Lady Morton fails to keep you entertained at Heatherfield?'

He chuckled. 'Rather. I'd wager there are crypts with more life in them.'

'I wonder, then, that you stay with her.'

'Ah! Duty. It's a bore, but what can you do? One cannot neglect such old ties.'

I smiled. 'It is to your credit, I am sure, that you are attentive to your family. Tell me, is Lady Morton unwell, that she does not venture out in public? I am sure she used to visit my late mother, years ago. Has she developed a sudden misanthropic disposition?'

Another man might have been offended. Sir Thomas merely took a sip from his drink and said, 'Sudden? I perceive you do not have siblings, Miss Truelove. I am her brother; she has been surly to me for years. But do not fear that Georgiana has forgotten you. She has spoken to me of your mother often. I daresay she would call, were it not for the hives.'

'Hives?'

'Dashed terrible hives. She comes up in them, great red belters like she's been whacked with a stick. But you did not hear that from me. You cannot imagine the wrath I would face if that gossip spread in society.'

For all his pretend insouciance, I believe Sir Thomas Biggleswade to be a sensible sort of man. His intellectual organs are large, as is the centre for Ideality, which will dispose him to prefer the straightforward things in life.

'What a misfortune for Lady Morton! Well, do not trouble yourself, Sir Thomas. I shall be the soul of discretion.'

'Shall you? You disappoint me. I had set my heart on gaining a secret, for the one I have given to you.'

I paused. His words seemed to release something dangerous into the room. Was this a flirtation, after all?

Cutlery chinked. The air was crisp with the scent of fruit and champagne. I took a breath.

'I fear you will be disappointed by the entire evening, Sir Thomas. These private balls must prove trying for a gentleman in your position.'

Another sip of his drink and a slow smile. 'I am sure I don't know what you mean.'

'Well, you being a baronet, and young, and unmarried. All night you are plagued with mamas pushing forward giggling, simpering daughters, praying they will take your fancy. It is no more enjoyable than being a worm on a hook.'

He stretched his jaw. No lady has ever dared to speak to him like that, I would wager. All to the good. I have found there is nothing more certain of turning a gentleman away than an honest tongue.

'Do you base this statement on your observation of me, Miss Truelove, or merely your own imagination?'

'On experience. Come, you do not need me to inform you that I am an heiress.' Mrs Pearce released her jangling laugh. The food soured in my stomach. 'I cannot tell you how tired I am of endless suitors and full dance cards.'

He was paying attention to me, now, but it was hard to tell whether he was interested or insulted. 'I am trying to make out,' he said, 'how you wish me to respond. You either mean to tell me you do not, on any account, wish to stand up with me after supper, or you are urging me to claim a dance by implying scarcity. It is easiest for me to say nothing at all.'

'Then I shall do the same, and we will enjoy our silence.'

He gave a little snort of amusement. 'I see. I am put into their camp, am I? The endless suitors after your money?'

'I should be sorry to think so.' I glanced significantly in the direction of my father and Mrs Pearce. Her hand clutched his sleeve; the cupid's arrow skewering her head pointed directly at him. 'Come, I *will* give you a confidence in return for yours. It is this: I fear that any man who pursues me in hope of a fortune is liable to a nasty surprise.'

'How so?'

I dropped my voice to a whisper, but it was a stage whisper, clearly audible. 'I do have *some* money, of course, from my dear departed mother. But it must be plain to you, as it is to me, that my father means to marry again.'

He regarded Mrs Pearce, her head thrown back in laughter. I was glad to see a moue of distaste. 'It does appear that way.'

'If they should have a daughter, my father's wealth would be split between us. That is the most favourable outcome. But if they should have several daughters, or a son …'

'I see.' He was not smiling any more.

'And I pray that if you hear any young men mention my prospects tonight you might, discreetly, put them right. It would be mortifying to be suspected of subterfuge.'

'Indeed.' He leant back in his chair, thoughtful. Lines marked his brow. 'Indeed it would.'

Success. I had thrown him off the scent, appearing to be candid and pure of motive the entire time. *You will wait a little longer, Mrs Pearce, for your romantic name.*

But Sir Thomas was not vanquished yet. 'Forgive me, Miss Truelove, but if this is the case, surely you would be wise to accept one of the legion of beaux clamouring for your hand? A match would provide security, would it not, and pave the way to contentment for both yourself and Mr Truelove? Or have you a fancy to play the step-daughter?' The look he threw Mrs Pearce suggested only a fool would be so disposed.

Heat suffused my cheeks. The mere thought of 'playing step-daughter', as he put it, filled me with anger, and its blaze was intensified by Sir Thomas's advice. Indeed, who was he to say I should marry? He knows nothing of me! But I could blame no one save myself for these unpleasant sensations. It was indelicate of me to speak so frankly with a stranger in the first place. 'I have no inclination to marry at present,' I replied stiffly.

After an awkward silence, he moved towards me again. 'I would be sorry to end supper on this note, Miss Truelove. Wreaks havoc with the digestion. Come, let us be cheerful and speak of something else.'

I smiled. 'Gladly. I have just the thing. Allow me to tell you, Sir Thomas, about the shape of your head.'

18

Ruth

Sewing at home, I'd been able to take breaks as I pleased, but not at Metyard's. If I so much as shifted my legs, the twins glared: identical, baleful eyes watching me over needles that dipped in unison.

My own eyes felt bone dry from unremitting concentration. Every stitch looked double. I began to worry that more women, innocently purchasing clothes I'd made, would find themselves going blind.

When the clock downstairs struck eight, Kate finally sallied from the room. The other girls began to tie off their stitches. Eight was the finishing time, then. Thank God. As far as I could reckon it, we'd been working since about five or six in the morning.

A red ring marked the top of my middle finger, where the thimble had sat. Cramp had set my hand into a claw shape. I was afraid to think what that claw might have done.

In the bustle of packing away, I risked a few words to Mim.

'What do we do now?'

Mim opened her lips to reply, but then there was a terrible pounding on the stairs. The floorboards shook. Nell, Ivy and Daisy all turned to look in our direction.

Mim's nostrils flared again, and her stance became rigid.

'What is it?'

The door answered me, banging back against the wall as if a gale had blown it in. Mrs Metyard stalked across the threshold, even taller and squarer than I remembered.

'Where is she? Where is that villain, that vandal, who broke my china?'

It wasn't china – only an earthenware plate – but no one dared say that to Mrs Metyard. Not when she spoke in a voice sharp enough to flay skin from the bone.

'Thought you could hide it, did you?' She swept over and gripped Mim by the wrist. It was the right wrist, the side with the missing finger. 'Thought I wouldn't notice? Devious wretch!'

'It was an accident!' Mim asserted, but Mrs Metyard struck the words from her mouth.

'There are no accidents, girl, only carelessness. You were born careless.'

I could despise Mrs Metyard, storming and screeching like the witch from a pantomime. But when I saw Kate, lurking in the shadows by the door – that's when I missed a breath.

She was all eyes and cheekbones. Chilling in her lack of expression. The peacock-blue dress didn't compliment her now. It was an incongruous thing, belonging to a different world; its bright colour grotesque against the sudden pallor of Kate's skin.

'Must I teach you again?' Mrs Metyard went on. 'Do you need the rules and regulations made clear?'

'No,' Mim said. Not a plea. I admired her for that.

Kate was clutching something: it moved forwards and backwards, in slow, contracted waves beside her thigh.

It was a poker. An iron poker fetched from a fireplace downstairs.

'I'll do it, Mother.'

'Very well. Twenty lashes. It's the only way they learn.'

Kate sloped into the workroom, seizing Mim's other wrist in her spare hand, so close to me I could have touched her. Lily of the valley wound up my nostrils, forced its way down my throat.

'No!' Mim cried.

They dragged her from the room.

Part of me expected the twins to laugh. They didn't. Even when the door closed upon us and we heard the sound of Mim's shoes, scraping across a distant floor. They were grave, staring at the wall.

'They won't hit her?' I whispered. 'I mean, not with that poker …' A tingle, a ghost of feeling in my ribs. I thought Rosalind Oldacre's boots had been bad.

Daisy pushed back the wisps of hair that had fallen over her forehead. 'Don't fret yourself. The black-amoors don't feel pain, not like we do.'

It was the stupidest thing I'd ever heard. Slowly, I pushed up the caramel sleeve on my right arm. My hand was still a claw – I made it into a fist.

'You did this. You and Ivy. You're the reason Mim—'

Nell touched my shoulder. 'Better her than you.'

I hated every one of them. If I could, I would have boxed their ears, but there was that tread upon the stairs again.

Mrs Metyard reappeared. Her cheeks were flushed, her beady eyes sparkled.

'Beg your pardon, Mrs Metyard, ma'am,' said Nell. 'It's past eight. Shall I dismiss the girls, or is there something else we can assist you with?'

Muscles relaxed in Mrs Metyard's jaw. She looked more collected, more as she usually did. 'As a matter of fact, Nelly, I had Lady Morton call on me today. The black satin and tulle must be finished by the end of this week.'

'A ... fortnight ahead of our schedule, I believe?' Nell was dead of expression. Dead of tone. I wondered what else had died, in this place.

A smile surfaced on Mrs Metyard's lips. The lines by her chin puckered. 'Just so. Fetch your embroidery needles, girls. It's going to be a long night.'

———

After that, I didn't care what I thought about while I sewed. Why shouldn't Mrs Metyard's clients see flashes of blood, or come up in the pox, if the girls who made their dresses were beaten black and blue?

Poor Mim. I'd never seen someone hit with a poker before. Just the idea of it made my skin tender. Would Kate heat the poker and burn her with it? I wondered if a brand would come up different, on skin so dark.

I soon found out.

The next day started very much like the one before: up at dawn, waiting for Kate to unlock us, the empty buckets. The only difference was in me. Something had broken. I was soft; I couldn't bear to see Mim suffer.

I had to help her undress to wash. The cuts on her back had scabbed and dried the linsey nightgown to her skin. Scars cross-hatched her shoulders, silvery-white. This had happened before. Who'd helped her, when I wasn't here? Had she struggled through alone?

No sounds of pity came from the girls around us; there were no flinches or cries. For the first time, I dared to stare at them properly, naked as they were. But what I saw unpicked a stitch inside of me.

They all wore scars of their own.

19

Ruth

We were sitting in the kitchen, finishing off breakfast. I'd wolfed mine down in very few bites. Back home, I'd thought we were poor, but at least we had thicker slices of bread. You could feed a sparrow on what we ate at Metyard's. The sparrow might turn his nose up, though.

I'd just emptied my mug and placed it on the table when there came a smart *rat-a-tat-tat*. Nell jerked to attention. 'That's the tradesman's door,' she said.

Mim's eyebrows bunched together in dismay.

'Hurry up, Miriam,' Ivy sang. 'You wouldn't want to be neglecting your duties.'

'I'll go,' I said.

I dived off the bench before anyone could stop me.

The tile floor was still damp. I picked my way over it, careful not to slip. It felt like ten years ago I'd shuffled into this room with Ma and wrinkled my nose at the smell.

This person at the door, waiting for me … It couldn't be Ma again, could it? Come back to say she'd made a terrible mistake?

Praying with all my might, I opened up the door.

It was Billy Rooker.

I expect you've read about him in the paper. Maybe you've even seen a woodcut. I can't say he was handsome, exactly, but he had a rugged charm. Rumpled hair, ill-concealed beneath his cap. Bright, blue eyes. Remarkable, the colour of them; they were the first thing you saw when you looked in his face. So very sharp. You could cut yourself on those eyes.

'Hello.' He offered a smile. It created a tiny dimple in his chin. 'You're new.'

'I'm Ruth,' I said, stupidly.

'So you are. Billy Rooker.'

He put out his hand. I shook it. I remember how warm it felt, encasing my bloodless fingers.

'Can you help me then, Ruth?'

'I don't know ... What do you want?'

He laughed. Careless, breezy. How long it had been since I'd heard someone laugh like that. It felt like a miracle.

'They haven't told you about me, then? I'm your draper. Well, Rooker Senior is. I bring all your material.'

'Oh. I wouldn't know where to put it. Mrs Metyard and Miss Metyard are in the showroom, but I could—'

He gestured over my shoulder. 'Sure, in that lumber room behind you will be grand. Come on.'

Jamming his hands into his coat pockets, he turned and walked across the yard towards the gate. Snatches of a melody floated to me on the summer breeze. He was whistling.

Leaving the house didn't strike me as an advisable course of action – not with the threat of Kate's poker. But the wrench I felt as Billy Rooker slipped from sight was strong enough to combat my good sense. To lose him would be like forfeiting the only gasp of fresh air I'd breathed in months. I had to follow.

The soil was dusty beneath my boots. I retraced the steps I'd taken with Ma two days ago, past the coal hole, through the battered gate. Billy stood at the side of the road next to a wagon. A sturdy piebald mare dozed between the shafts. She was tied to a hitching post.

'Autumn colours,' Billy told me. 'Already. They don't waste any time, your fine ladies.'

As he opened the back doors, I darted glances down the street, hoping against hope to see Ma. There were only milkmaids and bakers. Each time I thought of her out here, alone, another part of me withered. Already the world outside Metyard's felt bigger and noisier than I recalled.

'Here.' Billy was standing hunched over inside the wagon, pushing out a long roll wrapped in canvas. 'These are the bolts. You take that end, I'll grab the other.'

The canvas scratched against my palms.

The bolt wasn't heavy, really; more unwieldy. I could see why Billy would struggle to navigate it into Metyard's by himself. Gallantly, he walked backwards, allowing me to see the steps and the gate. But to tell you the truth, I couldn't turn my face up. It felt too intimate: staring down that roll of fabric at a young man. Like I was hot and too large for my body.

I'd never had a male friend, barely seen a boy my own age. And here, suddenly, was this dazzling person, in his early twenties, so friendly. New and alarming sensations rose up inside of me. My corset seemed too tight.

But if I was flustered, Billy didn't notice. He kept chattering away to me. 'You'll like this one. Striking colour; chestnut, like a conker. Or a bit deeper. Like ... Miss Kate's hair.'

'Nell has cinnamon hair,' I replied without thinking. My cheeks burned. I could have bitten my tongue off.

But Billy seemed pleased. 'Aye! So she does. I never thought of it like that. Cinnamon. And what about your hair? What will we call that?'

'A mess,' I said.

He laughed. 'You're all right, Ruth.'

We lumped about half a dozen bolts from the wagon and set them on the floor of the lumber room. My shoulders ached, but less than I'd expected. I already had more strength than I used to.

Billy and I stood together, catching our breath. His cap had slipped to a jaunty angle.

'Come on.' He produced a knife from his pocket. 'Fancy a peek?'

With a practised motion, he squatted and cut the canvases away. Burnt orange, hunter green, russet and merlot. Then the chestnut, just like he said.

'Look at that velvet! Trim it with sable fur and you'll have yourself a spanking cape.'

I reached out a hand to touch. It was soft as skin. I yearned to lean down and place my cheek against the pile. Would that make a difference – if I caressed material instead of stabbing it? It might. But this gentle, voluptuous feeling was hard to keep alive. It sparked out so much quicker than hate.

'I suppose you need to be paid,' I said, forcing myself away from the velvet. 'I don't know how it works here. Should I fetch Mrs Metyard? She might not like me going in the showroom ...'

'No. Better get back to your sewing before the old dragon catches you.' He winked. It caused an odd movement inside my throat. 'I'll be grand; Miss Kate will come and find me when she's ready.'

Disappointed, I shuffled out of the lumber room. Billy returned the knife to his pocket and followed me. It made a nice change to be walking at the front, instead of behind Kate and the other girls. But when I turned, heading for the kitchen where no doubt Mim would still be struggling with the plates, Billy started to climb the hallowed carpeted stairs. Easy as you like, the most natural thing in the world! I paused, confounded, wondering if I should stop him. He was already gone.

My step was less steady as I entered the kitchen. Suppose I got into trouble for letting him inside? What if he stole something? If Mim could be beaten over a cracked plate, my situation was dire. I remembered that missing finger ...

Mim was in the kitchen, as I'd thought, but so were the other girls. They lounged at the table while Mim washed up. We'd all be for it, if Kate found us dallying. But Nell looked relieved rather than guilty, her shoulders less hunched than usual. Even Ivy's scowl was gone.

'It's him, isn't it?' she asked me. 'Mr Rooker.'

'Yes. Why?'

Ivy threw back her head and exhaled. 'Thank goodness. That's her in a good mood for the rest of the day.'

I stared at them. 'Who? What are you talking about?'

Ivy waved her hand dismissively, as if she'd done with speaking to me.

Nell got up from the table. 'Mr Rooker is Miss Kate's fiancé. Didn't he tell you that?'

Rosalind Oldacre's boots: that was all I could liken it to, the swift drop in my chest. Of course Kate, with her tilted nose and tiny waist, had everything. That's why he'd compared the velvet to her hair.

Whereas I was just a silly, mooning girl of thirteen.

'He spoils her something rotten,' Daisy said. 'Lucky bitch. I wish someone would mix me drinks and buy me rings. Haven't you seen it, the sapphire on her finger? Must have cost him a year's wages. You could take someone's eye out with that.'

Mim shivered, as if she knew only too well.

Sapphire was the stone for Kate. Another deep, fathom-less blue. And Billy's eyes would rival the stone with their brighter, lighter hues.

'Well,' said Nell, moving towards the cupboard. 'If Mr Rooker is here, I'd better fetch the cocoa flakes.'

I never tasted cocoa. All I drank was the smell: sweet, seductive and a tiny bit peppery, wafting its way up from the rooms below. It was like a dream, like a sumptuous gown. You could feel the texture of it.

The girls said Billy Rooker mixed the best cup of cocoa in the land, even finer than the parlours in London. But how anyone knew that, I'm not sure, because he only ever made cocoa for Miss Kate.

When she returned to us that day, there was a brown smudge above her top lip. It looked erotic, almost obscene, as she went about smiling, humming to herself, unaware. Billy hadn't noticed the mark, he hadn't kissed it away. It seemed to me that was the sort of thing a fiancé should do.

There were no arguments, no beatings that afternoon. But I was mistaken if I thought the holiday spirit of Billy's visit would last.

The next week, as I stumbled into the attic, barely awake, it struck me that something was off. A taint in the air. That was unusual. Kate kept the workroom in pristine condition to protect the material; there was no fireplace to produce smuts, and spreading dust was counted as bad as speaking a curse. Still, there was some-thing. An odour.

Kate herself was downstairs, arranging the new bolts in the showroom window; otherwise, she might have noticed it. But I was too tired to give it more than a cursory thought.

I watched Nell open the drawers – she'd been entrusted with the key that morning – and picked out my needle and my spools. There were about three pieces of half-completed slop that I had to finish, within the hour, before we all started on bodices for the season's ball gowns.

I'd left my work pinned and tucked in a wicker basket the night before, which I put in an empty cupboard at the back of the room. No one else left work unfinished overnight, but I'd presumed this was due to impatient customers and Miss Kate's scolds.

I was wrong.

The basket felt heavier than I recalled. Weighted. I placed it on the work table, aware of the twins watching me. That wasn't odd in itself – I think my plain face was a form of amusement to them. So I carried on, dwelling more upon the strange odour than on Ivy and Daisy, and submerged my hands beneath folds of cotton, ready to lift my work from the basket.

'Ugh!' I recoiled, holding my fingers up. Slime. Faintly yellow, salty and sour. 'What …'

A quick gasp of breath. Daisy, smothering a laugh.

'What have you done?' Frantic, I tipped the basket over and rummaged through my half-sewn cotton petticoats. All of them were stained with the same phlegm-like substance. And there, sandwiched in the middle, two sets of bones. Fish bones from yesterday's dinner.

They hadn't been picked clean. Grey ribbons of skin snagged on the prongs; one of the creatures still had scales and eyes in its head. It gaped at me.

Anger filled me to the brim. I would have flown at her. Skidded across the table, torn the shears from their rope. But at that moment, Kate's foot creaked on the floorboards.

'What's this?' She looked just as she had that night with the poker: her features petrified.

I was a coward. I admit it. All the fire within me died under the cold intensity of her glare. 'I …'

No laughter, now. Everyone focused on Kate's quick eyes as they darted from the ruined petticoats to me and back again.

Surely she'd realise I hadn't done it. *Why* would I do it? Mim and Nell knew the truth; they would say the words that were congested in my throat.

Wouldn't they?

The silence began to ache.

When at last Kate spoke, her voice rang out like a gunshot. 'Coal hole.'

I gawked at her.

'Coal hole. Quickly.'

Before I could gather my wits, she'd crossed the room and twisted my arm behind my back. She pushed me, in front of her this time, from the room and down the stairs.

'Three more petticoats to pay off. You'll never leave here, Ruth.'

'I didn't—' She trod on the hem of my gown, jolting me back.

I was stronger than her, heavier too. If she didn't have my arm at such an angle, I might have broken free. But what then? Mrs Metyard's leniency would end the minute I assaulted her daughter. To hit out would be to sign Ma's warrant for debtors' prison.

We reached the ground floor. *Coal hole.* What had Kate meant by that? For a delirious moment, I thought she was going to take me outside and cram me through the narrow chute in the garden. But she swung me round and pointed me towards the kitchen.

There was a hatch in the floor. I'd failed to notice it, devouring my precious meals at the table while Mim bustled back and forth. Now I saw its terrible wooden slats and the darkness gaping between. I thought I might prefer the chute, after all.

With her spare hand, Kate undid a bolt and prised the hatch open.

'What—'

She pushed me, headlong.

I fell.

Pain sliced at my arms, my knees. I coughed. Bitter sulphur upon my tongue, powder on my chest. The hatch creaked again. My world turned black as pitch.

I couldn't see. I could barely breathe. Panicked, I groped with my grazed hands, trying to find a way out.

There was no escape, only hard, vaguely round shapes. This was where the chute in the garden led to, where the coal was kept. Dirty, sooty clumps of rock. And me.

The roof was too low to stand. Instead I curled up on the damp floor. The darkness expanded to swallow me. I welcomed it. Maybe I'd suffocate down there, amongst the coal.

20

Dorothea

'The master wishes to speak with you.'

Oh dear.

I blot my letter to Fanny and avail myself of the opportunity to arrange my face into a careless expression. 'Does he, Tilda? I wonder he does not come to me in person.'

Her florid countenance peeks around the door to my room, which stands ajar. She looks rather comical, half in and half out.

'That's none of my concern. I'm just fetching you, as I was told.'

I sigh. 'Very well. Where is he?'

'In the library.'

This is not auspicious. No doubt I am about to reap the consequences of my discussions with Sir Thomas Biggleswade. I would so prefer to face the argument in my own room, on my own ground. But Papa has summoned me: a sure sign of his displeasure.

Packing away my writing implements, I whistle to Wilkie. He chirps back, lending some encouragement. Tilda is less of a comfort. She idles by the door, waiting to escort me herself, as if I cannot be trusted to go alone. It is not so very different from New Oakgate Prison!

I stride downstairs with affected confidence, ignoring Tilda. My knuckles rap on the library door.

'Enter,' says Papa.

The library is one of the masculine rooms in the house, furnished in dark mahogany and a deep, gloomy red. It gives me a chill to cross the threshold, for there is a stuffed vixen in a glass case immediately on the left, and a raven beneath a bell-jar, which distract from the handsome tooled morocco of the book spines. Taxidermists never contrive to arrange animals in pleasant positions – they must be always gasping or snarling.

Papa sits in a leather chair behind the desk. Sunlight falls through the window and glints on his brass lamp. He holds a letter in his hand. 'Dora. Come in. Sit down.'

I take my chair, fully prepared for a scolding. Papa wastes not a moment in flourishing the paper at me.

'Well, Dora, you have done it. I do not know what you said to Sir Thomas, but you have truly done it this time.'

I open my dry mouth. What can I possibly say?

An envelope rests on the desk, with a Penny Red stamp in the corner and our address scribed in a hand I do not recognise. The sight of it fills me with confusion. Can it be that Sir Thomas was so greatly offended by my behaviour that he has written to Papa?

'You must have made quite an impression,' Papa goes on, 'for we have an invitation to dine at Heatherfield Manor!'

My sweaty palm slips on the arm of my chair. 'I beg your pardon, sir?'

'Yes!' He beams. 'Lady Morton rarely entertains, as you know. This is a great favour, Dora. Sir Thomas must have been prodigiously impressed with you.'

'I ... do not believe it.'

'It is here, in his own hand!'

Papa slaps the letter on the desk. Sir Thomas's writing is scrawled and a little smudged, as I might have expected. Oh, what a fool I have been! Only now does it occur to me that a man with Sir Thomas's head, careless of appearance and unimpressed by show, *would* prefer to be spoken to in a candid manner. He would *like* that I demonstrated my learning and refused to dissemble about my fortune. Why did I not think of it before?

'Goodness,' I say, using a bland word to fill the silence. 'I … I shall have to think of something to wear.'

Papa laughs. 'Good girl. I am proud of you, Dorothea. This is well done.' Somehow his praise makes me feel unclean. 'I knew you should pull it off, in the end.'

I return to my room, sick at heart. It would almost have been better to receive the scolding.

Still, it is only dinner. Perhaps Sir Thomas means to use me as an amiable flirtation while he is marooned at his sister's house. He is unlikely to have *serious* designs, after what I have confided in him. Admiring a woman and marrying her are two very different things. This only means that he likes me. Well, I do not *dislike* him.

Besides, it will be interesting to set foot inside the famous Heatherfield Manor and see my mother's friend Lady Morton, who I secretly believed had perished. Did Sir Thomas jest, or does she really suffer from hives? How curious, that Ruth should also mention a Lady Morton ordering from Metyard's dress shop when I last saw her. Can they be one and the same?

Now that I dwell upon it, I recall Ruth was worrying about Miriam and her punishment whilst embroidering the Morton gown. It could not be …

What did Sir Thomas say? *Great red belters like she's been whacked with a stick.*

No, it is too ridiculous!

Speaking of Ruth, I have completed further research into the tale she is spinning me. I scarcely see the other prisoners, I am so absorbed by this girl! At least with the dress shop, I have more material at my disposal (forgive the pun). Horrendous as it seems, I believe she is telling the truth for the main part.

Naturally there is a wealth of information about Mrs Metyard, because of what happened. I recall the case myself, although I was not at that time involved in the prison to the same degree. We had yet to pull down the old colossus and rebuild it. I wish, now, that I had interested myself in the criminals earlier.

Newspaper engravings show the exact face Ruth describes: square and formidable. It is hard to tell, in two dimensions, but I ascertain the lady had little top head, which is a sure sign of an immoral brute.

For all her physical prowess, Mrs Metyard did not follow the drum as a military wife. She preferred to stay at home, overseeing an exclusive mantua-maker and milliner business.

Captain Metyard's demise occurred in the Battle of Nsamankow, 1824. Accounts suggest that the soldier was scarcely more agreeable than his spouse: stern and fond of excessive discipline. He must have possessed knowledge of Mrs Metyard's deplorable employment practices – or even instigated them in the first place.

He answered for it with his unfortunate end.

I confess, I do not pay much attention to battles. I had no idea what happened at Nsamankow until I undertook to research it. Our men were attacked by the Ashanti unawares, and ran out of ammunition. It was a terrible defeat. Sir Charles MacCarthy, the governor at the time, decided to die rather than risk being taken prisoner. In retaliation, the Ashanti beheaded his corpse and *ate his heart*. Charming behaviour, upon my word!

Both MacCarthy's head and that of an ensign were kept as trophies by the enemy. I look up at the ceramic busts that decorate my shelves and find myself prey to an unwonted shudder. Flesh and blood are not so clean: there would be burst vessels, trailing veins. I dare not flatter myself that the Ashanti held an interest in phrenology.

I have no information to tell me whether Captain Metyard retained his head and his heart, but I do know he left behind an infant daughter, along with his widow, and this must be Catherine, or 'Miss Kate'. At first, I was disposed to pity the child: our parents both expiring in the same year, and her abandoned to such a mother! Yet it seems from Ruth's narrative that Kate was an apple fallen near to the maternal tree. Indeed, with the mention of the poker, she sounds more frightening than Mrs Metyard herself – which paints events at the trial in a different, more chilling light.

No doubt all discrepancies will be laid to rest on my next visit to the prison. My craniometer is prepared, my books are ready. Heatherfield Manor be hanged – I have an engagement that promises far more excitement.

Tomorrow, I will measure Ruth Butterham's head.

21

Ruth

Time passes strangely, in the dark. I couldn't have been trapped in the hole for too long; they wouldn't have been able to spare me from the workroom for whole days together. I know that. But it felt like an eternity. I swear I aged, down there.

You believe in purgatory, don't you, miss? I suppose it was like that. Dark as death but not dark enough, not the oblivion I longed for. Just enough consciousness remained to torment me.

Was this how the world appeared to Ma? Impenetrably black and chill? It occurred to me, as I lay there in the soot, that maybe Ma wasn't the blind one. She saw things as they truly were: cold and devoid of colour. The rest of us were fooled by chimeras.

I couldn't get it straight in my head why Ivy and Daisy would play this trick on me. At least Rosalind Oldacre had reasons. She despised my poverty, envied my sewing skills. And hurting me in front of the other girls made her look strong. But this ... I'd done nothing to either of the twins. They were parentless and destitute, just like me. Why couldn't we be friends?

I'd *hoped* to find some friends, at long last, in Mim and Nell. Something to make me feel less alone in the world, less isolated by my curse. But they'd stood there and said nothing while Kate dragged me away. It would have only taken one breath, three words to save me. 'It was Ivy.' They couldn't even spare me that.

Left there much longer, I would have fallen into self-pity. I might have turned to coal myself. But just as I hugged my arms tight around my chest, feeling the reliable solidity of my corset, a glint shot past my eye. Against the felted darkness, it was bright as a shooting star. Another. Spots floated in my vision, the effect of sudden light on eyes grown accustomed to the gloom. Through the chinks in the trapdoor, I saw the gleam of an approaching lamp.

Relief fought with fear. If this was Miss Kate come back, I might still be in for a beating. Yet it didn't sound like Kate's tread. It was too heavy, too slow.

A bolt slid, painfully loud. The hatch creaked. I felt a gust of air and then – light.

I squinted, covering my face with my hands, a wiggling creature unearthed. From above, a voice addressed me. It was kind, satin-soft.

'Are you all right, down there?'

In my surprise, I lowered my hands. The light still hurt, but I needed to brave it and make sure I could believe my ears. The person who had spoken was a man.

His features, articulated by the lamp, were not ones I recognised. Then I saw the eyes: shimmering, flickering blue.

'Mr Rooker? Is that you?'

He raised a finger to his lips. 'Quiet, now. Try and stand up. Slowly.'

All my torpor had gone. Replacing it was a glow, achingly sweet. Someone cared for me. Someone had cared enough to come to my rescue.

After hours cramped in one position, my body didn't want to unfold; the joints making a creaking noise like the hatch when it opened. When I gained my feet my legs trembled, but the corset propped me up.

'That's it. Good girl.' He placed the lamp on the kitchen floor. Shadows swam around us as he reached down. 'Can you give me your hand?'

I gripped his arm at the elbow. My skin appeared grimy beside his. I was too wretched to feel embarrassed about that, or the soot clogged in my hair and smeared over my face.

Billy heaved and I scrabbled up. I flopped on to my hands and knees on the kitchen floor and coughed. It was still the same kitchen, damp and dreary, but compared to the coal hole its air seemed pure, forcing the soot from my lungs.

'Thank you,' I spluttered. Billy thumped me on the back. I coughed until my eyes watered.

'Look at the state of you.' He said it with indulgence, like a fondly scolding parent. Producing a handkerchief from his pocket, he spat on it and began to scrub my cheek.

It reminded me of Ma. Now I was glad the cough had made my eyes stream; it meant he couldn't see me cry.

Gradually, I got my bearings. There was no light except the honeyed pool at the base of his lamp. It must be late.

'Well, at least I can see your face now.'

He dropped the handkerchief beside the lamp. Long, black streaks tarnished the cotton. 'I've ruined your handkerchief,' I lamented.

'You can owe me a new one.' Billy winked. He knew, as well as I, that I could never afford such a thing.

'How do you come to be here, Mr Rooker?'

'Call me Billy, please. The Metyards invited me to dinner. I'm on my way home just now.'

'But … how did you find me?'

He leant against the sink and pulled himself up. 'Miriam told me you'd run afoul of Kate. The poor girl was worried. She didn't know where you were.'

So Mim *had* fretted about me. She must have been in this very room, cooking for the Metyards, and neither of us had heard the other. That was an unsettling thought. Like knowing someone had walked over my grave.

'I reckoned you'd be here,' Billy went on. 'I've rescued Nelly from the coal hole a few times before.'

The way he spoke took me aback. As if this was an everyday occurrence, not to be remarked upon.

'She put Nell down there, too?'

'Aye, sometimes.'

The specks of soot seemed to form into Kate's shadow; a shade hovering between us. Billy appeared kind, heroic even, rescuing trapped apprentices. It didn't make the least bit of sense that he'd engage himself to someone like her. Could men overlook such glaring moral faults for a pretty face?

'Won't she be furious?' I whispered. 'Miss Metyard, I mean. When she finds out you've freed me …'

He extended his hand again, helped me to my feet. 'Not to worry. You leave Kate to me. Her bark is worse than her bite.'

The scars on Mim's back told a different story.

Billy didn't let go of my hand. Instead, he tugged me gently towards the kitchen door. Nell was waiting on the other side with a bucket of water and a linen towel.

'I thought you'd need to get washed up,' she explained. 'The mistresses are reading upstairs. Kate won't come to fetch us from the sewing room for about an hour yet. Shall I put this bucket by your bed? Then you can sneak straight under the covers and she'll not see you.'

God knew it was a feeble offering, but I'd never felt
more grateful to a living soul. Mim, Nell and Billy – the
three of them, considering my comfort. Almost like
friends.

'Thank you,' I said. It sounded inadequate.

Billy released my hand. 'Nelly will look after you.
She's a good girl,' he added with a smile. It was not
returned by Nell. 'Now I'd better be getting home. I've
a mother who'll worry about me.'

I couldn't help the small sob that escaped my lips.
Nell glared daggers at him.

Billy winced. 'I'm sorry. I shouldn't have said that.
You're from the Foundling, are you?'

I shook my head. 'No. My mother used to work for
Mrs Metyard. She … she had to sell me to her.'

A sigh. 'Poor lamb. I wager you miss her something
fierce.'

All I could manage was a nod.

I was glad he didn't say anything else; didn't try to
cheer me with platitudes. With a respectful incline of
the head and a pat on Nell's shoulder he walked away,
towards the showroom and the door that led to freedom.

Nell and I watched him go.

'He's a lucky bastard,' she said. There was no malice
in her words. All the same, I could tell it cost her pain to
see his liberty, the way he could waltz in and out of our
nightmare as he chose.

'He saved me. Right now he's my favourite person
alive.'

Nell gave a tight smile. 'You silly noodle. Come on,
let's get this bucket to the cellar before they catch us.
Otherwise we'll both end up in the hole.'

Nell left me alone in the cellar to wash and change as best I could, by the feeble light sneaking in from the street above. I was as filthy as a chimney-sweep. Again and again I passed a sponge over my arms, revealing what looked like brand-new skin beneath. Rinsing the sponge, I saw soot ribbons twisting into the water, turning it the colour of smoke.

I picked up the linen towel, rubbed it over my chest.

And then a strange thing happened.

The hooks of my corset gave way. For the first time in months, the casing slipped from my body and fell to the floor.

I stood there, naked, staring at it. At myself.

Lines marked my torso where the cording had pressed into the skin. I ought to have been relieved, but I wasn't. My stomach felt odd without its familiar pressure. Exposed. It wasn't a release to be out of the corset's clutches. It was lonely.

Hastily, I stuffed my nightgown over my head and picked up the corset, my dear companion. There were no stains. Soot lightly peppered the laces, but that was all. I folded it, tucked it under my pillow.

What could it mean?

I lay down.

There's nothing like hardship to make you appreciate the good things in your life. The pallet, which I'd loathed, was now a comfort. Better than the coal hole floor by far. But still I didn't fall asleep.

Most nights I spent awake, dwelling upon those I'd lost. My nightmares showed me visions of Naomi's throttled face, Pa's splattered brains; all the evil I'd done and couldn't escape. Tonight I saw a different image: blue eyes, sparkling by lamplight.

Billy. I whispered his name to myself, savouring the way it felt in my mouth. I hadn't met any other young men. Could it be that they were all as kind and bright as him? I doubted it. There was something different about Billy, something extraordinary, although I couldn't decide what it was. I only knew that, in the two times I'd been in his presence, I felt more alive than I usually did.

Pressing my ear deep in the pillow, I listened to my corset. No creaking, now. It slumbered.

Guilt itched at me. Did the corset know? Had it abandoned me because I'd found some friends?

Perhaps that was for the best. Perhaps, I thought, with these people at my side, I didn't need a corset to keep me strong. I could get by alone.

Well, miss. You see how that's turned out.

22

Dorothea

'They have set a date, you know.'

Matron sits at her desk with Ruth's character book spread out before her. Although it is upside down, I decipher the word *improvement*, written in pencil.

'A date?'

'It's our turn on the assize circuit. The justice has scheduled Butterham's trial.'

Her words produce a very odd sensation inside of me. It is as if I am tied to a rope, and Matron has suddenly jerked it backwards.

My time for analysis is running short.

'Oh. Of course. What with Miss Butterham's confession, I do not suppose her trial will last for long?'

'They keep gathering witnesses for the prosecution, in case she changes her plea,' Matron explains. 'Or in case her lawyer suggests the death sentence should not be passed.' Her short, pared fingernails tap on the character book. 'I believe he might.'

'And why should he not? Her youth speaks for her. I would be glad to see her in a penitentiary, or transported to the Antipodes, rather than dangling at the end of a noose.'

Matron presses her lips together. 'I will not argue with you, Miss Truelove,' she says, although her face is doing exactly that. 'However, I will say that, in my experience, a leopard doesn't change its spots.'

Leopards, indeed! As if she watches over untamed beasts, rather than human creatures in possession of souls.

'I should very much like to see Miss Butterham today. Will you take me to her cell?'

Matron closes the book. 'She'll be washing it down about now. That is something we like to have the prisoners do, Miss Truelove, to encourage industry. May I take you to the visiting room instead?'

My stomach sinks. That will not do at all. I can hardly produce my craniometer and measure Ruth before a hall of inmates and their lawmen! Yet to forgo my experiment, after all this preparation …

'No!' I cry. 'I mean, no thank you. You are considerate, but I am certain the cell will not be too damp for me. I prefer to see the women at home, as it were.'

Matron raises her judgemental eyebrows, but does not protest.

Never have I walked down the limewashed corridors with such a sense of anticipation. The tinkle of Matron's keys and the crunch of sand beneath my boots make a kind of music, delightful to my ears. Sunlight streams through the porthole windows, warming my hand as it holds my carpet bag. This is the moment, I am sure, that all my study has tended towards. Ruth – strange, passionate Ruth – will confirm my theories at last.

The enamel plaque above her door now bears her name in capital letters, but no sentence, yet. It is that blank space that cheers me most of all. There *is* still time, there is always time, to blot out our sins. The future has yet to be written.

I pull down the iron flap and place my eye to the hole.

A dishevelled shape grovels on all fours. For an irrational moment, I think of the beasts Matron mentioned: leopards and other cats with large teeth. But then I realise my folly. Of course it is only Ruth, down on her hands and knees, scrubbing the floor.

'Take care, Ruth,' I call. 'We are coming in.'

My voice startles her, but she appears pleased to see me and throws her brush into a bucket of water. Her face is flushed, her hair chaotic. 'Don't slip, miss. It's wet.'

Matron clunks open the door and Ruth shuffles back towards her bed. I step carefully inside. The air smells acerbic: vinegar and soap.

'I hope I shall not tread in dirt,' I say awkwardly. Matron's eyes are upon me, unblinking. 'You have worked very hard.'

Ruth shrugs, as if that does not matter much – and I suppose it has not, in her life.

Her hands look sore and cracked as she wipes them on her apron. The water in her pail is brown, a few diseased bubbles floating on top.

I take a seat and place the carpet bag on the floor, beside my skirts. It makes a satisfying *thump*.

Matron fumbles with the keys at her belt. 'Do call, Miss Truelove, if there is anything else.' I cannot tell if this is a sour or foreboding tone; I rather think it might be both.

The door clangs shut and Matron's footsteps beat a tattoo, taking her down another path.

'Well, Ruth, and what do you think I plan to do with you today?'

'Measure my head. Like you asked.'

'Yes!' Rising to my feet, I grab my carpet bag. 'That is a great deal better than washing floors, is it not?'

'If you say so, miss.'

Ruth's ambivalence does not endure for long. When I show her my books and the shining craniometer, her eyes grow wide.

'What's that? It looks like something a surgeon would use!'

'Oh, it is not painful!' I laugh, opening up the arms and placing them either side of my own head. 'It is like a calliper or a compass. Did you never use one at school?'

She gives me an odd look. 'I don't think I went to the same kind of school you did, miss.'

I sit Ruth upon the rickety chair and begin to position her. 'It is easier to measure, I find, with the subject sitting. Only you must take care to hold your head straight, in line with your spine.' Placing my hands under her jaw, I pull gently. Her back arches.

'If you were measuring me for a corset,' says Ruth, 'you'd tip my head forwards now. Then you'd find the biggest knob on my spine, and start the tape there for my back length.'

'Would I? Well, this is quite different. I use the craniometer instead of a tape measure. And I'm afraid I shall have to touch your head all over. I hope you do not object?'

Ruth shrugs again. The gesture pulls her neck forward and I am obliged to straighten it once more.

'Excellent. Let us begin.'

As I unbutton my gloves, a stinging blush creeps to my cheeks. Why I should feel embarrassed to remove my gloves before a common criminal I cannot say, but I certainly do. Without them, my hands seem as raw and naked as peeled prawns.

'The first organ,' I say brightly, to cover my nerves, 'will be Destructiveness.'

My index finger extends, hovering just beside the outer angle of her eye. *Blink, blink*, go the stubby lashes. I trace a line to the top of the ears and stop. There. Beneath the black, spiralling locks lie my answers.

I am holding my breath.

Gingerly, I uncurl the rest of my hand and touch Ruth's hair. It is soft and dry; for all there is so much of it, it feels insubstantial, like cobwebs.

Destructiveness is large, as I predicted. So is Secretiveness, three-quarters of an inch above it. However, the head becomes narrower as it rises, which implies the latter quality is less prominent. The numbers on my craniometer confirm this.

Indeed, Ruth appears to have many large organs in her brain. I rather wonder her head is not bigger altogether to contain them. When I place the balls of my fingers behind her ears and run them up towards the crown, I find Combativeness swelling there. Combined with her large Approbativeness – that is, the desire to excel and be esteemed – she will greatly resent all insults.

As with most female subjects, a hollow is apparent at Self-Esteem. Yet I do not find grooves where I expected them. Her Mirthfulness, her Moral Faculties – all these are bigger than I dared to hope.

'How long did you say you had been speaking with the chaplain, Ruth?'

'Only saw him two or three times.' Her voice vibrates through the skull. 'And at Sunday service, of course.'

Can reform take place so quickly? Such a substantial reform as to reshape the crania ... But she is a child, just sixteen years old. I must not forget this. Children grow and change with great rapidity. It may be that their skulls do the same.

'I will move above your left eye, now. This will tell me how skilled you are in your work!'

Colour, Neatness, Constructiveness: all the tools of Ruth's trade are written in her brow. It is little wonder that she excels at sewing. But one anomaly has me reaching for my craniometer: a curve slightly below the centre of the forehead.

Ruth does not blink. She stares forward as I look, huff, look again.

Eventuality: this is the memory of facts, the recollection of circumstances and passing events. Generally the organ is larger in children than in adults, but even so Ruth's seems particularly developed, denoting a wonderfully retentive memory.

Of all things, I least expected this. I had depended on her recollection being twisted and confused: it goes hand in hand with her torrid story. I thought her mind in trauma, fabricating tales of supernatural powers. But if she recalls all the events leading up to her crime …

She is lying to me. Reciting falsehood on purpose. There can be no other explanation.

'All done.' My voice comes rather stiff, starched by the thought of her treachery. I turn away from her deceitful eyes and begin to write up my observations. After all these visits, I still do not have her trust. Or worse: she looks upon me as a dupe. A silly spinster to make sport of with talk of magic needles. 'You may move now, Ruth.'

'Can I look at your books?'

'If you like.'

Whatever untruths Ruth has been telling, her enjoyment in my books and their coloured diagrams is genuine. As my pencil scratches away, she spreads my manuals out on her skirts and flicks through the pages, exclaiming now and then. Whenever she comes across a drawing of a head split into sections, she places a hand on her own skull, wonderingly.

'So our brain's all sewn together, like this?' She angles a picture in my direction. It is the side of the head, the organs divided into pleasant blocks of yellow, orange and purple. 'Like a patchwork quilt, isn't it, miss?'

'That drawing is just to make the organs clear for phrenologists. I expect the brain looks rather different, inside.'

Her mouth droops a fraction. 'Oh. That's a shame. I thought there might be one part of us that was ... beautiful.'

'The soul,' I suggest.

Her eyes remain on the book. 'Inside, most of the body is disgusting.'

Choosing not to pursue this line of discussion, I return to my work. A dismal business! The figures are not at all what I had anticipated.

How will I trace a line of improvement, if Ruth's moral organs are already mature? If they were to grow larger, they would be very big indeed. Yet they *must* grow, surely? For if this is the skull of a murderer, what does it mean for those with a smaller Conscientiousness, a smaller Contrition? They must be considered diabolical.

'If I'd stayed at school,' Ruth sighs, 'they might have taught me this. I wish I'd had a book like this all my life. It would have been so easy. I could have looked at this and known at once who was good and who was evil.'

Her words make me shudder. 'It is not as simple as that, Ruth. The whole *purpose* of phrenology, so far as I am concerned, is to ascertain which organs we use the most and repair any imbalance. It shows us how we need to change.'

'Change the lumps on our skulls?' The corner of her mouth twitches. 'How do we do that? With mallets?'

Usually, I would laugh. But in this cell, with the bite of vinegar and Ruth's deadly fingers upon my books, I cannot. I do not seem to have a sense of humour left.

'Please do not be facetious. This is immensely important to me.'

She looks away.

What a relief it is to pull my gloves out of my carpet
bag and button them back on! They are an armour of
sorts, these little scraps of kidskin. I find I have exposed
too much; laid myself open, in a dangerous place.

I wish I had never asked Ruth if I could measure her
head.

I wish I had never visited her at all.

23

Ruth

It's hard to think kind thoughts, sewing when you're tired. Sometimes it struck me I'd be a nicer person altogether, if I could only get more sleep. But the season was in full swing and all the ladies wanted dresses ready to take up to London with them, rather than pay extortionate prices in the capital. And being ladies, they didn't think of this until three days before their departure, and they couldn't understand why their gowns didn't appear overnight.

We had to *make* them appear. In half the time. *Or else*, Kate said. I didn't really know, then, how bad the *else* was.

She never asked how I got out of the coal hole. In truth I think she was too busy. The shop bell tinkled all day. Kate was needed in the showroom almost constantly.

Mim and I were both tasked with making the voluminous skirts of a tartan gown. It was to have two rows of hem ruffles – a gaudy addition, given the sulphur and lavender colours in the pattern. Without Kate to watch us, we could actually talk as we sewed. I was sure that must be better for all involved. The less I thought about my exhaustion and how much I hated Ivy for getting me thrown in the coal hole, the less harm would go into my work. And God knew this tartan dress was going to be distasteful enough. The lady wearing it would need all the help she could get.

'I was talking to Mr Rooker, the other day,' Mim said. Her eyes remained trained on her needle and I was glad. She didn't see my blush. 'He asked if I had any family.'

'He's nice like that,' I replied cautiously. 'He's got manners. Almost like a gentleman.'

'And he can read,' she added.

In my surprise, I made my stitch too big. Tutting, I put my needle down and unpicked it.

It had never occurred to me before that I'd enjoyed a better education than the other girls. I was sure the Oakgate Foundling Hospital taught its wards the skills they needed for employment, but perhaps reading was considered a step too far. If the girls could ply a needle and cook mutton, what else did they need?

Mim lowered her voice to a whisper. 'I always knew there was a word engraved on the fish my mother left. Just on one side, where it's rougher. I asked Mr Rooker to read it for me. He told me it says Belle's.'

All those nights she'd been flicking the fish over and over in her hands beside me in bed. I could have helped her to read it ages ago.

Wetting the ball of my thumb, I threaded my needle and recommenced my running stitch. 'And what's Belle's?'

'He says it's a gambling house in London.'

'Your ma was a long way from London, if she gave you up to the Foundling here,' I observed neutrally. It wasn't that I didn't care, but I didn't want to talk about our mothers in the sewing room. The lady wearing the tartan dress would feel my sorrow.

'But she was coming back,' Mim went on, excitement creeping into her voice. 'She wouldn't have left a token if

she didn't mean to come back for me. Now *I* can find *her*.
If I can just get to London, get to Belle's, I'll find my ma.'
   'And then what?'
   'I don't know.' She held her needle suspended, gazing
up at the skylight and letting her dreams unspool.
'Maybe we'll get on board a ship. Sail to ... Africa. The
matron in the Foundling, she used to say that's where I
belong: Africa.'
   Evidently the matrons in the Foundling didn't have
much education, either. 'That's ridiculous. You were
born in England. You belong *here*.'
   'Oh, I know.' Mim shook her head dismissively, more
forgiving than I would have been in her situation. 'She
was always saying horrible things to me. But it got
me thinking. They say the sun shines all year round
in Africa. Even when it rains, it's hot. People dress in
bright clothes and they eat fruit we don't have. It might
be nice. The Africans couldn't treat me any worse than
Mrs Metyard has.'
   So that was how Mim got along: she'd created a fantasy
for herself, a magic land where people would be kind. I
could see the attraction. But it was just a story. The real
Africa – if Mim had any connection to the place – must
be entirely different. Although I didn't have the heart to
take it from her.
   'You can come with us,' Mim whispered. 'If you like.'
   I exhaled. If I ever got out of here – and who knew
when that would be? – I didn't fancy risking my life at
sea. Ma would never survive six months on a ship.
   'You don't want to take me, Mim. I'm bad luck.'
   She placed a hand on my arm. 'You're my friend. My
only friend. You haven't been bad luck to me at all.'
   Words I had wanted to hear for so long, but they
didn't bring me the joy I'd expected. Instead I felt a

queasy dread. I thought of Ma, without sight, without a husband, without her baby.

'Not yet,' I said.

Feet clopped up the stairs. The five of us fell upon our sewing, our fingers moving faster than they had all day. The room was quiet, the perfect model of industry by the time Kate sailed in.

The colour was high in her cheeks and her mouth was open, panting a little from her swift journey up the stair-case. 'Ruth.'

Just my luck. Was I about to pay for my escape?

I raised my eyes but I didn't stop sewing. The constant motion of my hand steadied my nerves. 'Miss Metyard?'

'Put down your needle. Show me your arm.'

I swapped a look with Mim. It was an odd request, but I didn't dare disobey. Reluctantly, I let the needle go.

'Come on.'

I rested my elbow on the swathes of tartan in front of me and put my arm down flat.

Kate bustled over and seized me by the biceps. She held my limb out at my side. 'He's right.' Her thin fingers began to squeeze my muscles. Shaping, plumping. I might have been a beef steak. 'You are strong.'

Strength had crept up on me unawares. That must be the corset's doing. Kate's arm, gripping mine, looked puny by comparison. It made me feel monstrous.

'I ... suppose I am.'

'Then it must be you. Don't botch it.'

I blinked at her. 'I don't ...'

'Kate, what do you find? Is it suitable, will it serve us a turn?' Even Kate jumped at the sound of Mrs Metyard's voice. The old woman had stolen in like a cat and stood at the door, watching us with her gimlet eyes.

'Yes, Mother. It's just as Billy said. Ruth's arms are burly.'

Burly. Did he use that word? I didn't look at Ivy, but that was no comfort. I could *feel* the glee in her face.

'Stronger than Miriam?'

'I should say so.'

'Right. You'll do it then, Butterham, and you'll make a good job. Your mother will soon know if you don't.'

Her mention of Ma electrified me. Suppose I should blunder in this task – what wrath would I call down upon my mother? 'Please, Mrs Metyard ...' I began.

'What?'

'Can you tell me what it is I'm to do?'

Kate sniffed. 'We used to make baleen stays for our customers. We've had several ladies asking for them again today.'

'But I've never worked with whalebone,' I protested.

'Billy has. I asked him to teach someone how to whittle them, but the worker has to be strong. He said you were strong.'

Not *burly*, then. 'Just me? Making them on my own?'

'No. With Billy.'

Making stays with Billy Rooker: a prospect both wonderful and horrifying. How would I bear standing next to him for all that time? My heart would beat so fast it would be like running up and down the stairs all day.

'But take care you learn,' Mrs Metyard warned. 'His father can only spare him for a short time. After he shows you how to make a few pairs, you'll be doing it on your own.'

Learn? Good God, it was all I could do to hold a bolt of cloth in his presence. If I had to do something delicate I'd be all fingers and thumbs. And Ma would reap the punishment for every skewed stitch ...

'There's a little area just off the showroom,' said Kate. 'Customers go in there if they want to try on the ready-made goods. I'll set it up for you.'

Behind a curtain. Sitting next to Billy Rooker. His smiles, his laughter, his hand guiding mine.

Ivy wasn't grinning now. Her face was cold enough to give you frostbite.

———

Did you ever see a lace-making lamp? It's like a three-legged stool with five poles on the top: the one in the centre holds the candle. The others are shaped round it in a square, and they have glass bowls full of water on them. That's what we used to embroider by night. The water was meant to amplify the flame. Maybe it did, but it seemed very dark to me, working through the long night hours at Metyard's.

We looked like a coven, the five of us gathered around the lamp. A yellow glow fell over Ivy's face, and I could have sworn she had a halo of fire.

She began it, that particular night. I was minding my own business, deep in concentration on a rose motif. Golden thread against black silk, no clear line where the gown ended and the darkness began. I was sewing the night, sewing shadows with stardust.

But then the light wobbled.

I blinked, feeling giddy. Waves of gilt washed across my lap. When I looked up the sensation was intensified, like drowning in a golden pool.

'What are you doing?'

Ivy held Mim's work in her hands: a powder-pink jacket bodice. Mim tugged on the trailing sleeve, her eyes wide as inkwells. The legs of the lamp rocked against the floor.

'Stop it,' Mim cried. 'Let go!'

'What are you quarrelling about?'

Ivy didn't answer my question. But her eyes slid in my direction and her cheeks lifted with a slow, treacherous smile.

I should have been expecting this: my punishment for being chosen to work with Billy Rooker. Oh, Ivy wasn't stupid. She knew the best way to hurt me was through Mim.

'Give it *back*!'

'Careful!' sang Ivy, kicking the lamp stool. 'You wouldn't want to break something.'

Beside me, Nell caught her breath. She clutched her work to her chest. 'Stop, Ivy. I mean it. You'll set the place on fire.'

'*Will* I? And what will you say, Nelly; will you tell Mrs Metyard it was that nasty Ivy who did it? You know how she loves a tattletale.'

Nell's jaw set rigid. 'I'll tell her nothing. But I'd rather not be burnt alive, thank you very much.'

Ivy laughed. Hysterical: that's how it sounded. Maybe she was. Maybe she'd been in that place for so long it didn't matter to her if she went up in flames.

'Give the work back to Mim, Ivy,' I demanded. 'She's done nothing wrong.'

'It's not your concern. You work with Mr Rooker now, not us.' Ivy tugged the bodice, pulling it dangerously close to the candlelight. 'Such fine work. Would be a shame if something happened to it.'

'No!' Mim's hands were frantic, gathering up the material with all her strength. A stitch popped. 'She'd kill me, Ivy, she'd actually kill me.'

'No, not she. She'll thrash you until you wish you were dead, but she won't go through with it.' The candle

danced beneath her breath. Warm satin scented the air.
'She isn't that kindly disposed.'

Both Nell and I were on our feet, begging her to stop.
Even Daisy looked afraid. But Ivy paid no heed; she just
kept staring, staring into the flame.

Another tiny pop. One more stitch gone.

'Give … it … back!'

All at once, she did.

Mim crashed against her stool, sending it skidding
across the floor into the cupboards.

Daisy squealed.

'Mim!' I ran over to where she lay, stunned. Her face
was clenched with pain, but the bodice was safe, clutched
to her so tightly that her knuckles were turning white.
'Mim, are you hurt?'

I don't think even Ivy knew what was going to happen
next. I don't think she planned to do it. Her hand just
reached out in a kind of diabolical reflex, seized the
candle – and flung it.

Someone screamed. I don't know who. My eyes were
focused on the candle as it flew, impossibly slow, arcing
light through the room. The flame fell with a hiss on
Mim's pink satin.

My hand moved so fast that I didn't feel pain. There was
a spark, a putrid stench and then I was slapping, hitting
the material harder than I'd ever hit anything before.

A blotch: that was all that remained; dark pink at the
edges and brown towards the centre. It hadn't burnt
through. Yet the bodice was still ruined.

'*What* do you think you are doing?' Mrs Metyard's
shout echoed around the attic. Our ruckus must have
woken her. 'Ruth! Miriam!'

Both of us were on the floor, holding the satin. Mim
lay beneath it, me to the side. It looked bad. Very bad.

'Explain yourselves!'

I didn't dare raise my eyes to Mrs Metyard. If I had, it might have stopped my mouth. But I was looking at Mim, at her trembling nostrils, and the words came out before I realised they were there.

'It was my fault, Mrs Metyard. I dropped a candle. Mim had nothing to do with it.'

The coal hole, I thought. It wasn't so terrible. I could face the coal hole, for Mim, and maybe Billy would come to let me out again.

Mrs Metyard pounded across the floor and seized me by the hair. Pain screamed through my scalp as she dragged me past the table, out of the room and down the stairs.

Bump. Bump. I bit my lip, tasted blood.

Darkness span around me. I only saw one flash of her face, upside down. It was cadaverous, the eyes unnaturally bright.

I knew then that we weren't going to the coal hole, not this time.

———

After all those days longing to ascend the carpeted staircase, I ended up in the living quarters by a different route. Down, down, she dragged me and the only thing I knew about the carpet was that it burnt my cheek.

My nose stung. All the same it picked up a scent: lily of the valley. Notes of firewood and violets. This was where the Metyards lived and moved, where the good things were kept.

Cracking open an eye, I saw a skirting board, gleaming white. It came closer and closer until Mrs Metyard rounded a corner and I smacked my head against it. Pain flared bright in the centre of my brow. I didn't see for a while, after that.

Of course she waited. She bided her time until I stuttered into consciousness, unable to move. I was on my feet, my back hard against a wall, my hands bound together above my head. I couldn't pull them down. Something held them aloft, perhaps a hook in the ceiling.

Around me was a room I'd never seen before. The wallpaper had a muddy background, with a pattern like autumn leaves. Beneath my feet lay a brown carpet. There was a fire to my left, its flames winking off the fan-shaped screen spread before the grate.

On my right was a window, but the curtains were drawn. All the light came from the fire and a single floor lamp with a fringe around the shade. The furniture was made of dark, heavy wood: a wardrobe and a standing mirror.

And there ... a dressmaker's model, like we used in the window display. Only instead of a gown it wore a scarlet coat, ribbed with white, and pale trousers. Golden epaulettes adorned the shoulders, but it wasn't the glimmer of them that caught my eye: it was the scabbard, slung around the waist, showing the hilt of a sword.

Crowning the whole was a black, plumed shako, where the head should be.

It must be Captain Metyard's uniform, set up as a kind of shrine to him. The sight of it was melancholy, and a touch sinister. As if the captain had stood there in the corner and simply dissolved: his flesh had withered away.

I moved my feet. With my hands bound so high, I had to stand on tiptoe. It was uncomfortable, but at least it was warm in this room. I couldn't decide whether it was better or worse than the coal hole.

And then I knew.

The door opened slowly, creaking its way across the carpet. A hessian boot appeared on the threshold, followed by a cloud of tobacco.

'Attention!' Gruff. A man's voice.

He entered casually, smoking his cigar. He didn't wear an army uniform now but a country gentleman's suit, the kind of thing a rich man might put on to go shooting. Greying hair, oiled back from his forehead. Strange, misshapen facial hair. Jamming the cigar between his lips, he shut the door behind him. I saw then what he held in his other hand: a thin, leather whip.

I moaned: my mind going nineteen to the dozen. The captain, still alive? Did they keep him locked up here the entire time? I couldn't think; I couldn't see why they'd do such a thing. Unless he'd come back from the wars *changed*. Unhinged. Dangerous.

Uselessly, I tugged at my bonds.

'Insubordination,' he drawled. Smoke flowed with his words, choking me. 'It's a damned thing, soldier. I won't have it. I tell you, I won't.'

I couldn't speak. I could barely even see; I was so afraid that the walls seemed to soften and run like wax around me.

'You put the whole company in danger. The whole bloody company.'

He sucked on his cigar as he looked me up and down. The tip glowed. He was short, for a man, but that didn't give me hope. Ma said short men had the most to prove.

'I've known them hang a fellow,' he told me. 'String him up for failing to obey orders. But I'm going to give you a chance, soldier. A chance to redeem yourself.'

'Please, sir ...' I croaked. My arms were aching. I thought my shoulders would rip from their sockets.

'First, I'm going to take off your clothes. Then I'm going to flog you. And after … we shall see. We'll see if you've learnt your lesson.'

'No!' My feet kicked out. Useless. Every movement span me round, sending agony burning through my neck. 'No!'

The smoke wound closer. A throaty chuckle. 'Oh, I like it when they have some spirit.'

He caught me round the waist. With the cigar still between his teeth, his face came near. Too near. I screamed as he stubbed the smoking tip out on my neck.

It was then, in all that pain and fear, that I caught a snatch of it: something else, beneath the smoke. Powdery. Feminine.

I opened my eyes.

It wasn't Captain Metyard, back from the dead. It wasn't a man at all.

Mrs Metyard held me in her grasp, her eyes glassy with madness.

'Let's see if you scream as loud as my wife.'

I never took the blame for Mim again.

24

Dorothea

I could not enjoy this morning's perambulation as I usually do. There was no fault in the botanical gardens. I fear the sense of dissatisfaction had its origin inside of me.

Gardeners were turning the beds, releasing the fresh breath of soil. Here and there, a pink worm. The birds waited. They had their sights set on a feast.

I do not wish to believe my fellow creatures are all akin to these scavengers: ravenous, skulking in the shadows, awaiting their opportunity to strike. But after what has happened, I begin to doubt. Do we not treat inmates in New Oakgate Prison with the highest level of compassion? Do we not give them all we can to make sure they are comfortable and well occupied? Yet still they betray us with their behaviour.

So deep was my melancholy that I took Tilda's arm to feel the warmth of another soul next to me. She does not walk fast. Strolling at her slower pace, I was aware of the clouds moving in the wind, and the dampness in the air. It would have been better to stay indoors.

But no. That would mean forgoing my glimpse of David, however brief. Today he was on patrol, as I knew he should be, crossing the gardens at the regular time like a well-wound watch.

Dear David. *He* shall not disappoint me. Let other hearts be as black as night, I know *his* will never change. When he stopped and tipped his hat to us, compassion was written across his beloved face.

'Miss Truelove. Forgive me, but I heard what happened, at the prison. I must ask if you are all right?'

I rallied myself to raise a smile. 'Oh yes, I am quite well, thank you. I was not in the infirmary, you know, when the riot took place. But we have lost a window, and a quantity of bed linen in the fire. All of the committee are deeply distressed.'

'That's only natural. You've had a shock, and you must take care of yourself.' Perhaps he heard the tenderness creeping into his voice, for he quickly turned the subject. 'And what will be done, to punish those responsible?'

I wonder if I am not partially responsible myself. Had I continued to visit the sick in the infirmary, instead of neglecting my duty to converse with Ruth, I might have spotted signs of growing discontent.

'The leaders are confined to the dark cells for a week. But I am afraid all of the prisoners must pay a price. The committee has decided that we were too lenient, feeding them meat. Eating flesh only inflames the criminal mind … The diet shall be much plainer from now on.'

He raised his eyebrows. 'I shouldn't think they'll like that. But I can't say it doesn't serve them right. Someone could have been seriously hurt.'

'Thanks be to God, there are only cuts and bruises. Our staff are to be commended.'

'Indeed they are. It makes you think, something like that. Makes you realise that life doesn't go on forever.' He fixed eyes of entreaty upon me. 'And no one should delay an action they really mean to perform.'

Tilda cleared her throat. Odious to admit, but she was right. We had stopped quite long enough for a chance conversation.

David scratched his cheek. He looked boyish, abashed. 'Well, I'd best be getting along. Good day, Miss Truelove. I'm glad to see you unharmed.'

'Yes. Good day.'

I do not comprehend how my feet can ever bear to do it: how they turn and walk away from him without a stumble. And my eyes! What agonies it costs them to look upon something else, when they know that *he* is there.

David lacks my discipline, even with his police training. I always feel his gaze, warming the back of my shoulders as I stride from view. It is not cautious, it is not discreet. But I find that I love him better for it.

I wish I were the same: disingenuous and earnest with the Mental Vital, a head shape so rarely seen in a male subject. But alas, I am full of deceit. The first thing I said to Tilda when we were out of earshot was: 'I do not mean to tell Constable Hodges about my invitation to Heatherfield Manor. Please take care not to mention it in his presence, it would only upset him.'

'Me, miss? When do I even open my mouth?'

She has a point, I suppose. I find myself jittery, struggling to trust those around me. It is the riot, I expect, and the letter from Matron. Sometimes it is difficult to know what to do for the best.

The days are wearing on and Ruth's trial grows nearer, and still I am no further along in my studies than I was at the genesis.

The horror of her recitation! Such unspeakable occurrences ... from a girl of only sixteen. Once more, I am faced with the same question: is she telling the truth? For now I have read her skull, the waters become murky.

It seems preposterous to me that any woman should dress as a man, outside of the 'breeches roles' you see on stage, but then Mrs Metyard was manifestly not a healthy individual. And the work of the alienists leads me to believe there are more diseases of the brain than we have hitherto discovered. Once, we had an inmate who went by two names. You could not tell which alias she would choose, but her voice, her posture, her entire deportment altered dependent on her selection. I wished to measure her crania in both guises, to see if the organs shifted between the two, but alas she was removed to Bedlam before I had the opportunity.

Could Mrs Metyard be such another? Either these terrible events really happened, exactly as Ruth said, in which case I pity her from my very soul – or they are a deliberate falsehood. This sickening tale has come from her own imagination, for her own amusement, and what *sort* of a person makes up a story like that?

The answer is of more consequence than ever, now that I have received a request from Matron. With all the infirmary bed linen lost in the fire, she requires twice as many prisoners to work in the sewing room. So far, Matron has held off sending Ruth – neither of us like to absolutely force a prisoner into a task that upsets them. Yet now there is the need, and Ruth *can* turn a stitch.

I must be honest: there is a fear in me. However silly, however outrageous Ruth's claims about needles are, I hesitate to let her hold one. Could she really cause hurt?

There, see, I am talking nonsense! I have let her dupe me, I have let her make me believe such dross!

I will not be lied to any longer. It is time to take a firmer stand. Ruth *shall* go to the sewing room. We will 'call her bluff', as they say.

I shall write to Matron now, before I change my mind.

———————

Where do you think I have been today? I have taken myself off to debtors' gaol!

What with the riot, and my little upset over Ruth's skull, I found myself disinclined to return to New Oakgate Prison. Yet I must be occupying myself, so when Fanny Awning mentioned she was paying a visit to the captive debtors, I felt compelled to accompany her.

I wish that I had not.

The first sign of warning was the basket that Fanny packed shortly before we departed. She squeezed in some tinder, a bottle of wine, cheese, bread: all the usual provisions for the poor. Then she placed a sort of board over the top, and began afresh with several smaller bundles.

'Whatever is that?' I asked her.

'Why, it is a false bottom for the basket.'

'Fanny!' I cried. 'You are not *smuggling* into the prison?'

She gave me a wry smile and simply replied, 'You will see.'

Like most of Oakgate's institutions, the debtors' gaol is modelled on its larger London counterpart – although the Marshalsea Prison in the capital had the advantage of being pulled down and rebuilt about thirty years ago. No such arrangement has been made for our poor. A more sunless and chill place you never did see: every-thing studded with iron, more like a castle keep than

anything else. As we walked across the broken cobbles,
the shadow of a tall, iron-spiked wall fell over us, and
with it came a smell so sweet, so musky, that I thought
I should be ill.

'Remember your handkerchief,' said Fanny.

Obediently, I raised it to cover my nose and mouth.
She had bid me soak it in bergamot before coming – how
grateful I was that she did!

A dirty fellow stood beside the great iron door; or port-
cullis, I should say. He leered at poor Fanny. However,
she seemed to know his tricks, for she addressed him
immediately. 'Here I am again, you see, Collins.'

'And what have you got for me?' He peered into the
basket that hung from her arm.

'Why, this is for the debtors, Collins. I will give you
your usual sixpence.'

'You'll give me sixpence and that bottle,' he ordered.
'Or you ain't coming in.'

Fanny made the exchange cheerfully, having put a
cheap bottle of gin on the top of her basket. For myself,
I thought it a disastrous bargain. Sixpence, to be admitted into a prison yard little better than a cesspit, with
rats running about like dogs!

The yard was a square space, overlooked by a quad-
rangle of dull-brick buildings. Smudged faces appeared
through the windows, miserable and gaunt.

We passed a wagon in the centre of the yard, waiting
for its load. A boy of about ten years of age teased the
horse.

'Does that filthy conveyance bring the food and drink
supplies in?' I asked Fanny, aghast.

'It does,' she said sadly. 'And it takes the bodies out.'

They are not divided into male and female in this
prison: they converse in groups, with poor tattered

children hanging about their legs. Of course the women are allocated separate sleeping quarters, but these are above – of all places – a taproom.

The stairs we climbed to reach them were sticky and reeked of beer. No matter how close I pressed my handkerchief, it did not cover the smell. To think that we have murderers awaiting trial, fraudsters and thieves all kept cleanly in New Oakgate Prison, when these people live like animals simply for the crime of being poor! It embarrassed me that I had not been aware of the fact beforehand. No wonder Ruth's mother so feared this place.

The 'room', when we gained entry to it, was a dank, coffin-shaped space hardly big enough for a bed. Yet there *was* a chipped, worm-eaten bedstead in the centre of the floor, fusty with the sweat of no fewer than three sleepers. All of them were elderly women. I marvelled they had managed to survive so long.

Fanny was greeted as an old friend.

'She's a treasure, she is,' I was told by a scrawny, malnourished woman. 'I don't know what we'd do without her.'

She gave way to a hacking cough, which continued for so long that it frightened me.

As we began to unload the basket, I ventured to ask how the turnkey had dared to demand money and alcohol beside.

'They charges for everything!' the emaciated woman cried. 'For food, for coal. We pays rent, and for this bed, which Martha brought here herself!'

'And if they find out we get a gift, like this,' put in her room-mate, 'they take a cut of it too!'

'This is madness,' I whispered to Fanny. 'They are put in here because they cannot pay back their debts. How are they ever to do it, if they are granted no opportunity to make or save money?'

'They do *not* do it,' Fanny said shortly. 'Many only get out in that wagon you saw.'

A short enquiry informed me that the prices charged for necessities such as candles and coal were in fact double the price of those I could purchase outside the prison. It is nothing but extortion.

We helped the women tidy and air the room as best we could. The bedclothes were infested with lice. Imagine spending the winter of your life in such discomfort, without even liberty to cheer you. The poor on the street are pitiful, but at least they may wander where they please.

'You can see why the fellows get drunk,' Fanny said, aside to me. 'But they become disorderly, and more than one woman has been attacked.'

The old lady named Martha showed me a scar along her neck, where another prisoner had launched themselves at her.

Money – all this evil because of money! I smelt its coppery tang mixed with the urine and sweat, I heard its chink in the footsteps running outside. Even Martha's wrinkled eyes appeared, to me, like two dirty pennies.

David tells me money does not matter but – oh! – it does, it *does*.

25

Ruth

So that was Mrs Metyard's secret. Not just cruelty but all-out madness. Overnight the misery I'd suffered at Naomi's birth and Pa's death became raindrops in an ocean. My flashes were barbed, now. They were more than just blood.

I don't want to talk about that. But what I will say is that, after my experience, I began to understand the place a bit better. I realised why everyone was so heart-less and strange. The captain wouldn't rest.

That was why Ivy staged her spiteful 'accidents'. That was why Nell kept her head down and her mouth shut. He was always hungering, prowling for a victim: every girl had to make sure that it wouldn't be her.

Three days later I was still sunk deep within myself: my body patched with bruises, my mind full of sand. I felt nothing, not even a flicker, when Kate's voice came up the speaking pipe and ordered me downstairs.

I hadn't been near the showroom since that first day when I stood on the threshold, peeking in. Leaving my shoes outside, I opened the door and entered in my stockinged feet. Everything was just as I remembered: the duck-egg blue; the chandeliers; a warm, powdery aroma of satin. Great sheets of light fell through the bow windows and set the glass counters sparkling. Beautiful.

It made me want to cry.

'There she is!' Billy Rooker leant against the wall, beside the rolls of material, an incongruous figure amidst all that femininity. He'd taken his hat off, revealing a tumble of ungreased hair. The sight of his smile was the only thing in the world that could make me feel a fraction better.

'Whittling,' said Kate. 'You haven't forgotten, Ruth?'

'No.'

'Grand,' said Billy. 'I've brought everything with me. Wait until you see these knives.'

Kate flinched. She disguised it quickly, brushing down her dress in a no-nonsense manner. 'Go on, then. Follow Billy.'

Awkwardly, I went behind the counter and trailed Billy to a recess on the left-hand side of the showroom, covered by an aubergine curtain with gold tassels. Pushing the thick, piled velvet aside, we entered a small chamber.

'Bang-up job, isn't it, Ruth?'

True enough, it was a pleasant room, papered in white and gold. A mirror hung on the wall and more cream carpet covered the floor, only it had been overlaid with a sheet of black oilskin. One of the showroom's round tables sat upon it, spread with gleaming knives and a pile of yellow-white bones. There were two chairs.

I sat down heavily, too weary to stand.

Billy was much slower to take his seat. His brows were not arched and expressive now, but bunched together, straight, like two stitches on a seam. 'What ails you?'

His voice was low and soft. I wanted to tell him. I wanted him to make it better, but I didn't have the words to describe my ordeal. 'Mrs Metyard ...' I whimpered.

He just nodded.

We sat in silence for a time. Not an uncomfortable silence. It had a nap to it, like a fine coat. Gentle. As if I could feel the texture of Billy's sympathy through his lack of words.

I was reminded of another time and place. I saw myself sitting in the comfy chair at my old home in Ford Street, hiding my injuries under a cloak. How Ma had fussed around, bleating out cheerful, meaningless reassurance. Billy didn't do that, and it was better. Better to sit and just *be*, letting the despair gust around me until it ran out of breath.

'Have you heard from your mother at all?' he asked at last.

I shook my head. 'I don't know what's happened to her. She couldn't even see properly. What if ...' I trailed off. Could Ma's circumstances be any worse than mine were?

Billy didn't look at me but kept his blue eyes focused on the knives upon the table. 'I doubt you'll ever know, Ruth. And that's hard on you. But you have to keep thinking, she didn't just abandon you. She gave you up for what she hoped was a better life. Not her fault that it wasn't.'

It surprised me he'd thought so much about my ma. A feeling began to trickle through my sorrow; something warm and sweet. 'Of course it's not her fault. But that makes it worse. It means all her sacrifice was for nothing.'

Billy's jaw set. 'That's why you owe it to her. To survive.' There was a beat, and then the cloud seemed to pass from his face. He sat straighter in his chair, crossed one leg over the other. 'Come on, let's teach you how to do some whittling. I think you'll like this, Ruth.'

He was right. The tips of the knives sparkled. They had sturdy, thick handles and the thought of gripping one steadied me, as the thought of Pa's gun had done a thousand lifetimes ago. As for the whalebone, it was enchanting: translucent plates, strips like horn. Something natural and raw that I could shape.

'Mrs Metyard has already taken the measurements we'll need for this one,' he said, drawing out a scrap of paper. 'But Kate will show you how to do them yourself.' He grinned. 'Not really something it would be proper for me to demonstrate.'

I swallowed and felt my cheeks warm. Unbidden came the image of Billy measuring under my bust, passing his cloth tape around my waist. 'But ... how is it you know how to do this? A draper doesn't usually make corsets.'

His right eyebrow lifted as he reached for a piece of bone. 'Well, I wasn't always a draper, was I?'

'Weren't you? I thought ... Doesn't your father own the business?'

'Aye. But Mr Rooker wasn't always my father.'

What could he mean? Was it his mother's second marriage? But no, it would be unusual for a child not to keep their real father's surname, especially a boy.

He saw my puzzled face. 'Can you guess?'

'You were ... adopted?'

'That's it. Eventually. I was a foundling at first, just like the others.'

Suddenly I understood: the way he spoke of my ma, the look on Nell's face as she called him a lucky bastard. He had been lost, like me. We shared a connection.

I pictured a blue-eyed baby, lying swaddled on the steps of Oakgate Foundling Hospital. God above, what woman could bear to give him up?

With a small knife, he began to peel slithers from a strip of bone. 'It was here in this shop that Mr Rooker first saw me, spreading lengths for the customers. He used to watch me do it. One day I was cutting a particular bolt – champagne brocade it was, I'll never forget – and he says, "Always so neat with his cuts. That's a likely lad, that's the sort of lad I could use around my place." The next thing I know, there's Mrs Rooker coming in to take a look at me. God bless her, I loved her from the moment I set eyes upon her. And after a few months, and all that toing and froing and haggling with Mrs Metyard, they did it. They took me away.'

'*What?*' The word flew from my mouth with such force that I nearly slipped off my chair. I hadn't heard right, I couldn't have done. Billy, the shining, cheerful Billy – here? 'No. You couldn't have … '

'Couldn't I?'

'You really worked *here*?'

'Aye.'

'But then how can you …?' I stopped, afraid of saying too much. After all, Kate was in the showroom. But then the bell tinkled and I heard customers, voices beyond the curtain. I glanced at it.

Billy dropped his voice. He looked a bit graver, now. 'Ah, I see. You're wondering how I can marry into the family, after …'

Our eyes snagged. Something passed between us, some unspoken understanding that made his irises burn fiercely blue.

Kate's nasal tones drifted towards us, recommending a midnight satin.

'Kate never beat me,' he said, very gently. 'Skinny little whip she was, even then. We were all of us about the same age, and we were friends for a time: Kate, Nell and me.'

'Nell?' I couldn't comprehend what I was hearing. This was all too much to take in.

'Aye, we both came from the Foundling together. The twins and Miriam are a fair bit younger than me. I was long gone by the time they arrived here.'

My greatest wonder was that Nell could stand the sight of him, after all that had passed. By rights she should be eaten alive with jealousy. Fancy being friends with a boy – and a boy like Billy, for that matter – only to see him lifted to a better life, away from you. And then, to engage himself to your tormentor! She must be kinder and more forgiving than I had given her credit for. *Lucky bastard* was a mild term for her to use.

Selecting a knife and a plate of bone, I began to copy Billy's actions. The movement came naturally to my hands. Gently, gently. Little white spirals fell from the bone. Curls of butter.

'That's good. But that one's going to be for the shoulder blade so – come here. Let me help. Like this.'

The warmth of his hand guiding mine. His touch was tender and skilled, so why did it hurt to have it upon me?

'I still can't believe you worked here making corsets,' I said wonderingly. 'If I managed to get out of Metyard's, I'd never come back.'

He continued scraping the bone, our fingers a fraction of an inch apart. 'Goodness will triumph, little Ruth. I believe that. I was treated badly here, I won't pretend otherwise, but it all came right. You see ... if I'd given up, if I'd been sullen and resentful, Mr Rooker would never have taken to me. Kate would have been my enemy. But I won against them all.'

'You haven't won,' I protested. 'You still earn your money from Mrs Metyard, you still have to see her.'

'But who will inherit her property? All she's worked for?'

'Kate, I suppose.'

'And who will own Kate's possessions?'

'You,' I admitted.

'And who does Mrs Metyard love more than anyone else in the world?'

'Kate?' It was a guess. I couldn't say I'd witnessed a great deal of affection between mother and daughter.

'But who will have all of Kate's love?'

My hand twitched away from his. 'Her husband.'

'So Mrs Metyard might think herself better than me, but she's not. I'll walk away with the love of her only child and, one day, her shop. I'll beat her, Ruth, I'll have my revenge. And I won't even need to raise a fist.'

That wasn't the kind of revenge I wanted. I wanted to crucify Mrs Metyard.

I wanted to see her suffer.

26

Dorothea

You would not have occasion to drive out as far as Heatherfield unless you were visiting the manor house. Removed from the town of Oakgate and up steep hills, the journey thither is fraught with mud. Given the damp fortnight we have suffered, Papa was concerned for the horses on the slick roads, but I am pleased to report his fears were unfounded. We arrived yesterday unscathed, if a little shaken about.

For all its discomforts, the expedition proved worthwhile. Reports have not exaggerated the beauty of Heatherfield Manor: the grey and beige stone house, almost like a chateau in its design, and the cheerful red tiles that adorn its roof. There is a gravel sweep and a hexagonal lake, but these are the only signs of stately grounds. The sloping fields and valley beyond run in their own, rugged fashion, washed with the pink and mauve heather from which the house takes its name. The plants are beginning to bud: I caught their scent as Papa handed me out of the carriage.

'Is it not the most splendid place you ever saw?' he asked.

'Yes! Very fine.' It was not a lie.

'And it will all belong to Sir Thomas, one day.'

I was occupied with holding down my dress as we walked across the gravel. Foolishly, I had chosen something with a light, floaty skirt and was paying the price for it. 'Sir Thomas?' I said, distracted. 'Surely not?'

'Why, yes. Lady Morton has no children.'

'But the house came from her late husband. I expect there is an entail, or something like one, to keep the property within the family.'

'I am not sure there *is* any family, Dora. No one has taken the title, after all.'

There it was again: the reckless turn to my imagination. It painted me as Lady Biggleswade, mistress of Heatherfield Manor. I might sit at the window in that tower, there, my chest covered in diamonds, and gaze over the hills, remembering my lost love.

A romantic picture, but utterly stupid. I should be bored after an hour.

Existence as a society wife must be akin to standing in a bog. That slow, sinking sensation. I would be dragged down day by day, grow vacuous and preoccupied with frivolity like those around me. I should begin to resemble Papa or – God forbid – Mrs Pearce. At least with David I may strive to be a better person, practical and helpful to my fellow creatures.

We reached an arched door studded with iron. It opened before we could knock, revealing a line of powdered footmen clad in a purple livery. They bowed simultaneously before the tallest man said, 'This way, if you please. Sir, madam.'

A greater contrast to the fetid debtors' prison I could not imagine. Here was gilding and chestnut; there, chandeliers and oil portraits. As an heiress, I have always lived in comfort, but Heatherfield was something else: something elegant and full of joy. Small wonder Lady Morton is reluctant to leave the place, hives or no hives.

We were shown into a honey-coloured drawing room with gilded window shutters and a great frieze ceiling. Sir Thomas and a middle-aged, pudding-faced lady rose from separate sofas to greet us.

'Please excuse my sister,' Sir Thomas offered a shallow bow. 'She'll be down presently.'

I turned to the lady, who clasped her hands together and averted her eyes. Her gown was good, but out of fashion. I should say a year or two old.

Sir Thomas fiddled with his pocket watch. I cleared my throat.

'Ah!' he said. 'Yes, of course. You haven't been introduced. Mr Reginald Truelove, Miss Dorothea Truelove; Miss Selma Potts.'

'And how are you related to our dear friends?' Papa asked, kissing her hand.

Colour flooded the woman's fleshy cheeks. 'Oh! No relation. I am Lady Morton's companion.'

Papa rather lost interest in her after that.

I was by no means sorry to have an opportunity to converse with Miss Potts, prior to seeing the famed Lady Morton. From what I could glimpse of her Secretiveness, concealed by a lace cap, it was uncommonly small, and she should prove the ideal gossip.

Papa and Sir Thomas sat together, talking about coursing dogs and tiresome subjects, while we ladies moved nearer to the fire. Occasionally, I permitted myself a glance in their direction, but not once did I see Sir Thomas regard me with his sleepy eyes. Poor Papa – he shall be disappointed!

'I am sorry Lady Morton is not down,' said Miss Potts. 'It is rather embarrassing. She is so used to keeping her own time, you see. Then, of course, it does take her a while to dress …' She bit her lip, as if afraid of saying more.

I leant forwards. 'I do understand,' I began slowly. 'That is – Sir Thomas has alluded to … there is something to do with a skin complaint?'

Miss Potts put a hand to her throat and gave a nervous laugh. 'Dear me. Yes. I am glad you are prepared. We have all of us been uneasy, for her sake. The poor lady does her best to cover it with powder and so on, but it is quite mortifying. And she, such a beauty!'

I had not recalled Lady Morton being beautiful, only very rich, but I nodded as if I comprehended the depth of the tragedy.

'Excuse me for asking, but … there is no indication what caused the outbreak? No underlying health condition?'

'Not that we can observe. She had been perfectly well for months before the first bout. The doctors cannot puzzle it out, they just call it St Anthony's Fire, but none of their lotions work.'

'I do not suppose … it sounds foolish, but you did not notice any change after she wore a particular gown?'

Miss Potts adjusted her lace cap. 'Alas, no. I understand what you are thinking – it has crossed all of our minds: perhaps she reacts to a certain material, or a certain food. We have tested everything and cannot find the source.'

Before I knew it, the next question had slipped out. 'She never ordered clothes from Metyard's, did she?'

Silly, credulous goose that I am! But the idea, once conceived, would not leave me alone.

Miss Potts widened her eyes. 'As a matter of fact, she did order from there once or twice. I shouldn't wonder if the material they used carried some disease from a poor seamstress's house. I could credit almost anything, after the awful things that happened in that shop.'

You do not know the half of it, I thought.

Lady Morton descended the grand staircase to meet us just as we were finally walking to the dining room. Papa, who had been escorting Miss Potts, abandoned her for her mistress.

I could not glean a glance at the lady's skin. Only her head bobbed before me: sandy like Sir Thomas's, with the odd wire of grey. The shape of her skull was rather like my own, except in one particular. She had the same Amativeness that longs for conjugal bliss, and the Inhabitiveness that gives a profound love of home.

'How very sad,' I found myself saying to Sir Thomas, 'that your sister should be a widow! She does not have the type of head to flourish alone.'

'And she does not have the type of face,' he laughed, 'to marry again.'

Cruel – and yet, he was correct. When we were seated at the mahogany dining table, I took quite a turn to see the lady sitting at the end. She looked pallid and diseased. Powder coated her skin until it was white, but lumps remained visible, as Sir Thomas had said, for all the world as if they were welts from being beaten with a stick. Her high collar and long sleeves suggested the ailment ran further down her body.

Once, the features may indeed have been beautiful. She possessed Sir Thomas's languorous eyes and small nose. Yet suffering, and perhaps loneliness, gave her brow a cloud of hauteur.

'It is not often that Tom chooses to meet his friends at Heatherfield,' she observed, as she took a sip of wine. It left an awful red stain at the corners of her mouth, where

the powder had massed. 'I should take this as a compliment, if I were you.'

'Indeed,' cried Papa, 'how could we view your kind invitation in any other light? It is always a compliment, and an honour, to meet with your ladyship.'

He rather overdid it, I thought.

Lady Morton waited until the servants ladled the soup before recommencing. 'You have not enjoyed the honour, I believe, for some years past. Miss Truelove is quite grown. I remember you as a child, young lady. Tell me, what is your age now?'

I suppose she wished to distract attention from her own flaws, but I did not consider it polite of her. 'Five and twenty,' I said, aiming for the same insouciance as Sir Thomas.

'Indeed!' Her fair eyebrows had all but disappeared with the powder on her face, but there was a movement of muscle, as if she had raised them. 'Time does pass. Why, your mother was younger than that when she bore you. Has your father failed to find you a suitor, Miss Truelove?'

It was as well I had a mouthful of soup. Papa was called upon to laugh it off and say, with a fond sort of weariness, 'I fear Dorothea has kept herself too busy to consider marriage, as normal young ladies do. She has set herself a colossal list of good works to complete, when she should be concerned with performing other duties.'

'It is to Miss Truelove's credit, I believe,' Sir Thomas said to his bowl. 'Better than having your head full of gowns and pugs and other such fluff, as most ladies of my acquaintance do.'

'My dear boy, as if you would know!' laughed Lady Morton. She had a nasty laugh; abrasive. 'When you yourself can think of nothing but Ascot or the lineage of your pointer.'

'There's precious little else to think of, banished out in the country here.'

'I am sure I never saw a happier estate,' Papa put in, smoothing the way. 'I should be entranced by it forever. Tell me, your ladyship, do the hounds run in the woods in the valley?'

'Certainly. Do you and your daughter hunt, Mr Truelove? I do not recall … '

'In my younger days, you could not tear me from a horse. Alas,' he added, with a sorrowful glance at me, 'Dorothea has never learnt. She lacks that ladylike accomplishment.'

'Then she must come and ride with us. Tom and I shall teach her. She will take Miss Potts's horse.'

'How kind of you! You are all goodness. Dorothea would be delighted.'

Lady Morton returned to her soup.

I was fidgety and unhappy in my chair. How could Papa talk about me in that belittling manner? What pass had I come to, when the only person to speak a word in my defence was the feckless Sir Thomas!

As for hunting—! I could picture nothing worse than riding to dogs with Lady Morton. I did not see how that could be a suitable pursuit for me – how Papa could consider visiting prison unrefined, but be happy for me to gallop through the mud and watch a fox meet its bloody end.

While the servants removed the soup bowls and set the main dishes down, Papa enquired how Sir Thomas spent his time in Gloucestershire. Sir Thomas toyed with his wine glass and replied he was always up to 'this or that'. Lady Morton seized his hesitation as her opportunity to swoop in again.

'Did you taste nothing remarkable in that soup, Mr Truelove? It is a great favourite of mine.'

'It was certainly very pleasant, your ladyship. What do you call it?'

'It was white soup. I was sure you would recognise the mixture. I had the receipt from your wife.'

A hush fell over the table.

I looked up at Lady Morton. Our dining preferences are not a vast part of our general character, I admit, but still they are a detail. One of the intimate details I have forgotten about my mother. I was hungry for her to say more; all appetite for the actual food before me evaporated.

Lady Morton threw a slender, powdered hand in my direction. 'Did it not survive in the household cookbook, Miss Truelove? That is a pity. I will have my housekeeper make a copy for you. Your mother was wonderfully fond of this dish. She must have been, for I could often smell the almonds on her breath.'

'Well,' said Papa, clearly discomfited, 'she certainly did have an inclination for soup.'

I wondered if he recalled, as I suddenly did, that soup and broth were all she could swallow in those last days. The terrible pain even that simple fare caused as her weak body attempted to digest it.

'Indeed, most of the receipts in the Heatherfield kitchen were given to me by my lamented friend,' Lady Morton went on, but her eyes, the only animated spots in that white face, turned from me to Papa. They seemed to pin him in his chair. 'A more indefatigable little housekeeper I never did see. Were it not for her sad illness, I would have called her unstoppable.'

Papa muttered some words of thanks and dabbed his mouth with his napkin.

A brooding, uncomfortable silence followed. Even Papa's stream of toadying compliments dried up. You would have thought that Lady Morton, a widow herself, might have been more sensible of his feelings. How could it be that this woman was acquainted with my mother? Two more disparate characters I cannot imagine: the one all goodness, all delicacy; the other haughty and lacking tact.

I gazed from our disfigured hostess to the mute Miss Potts, all but invisible in her chair. Then I saw Sir Thomas.

He had set down his fork. A spark of worry lit up his tired eyes, there was tension in his jaw. I would have expected him to stare at his outspoken sister, to upbraid her with a glance for starting this mischief. But on the contrary.

Sir Thomas was looking straight at me.

27
Ruth

There's beauty in sculpting the human body. All that loose flesh pinned and transformed into something else. Naked, the female torso is a gelatinous landscape, varied in colour. But put it in a corset and you get strength, shape. A kind of armour. Vertical strips across the stomach, diagonals over the ribs. Wide bones to push up the bust, but something thinner for the shoulder blades, sewn in horizontally. Holding you steady, holding the jumbled parts of you in place. There's no other garment like it.

I know it sounds peculiar to rhapsodise about a piece of clothing. But when you're sat on your own for hours at a time, whittling plates of bone, backstitching sheaths, measuring busks, these thoughts wander into your fancy.

I learnt much in the year that followed, and not all of it from Billy. I'd picked up a thing or two making my own corded corset in the dark, before Naomi was born. Many was the time my mind drifted down the stairs to our cellar bedroom and that poor creation beneath my pillow. How I'd remake it now! Metal eyelets, spiral steel bones. Grosgrain ribbon for the laces and coutil for the body. But that would have to wait. With the captain always lurking in the shadows, I didn't dare plunder supplies. I'd only dream and sigh, and sometimes I could hear my corset, sighing back.

There was demand for my trade. So much easier, the ladies said, to have everything ordered in one shop. It wasn't easier for my fingers. But it got me out of the attic room for a few days a week, so I suppose I should be grateful.

The attic wasn't a place for winter. No fires, no carpet. Delicate work was next to impossible with numb fingers. The only thing worse than the numbness was when you finally went downstairs for a cup of tea and the feeling came back; Nell would cry, sometimes, with the pain of that.

So it was in the winter I turned fifteen that I sat in my curtained alcove, taking as much time as I could over the pearl-cotton flossing on my latest corset. When I was done, I would have to climb up to the attic and face its cold claws.

I added another flower here, another swirl there. Anything to draw out my time.

Just then, the bell tinkled. I didn't think much of it. Kate and Mrs Metyard were in the showroom; they would deal with any customers.

'My daughter is to be married,' a lady said, her voice ripe and smug. 'Married in the new year, on her sixteenth birthday.'

The Metyards cooed with the usual congratulations. I tied a knot in my thread and pulled it, tight. Another trousseau. God, how I loathed the wedding trousseaus.

Tidying up my bits and pieces, I didn't pay attention to what passed next. But then I heard something that stopped me, stock-still.

'I want only your finest materials. Cost is of no importance. Do not show me anything less than the best.'

Haughty, spoilt – it might have been the voice of a dozen young ladies. So why did gooseflesh skitter up my arms?

A clearing of the throat beyond the curtain. 'You do realise, dear, that Papa will have to pay for this and not Mr Green—'

'Then I will pay him back! I could do it with my first quarter's pin money, you know that.'

'My daughter's intended, you must understand, is well placed in society and exceedingly rich,' the mother explained.

'Indeed,' said Mrs Metyard, affecting the same self-satisfied tone, 'I had the pleasure of clothing Mr Green's first wife.'

I smiled. It wasn't often I took Mrs Metyard's side, but I had to give her points for that hit. There was something I couldn't put my finger upon in the voices of the customers outside. They made me feel ill. Especially the girl. Where *had* I heard that girl before?

'The old Mrs Green was a dowd.' A rustle of material. Evidently the young lady was not cowed by Mrs Metyard. 'I mean to put her quite in the shadows. But I must have green, nothing but green. They shall remember my name.'

At this Kate piped up. 'We have some wonderful shades of that colour. Let me show you the *tarlatanes* in Scheele's green.'

The elder women were silent for a moment, letting Kate spread out the materials.

'A sweet fancy, madam,' Mrs Metyard observed, 'your daughter dressing to match her husband's name. I married a soldier myself. Ah, it was nothing but scarlet for me many years after.'

'But scarlet is not becoming to the complexion.'

'It is not, Mrs Oldacre.'

The golden walls crept in on me. Rosalind Oldacre. My schoolyard nemesis.

Suppose she saw me? Wretched, as good as orphaned, working for my bread. She'd thought me contemptible three years ago but *now* ... I would rather die than have her see me like this.

'My daughter, also, is to be married,' said Mrs Metyard. 'She and her intended are choosing their date.'

It was like Mrs Metyard to press on a wound. Not that she realised she was doing it. Couldn't I just picture them now: Rosalind and Kate, both brides, decked in white like the Queen with orange blossom in their hair? Laughing at me.

'I expect it is rather different with your sort of people,' drawled Mrs Oldacre. 'Your daughter must take her bridal day at a time when ladies will not require her services. And then there is the misfortune of you losing a hand, in your little shop! I expect you will miss her terribly.'

Mrs Metyard was achingly polite. 'Oh, but there we are the same, madam. You will be equally bereft when Miss Rosalind leaves your home.'

'Yes.' She didn't sound very sure.

'Mama, come and look at this.'

What an affectation! *Green, nothing but green.* I sat on the chair, growing angrier and angrier as I heard Rosalind reel off the list: green gloves, green parasols. Emerald, hunter, white muslin piped with mint. I should like to show her green. I should like to drown her in it.

Creak. A noise inside of me, rather than without. My injured corset, the corset Rosalind had broken with her boots, cried out for revenge.

Green feathers, green ribbon.

'It is to be a very large order, you understand. Your girls shall have to work around the clock.'

Slowly, a smile surfaced on my lips. My stitches would go into each dress. It would be my cotton, my web, holding it all together, with Rosalind Oldacre pinned at the centre.

Oh, I would work around the clock, all right. I would work until I dropped for just one clear shot at her.

'They will remember you, Rosalind,' I whispered. 'I promise. They will all remember Mrs Green.'

I wasn't the only one making plans.

That night Mim was restless, shifting constantly in our bed. Every toss and turn sent the straw jabbing into my skin.

'Lie still, won't you? I can't sleep.'

'It's too cold to sleep.'

She was right. My limbs were frost-burnt and my toes itched with chilblains. Outside a foghorn sounded in the distance, somewhere on the dark river winding towards my old home.

We had fog of our own in the cellar: our breath steaming in the frigid air. When Daisy snored, wisps plumed up from her nose as if her soul was escaping.

'Well, the twins have managed to drift off.'

'They don't feel the chill,' Mim whispered bitterly. 'On account of their cold hearts.'

I lay still on my back, listening to the wind. It blew fiercely tonight, strong enough to pare the skin off your face. How they must be suffering, in that boat upon the river!

Creak, creak. Lumpy, beneath my head, my corset sang a lullaby. It whispered of revenge and power, of taking back control. As I listened, my eyelids drooped, my head grew heavy.

'I'm going. Soon.'

My eyes snapped open. 'What do you mean?'

'I'm going. I'm getting out. Everything's planned, I'm just waiting for the right moment.'

She'd always told me that she meant to do it. I'd imagine her, sometimes, on a great silver vessel that cleaved the water as it sailed for Africa and the desert land. In my dreams, I felt a rush of triumph. But not now. Not in reality, with the corset's whispers on the back of my neck.

'Why?'

The whites of her eyes flashed in the dark. 'Why? Can you really lie there and ask me *why*?'

'No … I mean, why now? When it's so bitter and wet outside? We'll have snow before New Year. Better to wait for summer.'

'No. The days are longer then and people stay abroad at night. No one looks at you in winter, they just pull their collar up and hurry past.'

'But you don't have a collar,' I pointed out. 'No kind of cape at all.'

'Never mind. I can face a bit of cold, to find my ma.'

I shivered just thinking about it. There was a beggar once, on the street near our school, with stumps at the end of his legs. The girls said he'd lost his feet to the frost. The thought of it haunted me: a rapacious cold, with teeth that gnawed through flesh. Was that better or worse than the captain's room?

'Mim,' I whispered. 'I want you to think about this. I know it's rough now, but in a few years you'll be twenty-one. An adult, not an apprentice. You can leave here in broad daylight and no one will stop you.'

She laughed sourly. 'Is that what you think? She'll just let us go? Come on, Ruth, you don't believe that. Has she let Kate go?'

'That's different, they're family. But with you ...' I trailed off. What did I know, after all? I'd only been there a year and a half. And now I thought of it, it struck me that Nell must have turned twenty-one, and she wasn't going anywhere.

'Come with me,' said Mim.

Into the claws of that wind? Despite the howl it made as it battered the streets, I must admit I was tempted to brave it for Mim's sake. Her courage was infectious. A fresh start with a true friend. Wasn't that what I'd always wanted?

If I stayed here, life would only become more miserable. Admittedly, I'd still have Nell and Billy, but they weren't like Mim. They saw no farther than the confines of this shop, this town. Mim was going to London. Maybe Africa.

Mim and I could build a life where we needed only each other.

But how could I go back on the document Ma had signed; abandon her while I sought a new life under a foreign sun? And there was the corset, creaking softly under my head, reminding me of pleasures yet to come. I couldn't throw up this chance to hurt Rosalind. Not now.

'You know I can't go. The old hag will send Ma to debtors' gaol if I run away.'

'If she can find her! She still hasn't written, has she?'

'No,' I admitted, begrudgingly.

'Well, then.'

Common sense told me that my ma was probably dead, but everything inside me recoiled from the thought. To have Ma die would bring a new desolation, a new shrieking loneliness to my existence, beyond anything I'd endured so far. I had to hope she was still alive.

'You believe so fiercely that your ma is out there, in London.' My voice came a little shaky. 'Why can't you believe in mine?'

I heard her exhale. Her hand found my own. 'You're right. I'm sorry. I just … I'd rather go with you.'

'I know. But look, if I'm here, I can help. Distract them. Today Mrs Metyard was talking about setting a date for Kate's wedding. There's got to be a chance then, hasn't there? With the celebrations and all that?'

Mim squeezed my hand. 'Yes,' she said. 'Yes, I'll do it then.'

We didn't talk, after that. I lay open-eyed on the pallet, knowing sleep had gone to the devil for me. The day Kate married was to be the day I lost every faint ray of light in my life. What would Metyard's be without Mim's terrible tea, Billy's whistle, Kate's peacock-blue dress?

At the far end of the cellar, Nell cried out in her sleep. I pressed my left ear to the pillow, listening to the corset creaking, and under it the sound of the steady flick of Mim's bone fish.

28

Dorothea

I have expended much thought upon Lady Morton. Courtesy dictates we return her invitation to dinner, although I scarcely expect her to come. Imagine that skull-face, crossing my threshold; shedding a cloud of powder and dead skin over my carpet! No, I do not want that woman in my house, any more than I want the inexorable Mrs Pearce.

Papa once told me that all good company forsook him once my mother converted to Catholicism. This I have used to explain the absence of family friends, anxious for my upbringing, and the sad state of affairs that led my father to set his sights as low as Mrs Pearce. Yet now, I wonder.

Lady Morton did not speak disrespectfully of Mama. Indeed, there are Catholic ties in the Morton family which would make it hypocritical of her to do so. The more I think upon that dinner at Heatherfield Manor, and the tea we shared after the meal, the more I believe Lady Morton's distaste has sprung from another source. She no longer calls because she does not like Papa.

Mama and Lady Morton were friends. Searching through her remaining belongings – the silhouettes and the dried flowers, the little handkerchiefs half-embroidered – I have found several notes from one to the

other, signed *Your Affectionate G.M.* I have memories of
Lady Morton calling at the house, so she could not have
deserted us, as Papa would have me believe. But she has
not set foot here since Mama died.

Do you not consider it strange? Illness aside, I would
expect a letter from time to time. *Something.* A woman
– a childless woman – does not watch her dear friend
die, leaving an only daughter, and take no interest in the
girl's welfare. Not unless a weighty consideration keeps
her away. And Papa, I am increasingly convinced, must
be that consideration.

Papa has been nothing if not civil to her, yet I recall
the satirical look upon her face as she spoke of Mama's
'sad illness'. As if she blamed him for failing in her care.

Last night, as I was preparing for bed, I decided to
quiz Tilda. I sat in my nightgown before the dressing
table, where two candles burnt in their holders. My hair
fell about my shoulders, loosened from its ties. Tilda
worked it with the silver-backed brush, preparing to
weave it into plaits.

'Tilda,' I said, watching her in the mirror, 'you worked
for us, did you not, at the time my mother passed away?'

The brush slowed in its path. 'Yes, miss. I was in the
kitchens, then.'

'Indeed you were. I recall it now. Not a great deal
older than I was.'

'I was … fourteen, I believe, miss.'

Fourteen years to my seven. Much may escape the
notice of a child, but at fourteen Tilda would have the
ability to look about her.

'Do you remember much, Tilda? About how my
mother died?'

A tug on the end of a lock. My scalp prickled. 'I can't
say I do. It was very sad, of course. But I was busy

downstairs, in the scullery. I daresay you remember more than I do, miss.'

What *do* I recall? Vomiting. Terrible circulation. I used to hold Mama's dear hand in mine and chafe it, breathing hard upon the skin, in an attempt to warm the icy fingers.

'That is the difficulty. Certainly I nursed her, young as I was. Yet even now, I do not comprehend exactly what complaint she died from. What did they say in the kitchens?'

'A … wasting disease, I think.'

Tilda threaded my hair between her fingers and began to plait. Her eyes were focused on her work; they did not meet mine in the mirror.

'But the name of the disease? I do not suppose any of the servants saw what was written upon the death certificate?'

'Oh, I wouldn't know that.'

'There was no inquest, no examination of the body?'

She pulled the plait, tight. 'No. Dr Armstrong was in attendance, wasn't he? He's always been the master's friend. He saw the poor thing all the way through her illness.'

I am not a devotee of Dr Armstrong. He appears slapdash, uninterested, as if medicine is a great inconvenience to him. Indeed, I believe it is, for he has told Papa on more than one occasion that he wished he had gone for a soldier instead.

Perhaps that forms the basis for Lady Morton's dislike? She would have employed a better doctor, but Papa, of course, went straight to the friend he trusted.

Tilda *must* know more. Servants gossip; it is in their nature.

'I worry, you see,' I said, trying a different tactic. 'I am approaching the same age. Suppose the condition should be hereditary? I must know what symptoms to watch for.'

By the candlelight, I saw her fumble. A lock of my hair sprang free. 'Nonsense. You're stout and hearty.'

'I am sure that is meant to be a compliment.'

'What I mean, miss, is ... well, your mother. She had those big glittering eyes and roses in her cheeks. Ladies like that never last long.'

'You think it was consumption, then?'

Tilda's fingers regained their rhythm. 'Maybe. I'm not a doctor, am I?'

'There was no cough,' I muttered, casting my mind back. 'It was more like acute gastritis.'

'If you say so, miss.'

We were silent for a moment. I watched my reflection, shimmering by the flames of the candles, and tried to trace Mama in my face. Very little of her remains, either there or in my skull. It is in *temperament* we are alike. Always busy. Always active. Until ...

'Perhaps I should ask my father to see the death certificate.'

'I wouldn't do that, miss,' Tilda said quickly.

She is right. It will only upset him. Papa is not the bravest of men. He has a terrible aversion to talking of sickness and death. I slept in Mama's chamber every day of her decline, yet he hovered on the threshold, peering through the doorway. Cautious.

That could be another reason for Lady Morton's disdain. If you did not know Papa, as I do, you would think it cowardly, or even heartless behaviour.

By now, my temples were beginning to ache. 'Enough, Tilda. You have pulled that exceedingly tight.'

'Sorry, miss.' She handed me my nightcap. 'Will there be anything else?'

'No. Goodnight.'

A hasty curtsey, then she was gone.

Without a doubt, Tilda knows more than she has told me. She has a well-developed organ for Secretiveness, which has not gone undetected by my watchful eyes. But I must not blame her. People do not always conceal facts through base motives; perhaps she fears distressing me with talk of my mother's demise. And if Lady Morton and my father *did* quarrel, Tilda would hardly tell me.

All the same, I am uneasy in my spirit. I do not like to think, even in supposition, that Lady Morton blames Papa for Mama's death.

But grief, as I have often observed, is a strange distorter. It makes one believe the most fantastical things.

Look at Ruth Butterham. Her tale spins ever more wildly, veering out of control. Her fantasies of punishing her childhood tormentor. It is bordering on puerile, even for a girl of sixteen.

Ruth may amuse herself in this manner as much as she pleases; it is nothing to me, so long as I can measure her head. She takes me for a credulous fool – I have forgiven her that. But at the end of the day, I am not the one who suffers.

It is she who needs to confess and repent.

With the trial approaching, this is no time to evade God's mercy. The days are running short. Ruth must be purged with hyssop, daubed with sacrificial blood, before she takes the last drop.

How long, really, can a person continue lying to themselves?

29

Ruth

Kate took all the measurements for the Oldacre trousseau, wrote out the many orders for us to complete. It was the first commission that had ever given me true pleasure.

For her corset, Rosalind had chosen a shade that oozed, that made you feel ill. I couldn't have picked it better myself.

My hands hovered over the panels I had made. They seemed to hum, slowly warming, as if I'd held them before the kitchen fire. I knew what I must do. I knew it before I'd sewn a single stitch.

On the table, to the right of the half-completed corset, lay my own dear creation: the garment Rosalind had ruined, so long ago. She'd called it a weak thing, but now it was strong, as strong as my hate for her.

Lovingly, I spread it out. How small it looked. My body had grown considerably since the days the cords held me tight in their embrace. Now it was time for them to cling to another. Drag her down.

The square I cut was not large. A single patch of the brown jean material I'd hidden beneath the floorboard under my bed. I ran a finger around the edge of it, feeling the caress of the fibres. Raising it to my lips, I placed a kiss at the centre. Then I slipped it into Rosalind's corset, between the green material and the lining. A rotten secret at the very heart.

The unfinished garment seemed to come alive with that addition. Perhaps it was their lurid colour, but the panels appeared to pulsate on the table. Breathe, in and out.

'Where is she? Where's that girl?' I started as the aubergine curtain swished back, revealing Mrs Metyard's solid form. 'I am going to the privy, Butterham. Watch the showroom.'

'But—'

'No arguments,' she barked.

Sighing, I folded my acid-green panels away. It would be just as well to spare my eyes for a while.

Mrs Metyard disappeared, leaving me to walk out, uncertainly, on to the cream carpet. Winter it might have been, but the showroom blazed. I stood behind the gleaming glass counters, beneath the chandeliers, mistress of it all. The feathers, the fans, the scent bottles, the rolls of silk on the wall: they were mine alone.

Or perhaps not.

Billy hovered by the window. He was jamming his cap back over his hair, which looked limper than usual, as if he'd run his hand through it many times. My heart jumped at the sight of him.

'Good day, Ruth. You ... heard all of that, I suppose?'

I reached beneath the counter and began straightening the display, trying to hide my surprise. 'Heard what?'

'Mrs Metyard and I were talking. About the wedding. It's really happening, after all this time. The first banns will be read next Sunday.'

Thank God my hands were under the counter. He couldn't see them tremble.

Billy had been outside the whole time, a whisper away from me, and I was so absorbed in my loathing

for Rosalind Oldacre that I hadn't even heard his voice.
I might not hear it at all, in the future. As a married man
he would be in the shop far less. At home with Kate and
their blue-eyed children, rather than running around
rescuing me and Nell from the coal hole. Another friend,
lost to me.

'Well? Aren't you going to say something?' The blue
eyes bored into mine.

'I …' It was the wrong way to start the sentence. The
last thing I should talk about was myself. I needed to
turn this back to him. 'I imagine that's a great relief to
you both. How do you feel?'

He chuckled. 'Ah, I won't lie. I'm nervous, Ruth, of
course I am. But very happy.'

I didn't want to hear any more.

Perhaps he knew this, deep down. Perhaps my face
revealed the truth. Either way, he changed the topic
pretty swiftly.

'You must have been working like a Trojan if you
didn't hear me come in. Another corset, is it? You've
been doing a grand job, they all say so. Better than I ever
did. Can I go behind the curtain and take a look?'

I pinked, pleased in spite of myself. 'No … it's not
ready, yet.'

'Well you can't rush a masterpiece. Split busk, is it?'

'Oh no, not this young lady. She doesn't want to wear
anything she can put on without a maid. I've got a solid
wooden busk of twelve inches wrapped in wash leather,
but it looks bulky to me. She'll have a shock when her
maid pulls the laces. It'll squash her stomach flat enough
to touch her spine.'

What a wonderful image: Rosalind flattened, Rosalind
pressed with a hot iron. But even that wasn't as good as
what I had planned for her.

'These fashionable sorts.' Billy winked. 'I daresay she wants lots of boning put in it, too?'

'Her corset,' I said honestly, 'is like a graveyard.'

He laughed. Maybe he wouldn't, if he knew.

I flicked my eyes to the speaking pipe. We were standing well away from it; they couldn't hear us upstairs.

'It will be strange,' I said softly. 'Come this time next month … I can't imagine it.'

'What, can't imagine me married to Kate?'

Oh, I could imagine *that* rather too well for my own peace of mind. But my brain only taunted me with pictures of embraces, not day-to-day life. I struggled to think how they'd rub along together.

'You're … rather different.'

'We are,' he agreed. 'You need that in a marriage. You know, Ruth … Kate isn't her mother. Sometimes I feel you think badly of her.'

I paid very close attention to the ribbon cards. It was on the tip of my tongue to tell him about the poker, but what good would it do? His honour was pledged.

'Perhaps I'll make her a corset,' I muttered. 'A little going-away present.'

'Aye! She'd like that.'

Lord bless him, he thought I was serious. I allowed myself a smile.

No, Billy. She wouldn't like one of my corsets. Not in the least.

30

Dorothea

It has become my duty to relate a most alarming circumstance.

When my carriage ground up to New Oakgate Prison this afternoon, there were no porters to open the gates. Graymarsh was forced to dismount the box and leave the horses, while he went to locate assistance. Fortunately it was a dry day, warm when the sun peeked out between scudding clouds. Our two bay mares were content to lower their heads and swish their tails while they waited.

At last a man returned with Graymarsh: a hook-nosed, flat-headed fellow. He opened the gates with much bluster, and seemed about to disappear again, until I pulled down the glass and accosted him.

'The gates must be guarded at all times! What are you about, there?'

'Sorry, madam,' returned the insufferable man. He did not sound the least bit sorry, only harassed. His forehead was low, rendering him deficient both in reasoning capacity and moral power.

'Explain yourself,' I demanded, drawing myself up. 'I sit on the prison board, you are accountable to me.'

'Good. P'rhaps you can do something about all this, then.'

It was not until I had gained the entrance that I could make sense of his cryptic words.

The place was in disarray. No sand crunched underfoot, no prisoners exercised in the yard. Even the windowsills bore a rime of dust.

Clogging the air was the reek of vinegar and something else, something burning; a cauterising smell. For an instant, I feared there had been another riot. But then a little seed nudged the soil of my memories, pushing up a shoot. *Camphor oil.* Yes, that was it: the very essence of Mama's stuffy, airless sickroom.

'Miss Truelove!' The turnkey Mrs Jenkins bustled towards me, her face alight with excitement. 'You will never guess what's happened! We have a plague.'

'A *plague*?'

She nodded, eager. 'Blotches on the skin, diarrhoea. The poor women are dropping like flies.'

Dread wrapped its icy fingers around my shoulders. I hastily removed the bergamot-scented handkerchief from my reticule and covered my nose. 'No one has died?'

'No,' she conceded, a touch disappointed. 'Not all of them have it. Your Ruth Butterham is well enough.'

Somehow, I knew that would be the case.

'I can allow you to visit her, Miss Truelove, but I dare not let you at the rest. Can't have a young lady like you taking the sickness.'

My breath came short as we walked through the corridors; a nagging pain set up beneath my ribs. Fortunately, Mrs Jenkins did not require me to speak; she only wanted to be talking herself.

Apparently it started in the laundry, when one of the women fainted in the course of her work. Not much attention was paid; the laundry is always sweltering, full of steam, and with warmer weather on its way we might expect a swoon or two. But the prisoner remained despondent, lethargic even, when she regained consciousness. Matron noticed an odd mottling to her skin. By then, three more women had fallen down.

'It's all hands on deck,' Mrs Jenkins enthused. 'We have twice the laundry and half the prisoners to wash it. Thank heaven none of the staff have been taken ill!'

I caught her arm. 'It only afflicts the prisoners? Are you sure? You suffer no ill effects from the miasma?'

'No,' she said. 'It's the strangest thing.'

We had reached Ruth's cell. The enamel plaque swung gently, although there was no breeze.

Shaking myself, I entered to find Ruth picking at more of that awful oakum. Its musty, fibrous fragrance only added to the general taint of the air. Even my bergamot-scented handkerchief was no defence.

I coughed.

Ruth gazed up at me. 'Miss. I didn't think you'd come, with the sickness about.'

'I was not aware of it. Do put that rope down, Ruth, I hate the stuff. I thought Matron had moved you to the sewing room?'

Shrugging, Ruth dropped the pile of oakum and dusted off her hands. Black motes rose around her like soot. 'She did, until the bed linen was done. But we're not to mix together in the workrooms, now. Might get infected.'

Was it my imagination, or did the corner of her mouth buck, ever so slightly? Did she not handle the word 'infected' with a touch of scorn, as if she knew …

But I am becoming nervous; I am supposing the most outrageous things!

'And how did you find it?' I asked, keeping out of her reach. 'Sewing, once more? I understood you were no longer inclined to that employment.'

'Well I'm used to having to sew, even when I don't want to. It's all the same to me, really.'

She clasped her hands together. Dirty, black. Broken nails. The words of her story came flooding back; I recalled the venom with which she had spoken of Rosalind Oldacre. Could it be that she nurtured similar grudges against her fellow inmates? That she had tried …

Foolish, trusting girl that I am, I found the words spilling from my lips. 'And what did you dwell upon, while you sewed the bed linen? I hope they were edifying thoughts.'

Her head tilted, spilling elflocks across her neck. 'What do you think?'

Tingles, all down my spine. Silly Dotty, caught again! This was just what she intended, of course. She has been lying to me for the thrill of it, for the expression that crosses my face when I am simple enough to believe her. What use is all my learning, if I am to be fooled by her tales?

'I have not the slightest idea. I only asked out of curiosity. Sit in the chair, would you, Ruth? I should like to take some more measurements.'

Patiently, she submitted to my hands and the craniometer. Rope fibres tangled in her hair and had to be removed before I could commence.

My eyes were a little cloudy, dazed by my concern for the ill prisoners, and the prickling dust, but they saw clearly enough: the readings had not altered. Not a fraction of an inch.

Surely there should be a shift, however small? Even supposing Ruth's visits with the chaplain to be a total sham, she has been lying to me, day after day. I would expect the baser organs to grow larger from overuse and the moral faculties to shrink.

Unless my theories have been fallacious, all along …

'You're very quiet,' she said. 'Haven't I got enough bumps today?'

I clapped the craniometer shut. 'No, no, everything is in order. Do you feel well, in yourself? I am most concerned about this sickness in the prison. I should hate for it to reach you.'

'That's kind, miss. But I shouldn't worry. It might be better for me to be taken, suddenly, like that. Better than hanging.'

'The illness is not fatal, Ruth. It has not killed any of our prisoners,' I pointed out.

She looked down at her stained hands. 'No. Not yet.'

31

Ruth

They were strange days in the attic room. We sewed in an atmosphere of smothered excitement, snatching at hints and portents of the new world to come. Often we would hear Mrs Metyard whisper about cold meats, or say to Kate that 'the girls must do it, if we can make them presentable'. Under all her smiles lay a sting of hostility. She wasn't really pleased about Kate's forth-coming marriage. She resented it.

Kate herself became jittery, her cutting faster, her orders more distracted. Yet it seemed to me there was another change to her. She was more beautiful, more human.

I hated her.

We got away with the odd whisper, in the week leading up to the first banns, so long as Mrs Metyard was down in the showroom. Mim and I would sit at the end of our table, apart from the other three, and put our heads together as we tackled scratchy, horsehair petticoats.

'They're having a supper party,' I told her, my eyes upon Kate. 'Next Sunday, after church.'

'Mrs Metyard didn't say anything.'

'No, but she will. I've been listening. They mean to have all their friends over and make us wait upon them.'

Mim's sewing hand slowed to a stop. It was the right one, with the missing finger. 'They'll be ... busy.'

'Distracted,' I agreed.

'They won't be able to keep an eye on us. Not all night.'

'No.'

A sore on my middle finger burst. I raised it to my lips, ready to suck out the pain, but the smell of it made me stop.

Mim tossed me a scrap of linen and I wrapped the seeping wound up. I couldn't wrap my uneasiness away with it. My hands were growing rougher than I'd ever known them, ulcerated around the nails. Often, I had a headache. I couldn't remember when it started, exactly, but I thought it was about the time I began working on Rosalind's trousseau.

My loathing for her had swollen like a monstrous abscess that must be lanced. Could it be I was growing ill with the force of it?

'I'm going.' Mim smoothed out the horsehair petticoat. Her lips were set with determination. 'I'll do it on the night of the party.'

Another sting, but this wasn't in my hand. Mim was right – it was the best chance to get away. But without her I would be ... I'd be like the threads left behind once a bead falls from a dress.

I picked up my needle again. 'Don't count on the twins. If Ivy sees you running, she'll tell.'

'I'll have to go in the small hours. Just as the guests are leaving.'

'Maybe we should tell Mr Rooker.' Doubt tinged my voice. He'd helped me escape the coal hole, but never the captain's room. Could I really persuade him to hoodwink his fiancée at her own party? 'Or Nell ...'

Mim shook her head vehemently. 'No. Don't breathe a word to anyone else. I only trust you.'

'I promise.'

She shot me a brief smile. I thought of that first day I'd seen her, so wary and unsure, pretending to fetch Mrs Metyard from the showroom. Whatever was left of my heart jerked behind my ribs.

I wanted to say that I loved her, that she'd been the best friend I ever had. I wanted to say that I forgave her for witnessing the document that bound me to Mrs Metyard. But just then Kate looked up.

'Miriam! Ruth! Stop dallying! Don't make me fetch my mother.'

And that was enough to seal our lips for the rest of the day.

Since coming to New Oakgate Prison, I've thought a lot about death. I mean the experience of it, not the afterlife. They'll hang me, probably, for what I've done. Hanging's not the worst death I've seen.

Sometimes I wonder how I'll feel, waking up that morning, knowing it's the day I'll die. Maybe I'll weep. But the more I think of it, the more I believe I'll feel just like I did that Sunday, the day of the banns and Mim's escape.

Dawn came bright and frosty. We washed to the persistent trill of a robin in the tree. New gowns to wear, for we'd be on display at church and in the evening, serving the visitors. They were nothing to be excited about: cheap things, the colour of mud. Still, it unsettled me to fasten an unfamiliar dress over my stays; as if it was a costume for a play.

I had to use the privy three times before we left. Terror
trod on my heels all through the house and out into the
street.

White crystals made a lace between the cobbles. Even
the dead leaves and piles of manure were sugared with
frost. To my eyes it was all too sharp, too vivid, the bird-
song full of spite.

I walked with Mim and Nell, unable to speak. The
twins strode in front and Mrs Metyard and Kate saun-
tered at the back, arms linked, as they always did. They
had to let us come to church on a Sunday – it would
look odd if they didn't – but they lent us to God once
a week with ill grace. They were always hovering close
by, watching us, making sure we didn't bolt off.

And that was just what Mim meant to do: bolt. Less
than twenty-four hours would see her here, on these
very cobbles, alone and running for her life.

I wanted the privy again.

Church was busy, stuffed with the odour of damp
wool. We shuffled into a pew, crammed close together
and, for once, glad of it. Little by little, we warmed up.

The congregation chattered as they waited for the
service to begin, but our party sat in strained silence.
Kate perched on the end of the pew, her cheeks glowing
from the walk. She looked radiant, like the stained-glass
window of the Virgin. Only, I noticed, her lower lip
trembled.

I was trembling too. Mim pressed next to me but I
couldn't look at her for more than an instant. She'd kept
the veil down over her bonnet. Every time I saw it, I
thought of a shroud.

At last the service began. The readings, the hymns and
the slow, familiar chants coated my frayed nerves. My
pulse slowed. I might have calmed down altogether, if

the vicar hadn't chosen that moment to say: 'I publish the banns of marriage between Catherine Maria Metyard, spinster, of this parish and William Rooker, bachelor, of the parish of St Luke by the Water. This is for the first time of asking. If you know any reason in law why these two may not be married, you are to declare it now.'

No one knew what I suffered in my heart as I sat there on that pew. Well, maybe God knew. But He didn't do anything about it.

Sunday was never a day of rest for us. As soon as we got back from church, we were expected to work. Today was only a little different. Instead of the cold climb to the attic, we bustled into the kitchen. Nell laid the fire, Mim began to sweep, and the rest of us beat out carpets.

'Aprons,' announced Mrs Metyard, marching into the kitchen with an armful of white cloth. 'And these caps – *after* you have done the dirty work, Miriam! They must look clean for the guests.'

She piled them upon the table with swift, decisive motions. Her square jaw clamped tight, deepening the wrinkles around her mouth. Her eyes, usually beady and small, protruded. I'd seen the expression somewhere before. Yes, that was it: on the boy driving the hay cart, when his pony spooked. The look of someone hurtling down a road, too fast, the reins slipping from their hands.

Kate was nowhere to be seen. I expect she was fastening herself into one of those dresses with the twenty-inch waists. We didn't know what she was wearing; she'd ordered it from one of the other fashion houses in town, much to her mother's displeasure.

Soon the house warmed with the scent of cooking food. Not what we made do with: the guests had bacon, white bread, potatoes coated in breadcrumbs and parsley, game pie and seedcake.

Daylight didn't last for long. Before we knew what we were about, the sun began to set in a powdery cascade of blue and pink, streaked with mackerel clouds. Shadows stretched and lengthened. The carriage clock in the showroom pinged. It was time to put on our caps.

How odd we looked, how insubstantial, with our hair covered and our necks bared to the firelight. A line of maidens, sentenced to the guillotine. Mim paused beside me as we collected our trays. Her hand reached out and tucked one of my unruly locks back behind my ear.

I knew this was goodbye.

At last, I was permitted to climb the carpeted staircase up to the living quarters. The tray wobbled in my hands as the scents flooded back: lily of the valley, violets, wood and coal. No longer pleasant fragrances. They put me in shackles, in the captain's room, even though that door was closed and locked.

Food and drinks were served in the drawing room. I'd never been in a space so fine. Beeswax candles blazed from sockets on the walls, the light gleaming on the mirror and the mahogany mantelpiece. Warm paper, patterned with poppies, covered the walls. Marble-topped tables stood waiting for the food, while here and there were sofas for the guests to sit. Kate had filled vases full of hothouse flowers. It was perfect: a stage, ready for the actors to arrive.

I stood by the wall, watching the wings, twitching the curtains.

Waiting for one player to depart.

32

Ruth

'We were blessed once, so we were, a long time ago, but the angels took the poor dear home. Ah, it was a sad thing. But when I first saw Billy! Lord love me, I says to Mr Rooker, if he hasn't just the look of our Alfred about him.'

Billy's adopted mother wasn't what I expected. She was Irish – and it occurred to me that Billy *did* have a turn of phrase, and an Irish way of speaking, even if he didn't have the accent. Mrs Rooker was also fleshy, with apple cheeks and a bosom that could knock you for six if she turned around too quickly. She chattered happily to the guests, waving her hands, while her husband – a small, balding man with spectacles – smiled fondly on.

'Why yes, to be sure, we were surprised when the young people took it into their heads to marry. But why shouldn't they? He's every bit her equal, and,' dropping her voice, 'a bit more so, between you and me.'

From my position, pressed like a piece of furniture against the wall, it looked like a jolly party. People drank champagne, smiled and laughed. Kate shone at the centre, a different creature to the one I saw by day in the shop. Her skin had lost its tension. Paste diamonds sparkled at her neck and lit her eyes. The dress, which had so disgruntled Mrs Metyard, proved to be made in midnight blue, spotted with silver. It complemented her dark curls, now bound up with silver ribbon, and made her complexion more brilliant than ever. She was perfect, from the bones in her bare shoulders to the toes of her slippers.

My old, relentless yearning flared up. *Envy* is too weak a word for it. I didn't want what she had, I wanted to *be* her. If I could have taken Kate's soul from her body and replaced it with mine, I would have done it in an instant.

To look as Kate did now, as she raised her glass and smiled at Billy, was to be invincible. Nothing could touch her.

Meanwhile, I sagged and shifted the weight between my aching legs, unused to standing for any length of time.

The hour was late, but the guests showed no sign of leaving. One of the lads from church struck up a tune with his fiddle. There was no space to dance, yet gentlemen hummed and tapped their feet.

Billy caught my eye and tipped me one of his winks. It didn't look like him, standing there. A starched collar rested its points upon his cheeks. He wore a frockcoat and a plain, velvet waistcoat instead of his usual checks and stripes. His hair, which I loved to see tumble about, had submitted to the comb and grease. He was still charming, but he wasn't Billy.

Ivy's sour face glared at me from across the room. Nell, Daisy and Mim had been down the stairs a few times to fetch bottles and remove plates, leaving the pair of us to attend the guests. But how closely did Ivy look?

Had she noticed the determination in Mim's chin? How long it had been since Mim last came up from the kitchen? I would have given much to know what Ivy thought. Something in her brow made me shiver.

When the clock struck three in the morning, people finally began to take their leave. Whoever dreamt they'd stay so late? Nell and I were sent to gather up armfuls of the guests' shawls, wraps and overcoats. On our way back to the drawing room, we passed the twins. Ivy frowned at the sight of us, as if something were amiss, but she didn't speak.

I thought I might be sick.

Downstairs, all lay in silence. Mim wasn't in the kitchen. She wasn't in the house – I could feel it.

Too late to cry. I made myself walk with a steady step, back to face the guests. Without the fiddle and the clink of glasses, you could hear wind howling through the streets, rattling at the windows.

She didn't have a cloak.

I handed out shawls to young ladies and tidied up the glasses in a kind of panicked alert. Any minute, I thought. Any minute now, someone will ask me where she is. Someone will raise the hue and cry, and they'll fly after her like a pack of dogs.

But when I left the drawing room to take the glasses downstairs, Mrs Metyard was still smiling.

On my way to the kitchen, I stole a peep out of the window. A full moon glowed through tatters of grey cloud. Stars shone, bright as needle points in the cold sky. Snow dusted the ground.

She was only wearing thin shoes.

One by one, the company departed. I shivered, ever fiercer, as the seconds ticked away.

Finally, Nell stacked some plates in the sink and asked, 'Have you seen Miriam?'

I shook my head. Too fast.

We hadn't even gone to bed when the blows fell on the showroom door: not in pairs or trios, as knocks often are, but a steady barrage of open-handed slaps.

I felt them on my body.

'Who can that be, at this hour?' asked Nell, up to her elbows in suds.

My temples pounded from lack of rest. 'Probably some fool in his cups. We should ignore it, they'll go away.'

They didn't go away. They didn't stop to rest their arm but hit louder and louder until I thought my brow would split.

'You'd better answer the door, Ruth.'

I took a few hesitant steps out of the kitchen. Kate ran down the staircase at full pelt, skirts hitched up her calves, her curls tumbled from their ribbons. Mrs Metyard followed at a slower, more ominous gait, each footstep resounding.

Billy and the other guests were gone. There was no one to see me slink after them, silent in the dark.

I stood as I'd done on that first day: at the threshold of the showroom, peering in. It wasn't light and heavenly now. The poppets and dressmakers' models loomed, ghostly in the shadows. Coloured feathers became the plumes of carrion birds. The glass counters winked, malicious.

Kate unbolted the door.

Freezing wind rushed inside. Ribbons flailed, feathers flew. Then I saw the man standing upon the steps, and the writhing figure that his arms struggled to restrain.

'Found something that belongs to you, Mrs Metyard.' It was our milkman, Mr Brown: a bull-necked, florid fellow. 'I says to myself, that's the dressmaker's Negro all right, by the coaching inn. We don't get many of them in these parts.'

Mim's dress clung to her tall frame. She was bedraggled, cold and her cheek bled – yet for all this, she'd never looked more beautiful.

'Thank God,' Kate babbled, 'I thought we'd never find her. My mother only just noticed …'

'Silly mare wouldn't get far, not on a night like tonight.'

Mim twisted in Mr Brown's grip, gasping for liberty.

'Fierce one, ain't she? Nearly gave me the slip. Have you something to tie her, miss?'

'I think – yes, here's some cord.' Kate shivered as she moved, her shoulders bare in her evening dress. 'Help us, Mother.'

Mrs Metyard didn't speak. Didn't move. In the midst of the foraging wind and Mim's desperate bids to break free her stillness was appalling.

'Careful, miss, she'll catch you.'

Together, Mr Brown and Kate bound Mim's wrists. Her skin paled where the cord tightened.

'Let me go!' screamed Mim. 'You don't own me!'

'I've got papers here that say otherwise.'

Had it been worth it? The fear and the pain for an hour of freedom? I should've stopped her. A true friend would have stopped her.

'I can't thank you enough, sir. You've been my saviour.'

Mim's scoff covered my own. Why couldn't the bastard mind his own business? Why couldn't he look the other way?

Silently, Mrs Metyard moved behind the counter and reached for something. A purse. She opened it, produced a coin and gave it to the milkman.

'That's mighty decent of you, ma'am. I was just doing my duty. But I can use this for a spot of rum to drive out the cold.'

'You'll have breakfast here when you deliver the milk next,' Kate promised. 'Miriam might have frozen to death or been attacked by desperate types if it weren't for you.'

He laughed. 'Not her, miss. She'd fend them off.'

Mrs Metyard stepped forward. Between them, she and Kate took hold of the hostage.

'Thank you again.'

It was only when the door was shut on the milkman and the wind died down that Mrs Metyard uttered a word.

'Deserter.'

It came from the chafed red lips and the bracketed mouth, but it wasn't Mrs Metyard's voice. This was deeper.

'I ought to have you stood against the wall and shot.'

She dragged Mim into a pool of light from the streetlamp outside. My stomach clenched.

He stood there, clutching Mim.

The captain had returned.

33
Ruth

First, they beat her with the broomstick. The captain held her by the hair while Kate administered the blows. With every swing, her sapphire ring flashed. Mim refused to cry out.

When the hollow thwack of wood had faded away, we were sent to bed: the twins, Nell and I. My pallet felt large and achingly cold without Mim.

'What was she thinking?' Nell said into the darkness. 'She must have known she'd never make it, especially in the frost.'

Daisy cleared her throat. 'I don't think blackamoors feel the cold. Not like we do …' But you could tell that even her spiteful soul didn't believe it.

Very soon, the sun would rise again. None of us pretended to sleep. We lay there, staring at the mouldy ceiling, wondering what was taking place above our heads. I listened to the house, every creak and every groan, but I didn't hear Mim. Whether that was a good sign or not, I couldn't decide.

In the days that followed, Nell abandoned the attic to take over the cooking and the cleaning. She was good at it. If I'd had anything but bile in my stomach I would have appreciated the stronger tea and the eggs that didn't run. But now every moment only served as a reminder that Mim wasn't there: not in the sewing room, not in the kitchen, not in my bed.

We were all of us stunned by the loss of her. Even Ivy and Daisy fell quiet. I missed their barbed glances, their astringent remarks. At least they'd made me feel alive.

Now I only had Rosalind's corset to punish and I did it with relish – but upstairs, with the others, rather than down in the showroom. By the time Rosalind's trousseau was complete, all our nails were yellow, stained from the emerald-green dyes.

'I hate all the brides,' Ivy flared, 'but I hate this one most of all. Look what she's done to me! I hope the gowns rot her skin off.'

I smiled.

I suppose it was a week after the party that Kate brought us all down to the showroom, to pack up Rosalind's dresses in boxes and tissue paper. She'd never done such a thing before.

She was wearing her striped humbug gown and looked, in all honesty, dreadful as she stood amongst the fine silks and parasols. Her nose seemed to tilt even higher, as if she had dung stuffed up it. Grey shadows sat beneath her eyes. Her waist, always tiny, had shrunk again. I didn't feel any pity.

'Come on then,' she barked. 'Ivy folds, Daisy – tissue paper. Ruth, you put on the lids.'

'Green tissue,' muttered Daisy. 'Green ribbon. What a surprise.'

Kate pinched her. 'Get on with it.'

In fairness to Rosalind, she always had taste. The cuts were à la mode: tight sleeves, long bodices, all manner of intricate pleats and flounces. As Ivy fussed over the arrangement of a neckline, I wondered what Billy would think of the Oldacre trousseau and my serpent-green corset.

Why hadn't he delivered to Metyard's since the night of the party? If there was ever a time we needed him to come and rescue us, it was now. He'd lived in this house. He must have known the horror of the captain's room.

All I could think was that Kate had written and told him not to come. But surely he must suspect something was wrong? I didn't like the idea that he was falling under Kate's power and doing her bidding despite his better judgement. Becoming one of them, instead of one of us.

My work continued while I thought about Billy. Pale blue boxes, olive ribbon. Last in the line, I secured the lids and tied the bows. Throttled them.

For a time there was peace: the rustle of material and tissue, the slide of my ribbon against the box. The carriage clock ticked. But then the inside door opened, and Nell's freckled face appeared.

'She's not moving.'

'What?' Kate snapped to attention.

'I went to fetch her chamber pot. There's black in it and … she's not moving.'

All hands fell still.

Something curious was happening to Kate's face. Her skin wasn't peaches and cream now: it was old milk.

'I'll *make* her move.'

She flew around the glass counter in a whirl of black and white stripes. Pushing past Nell, she stomped up the carpeted stairs. A door slammed above us.

'Who, Nell?' I demanded. 'Who hasn't moved?'

Her throat worked beneath her high collar. 'Miriam.'

Of course there *must* have been someone going up to the living quarters day by day, to empty the pots and fetch the food. Nell. Nell had seen Mim and Mrs

Metyard, on a regular basis, ever since the escape – yet she'd said nothing.

'Why didn't you tell me that you saw her?' I cried. 'Why didn't you offer to pass on a message?'

Nell shifted against the half-open door. 'You know why.'

'Because you're a coward.'

Hurt in her eyes. I remembered then what she had risked to bring me the pail of water, that night I'd emerged from the coal hole. 'Go ahead and think that, if you like. But if you were up there every day, Ruth, watching that woman strut around in men's threads, you wouldn't say a word either.'

'She's still dressed as the captain?' Ivy asked.

'All week. Why do you think she hasn't been down here? She's not fit to see the customers. She's cracked.'

'But what about Mim?' I insisted. 'What have they done to her?'

Nell blinked her pale lashes. 'God, but it's terrible,' she whispered. 'They won't let me give her any victuals. The way she's tied, she can't sit, but she can hardly stand either ... '

I wanted to brain her, I wanted to shake her until her cinnamon head rattled. 'They won't *let* you? What, and you obey them? You can bear to see her like that, starved to death, and not slip her a cup of water?'

'I *can't*!' Nell cried, slapping the door. 'Every time I go in, she's there – *he's* there – with that bloody great sword ... There's nothing I can do.'

Behind me, Daisy rustled some tissue. Carrying on with her work, as though Mim were nothing.

I rounded on her. 'I suppose you're about to tell me blacks don't need food, aren't you? They don't *feel* starvation?'

All those lustrous gowns hanging in the showroom; the white gauze spread out across the counter like gossamer: they made me sick. Could nobody see the brutality that lay beneath the stitches? Didn't the customers realise that death lurked under every hem?

Daisy cast me a venomous glance. 'Careful with your mouth. If Miriam kicks the bucket, the captain will be after fresh meat. I tell you now, it ain't going to be me.'

'Nor me,' Ivy spat. 'Devil take the hindermost.'

Nell rested her head against the door. At least she had the decency to look tearful.

'There's nothing we can do, Ruth,' she repeated.

But of course there was.

Mrs Metyard in the regiment, Kate in the showroom, Nell all about the house. There was no one left to lock drawers. There was no one to notice if I slipped a few needles up my sleeve at the end of the day. I took three.

The sun set early, as it does in the winter. Black as the coal hole, black as Mim's hair. We finished sewing at eleven. Kate appeared in the attic, gaunt by the light of the lace-maker's lamp, and took us down to our chill, dank beds. I dressed in my nightgown, lay on my back.

Then I waited.

I waited a long time, staring blindly into the dark. Little by little, my eyes adjusted. Grey, fuzzy shapes showed me where the steps were and where the twins slept.

Rain tapped at the windowpane above my head. I heard it trickling down the street outside, trickling down our walls.

The air felt poised, as though it were waiting with me.

At last, I shuffled across the pallet and rose to my feet.

The snores carried on.

I wound my way carefully across the cold floor, making sure to avoid the chamber pots. The needles were tucked in my right hand, warmed by my flesh; I used my left to feel about me.

Scratches on my palm: the wooden steps. There was no banister – I would crawl up, for safety. What a notion: *safety*. When I was going straight into the lion's den.

Hitching my nightgown up to my waist, I fumbled on my hands and knees, inch by inch, up the steps. The third one down was rotten – I must remember that – but I hadn't kept count of the treads. If I should fall through—

Suddenly it was there beneath my fingers. Something creaked, ominous. Ivy snorted in her sleep.

I held myself rigid, listening. Surely she'd hear my heart, hammering in my chest?

'She'll kill you if she catches you.' Nell. Quiet as a whisper.

'I know,' I said softly.

'You won't be able to free her. It's not like the coal hole.'

'I just want to give her some food.'

I heard her turn on her pallet. 'I know,' she said, echoing me. 'I left some in the kitchen for you.'

After a few attempts, I managed to pick the lock with a long needle. Gently, I edged out into the corridor and pushed the door closed behind me.

Everything lay wrapped in velvet silence. Only faintly, in the distance, the carriage clock ticked.

I turned my head. This wasn't the place I knew: it was a funereal version, a ghostly version. Familiar objects appeared changed. I was lost and alone in the dark.

It was scent that led me in the right direction: burnt bread and fat, reaching out to me through the night.

Stumbling into the kitchen, I heard the sullen patter of the rain outside and the wind, sighing in its wake. My hip smacked, hard, into the corner of the table. I blew out my breath between clenched teeth. Something wet on my nightdress. Not blood? No – it was water. Nell had left a roll of bread and a mug of water close to the edge, where I could reach them.

Clutching the little supper took both my hands; I couldn't even grope my way through the darkness now. The mug handle burnt cold against my fingers. Shakily, I rounded the newel post and began to totter up the carpeted stairs.

The water sloshed in its mug, *lap, lap*, against the clay. It was the loudest sound I ever heard.

My hand tightened around the bread, squeezing the life from it. It wouldn't be any less wholesome for being crushed. But if I should leave crumbs on the carpet … Better not to think of that. Better not to think at all.

I'd resolved in my mind that it didn't matter if I died, that I was willing to run any risk for the sake of Mim. Yet when I gained the top of the stairs and the floorboard creaked, my body let me down. I began to tremble. Not just tremors: fierce, uncontrollable shaking that chattered my teeth.

What was I doing there? Was I mad?

I couldn't remember where the captain's room was. I only remembered the whip. Did I turn left or right? Suppose he'd heard the floorboard, just then, beneath my feet? Suppose he was already waiting for me?

Biting back the tears, I flew forwards in desperation. I thought – I *thought* – it was to the right. Why did it all look so similar in the dark?

Water dripped on to the carpet. I was too flustered to care about that. Two doors stared back at me, blank and

secretive, showing nothing of the horror that lay within.
There was no time: I had to choose.

I took the one on the right.

It was unlocked. Slowly, slowly, the door swung on
its hinges.

My vision flickered. The images came disjointed:
bulky shapes; a fire, swooping in the grate. A length
of rope hanging from the ceiling. Drooping against the
wall, her hands tied, as mine had been, a figure.

'Mim?' I croaked.

A sigh.

It was her. I'd heard her breath a thousand times: at
my side, sewing; sleeping in our bed.

Relief loosened my grip on the mug. And then something moved.

It uncurled gradually in the corner, something dark
and slender. With it came a powerful scent, sickly sweet,
slicing through the fug of the captain's tobacco.

Lily of the valley.

'Get out.'

'Kate?'

'Get out, do you hear me?'

I did, but only vaguely; her voice crackled in my ears.
I fought to keep my feet, to stay upright. 'What are you
doing to Mim?'

Kate took a step forward and I saw her, draped in
flickering orange light. Soot flitted out of the dwindling
fire, into her hair. It wasn't curled now but plaited, thick
down her back. She looked like an angel fallen in flames.

'Get out,' she growled. 'Or do you want me to call
my mother?'

Her hand reached for the fireplace, for the poker.

God forgive me, I couldn't hold my ground.

I dropped the roll and the water, and I ran.

34
Ruth

You didn't come to me for a happy ending. Obviously, she died. But the chaplain says death isn't the worst thing that can happen, and I believe he's right. For what befell me in the time that followed was much, much worse.

They waited until Sunday, when the shop was shut. Never a word to me in the meantime about my visit upstairs, or how Mim fared. Nell said they'd forbidden her the captain's room, and she hadn't heard them talk about Mim. None of us had an inkling the poor girl was dead, until that Sunday.

We were gauging cartridge pleats in the skirts of ball gowns. It was an awful business, trying to line up the rows precisely and gather them together. Oppressive shelves of cloud pressed down outside. There was no real light. Every time my needle reappeared from beneath the fabric it seemed like a miracle: shining, despite the dull matt surface of all about me. We'd been working even longer, with Mim absent and Nell engaged elsewhere. One day it was five and twenty hours, straight.

I was almost relieved when I heard feet thud into the workroom; it was a chance to pause and rest my sight. But then I looked up, saw Kate, and my relief vanished as quickly as it'd come.

Beneath her arm lay a rolled-up bundle I knew well: the knives Billy brought me to do the corsets, and the small saw. *My* things. Seeing them in her clutches was invasive, like watching her hold up my drawers.

'You're needed, Ruth. Come along.'

I pushed out my stool, grating its legs against the floor. 'Does someone want a corset?'

'Come *along*!'

There was too much work to leave, but I didn't dare argue with her – not after that night. Clear in my mind was the image of Kate, wild-eyed and gilded by fire. She hadn't punished me for sneaking up the stairs.

Not yet.

With the malevolent gaze of the twins upon me, I followed Kate out of the attic, down the stairs to the living quarters. How different they looked by day. Bright, richly furnished – but no less sinister for that. Something tainted the air. Not the powdery, floral scents I'd come to expect. They were gone, submerged beneath this other smell. No, not a smell. It was a *stench*.

It throbbed with more and more power, until at last we stopped outside the captain's room. Here the odour coated my tongue, unspeakably strong.

'Mim,' I whispered.

Kate's hand trembled as she turned the key. Blue veins stood out above the fragile bones. I had cause to remember them, after. To remember how different veins looked, with something flowing through them.

The door creaked open.

I'll never forget the blast from that room: ripe, fetid. There was a solidity to it. Both Kate and I choked.

'About time! In, in. Quick march.'

Kate shoved me before her, into the claws of the reek. She came in behind me, closed the door and locked it again.

Only then did I begin to see.

The captain bent over the fire. Flames capered, giving him a grotesque, gleeful look. The false hair stuck to his face wilted in the heat.

'The fire takes all,' he crowed, 'the fire tells no tales.'

It was too much: the heat, the smell and the fear. I fell to my knees.

'Up, up!' Kate tugged at my sleeve, dragging me across the carpet. I didn't mind how the friction hurt my skin. I would rather have been pitched into the fire myself than see what I saw, on the other side of the room.

Mim was in the wardrobe.

Crumpled, swollen about the abdomen. No hair left on her head. One of those monsters had taken a razor and cropped it close to the scalp. I didn't need to touch her to know that she was dead, and had been for at least a day. The stiffness of death had worn off. In its place came a juicy, overripe look. My beautiful Mim, reduced to this.

'What have you done?' I wailed. 'What have you done?'

I wished that I could cry.

There was a thump by my side. Kate had dropped my tools.

'You were her friend,' she said haltingly. 'Your hands have the greater right to touch her.'

Even then, I couldn't follow the diseased, twisting course of her mind. I stared blankly at the knives and the saw, as if they were memories from a former life.

'Cut it off!' the captain ordered. 'We need to incinerate it. Too easy to identify the body, with the missing finger.' Seizing a poker, he stirred up the blaze.

The harsh crackle of the logs filled my ears. Everything seemed to be happening in a reality separate from my own. 'Cut …?'

'You need to cut off her right hand with your bone saw,' Kate explained. As if she was telling me how to make a stitch. 'We're going to burn it in the fire.'

The words sank through me, dragging me down with them, stone weights in my stomach. I may have done terrible things in my life, but this was beyond the pale. They wanted me to dismember my only friend.

'I won't do it!' I shrieked. 'You can't make me do it!'

Beneath his monstrous facial hair, the captain smiled.

Kate was matter-of-fact. 'You have to. If the skeleton is found with that hand still attached, it will be quickly identified as Miriam and traced back to us. It needs to be done. You're the only one who can do it.'

'I won't. I don't care what happens to me!'

'But you do care what happens to your mother. Don't you?'

It winded me. In my mind's eye I saw poor Ma, lifeless like Mim. 'But … you don't even know where my mother is,' I stuttered.

The captain leered. His breath was a blast of tobacco. 'Oh yes I do. I've got my eye on the blasted wench and I'll be sure to make her pay. Wasn't she considered a beauty once? Pah! A damned scarecrow she is, now. She sold her hair. It will be her teeth, next.'

They hauled me to my feet. Strong hands, clamping each arm.

What could I do?

Desperate plans rushed through my mind. Suppose I grabbed my knives and stabbed them? Could I manage to kill both of them? It wouldn't bring Mim back. It might even put Ma at risk. But God, dear God, how I wanted to make them pay.

Strange to say, what I remember most are the touches of beauty. A fine web of veins. The inside of Mim's palm, which was once so pink against the brown, set like grey marble. She was more beautiful than Rosalind or Kate would ever be. Even in death she put them to shame.

When I'd finished, the captain offered up Mim's severed hand to the fire's blistering embrace. Orange tongues licked around the fingers, charring them, releasing the most terrible fumes.

I collapsed, vomited all over the hem of Kate's dress.

Revenge is a dish best served cold. That's what they say, isn't it? I tried to be cold, crouched there on the floor. To think, to let all my hate burrow deep inside like maggots.

I had a way to inflict pain: my own, special way. Hadn't it landed me in this mess in the first place? Perhaps now it would be my salvation. My escape.

No one would suspect. If I rushed headlong in my fury, slicing my way out of Metyard's, I might end up on the gallows. Ma might die. But if I bided my time … I would punish them. I would punish them without leaving a trace.

Kate was slowly turning the green of Rosalind Oldacre's wedding trousseau. 'We can't burn it all. The smoke, the smell … All the neighbours will be round. We'll have to think of somewhere else to put her.'

'God damn it all, you're right.' The captain stared at the conflagration, pushing Mim's hand in ever deeper with his poker. Something spat and sizzled.

'We can't carry her to the river. We would never make it that far. And if a boat found her … It would be clear she hadn't drowned.'

All things Kate should have considered, I thought furiously, before she killed Mim.

'Could we bury her?' Kate continued to fret. 'There isn't enough ground in the yard. But if ...' She froze, staring straight at me. 'That's it! The coal hole. Captain? Do you think the coal hole is deep enough? We can put her in there with some quicklime, just until the flesh rots and we can bury the bones. Would the neighbours still be able to smell her in the coal hole?'

To them Mim was no more than that: an odour to be concealed. Not entitled to her final resting place in a churchyard or beneath a marble urn, but rotting in the darkness of the coal hole with spiders scuttling around. It was even worse than Pa, buried on the Devil's side of the church. At least the sun touched his unmarked grave, now and then.

'It's the only defensive position we can take.' The captain dropped the poker, letting it clang against the fireplace. 'I'll be vanguard, you bring up the rear.'

Flicking out the tails of his red coat, he seized Mim's left arm and the stump of her right hand. I'd wrapped a swathe of muslin around it but fluid leached through, an accusation against him.

'We won't make you come with us,' Kate told me as she swallowed her gorge and hoisted Mim's bloated legs.

As if that was some kind of mercy. As if I wouldn't have to sit in the kitchen and eat my meals with the knowledge that my friend was festering beneath my feet.

'Isn't your young man going to come and help you carry it away?' I spat.

To my surprise, Kate flinched. 'Billy mustn't learn of this. Do you hear me? Not with the wedding so close.'

I snorted.

What *would* he think, seeing the tools he'd given me put to such use? Would he shrink from the stained bundle, rolled up with my blood-gummed saw? Would he even care?

At that moment, I despised him. I despised him for understanding what Kate was, and agreeing to marry her all the same.

'I think Billy knows what goes on here.'

The muscles in Kate's cheeks trembled. 'He doesn't know this, Ruth. No one has ever died, before.'

They lumped Mim's poor body out of the room, staggering under her dead weight. I was glad she was making them retch. Getting back at them, in the only way a corpse could.

They deserved far worse.

Once more, I found myself alone in the captain's room. The terrors of whip and rope seemed trivial now. Blood and vomit patched the brown carpet. They were the only suggestions that Mim had ever been alive.

The Metyards had taken everything from me. There was no memento, nothing to hold. When Naomi died, Ma had cut off a wisp of her downy hair. I would've liked to do the same with my friend, but even that was denied to me. All that remained of her here was a clump of damp carpet. The hand in the fire was already more charcoal than skin.

That hand … I'd seldom seen it empty. Even at night it was occupied, turning the bone gaming fish that her mother had left to her.

Where was the fish?

Frantically, I rifled through the wardrobe. She must have taken the fish when she ran away; there was no chance that she would leave it behind. But had she dropped it in her struggle with Mr Brown? Or was it still tucked in a pocket on the body, headed for the coal hole's sulphur depths? I searched as though my life depended on it. I think, in some strange way, it did.

There. A scrap of white, deep in the corner. Reaching in, I took the fish reverently into my hands. A fin of the tail had snapped off. Blood must have spilled on it, trickled into the cracks of the engraving. The word *Belle's* stood out now, bold in brown.

'I swear to you,' I whispered, addressing the only part of Mim I had left, 'they'll suffer for what they've done. All that you've endured will look like nothing – *nothing!* – after I'm through with them.'

35

Dorothea

I am more disturbed in my mind than I can possibly express. How could I be otherwise, with a recital such as this?

That poor girl.

Is it not odd, how print distances you from an event? You read an account in the paper and it looks just like a novel, a story that someone has invented. *Dressmaker Slays Apprentice*. Very well. On the next page you half-expect *Knight Vanquishes Dragon*.

But Miriam did live, and she also died. Horribly. I thank heaven the remains have since received a proper Christian burial!

I try to push the unpleasant images from my mind and do useful, everyday chores like changing Wilkie's water dish and blowing the husks from his seed bowl. Yet in every action I perform, I am dreadfully aware of my hands. I see Miriam's hand, melting in the fire. I see Ruth's fingers, about the saw.

I wondered, did I not, just what those stained hands, picking at the tar, were capable of? The truth is an unbearable weight upon me. It is much worse because, in this instance, I find that I believe her.

Not necessarily in all particulars. I have nothing but her own assertion that Mrs Metyard was either so enamoured of or abused by her husband that she attempted to assume his likeness. This may be the imagination of an overstimulated girl. But the manner of the death, and interference with the body ... This much I know is true.

Would that Ruth's were the only macabre tale dogging my thoughts, but David is full of another story, fresh from Putney. There, a female *trunk*, without limbs or head, has been discovered in the stables of one Mr Daniel Good. The man himself remains at large, much to the confusion of the six police divisions intent upon catching him. This would be horror enough, yet the circumstance which perturbs *me* is the fervour it has sparked within David.

'It's exposed the weaknesses in the system, Dotty,' he told me, eyes ignited with purpose. 'The police of our very capital, flummoxed! It's an embarrassment. There's no organisation. They need more men. Good, hard-working men to put the ship in shape.'

And before I could ask him what this signified, he informed me he had already taken action. Applied to transfer, to work in London 'where a man can make his name'.

This is my fault. I told him, did I not, that we should need to relocate in order to marry? That we required a larger income. I have forced his hand, and now I shall be obliged to leave behind my mother's house, my friend Fanny, Ruth, perhaps even Wilkie ... However, I must not fret. Not at present. It may all come to nothing. If the Metropolitan Police are truly as inept as he implies, they may make a mistake and reject him.

Am I selfish to hope that they shall? That by some miracle, I know not how, I am able to retain both the man and the house? It does not seem so *very* much to ask. But then poor Miriam only wanted a trip on the stagecoach and a meeting with her mother. I can see by these documents how she was served.

I take a shawl and wander with my papers into the garden. There is a little swinging seat, shaded from the sun. Bees tease at the opening buds of roses and geraniums. A dry, warm scent rises from the grass and I think I will be comfortable out here, with old Jim working at the hedges over the back. Nothing will appear terrible by the light of day.

I am wrong.

All these weeks I have wondered why the name 'Mrs Green' from Ruth's story rang a bell in a distant chamber of my mind. A common enough surname; no reason it should stick with me. But of course, it was the *colour* I remembered, from that year – the season Fanny, Rose and I vowed never to wear emerald green again.

We discovered that they manufacture the green dyes with arsenic. Some of it is simply brushed on to garments in a liquid solution with no treatment to fix the colour. Sweat activates the mixture, leaching the hue into the skin, and if that skin should peel and blister (as well it might) the arsenic enters the bloodstream. Frightful! To expire like a poisoned rodent!

Thank God, it never happened to anyone of my acquaintance. Our dressmakers used good-quality dyes, which never hurt us.

But it happened to Rosalind Green.

She was enamoured of green: green paper hung in her bedroom and her boudoir; there was green threaded into all that she wore, just as Ruth has said. She meant it as a tribute to her husband and the great wealth he brought her. By all accounts, she was a beautiful creature, suiting the colour so perfectly.

Until it began.

At first there were dry spots around the eyes, nostrils and lips: just peeling skin, which she thought little of. But then there came the blisters that burst and left craters. Her fingernails rotted.

By the time the doctor arrived upon the scene, she was vomiting green waters and passing green motions. Would you believe it, it was even said the whites of the poor girl's eyes turned green, until she wailed that everything she looked at was tinged with the colour.

Such a painful death, detailed before me. Convulsions – oh, I remember those well from my own poor mama! – but also foam. Green foam, from the mouth, nose and *eyes*. Almost as if ...

Ruth must know of this.

She has read the papers; this is another of her ruses, designed on purpose to frighten me. Why, she herself confessed to the marks the dye had made upon her nails and her fingers! Poison, sheer science, killed this girl Rosalind. It is folly to imagine otherwise.

But why do the hairs on the back of my neck prickle so?

Rosalind Green was a sad victim of her own mania. It has often been noted that bedbugs forsake rooms papered in bright green. In addition, mould grows between such paper and the wall, releasing an unpleasant-smelling gas. Faced with a combination of poisonous paper and deadly clothes, hour after hour, day after day, it is hardly incredible that unfortunate Rosalind succumbed. A frightful death, to be sure, and one that must have pleased the bitter, vengeful Ruth. But she did not *cause* it.

Goodness me, this case! Whyever do I pursue it? I gain neither progress in my studies nor good works for my soul! It seems clear that the prisoner is twisted and stubborn, beyond the reach of redemption. Her head does not change shape.

I am beginning to fear that evil is unavoidable.

That I should elope with David, now, before it is too late.

A bell rings inside the house. I tuck my papers away, and by the time I am done one of our footmen is crossing the lawn, carrying a silver tray.

'Letters for you, Miss Truelove.'

There are two. One in a cheap, slightly dog-eared envelope addressed in a hand I recognise as Matron's. The other is lavender-coloured and scented. Bold, blotted letters.

'Thank you,' I say, dismissing the footman with a wave. Pain darts across my knuckles. 'Bother!' I have caught one of the buzzing wasps – the blasted fellow has stung me.

'Are you well, Miss Truelove? May I fetch you something?'

'No, no, I am quite all right.'

I busy myself with the envelopes, resolutely ignoring the swelling on my skin. It itches like a thousand needle-tips.

Matron's letter first. News of the approaching trial, perhaps, or another murderer admitted? I rip it open, read the sparse lines.

I have to blink the sun from my eyes and read again.

I regret to inform you that New Oakgate Prison has suffered its first death. Jenny Hill expired at six of the clock this morning despite our best efforts. The doctor has been summoned, before this mystery illness can claim more lives.

Jenny!

I cross myself, say a prayer for her. The words are like paste in my mouth. How I have forsaken her, abandoned her, to follow my own selfish studies. Now I shall never have the chance to meet with her again. Poor woman. Did she die as lonely as she lived? She was serving time for attempted suicide. How awful that she should be saved, only to pass from the world in this manner.

I blame myself.

I blame Ruth.

It takes me a good while to shake off the tears and put aside personal considerations. Only then can I reflect upon what this will mean for the prison. Of course gaol fevers are commonplace, but we had hoped, with our attention to cleanliness and the new facilities, to avoid this sad misfortune. It seems to have found us, all the same.

At least the doctor will be able to advise us on the best course of action. It will have nothing to do with the bedsheets.

It is *not* Ruth.

The second letter. Yes, hopefully this will cheer me. I will read it, just to raise my spirits, and then I must dash inside to put cool water on this hand. Bless me, it itches!

The paper is hot-pressed, thick to hold. My eyes fly straight to the bottom, to the signature, seeking out the owner of this slapdash writing.

Sir Thomas Biggleswade.

The garden retreats around me.

Birds no longer call. Even the pain of the sting becomes dull, detached from me.

There is only one reason a gentleman would dare to address a young lady.

He has spoken to my father, he writes.

He is making an offer of marriage.

36

Ruth

I chose blue. Peacock blue. Could I really pick any other colour?

It hung neglected, towards the back of the lumber room, almost concealed by worsted and gaudy chintz. But it caught my eye, beckoned to me. And when I ran my hands over the grain, it was like brushing my own skin.

Perhaps it had been there all along, waiting for me in the room where I last saw my mother. Ma was in my mind as I unfurled ripple upon ripple of that blazing blue. It yielded easily to my scissors; thread and fibre parting to make way for the blade. Pliable. Unlike flesh.

Was I out of my wits? Maybe. But at least I wasn't afraid any more. The horror had set me free in a strange way: knowing I'd reached the abyss.

With the greenish-blue material folded into waves over my arms I marched, determined, through the show-room and into my alcove.

'What's that?' Mrs Metyard boomed. It *was* Mrs Metyard, stripped of her facial hair and, it seemed, the memory of what she'd done 'Come here! Girl!' She flung back the curtain. 'What do you think you are doing?'

'Working.' I sat myself at the table, unfolded my roll of knives. A dark crust remained on the blades. How far

I'd come, I thought, from my little cloth book of needles at home.

'There's plenty of work for you upstairs. Do you think I am going to let you dally about down here, when there's so much to do for the wedding?'

I gripped a knife in my hand. 'It's not my fault if you insist on killing the help.'

Something happened to her features then: a swift blast of the captain, fighting to resurface. She mastered him, pushed him down. I don't know what she would have done next, if Kate's peevish tones hadn't stopped her.

'Mother, I need you. Come quickly.'

She gave me a long, cold stare. Then she left.

It was time to begin.

No shoulder straps on this one. Front-fastening, split busk, lightly boned. Lace at the top and bottom. Then over the breasts, and in the curves of the waist, I'd embroider peacock feathers in brown, purple and green. A masterpiece. Like Pa said, the art that was the true me: beautiful and deadly.

I knew the measurements by sight. That waist of twenty inches. Why not make it eighteen? Sixteen? Squeeze the evil out, crush it, until there was nothing left but a tightly wound shroud of my stitches.

Blue. Endless blue before me. It might have been the sea for Mim to sail across. She might have been safe and happy, if it weren't for Kate. Kate must feel her pain. Kate would feel it all, and Mim would help.

For it wasn't just whalebone in that corset. I added slithers. Little pieces of Mim's bone fish, shaved down, pushing back against her oppressor in the only way she could, now. Scraps of the old corset, spotted with my own blood. The both of us, against Kate.

Through all the long hours I worked, my hand didn't shake. Not once. Nor did my eyes tire. I refused to take meals with the other girls, only creeping to the kitchen to grab crusts of bread and a sip of water when all lay quiet. How could I eat in that place, knowing what lurked beneath?

'What have you been doing?' Ivy would rail at me, when we went to bed. 'Too good to work with us now, are you?'

I laughed in her face.

'She's lost it,' Daisy said, edging away.

'Best leave her be,' decided Nell.

Not once did they ask what Kate had wanted with me and my tools that day. Not once did they hear Mim's poor blood, calling out for justice while they ate.

I wonder if they heard, as I did, the creak that came at night.

It might have been the old corset, beneath my pillow.

It might have been the rotting timber of my heart.

37

Dorothea

Am I overexerting myself? I can think of no other explanation for the poor health I have experienced. These past days have seen me harried and muddled in my thoughts. I begin to fear I am becoming nervous – a silly, girlish complaint that I never held truck with before.

Yet today, as I sat in the carriage with Tilda, I could not concentrate on the pleasant landscape sliding by or the trill of the birds. My gaze was turned inwards, and I did not care for what I saw.

I touched my hand to my breast, where Sir Thomas Biggleswade's letter lay concealed. Do not think I have turned sentimental and wish to press it to my heart! But Tilda can be sharp, and I have found it best to hide secrets about my person, rather than risk her discovery.

Poor Sir Thomas. He really does write well, with a great deal more eloquence than I would expect from a man such as he. His attachment cannot have any solid foundation. We have met on all of two occasions! Yet he is not a man I would wish to slight. Part of me is tempted to confide in him about my David, the real reason I cannot accept his offer; somehow, I feel Sir Thomas would understand my situation. But of course that would be careless. I cannot risk word getting back to Papa. If David attains his position in London, I may be taking my leave, eloping within the next month!

Guilt worries me like a rotten tooth. I do so wish to be a good daughter, to please Papa. Any other girl would be grateful to her father for seeking out an eligible husband like Sir Thomas! It is not as if he has chosen an ogre for me. I almost wish that he had. The letter of rejection would flow effortlessly, then.

As we approached the iron fences of New Oakgate Prison, I was surprised to observe the scaffolding on the male wing had been removed. White, newly minted stone shone in the spring light. Porters ferried supplies across the lawns. The gates swung open without waiting for our carriage to stop.

'This is more activity than I have seen for many days,' I told Tilda. 'What do you think has happened?'

Tilda looked up from her lopsided square of knitting. 'I wouldn't know, miss.'

It was as though a spell had been lifted. Even the air was less pungent, tinged with lime.

Could it be? Was the illness over?

In a flurry of anticipation, I flew to Matron's office. She was at her desk, writing in the character books. She nodded and stood – somewhat unwillingly, I felt – to greet me.

'Has the physician attended?' I asked, my words tumbling over one another. 'What does he say?'

'He called yesterday, Miss Truelove. I was on the point of writing to tell you. Yet here you are. Again. So I may have the pleasure of speaking in person.'

I nodded eagerly.

'It was scurvy, Miss Truelove.'

The breath left me in a rush. 'Scurvy?'

'Yes. You recall, naturally, that the prisoners' diet suffered some alteration after the riot? The new provisions were insufficient in nutrients. Today we have distributed oranges and put in a plea with the committee to reintroduce a meat allowance. I trust all will be well from now on. It's just a misfortune that poor Hill had to die, before it was resolved.'

I could have laughed for joy. Only the mention of Jenny Hill sobered me. 'Scurvy! Of course, scurvy. Why did we not think of it before?'

Matron lowered her brows and appraised me curiously. I daresay I appeared quite beside myself, but I could not help it; the liquor of relief was so strong. In my avid fancy, I had thought …

Never mind.

'It does explain why none of the staff fell prey to it,' Matron agreed. 'Although some of the prisoners were hardy enough to resist the disease, too. Your Butterham, for instance, remained in perfect health.'

The smile snapped off my face.

'I expect you would like to see Butterham?' Matron touched the keys at her waist.

'No!' The word flew from my lips, surprising me with its force. 'Not presently. I merely called to learn of the physician's findings. Thank heaven he has gifted us with such good news.'

'I am not certain I would call scurvy good news, Miss Truelove, but at least we can cure it. It is better than a fever.'

And better than a curse.

38

Ruth

Rosalind's corset marked me: an ulcerous finger, head-aches, yellow fingernails. Even the whorls on my skin became patterns of green. Yet with Kate's corset, there was no trace. My palms, which ought to have been bathed red, showed clean. A little calloused, perhaps.

I left it in the showroom, set out in an open box. How exquisitely it nestled against pale cornflower satin. A touch of gold thread in the eyes of the peacock feathers. When you moved past them, they winked.

With a hand more accustomed to holding a needle than a pen, I wrote awkwardly on a card: *To the future Mrs Rooker*. That was all.

Mrs Metyard decreed that we would all attend the wedding; not out of any spirit of generosity, but rather for the sake of appearances.

'I'm not going,' I told the girls. 'I don't care what she does to me.'

Nell's russet brows drew together. 'I'd rather not go. But we have to, Ruth. We don't have a choice. Don't give Mrs Metyard an excuse to hurt you.'

Ivy derided us, called us simpletons for not wanting a day off work.

'I wish I had the courage,' said Daisy, 'to stick my foot out and trip her up as she goes down the aisle.'

We woke a little later, on the bridal day. The sun didn't smile upon Kate and Billy. Veils of rain obscured the sky and the wind moved, restless.

Besides unlocking the door to our bedchamber, the Metyards paid scant attention to us that morning. The girls washed unsupervised and fetched their own clothes. Or at least, that's what Nell said. I don't know. I wasn't there.

I remained on my pallet, eyes open, staring blankly at the wall. After so much rage and pain, I couldn't feel anything at all. I couldn't summon the courage to climb to my feet, or even dread the consequences of staying put. Everything vital inside me had passed into the corset.

I never saw Kate in her wedding outfit. I didn't behold that figure I'd pictured, all those years ago, sewing the Lindsay gloves. But at the end of the day, I'm not sure Kate would have matched the pretty bride in my imagination. Over the recent weeks her skin had been a shade too grey, her cheeks pinched with stress. The petite waist looked unpleasantly sharp. Her eyes, which used to sparkle, began to glitter with something fierce.

'Where's the Butterham girl?' Mrs Metyard cried at last.

She'd barely finished her sentence before Ivy piped up. 'She's still slug-a-bed!'

Pounding footsteps on the floor above me. It would come at any time now: the fear. Wouldn't it? I heard Mrs Metyard draw nearer and nearer, heard her bawling my name. Still I felt nothing. I was somewhere safe, outside of my body, looking on.

'Get out of bed this instant! Don't make me come down there and—'

'Mother, Mother!' Kate's voice pleaded. 'There isn't time!'

'Does she think she can disobey me? I ought to—'

A rap on the showroom door cut her off. Just in time. Her tones had been sliding south, deeper, into the captain's territory.

'The Rookers are here,' Nell called.

A pause. They must've been at the cellar door, staring down the stairs at me, mother and daughter together. I didn't turn to look at them.

Instead, my imagination painted Billy on the steps outside the shop. Waiting for his bride. I'd thought he was my friend, but he hadn't been here when I needed him most. He'd chosen his side. He was part of Kate, now. And no one would ever rescue Mim from the trapdoor and the piles of coal.

'Make haste, Mother. Leave her.'

'What if she runs off? Or,' in a whisper, 'what if she goes for the police?'

Under the covers, my leg twitched.

'Every window is bolted. She won't get out. Hurry! It's my *wedding*, Mother!'

Mrs Metyard grumbled.

The door slammed.

And I knew, at last, what I must do.

———

Mrs Metyard hadn't locked the cellar. I would be able to get all the way into the showroom. To the front door.

Could I pick the lock? I'd managed with a needle on the cellar door, but that was a small, rickety sort of thing. I'd need a bigger tool, like a stiletto or a thin knife. Like my corset-making tools.

Once I was out, I could tell the bluebottles everything. Direct them to Mim's body, ensure it was buried properly. They'd clap Mrs Metyard in irons before she even had the chance to whistle at my mother.

Dare I?

Shakily, I pulled myself out of bed and began to dress. My old corset, the child of my creation, was too small for a girl of fifteen, but I couldn't leave it behind. I used it to wrap up a crust of bread and the remains of Mim's bone fish and carried it in a bundle.

Madness. Surely it was madness to take such a risk, and yet I saw myself do it: saw myself walk, trembling, to the curtained alcove and retrieve my grimy tools. Mim's blood still crusted the occasional blade; Mim's blood would help me. If this worked, both of us would escape.

I trembled back into the showroom, my pulse beating so fast that it made my head ache.

And then I saw it.

Kate had taken the corset from its box. Somewhere deep inside, my black heart crowed.

I'd never been allowed to enter the house through the showroom door, but I intended to leave by it. Selecting a long, thin knife, I inserted the tip into the lock. This was a superior mechanism, made to secure an outer door from housebreakers, not the rusty old lock on the cellar. The metal made a grinding sound. I couldn't tell if I was making progress.

My hands were slick. The handle twisted, twisted …

I dropped the knife.

Only luck made it miss my foot. Stuck upright by the tip, the blade trembled, flashing against the carpet.

I selected a stiletto this time, the tool I used to punch the eyelets in my corsets, and tried again. Sweat was pouring off me. Too far to turn back. If Mrs Metyard came home and found the lock scraped like this, she'd know what I'd been about …

Clunk.

The door opened a crack. Cold air rushed in and touched my cheek. There was the street, windblown and empty, waiting for me. So much bigger than I remembered it.

My breath came ragged and raw. Even after all that had passed, I was afraid to leave.

But I had to. Ma was out there.

The doorbell jangled, celebrating my liberty as I stepped over the threshold. The rain fell, fine and diagonal, hazing the streets. Carts rumbled along, passing a few brave pedestrians. God grant that Mr Brown the milkman didn't stop by and catch me.

I began to walk, shivering, unsure of where to go. It was hard to move like a regular person, an innocent girl about her business. Every closing door in the street, every whinny from a horse, made me jump.

I was heading in the opposite direction from church, on streets I'd never traversed before. Away from the river and my old home in Ford Street, away from school. In all my years living in Oakgate, I'd never known where the police station was. I'd just have to keep searching, keep going until my feet bled.

After roughly a mile, the pavement ended abruptly at a crossroads. The sweeper boys hadn't been out. If I wanted to pass to the other side, I would need to wade through mud and dung. So be it.

I stepped down and let my shoes sink into the sludge. I was lost, cold and beginning to grow numb. All the same it was glorious. These were free steps I took towards the other side; this was free moisture blessing my upturned face. Even the sound of horseshoes, ringing against the cobbles, was a kind of music.

A discordant music, out of key.

Growing wilder.

A whinny.

Snapping my head back, I looked down the street and saw a hansom barrelling towards me.

Sweat foamed on the horses. Clods of mud flew as they approached. I jumped out of the road, blessing my lucky stars that I'd seen the cab coming before it flattened me.

I was still blessing them when the whip cracked.

Pain. Red hot, across my face. I stumbled, fell. Dropped the corset.

Dimly, I heard the wheels skid to a halt. Hooves flailed, doors opened. A voice.

'That's her! That's the girl, damn her!'

Rough hands pulled me to my feet. Through the mist of my own blood, a face floated to the surface.

'We were just in time,' gloated Mrs Metyard. 'The ungrateful wretch was trying to run.'

39

Dorothea

I must conquer these superstitious whims! But even now that I am returned home, with my papers spread over my desk and Wilkie climbing the bars of his cage, my sense of dread remains.

With many inkblots, I scratch out my answer to Sir Thomas's letter. Time and time again, I must cast a draft aside and start afresh. Few tasks can be as distressing as this. It is an offer that, were I not engaged in my heart to David, I might well have accepted. There can be no doubt that Mama would have rejoiced to see me allied to her friend's brother.

I do not know that Mama ever met Sir Thomas herself. His living in Gloucestershire makes it unlikely. And yet, as I write, the facts seem ever more curious to me. Why, after all these years, has he suddenly become acquainted with my father? Why has Lady Morton summoned her brother to Heatherfield, if she did not deem it necessary while my mother lived?

Doubt nibbles at me, whispers that Lady Morton is behind this proposal. Perhaps she is low on funds, and wishes her brother to marry into money? Yet I *did* confide in him about Mrs Pearce and the change to my fortune, should progeny spring from the union. Unless

Sir Thomas thinks, as Papa's son-in-law, he would have the power to stop the marriage?

I cannot satisfy myself with this rejection. Language is clumsy and gauche. I cannot command it as I must. Putting aside the current attempt, I turn my thoughts to Ruth instead.

From the archives, I have successfully obtained many articles relevant to the next period of her story. Bursting with scandal, the tale travelled beyond local journals to some of the national papers. I must say, it appears a very fortunate circumstance that the police did finally arrive at Metyard's, prompted by a civilian tip. I cannot imagine what would have become of Ruth otherwise.

Whether she really did try to escape, I cannot prove, but she was certainly found locked in a room on the first floor of the property, in a death-like state. Her condition does not make for pleasant reading. There was a fear of gangrene and acute dehydration.

It is little wonder that Ruth has grown into such an unnatural child, passing as she did from a drunken father's care into the Metyards' torturous clutches for the duration of her formative years. A child cannot abide with a murderer and remain untouched. Evil thoughts float about the house like smuts from a fire. They speckle, they smear, they find a way in.

One murder has brought on another.

But could it have been avoided? *That* is the question I must ask myself: whether it is the innate nature of a person to kill, or if moral turpitude arises from insufficient nurture. Had Ruth enjoyed her youth in my house, with my faith, would she still have committed this outrage?

I open the bottom drawer to my desk and cradle the human skull. It is a comfort to me no longer. Beneath my fingertips, the bone feels immovable. Constant in its purpose. Today, for the first time, I consider the possibility that each head is predestined, just as Judas was predestined to betray Our Lord. We are trapped within them, flies caught in a jar. Some skulls have an unwavering, malignant will, and they must see it through.

Like Mrs Metyard.

She did not linger, awaiting her fate in the manner Ruth has done. Her capture coincided neatly with the assizes and she was tried almost immediately. So little time for her to be reclaimed – if indeed such a thing were achievable. Unchristian as it sounds, I am doubtful salvation could reach this woman. She appears more goblin than flesh and blood. But perhaps I have been influenced by Ruth's recital. There is no alienist report amongst my papers, nothing to inform me whether she ever truly took on the guise of 'the captain' – I rather suspect this to be the embellishment of Ruth's youthful fancy. All evidence suggests the original man was a distasteful fellow, not the kind of husband and father you would wish to resurrect. Yet *something* drove her to kill, to mistreat those girls …

Was it two bumps, above the ears?

I wonder where she sat in the old Oakgate Prison, which cell contained her wicked skull.

Would I have visited her? Would I have placed my fingers upon her head, given the chance?

40

Ruth

I don't remember much. I wish I'd been awake to see the policemen pile into the house and hear their rattles clacking our freedom, but I was in a pitiful state.

No one ever told me, but I presumed it was someone from church who raised the alarm. When Mim didn't show up to services any longer, and then I disappeared too, it would have begun to look suspicious.

Luckily for me, the case attracted widespread attention. My plight became known to the charitable types and I was voted into a voluntary hospital at once. Not that I knew anything about it, then.

My first clear memory after the capture is lying in a stark, white room, pressed up close against two other iron bedsteads. I thought perhaps I'd died and gone to heaven. But then I remembered all the people I'd killed, and I noticed the bedsheets were scratchy and marked with stains – surely the laundry was better in Paradise.

There was pain, too, rising to greet me. My left foot throbbed. Straining my neck, I tried to look down and see it, but I was too weak.

Over in the corner, someone retched.

The nurse who stumbled up to me reeked of port; I detected it, mingled with the other sickly scents. 'Need to change the dressings,' she blared.

Her hands were rough.

Forty lashes to the back and a missing little toe. It could've been much worse. And though the hospital wasn't a nice place by any stretch of the imagination, it was better than sleeping in the cellar at Metyard's. There was light and food and the bed was more comfortable. Best of all, they gave me laudanum for the pain.

When you're in pain like that, it takes up all the space. Gnawing at you, stripping the skin from your bones. My mind didn't comprehend that I was finally free, or dwell upon how I'd got out of the captain's room. I didn't begin to think coherently about my future and the world around me until Nell came to visit.

She was dressed in an umber gown, a straw bonnet and a tatty grey shawl. Soot flecked her copper hair. She wore gloves on the hands that clutched at her visitor's ticket, but they were coming loose at the seams.

'Nell!' She looked out of place here, decked in second-hand clothes rather than her work dress. Much more alive. The sight of her familiar features made me want to weep.

'How are you?' She fussed over me, tucking in the blankets.

'I'm ... alive.'

'No thanks to Mrs Metyard for that.' Concern was etched on her face. 'But you'll be revenged, Ruth. That's what I'm here to tell you. They're going to hang her.'

A stab, deep in my stomach. Something like satisfaction. But they weren't hanging Mrs Metyard for what she'd done to *me*. I needed to know if they'd found Mim, set her free at last.

'On what charge?' I demanded.

Nell watched me anxiously, searching for a hint that I knew. 'She's charged with ... murder. The murder of

Miriam.' Somehow, hearing the words on her lips intensified my grief, made Mim's death real in a way even the
sight of her body had not.

'Good.' My voice scratched. 'They should both rot
in hell for what they did to her. That's where Kate took
me, that day she came to the attic with my tools. Up to
the captain's room and Mim's body. They made me … '
I shook my head, could not continue.

'You should've told us,' Nell said softly. 'You
shouldn't have dealt with the burden of that alone.'

As if Ivy or Daisy would have given a halfpenny piece!
And as for Nell, she'd done nothing to help, had she? If
they didn't care for Mim in life, I felt they didn't deserve
to know about her death. But I couldn't explain that to
Nell. Especially when she'd come to visit me with such
welcome news.

Imagine Mrs Metyard, swinging from a rope! Like an
opiate, it alleviated my pain – but not enough. Something
was missing.

'What about Kate?' I asked.

Nell sniffed. 'What about her?'

'Aren't they going to hang her, too?'

'No. They haven't any evidence.'

'Couldn't you say something?' I cried. 'If you don't,
I bloody well will!'

'Who'd believe you?' she shot back. 'She's a respectable married woman as far as the jury are concerned.
She even testified against her mother. You should hear
the way she paints it. Innocent as pie, she was, apparently. You'd think she never took a stick to us in her
life.'

I gritted my teeth. I'd been in hospital for too long.
Missed Mim's body leaving the coal hole, missed the
trial. I'd be damned if I missed anything else.

'I want to watch,' I told Nell. 'I want to see that bitch hang.'

'Me too. We'll go together. I'm sure you'll be ready to leave soon. These charity subscriptions never last for long. They lose interest, move on to something else.'

'I *have* to leave. I have to find my ma.'

Silence fell as we both absorbed the enormity of that. Life, real life, waiting outside these walls.

The patient opposite me coughed.

'Is it really true, Nell? Are we really to be free of her?'

'Yes.' She gripped my hand. 'No one will employ me. I've been living in dossing houses ever since. But I tell you, this is the best life I ever had. I've never been so happy, Ruth. I'm free. We can be free together.'

I smiled. 'Let's talk to the nurses. I'm sure the sight of Mrs Metyard strung up will cure me at once.'

———

As it happened, the hospital staff were only too happy to hand me over to Nell. The six weeks my admission ticket entitled me to stay had passed, and none of the subscribers who voted me in were willing to take responsibility for me. It was as Nell said: they'd moved on. A mill catastrophe in this case. Dozens injured and stained with black grease, cotton fibres meshed into their wounds. My missing toe wasn't so interesting, compared to that.

I don't mean to sound ungrateful, miss. Charitable people like yourself saved my life. But I wish they'd thought a bit more about what I was to do with it, once it was safe. My old home was a crime scene and my employment had gone. I'd no clothes besides the torn and bloodied dress I wore when I tried to run away; the dress I'd continued to wear, and sweat fear into, during those long days in the captain's room.

Nell wasn't much better off. On the morning she came to collect me, a few days later, she was sporting the same gown and unravelling gloves. Red dots peppered the skin on her neck. Flea bites.

Still, her face was cheerful as she took me by the arm and said, 'Ready?' like we were off for a day of pleasure.

'I'm not sure. I think so. It all feels so … strange.'

She patted my hand. 'No, Ruth. Your life up until now: that's what's been strange.'

Together, we made our way through the doors and on to the streets outside. I felt like I'd been hit by a cannon ball. Never had the day seemed so bright, the air so cold. About twenty people were lined up by the entrance of the building in various states of distress; a man bleeding from the mouth, a young mother with two black eyes shushing her baby, an elderly woman coughing so fierce she could hardly stand. All of them praying for the chance to be let inside.

Watching them, I missed my footing and staggered.

Nell caught me. 'Take care! It's all a bit much, I expect,' she empathised, 'compared to in there.'

That was an understatement. The exhilaration that had taken hold of me when I picked the lock and escaped from Metyard's had long evaporated. Now I didn't feel free, but vulnerable. Walking was an effort I hadn't expected. My feet didn't balance the same way without my little toe.

And there were so many people. I clung to Nell as for dear life, sure I'd be unable to take another step without her. We passed a rag-and-bone shop and a man sharpening knives. It was only then that it occurred to me I had no idea where we were going.

'Are we walking far? Forgive me for being so slow.'

'It's a fair distance yet, I'm afraid. I couldn't afford to stay in a fancy part of town like this.'

Just then a rat scuttled past my foot. I wobbled, straightened again with a lance of pain. If I had to dodge vermin in this respectable area, I didn't like to think of the district I was headed to.

Could I really survive out here? I was better, but hardly fit to work. My plan had been to spend my days calling at dossing and sponging houses to find a trace of Ma. How would I gather the strength for that?

'Is it honestly all right for me to stay with you, Nell? I don't want to cause you any trouble. I haven't money to pay you ...' I trailed off, wondering what on earth I would do if she said no.

But Nell squeezed my arm. 'We're in this together, now. The survivors of Metyard's.'

'Do you have some money, then?'

'A little,' she answered, a bit cagily. 'It won't last us for long. We need to find work as soon as we can.'

'But where did you get it?'

She became very interested, of a sudden, in the pavement beneath our feet. 'Never you mind.'

I'd feared as much. A well-shaped girl like Nell, with her pretty hair. I didn't blame her. Only it caused a sort of spasm within my heart, to think of her selling herself to a man. Hadn't she suffered enough? And was I really to live off that hard-earned coin?

We went along in silence after that, awkward with one another. Little by little, the streets became darker. Soot stained the brick walls, which were chipped in places. The buildings seemed to grow higgledy-piggledy, their uneven rooves making a thatch that covered the sky. Every so often a window opened and the contents of a chamber pot splashed into the road. Nothing hit us, but that was hardly a comfort. There was nowhere safe to put your feet.

Street urchins tossed stones at one another. Some of them shouted at me, called me 'hop-along'. I grappled against a wave of giddiness. Already, my stomach had started to gurgle with hunger.

Had Ma been living this way since the moment she left me?

By the time Nell tugged at my elbow and said, 'Just here,' I was fit to drop. The area didn't look nice: a narrow maze of streets with an open sewer running down the middle of the road. Still, I limped the way she indicated, looking forward to a sit-down and maybe something to drink.

I was wrong.

Before we'd taken two steps inside, a hefty man erupted from the shadows. Broken veins purpled his skin.

'Thruppence each.' He thrust out a hand gloved in dirt.

Nell rummaged and produced some tarnished coins. He took them so quickly, it might have been a parlour trick. He bit each one, eyeing us warily the whole time. 'That's one night. First on the left.'

Later, I'd learn that there were four lodging rooms, each sheltering a score of people per night. But at that moment, I was too tired to take stock of the house as a whole. I just followed Nell.

You couldn't see much, with the grime coating the window. That made it seem dark as night inside, even though it was only early afternoon. But I could see enough to understand it was sheer robbery to charge a person threepence to sleep here. The place was more suitable for keeping pigs.

We shuffled to the far corner, where there were no people. We did sit down, but not on any kind of chair: only the hard floor and a pile of bedding that felt, and smelt, damp. I had to stretch my bad leg out in front of me. Something kept dripping from the ceiling on to my head, like rain. I looked up, but it was too dark to tell if there was a hole in the roof.

'Have you been staying here all this time?' I asked Nell in disbelief.

She shrugged. 'I'm used to it now.'

I didn't think you *could* grow used to it, that kind of filth and squalor. Pestilence stifled the air. Over the other side of the room, two old men with monstrous beards were beginning to squabble. I heard a thump, a curse. Those sitting near to them edged away.

To tell you the truth, I would have preferred the coal hole at Metyard's.

'Where's the privy?'

'There's a pail, in the middle of the room.' Nell pointed. 'Do you see it?'

I stared at her. 'One bucket, for all these people? You just … go in front of everyone?'

She shot me a rueful smile. 'I told you we need to find work.'

A thin wail echoed through the darkness. A baby. Living here. God above, I'd thought Naomi's life was bad.

I peered around the room at the desolate, pinched faces, hoping even now to find Ma's features under the grime. After more than a year of want and deprivation, she might not look the same. It terrified me to think I might tour all the lodging houses in Oakgate, stare over the paupers and fail to recognise her.

Still the baby cried.

My arm was itching. I scratched at it. Heaven only knew what sort of lice lived in this place. 'So have you tried to get employment yet?' I asked Nell.

'Of course I have!' she flared. 'I've been to nigh on every seamstress and milliner in this town. They won't have me. Not with the taint of Metyard's on my needle. Looks bad for their establishments, they said.'

Trepidation bloomed in my breast. Would the same trouble dog me? I'd counted on making a living and supporting Ma with my embroidery. There was nothing I could do well to earn my bread except sew.

'Why did you tell them you'd worked at Metyard's? You could have pretended you'd come from somewhere else.'

'Not in this town. They would check. Besides, I could hardly hide the fact. The journalists printed all our names in the newspaper.'

I hadn't realised that. Just when I thought I was free of Mrs Metyard, there she was, pressed into my skin like a branding iron. 'Make up a name?' I suggested.

Nell sighed, closed her eyes, as if she were explaining to a child. 'They still want a reference, Ruth. A character letter. Haven't you gone for a position before?'

Of course I hadn't. Nell's words made me feel hopelessly naive. As if the world I'd imagined was shrinking around me to a space no bigger than this awful rat's nest. 'Perhaps it would be better for us to move on to another town,' I said, a little shy this time. 'One where they won't recognise our names. Mim was going to London.'

Nell snorted. 'No, she wasn't. I'm sorry, Ruth, I don't mean to speak badly of her, but she was a dreamer. She had no money for the stagecoach. She might have tried to tramp it on foot, but without food and drink, she never would have made the walk.' She nodded significantly at my outstretched leg. 'I doubt *you* could walk to the next town. And even if you did, you'd be in such a state, no one would want to employ you. You'd look like a beggar by the time you got there.'

I swallowed painfully. Of course it was the truth. The steely, cold truth of a girl abandoned from her very birth, who knew life was tough and no one was going to grant her any favours. Beside Nell I sounded like Ma, with her hope that people possessed good hearts.

'What are we going to do, then?' I was ashamed to hear that my question sounded like a whimper. 'I already look tattered. A few more nights here and I'll be ... '

'Alive,' Nell finished, stern. 'And free. Which is all that matters. Come on, get some rest. You're still poorly. Everything will look better tomorrow.'

I doubted that. With the baby squalling, vermin scratching and the old men grumping, I'd never sleep. 'How?' I sulked. 'How will things possibly be better tomorrow?'

'Because tomorrow,' Nell grinned, 'Mrs Metyard will be hanged.'

41

Dorothea

How swiftly a day can turn from joy to utter, utter sorrow!

The early showers had cleared, leaving silver pathways and a sweet, dank dew. Graymarsh prepared the carriage and we drove to the post office, that I might send my letter to Sir Thomas Biggleswade without Papa's detection. A great weight lifted from my shoulders as I passed the envelope across the counter to the old postmistress, who pushed her spectacles up her nose to read my direction.

'Will that be all, *miss*?' She savoured my title, hoping, no doubt, to unsettle me. An unmarried lady, writing to a man! Her beady eyes said *I know very well what you are up to*, but I did not permit myself to become flustered.

'That is everything, thank you,' I said, doling out my coin and leaving the office.

Air rushed into my lungs, tasting of freedom. How pleasant it was to know the thing was done, and Sir Thomas rejected! Compassionately rejected, with much delicacy and gratitude threaded through the words. He can be in no doubt of my regard, even if he does not possess my heart. Mama would not blame me for such a kind answer to her friend's kin. Papa, however ... Yet

I hope David and I shall be safe in London before he makes the discovery.

From the post office we headed to the botanical gardens, where all of nature's beauty began to unfold. Wet spiderwebs hung in sparkling chains across the hedges, concealing the violets and primrose within. Petals of blossom flecked the lawns, a white and pink confetti, but none remained in the trees. Buds had exploded into leaf, bulbs had pushed their heads far above ground, and nothing remained buried beneath the soil.

My conversation with David was short, but no less satisfying for that. Our seconds together hung like the raindrops on the branches. He had not heard any news about the position in London, but for the first time the future felt truly within our reach. Palpable, our new life as a married couple an event that would certainly happen, and soon.

'You look mighty bright today, Miss Truelove,' he smiled.

I did! Would that I had stayed there all afternoon with the damp-wool scent from his coat on the breeze, and Tilda clucking behind us. But I came home.

And everything went awry.

The carriage caught my eye long before we had reached the house. I recognised those matched greys with a sinking feeling. What business had *she* in my home? It was not my time to receive calls, she should know that I was out on my errands.

But then my cheeks glowed hot. Perhaps she *did* know. I peered through the glass and saw that her carriage was vacant. They would have told her at the door that I was not present, yet she had crossed the threshold all the same.

Gone inside to be alone with Papa.

'Looks like you have a visitor, miss,' Tilda remarked. She did not sound overly surprised.

We walked in silence through the front door into the reception hall. Nothing looked real. It was a doll's house, not my beloved home. As Tilda took my bonnet and gloves, a high-pitched laugh jangled through the corridors and sank into my back teeth.

'I will go to my room,' I announced.

But fortune did not favour me. They must have heard the carriage pulling round to the stables, or my feet clacking across the floor, for Papa's voice boomed behind the closed library door.

'Dora? Dora, is that you?'

I paused at the bottom of the stairs, trapped. My instincts told me to ignore him and run, as fast as I could, to my room and shut the door like a little girl. Yet there was Tilda, watching me, and a footman standing on the landing. How could I disobey Papa before them?

A bump from the library. 'Come here, Dorothea. I wish to speak with you.'

Every step cost me the agony of walking upon broken glass. I remembered Ruth, relating how she had trembled her way towards the captain's room alone in the dark. That was how I felt now.

I opened the door.

The red curtain had been pulled across the window. Steam misted the cases containing the raven and the snarling fox.

Papa stood behind the desk with Mrs Pearce, their hands clasped.

'My dear Dorothea!' she beamed.

Her lantern jaw, her mustard gown, the ridiculous hair sculpture fallen crooked on her head: all of these were an affront to me. But to hear my Christian name, my mother's name, upon her lips – that was the sting.

It was only with great difficulty that I composed myself sufficiently to bob a curtsey and wish her good day.

'I have glad tidings for you, my dear,' said Papa. His collar had not been buttoned on properly. A sheen of sweat sat upon his forehead. 'Prepare yourself for something wonderful.'

I knew what he was going to say. Part of me yearned to dash over, place my fingers upon his lips and beg him to never, ever speak the dreadful words. But I could only act in this manner towards my papa. And this was not him. I saw another man, a base creature, no relation to me at all.

'I am delighted to inform you that Mrs Pearce has agreed to become my wife. I am the happiest man alive.'

She simpered. 'Oh, Reginald.'

Curious, to look back upon it. What shocks me most is my detachment. I felt dispassionate, cold, removed far from the scene, and these people, who were strangers to me. Only my lips, curling back from my teeth in disgust, betrayed any emotion. 'Well, fancy that.'

Papa's eyes turned a deeper shade of grey.

'Will you not congratulate us?' he demanded, straightening his jacket. 'Will you not kiss your ...' Our eyes met.

Do go on, a wicked part of me willed him. *Say it, say what you truly mean.*

But it was Mrs Pearce who bumbled forward, thrusting out her nauseous cloud of jasmine. 'Come and kiss your new mama.'

42

Ruth

Have you ever been to a hanging? The strange thing is, it's rather jolly. There were hordes of spectators that day, blotch-faced and drunk, all shoving for the best place. Children skipped and clapped, singing in high voices.

Here comes a candle to light you to bed
And here comes the chopper to chop off your head.
Chip chop, chip chop, the last man's – dead!

Woodsmoke and meat warmed the air. I couldn't smell them now without feeling ill, remembering Mim's hand on the fire.

Nell wasn't troubled by my memories. 'Wish I could afford some chestnuts,' she grumbled, gazing doe-eyed at the hawker.

I held her arm close in mine, still dizzy from pain and hunger too. Rough men pushed past me. Everywhere I turned were bobbing heads and bared teeth. I thought I might faint.

The scaffold waited before us, dangling its nooses as a promise of treats to come. Three. Who else would die beside Mrs Metyard?

It should be Kate.

It should be me. Justice for Naomi, Pa, Rosalind and whoever else had worn my gowns.

I felt a strange thrill then, imagining the weight of the hemp around my own neck. Would hanging hurt as much as losing my toe? I hoped it would hurt a lot more.

Sunlight slid free from the clouds just as wheels clattered on the cobbles.

A roar.

'Where is she? Can you see her?' Nell cried.

I couldn't. I only heard the sound of that tumbril, driving relentlessly towards death.

Figures massed around the cart, spitting and clawing. A man yelled, 'Give me a kiss, sweetheart!' There was laughter, shouts of joy. It looked like a lark, not a prelude to the grave.

'That must be them!' Nell exclaimed. Her eyes were wide as a fanatic's. 'Let's get close to the scaffold while everyone's busy.'

I let her tug me along. She chose a pitch close enough to hear the rope twisting in the breeze.

'Perfect.' Nell gazed up with relish. Her hair shone in the sunlight. 'You don't know how long I've waited for this day, Ruth.'

Even longer than me. No wonder she was champing at the bit.

Finally, the cart lumbered to its destination. The three prisoners unloaded were dishevelled and pulled about by the crowd. Mrs Metyard stood at the back, her hands bound as if in prayer. Although she'd lost weight, she had the same figure, the same upright bearing.

'There she is!' Nell's nails buried themselves in my arm. 'I hope she pisses herself!'

To our disappointment, she didn't look afraid. Drawn, perhaps, and weary, but not like the others. One was a broad woman with hands like hams. She swore and fought with the guards. The third was a girl a little older than me, perhaps eighteen, and her face was drenched with tears. But Mrs Metyard stalked through it all with her head held high, her features fixed in a terrible scowl. I recognised it. She was the captain, facing enemy fire.

She refused the hood. The other prisoners had their heads covered with sacks, but she remained indomitable, the noose tied close to the skin of her neck.

'That's a bit of luck,' I whispered to Nell. 'We can watch her suffer.'

She nodded. We were each of us as bloodthirsty as the other.

The chaplain shouted a prayer, but few words were audible. Raucous cries of 'Amen' came back from the crowd.

There was a clank, which vibrated through my ribs, and the trapdoors lurched open. Three pairs of feet dropped.

I'd read, at some point years ago, about a hanging where they'd tied the rope too long. That prisoner had their head pulled clean off. Part of me hoped that would happen to Mrs Metyard, but it didn't. She wriggled and danced with the rest of them.

My eyes never left her face. I saw the skin turn puce, the features swell. Blood vessels burst in her eyes. The crowd huzzaed and cheered.

The captain. Mrs Metyard. The captain again. Two personalities flickered across that tortured, bloated face. Then, at last, there was foam at her lips. Her feet lost their momentum.

Either side of her, the hooded women drooped. They looked like scarecrows. Slowly, the movement sputtered out, subsided from kicking to twitches.

Everything fell still.

The rope turned and creaked.

The thing hanging there wasn't Mrs Metyard now. It wasn't even the captain. It was just a bit of meat, ready to be picked by crows.

———

It was slow going to get away from the scaffold. The crowd that had piled into the square so readily took twice as long to filter out.

'I need to sit down,' I croaked to Nell. 'I'm that dizzy.'

She put her arm around my waist.

Damn Mrs Metyard. Her blows still hurt, even after she was dead. Watching her choke had been good, but it wasn't enough. It would never be enough. The idea that she was gone from the world, beyond the reach of injury, was an insult to me.

'It'll be a while yet,' said Nell, looking out over the sea of hats and viewing the startled horses that edged the sides of the square. 'If I sit you down here you'll be trampled. Just lean on me.'

Everyone was lazy, sated from bloodshed. They shuffled their feet. Someone kept treading on the hem of my gown.

'Keep going, Ruth.'

Thank God for Nell. When I thought about it, she had no reason to be good to me, to help me through the streets and pay for my lodgings. Maybe at last I'd found what I always wanted: freedom and a friend.

If only I could find food and work, too.

Finally we approached the south edge of the square, where the carriages waited. Rich people were too genteel

to watch a hanging from the street; they had to sit in
their coaches and peer out of the window. Horse dung
proved a new obstacle to negotiate, especially with my
bad foot. I was looking down and concentrating, so I
didn't see why Nell suddenly stiffened.

'What is it?' Her hands gripped my gown so tight, I
thought it might rip. 'You're hurting me, Nell!'

But just as her name left my lips, I heard it echoed by
another voice. A voice I knew well.

'Nell! Ruth! Over here!'

Billy sat on his wagon, about thirty yards from us,
waving.

My heart felt like it had gone through a mangle.

'Should we ...' I stopped, unsure how to go on.

He isn't your friend, I tried to remind myself. That
man, with the open face and the cap sat lopsided on his
tousled hair, was Kate's husband. A traitor. He kissed
the hands that had beaten Mim to death. I hated him.

But of course, I didn't. Not really. His smile still gave
me that feeling of rescue, of breathing clean air. I remembered him delivering bolts of material to the trade door
and saving me from the coal hole. Teaching me to make
corsets.

'We'll go over,' Nell decided, wariness in her eyes.
'He might let you sit on the wagon for a bit.'

We got there just in time. My trembling legs gave out
and I gripped the wagon for support.

'Steady on, Ruth! Come here.' His hands were at my
waist so briefly, I didn't have a chance to savour them.
Within seconds I was hoisted up on the wagon, sitting
by his side.

Did Kate sit there, now? Had her wickedness leached
into the wood? The thought kept me from relaxing,
from gathering my strength.

Nell must have read my mind, for she put her hands on her hips. 'The missus didn't come and see her own mother off, then? Don't tell me she hasn't got the stomach for it?'

Billy shifted beside me. 'No. She – she didn't want to see it, in the end.'

'Funny. From the way she went on at the trial, I thought she was keen as mustard to watch the old lady swing.'

'Well,' was all Billy said. His mare swapped the leg she was resting.

Chatter from the passers-by tumbled into the pause. I didn't feel better sitting there, only more agitated. Stuck between my wronged friend and the man who, God help me, I still nurtured a tenderness for. The atmosphere was too dense to bear.

'I'm all right now,' I lied, trying to clamber down. 'Best be getting on. I need to find my ma today.'

Billy put out his warm hand. 'Whoa! Rest a bit longer, won't you? I can drive you wherever you need to go.'

'I don't *know* where I need to go,' I admitted. 'And nor does Nell. We've nowhere.'

It occurred to me for the first time how shabby Nell appeared, after all those nights in the lodging house. Her bonnet was wilting like cabbage leaves. I must look even worse. We had nowhere to wash, nothing to change into. We stank. My cheeks glowed as I thought how Billy must view us; the contrast between us slatterns and his wife.

'You can't find work,' Billy guessed. He peered down at the reins in his hand. 'I should have expected that. It's been the same with Kate, we've had to keep her from serving in my father's shop. Just until it all … dies down a bit.'

'Well ask her to write us a character, won't you?' Nell's hands dropped off her hips. 'I've no references to show employers. At least a letter from Kate would have a different surname on it, now. It might help us.'

Billy thought for a moment. 'I can do better than that, Nelly. *I'll* employ you.'

'What?' she scoffed.

'We've got our own place now, across from my parents. We'll need some maids.'

The wind picked up and stirred the horse's mane. Nell and I exchanged bewildered looks. Was he serious?

Something sifted through me. What might it be, to see his face every day? To have a cheerful and kindly master? But no. I'd also have to see Kate. Do her bidding. She'd already put me in the coal hole and made me mutilate Mim. What would she ask of me next?

'You know better than anyone what I've suffered at that woman's hands.' Nell's cheeks flushed, angry. 'And do you really ask me, Bill, to put myself under her charge again?'

'*My* charge. Just for a while. Until you can find something else.' He wet his mouth. 'We go back a long way, Nell. You know I'd never let her hurt you in my house.'

Nell bit her lip.

'I still need to find my ma,' I said, sensing her weakening. 'I can't think of employment until I've found her.'

'Why not?' asked Billy. 'I'd give you an afternoon off every week; you could go looking then. And it might be easier to get information out of folk if you've coin in your pocket.'

He was right about that. But still … could I endure it? Living with Kate? Watching them as man and wife? There was no guarantee I'd even be safe. If Mrs William Rooker took it into her head to kill me, like she killed Mim, would her husband be able to stop her?

I darted a glance at him, saw the concern in his blue eyes. My heart squeezed. It wanted to trust him.

'What about Ivy and Daisy?' asked Nell, still sour. 'Employed them too, have you? It'll be a regular reunion at the old Rooker house.'

'Ah, you haven't heard?' Billy offered his winning smile. 'Daisy took up with one of the coppers. Got him eating out of the palm of her hand, she has. Even secured Ivy a place, working in his brother's pub.'

That, at least, was enough to make us all laugh. The idea of sniffy Ivy, pulling pints for the working man, was almost as good as watching Mrs Metyard hang.

I must have chuckled too hard, for my back complained and I winced.

'Look at you,' said Billy softly. 'Just out of the hospital. Sure, you aren't fit to tramp about. Come back with me, both of you. Have something to eat.'

Morals, self-respect – these things are all very fine. But when you're cold and hungry, it's astonishing how quick you can be tempted to exchange them. Clouds drifted over the sun, lowering the temperature. The clock in the square chimed four. We hadn't eaten all day. The thought of returning to that fetid lodging house was worse than prison.

Perhaps I shouldn't have laughed at Ivy. At least she was warm and fed.

'Don't you think you'd better ask your *wife*, before you invite us to your home?' Nell pressed on the word, like a bruise.

'I told you, I'm master of the house. And I think she'll be glad to see you.' Billy turned his face to me. The dimple showed through the stubble on his chin. 'She talks of you, Ruth, and your talent. That grand corset you made her! She's worn it every day.'

Heat crept up from my stomach. How did I forget? Peacock blue, the bone corset: my deadliest creation.

Mrs Metyard's pain had been all too brief. But Kate ... I could relish her suffering. Let it brew as I remembered that night I'd crept upstairs, and seen her hurting Mim. She'd pay for it. Oh, how she would pay.

'Has she really worn it?'

'Aye. It's her favourite. Come on, climb up, Nelly. You needn't stay at my house if you change your mind.'

I looked to Nell. 'What do you think?'

She shrugged. A quick, irritable motion. 'Go on, then. Just for a cup of tea.'

Billy's house perched close to the muddy banks of the river; a plain, two-storey terrace of grey brick, across the water from my old home in Ford Street. Drapes hung in the windows and the step was swept clean. Little surprise, with Kate as the mistress. I remembered how spotless she'd kept the workroom and flinched. Could I imagine myself as a maid under her supervision?

The wind was keen, near the water. Billy's piebald mare threw her head up and snorted. On the slick incline to the river, children scavenged in the dirt while boatmen repaired their nets. Circling above were gulls, calling in a forlorn tune.

'Here we are,' said Billy. 'Climb down. I'll take you in, then I'd better go and see madam here to her stable.'

Shoulder to shoulder for comfort, Nell and I followed him inside.

It was a modest home, but after the hospital and the lodging house, it looked like a palace. The chambers smelt of cocoa and warm oats. Our stomachs growled in unison. This house was bigger than my old home over the river; Kate and Billy had a bedroom each, a kitchen with a larder, two parlours and a housemaid's closet. Not that I saw all this, that day. Instead we trailed Billy into the parlour at the front of the house, where Kate and her mother-in-law sat on a worn, tapestry sofa, clutching at each other's hands.

'There, now,' Mrs Rooker sang, as if Billy's entrance were the answer to a question Kate had asked.

Beneath my lowered eyelids, I sneaked a glance at Kate. It felt odd seeing her again, like a waking nightmare. But I had to be brave and look. I had to see if my curse had worked.

Was she any thinner? It was hard to tell. Beside old Mrs Rooker, anyone would resemble a waif. Her shoulders were hunched, and she wore the black and white humbug dress, which sucked the colour from her skin. As she swallowed, I saw the tendons of her throat. Well, perhaps she'd lost a *little* weight, but it might just be the strain of the trial.

'Is it done?'

Billy folded his hands in front of him, lowered his chin to his chest.

'Good,' she said, though her voice wobbled.

'And who are these you're bringing in, Bill?' cried Mrs Rooker. 'Hadn't you better leave your friends for today?'

'No, Mammy, Kate asked me to find them.' He took off his hat and came into the room, revealing the pair of us cringing behind him. 'This is Nell and this is Ruth.'

We looked at each other, rather than Mrs Rooker. Kate *asked* him to find us? When was he planning on telling us that? Misgiving wallowed in my stomach. Kate could have no good purpose for us.

Kate scrubbed at her eyes. 'Yes, of course. It's good to see you, girls.'

We couldn't return the compliment.

'Bill said there'd be tea,' replied Nell, sullen.

'Yes, please go and ... help yourselves.' Kate waved a hand at us. At least this was a gesture we were used to, from her.

Awkwardly, we followed Billy to the kitchen. It was warmer and brighter than the one at Metyard's, but it carried the stink of pond water. A dozen dead flies lay mummifying on the windowsill.

'Bit of a fly infestation,' Billy said, noticing my gaze. 'Being close to the water and all.'

If he knew the state of the room we were sleeping in, he'd feel no need to apologise.

'Perhaps you could see to it, Nell, if you worked here? You could get some flypapers from the grocer round the corner.' He opened a cupboard and unlocked a small box with tea leaves inside. 'I was thinking the kitchen might be your domain. You're handy with cooking and such.'

The whole scene felt mad, like one of my drugged dreams in the hospital. Were we really contemplating entering into voluntary employment for *Kate*?

Nell watched Billy's preparations closely. 'Here was me, thinking we might get treated to your famous cocoa.'

Billy laughed, hoisting a pan of water above the fire. It didn't sound like his usual laugh; it was taut. 'Did you, now? This is the only time you'll have me serving you, Nelly. If I'm paying you a wage, you'll be making tea for *me*.'

'Nobody said I was going to work for you. I'm still thinking about it.'

I felt out of place, beside the two of them. As the water began to boil, the atmosphere between Billy and

Nell seemed to congest. I imagined them as children together at the Oakgate Foundling Hospital. Arriving at Metyard's, hand in hand like brother and sister. No wonder Nell was on edge. How must it feel first to see your playmate fall to a woman you despise, then have him offer to rule as master over you?

'What would you want me to do, then?' I asked. 'Polish your silver?'

This time his smile was its old, easy self. 'None of that to be had, Ruth! I thought you'd be Kate's maid.'

I baulked. He had to be jesting. I'd give much to sleep somewhere clean and dry again, but that price was too high.

'Seeing as you're so good at mending and sewing and all.' Billy chattered happily to himself as he stirred the tea. My stomach went round and round with the spoon, the same whirring motion. 'You'd be the perfect lady's maid, wouldn't you? After you've found your mam, of course.'

He turned to us and pressed the warm mugs into our hands. Nell peered into hers, frowning.

The tea looked perfect to me. My throat was parched dry. Suddenly I wasn't so sure I wanted to refuse his offer. My body was betraying me. Picturing a life where it could drink tea and eat good food every day.

'Thank you,' I said, ashamed at how grateful I was.

'Well then.' He dusted his hands together. 'Better see to that horse. I imagine Kate will speak with you when she's had time to …' He tailed off. *Grieve* wasn't the right word to use. But then what was? What *did* Kate feel after the grisly events of that day? Clearly Billy didn't know either: he left the sentence unfinished.

The kitchen felt empty and stale after he'd gone. I watched the steam rise from my mug. A trapped fly butted against the window.

'So,' said Nell. 'Miss Kate's maid. That would be a lark.'

I took a big mouthful of tea. It was the best thing I ever tasted. That made it all the harder to laugh, to scorn Billy's idea. 'Can you imagine it? I'd stick pins in her dresses. And you'd probably spit in her dinner.'

Nell smiled weakly. 'Still ... it's an offer.'

I shifted my weight from my bad leg. The tea, Nell's words and Billy's smile: all of them seemed to be drawing me in like a snare. But I *couldn't* go back to Kate. Not after all that had happened. Could I? 'Maybe we should go and be maids somewhere else,' I bleated. 'You said the dress shops wouldn't employ you, but we haven't tried households.'

She looked doubtfully at her hands, clenched around the mug. There were strips of torn skin. Dirt, soaked in deep, and black crescents under the broken fingernails. They weren't the hands of a person you'd want to let inside your house, let alone work with your linen. 'We haven't any experience of being maids. They expect that.'

Another door slammed in my face. Getting out of Metyard's hadn't set me free, I realised. I was simply caught in a new trap, and this one was called poverty. Not the genteel poverty I'd ploughed through living with Ma and Pa. Real desperation.

'I just don't think ... I'm not sure I could do it,' I admitted. 'Dressing her, combing her poxy hair.'

Nell caught my eye. Her face seemed to crumple like crape. 'No, me neither. I wish I could. But ... I don't know what else to do.'

A cold shiver ran over me as I imagined Nell opening her legs for another man. I couldn't ask her to do that. And I certainly couldn't make a good living that way myself. All my life, people had told me I was ugly. I wouldn't take half as much in a night as Nell would.

'Let's tell Billy we need time to consider it,' I said. 'Then the option is open to us, if we grow desperate.'

Nell nodded. Trying to be brave.

I wasn't sure we *could* grow more desperate.

43

Ruth

We didn't hold out for very long.

One housekeeper said there was a vacancy in her scullery, cleaning the plates, cooking pans and chamber pots. She got us in, sat us down and said she would fetch her mistress so they could interrogate us together. Well. She clearly knew her mistress. The young lady came tearing down the steps to the kitchen, eyes agog, crying, 'Are you really them?'

She didn't want to know if we could scrub, or who would vouch for our honesty. Her questions were more tasteless. *Tell me about a time she beat you. Did she ever ... interfere with you? Did you know the Negro girl well? Did you not smell her body, under the house?*

At least Mrs Metyard had madness as an excuse for her depravity. This lady was just downright heartless.

'We're not here to talk about that,' I answered testily. 'We want a place.'

But the lady would only employ us under one condition: that we would come upstairs whenever we were summoned and talk to her guests about Metyard's. Tell them every gory detail. In short, cheapen our lives, cheapen Mim's memory, so the gentry could get their thrills.

Nell held her chin in her hand; looked, for a moment, as if she might consider it.

'Absolutely not.' I stood, with as much dignity as I could manage, on my wobbly leg. 'We might be poor, but we have *some* pride. Good day to you. Come on, Nell.'

I regretted it afterwards. For I didn't have the pride I'd spoken of. Each day passed with no trace of Ma and ended in begging strangers for food. Nights were torments without sleep. And then the worst thing of all happened.

We were wandering aimlessly, as we did now, knocking on doors and looking for shops to ask about employment. Nell led the way, for she knew the streets better than I did. That particular morning, she took us through a shadowy court I'd never seen before. A great, hulking building rose up to our left. Vicious iron crowned the walls. It gave me a strange, unsettled feeling, like I'd seen it in a dream.

'What's that?' I asked.

Nell slowed her pace, followed my gaze. 'Oh. It's the debtors' prison. We won't find work there.'

My teeth began to chatter. Perhaps it was just the cool morning air, not yet warmed by the sun. I took another few steps, but I couldn't tear my eyes away.

Have you ever seen a building that seems to gloat? I can't say how it did that, exactly. But the barred windows were glinting at me, malicious, and the very bricks seemed to whisper, tempting me to share their dark secrets.

I came to a halt. 'Can we ask, Nell? About my ma?'

She sighed, looking back over her shoulder. 'If we don't find a place to work soon ...'

'Please.'

The agony in my voice stopped her. Reluctantly, she nodded. 'All right. I'm sorry. My ma ran off and left me, you see. I forget how much other people love theirs.'

Nerves gripped me as we approached a thick iron door. My knuckles trembled as I knocked, their raps swallowed by the metal. Of course, it was silly of me to get so nervous. Hadn't Mrs Metyard promised not to call in Ma's debt? I'd sold myself so she would never have to come near this chilling place. And yet ...

A grate opened. A bloodshot eye stared through it. 'What d'you want?'

'I – I'd like some information.' I sounded impossibly young. 'Can you tell me if there is a Jemima Butterham within?'

'Might be able to.'

'Please,' I begged. 'It's important. She's my mother.'

He stared back, unmoved. 'It'll cost you.'

'What, just to check a name?' Nell pushed me out of the way and shouted at the man. 'What if she's not in there, and we've handed over our money? We'd get nothing for it.'

'You'd know she ain't here,' the man behind the door leered.

I glanced at Nell. Uncertainty was nibbling away at my guts. 'How much?'

'Sixpence.'

I nearly fell into the door. The amount it cost for both of us to lodge for the night! Turning my face down, I tried not to let Nell see my distress. I couldn't ask her to give up a night's shelter.

'She's probably not in there anyway,' I said, sniffing back my emotion. 'Mrs Metyard said ...'

But Nell was rummaging in her pocket, then pushing coins across her palm. She fixed anguished eyes upon me. 'I have sixpence. But ... that's it. It's the last of our money, Ruth.'

My head throbbed. An impossible choice. Give up on searching for my ma, or beggar my only friend? I needed somewhere to sit down. I needed to scream.

'Haven't got all day,' the man barked from his grate.

I took a step away. I couldn't ask it of Nell. Not after the way she'd obtained that money.

But I didn't need to ask.

She made the decision for me, thrust her handful of coins at the grate. 'Tell us,' she insisted.

Ma was dead. I guess you knew that already. Mrs Metyard tricked her. They both signed a paper, and Mim witnessed it, but the amount shown on that document wasn't Ma's full debt.

That bitch slung my poor mother into debtors' gaol for the remainder, despite all she'd said, and let her die there like a dog. So my suffering, every minute of it, had been for nothing. I might have left Metyard's on the first night.

Nell and I sat by the river afterwards, speechless, looking down at the sludge. Gulls shrieked like lost souls. There was no moisture in my eyes. I was too sad to cry.

It smelt of ordure and iron, this landscape of mud. Compared to the reek of debtors' prison, it was a bouquet of flowers.

I didn't want to imagine the horrors poor Ma had suffered in that loathsome gaol, but I kept doing it, tormenting myself.

Miss Jemima Trussell. No one would dream that such a fine young lady could meet her end in gaol. She should

be in some country church, resting in a family vault. But
she wasn't. The turnkey at the prison said they burnt
the bodies if no one claimed them, to stop the spread of
disease.

My lovely ma was just ashes and bone. Discarded on
the dust mounds.

I wondered what had happened to Ma's old handkerchief, the one with the loose threads. I wanted to hold it
between my fingers and think of her. I wanted to use it
to smother Kate.

Before God, I swore I'd kill her. Not only for what
she'd done, but for her mother's deeds too. I would kill
her if it was the last thing I ever did.

Billy wanted me to work as her maid, did he? Mend
her gowns? Gladly. I'd create agonies for her in red silk,
livid horrors in mauve cotton.

I turned to Nell. Gnats hovered in a haze around her.
Poverty had taken its toll. Her beautiful hair was dull,
her skin pale beneath the patches of dirt. I'd be damned
if I let her die too.

'We must do it.' My voice came hard, determined.
'Let's go to work for Billy and Kate. There's no other
choice.'

She bowed her head. 'I can't believe it's come to this.
If I had a penny left, I'd scorn them, but ... God, I'm
famished, Ruth.'

'I know.'

She took my hand in hers. The gulls kept up their
lament. 'I can get through it. It won't be so bad for me
in the kitchen. But being her personal maid ... Are you
sure? Are you really sure you can do it?'

I pictured the corset I'd made: the bone channels, the
gussets reinforced with hate. Squeezing, pressing. Kate's
lips, dusted with peacock blue.

'Oh yes.' My mouth twisted. 'I can do it. I think I was born for this.'

———————

Dusk had thickened over the river by the time we stood and made our sorry way to Water Mews. Lamps flickered on the boats, casting halos on the oil-black surface of the water. It wasn't hard to find Billy's house again; we recognised the green door. Stared at it, as the temperature dropped.

It's a fearful thing, knowing you must perform an action that your whole soul revolts from. I knew I'd have to pass through that door into *her* house, as surely as we all must pass into death. For a moment, the second option seemed preferable. Even Nell was eyeing the green paint strangely, as if it hid the portal to some secret hell.

'Best go round the back and knock on the kitchen door,' I suggested. 'She's less likely to answer that, don't you think?'

Wordlessly, she nodded.

It would be a strange reverse, I thought, of all the times I'd let Billy into Metyard's through the trade entrance.

I was wrong.

When the door swung open, it revealed a fire blazing beneath an assortment of small pots. A woman stood before us with a spoon held aloft. Smuts streaked the apron that covered her gown.

It was Kate.

The sight of her was like a physical blow. Tearing pain in my chest and in my throat. I'd thought I could put everything aside and concentrate on punishing her, but that had been a vain hope. To see her face, smiling at me, so soon after learning of my mother's death! She was lucky I didn't have enough strength to throttle her there and then.

'Come in, girls.' She stood back from the door, her smile wavering under our stony gazes. Curls had stuck to the sweat on her forehead. She pushed them back with her free hand. 'Come in. Shut the door quickly. Don't let any more flies inside, they'll be drawn to the light.'

We shuffled across the threshold. Heat from the fire kissed our chilled faces. I didn't know what she was cooking, but it smelled glorious.

Kate stirred her pots and lifted one from the flames. 'You're filthy,' she observed.

'Just as well we came in the back, then,' Nell retorted. 'Wouldn't want to be ruining your fine house, *Mrs* Rooker.'

Kate turned back to the fire. 'No indeed. You know my ways, Nelly. If you've come here to take the work, you'll be having a bath before you leave the kitchen.'

Oh, we knew her ways all right. I was too angry to reply, but Nell spoke for me.

'It'll take a good scrub to get the dirt out. Especially the smell of the debtors' gaol.'

Kate's face blanched above the pots. Before she could muster a response, the door to the hallway opened and Billy appeared.

'I thought I heard Nell's voice!' He beamed at us. 'How grand it is to see you both. Have you come to be our maids at last?'

'They've finally swallowed their pride,' Kate affirmed.

From the way both our throats were working, I wouldn't say we'd swallowed our pride. We were gagging on it.

'Let's get them fed and watered, Kate; there's barely anything left of them.'

Kate passed him the spoon, brushed her hands on her apron. 'In a moment. I've got something of yours, Ruth. I found it when ... I found it after the wedding.'

After her mother had horsewhipped me and strung me up, she meant.

She opened a cupboard and rummaged within. What she produced made me shiver, like when you rub the pile of velvet the wrong way.

A garment of brown jean and peach sateen. Fraying where I had cut squares out from the bottom. On top of it, tangled in the laces, were the remains of Mim's bone fish.

I thought they'd been lost, along with my little toe. I didn't like to see Kate's hands upon my precious things. Snatching them from her, I hugged them to my chest.

'I found those in the road,' she explained, without meeting my eye.

Perhaps she expected me to thank her. I didn't. Couldn't. The silence spun out between us.

'Only right you should have your corset back,' Billy chirped up from by the fire. 'After that wonderful one you made Kate.'

I wondered what Billy saw, on those nights he visited her bed. If he caught a glimpse of my work, and admired it.

'It's the best piece you have done,' Kate agreed, still awkward. 'You've a real talent, Ruth. I'm looking forward to having you as my maid.'

If only she knew.

44

Ruth

It was an odd existence, working as a maid in the Rooker house that summer and autumn. The room I shared with Nell was small, tucked under a gable. We had an iron bedstead and a washstand. Compared to our previous quarters, at the lodging house and at Metyard's, it was luxury. There were no lice. We had plenty of food to eat, which Nell cooked with skill. But still there was an undercurrent. A force exhaling misery and unease. Only Billy seemed immune to it, but he was hardly ever there.

Most days Kate sat in her parlour, playing the lady, complaining of boredom. She was desperate for the Rookers to let her work in their shop. Yet that seemed to be her only vexation: my corset wasn't bringing her to her knees. I couldn't understand why it was so slow. Every day, I encouraged her to wear it. And every night, the hooks and laces gave way easily to my touch. It disappointed me. I'd hoped it would stick to her, like mine had done: squeezing, crushing, making her cry out with its percussive crack. But it bided its time.

One evening, shortly after we'd arrived, I let myself into her room. Part of her lingered: lily of the valley, insinuating itself into every fold of fabric; the pots of cold cream on her dressing table; a brush snagged with her dark hair. Outside, I heard a lamplighter going about his trade. I closed the door behind me.

There must be something I could do. An item in the shadowy press looming beside the window that needed re-stitching. Maybe I'd take her dresses in an inch around the waist and see if she'd really lost weight. The more items with my loathing worked in, the quicker my curse would take effect.

Cautiously, I creaked the door of the press open. Rosemary welled in my nostrils. All of the dresses looked black and grey in the twilight, a spectral parade of mourning. She never asked me to dress her in weeds for Mrs Metyard. Perhaps she didn't dare to.

This must be her wedding gown. The palest, webbed with lace. Bone buttons at the cuffs. Did Billy unfasten them, that night?

I pushed the other dresses aside for a better look. The wedding gown appeared wrong hanging there, a bodiless bride. Lonesome, too. There'd been no bridesmaids, no one to give Kate away.

I opened a drawer. Folded stockings, row upon row. It must be nice to put them on each day and not feel a gap where your little toe should be. I ran my hand over the bundles. Heard a rustling sound.

Peering closer, I saw patterns at the bottom of the drawer. Scraps of something. Piling all the stockings into one corner, I uncovered a lining of newspaper clippings.

The light was low. I picked up the scraps and took them over to the window, to see by the streetlamp. The taste of copper spread over my tongue.

GRISLY MURDER OF SEAMSTRESS
BODY FOUND IN CELLAR
METYARD SENTENCED TO DEATH

I hadn't read of the trial. What was there to know? I'd seen Mim's body, inhaled its putrefaction. But Kate had kept every article.

Below the headlines, the print was too small and smudged to read. Water, perhaps tears, had dripped on it. But the illustrations loomed out at me: the trapdoor to the coal hole, Mrs Metyard in the dock. My life turned into a penny dreadful.

A click.

'Ruth?'

I nearly jumped out of my skin. Soft light glowed from the doorway and, behind it, Kate's face sculpted with shadows.

'I …' My skin flushed hot and cold by turns. 'I was just looking for …'

She came in and closed the door behind her.

All my courage unspooled. The old fear of her returned. I remembered her with the poker that night, her eyes sparkling like jewels.

'You found them,' she announced stiffly.

'They'll rub print on your stockings.'

'I know. I shouldn't keep them.' The tip of a shadow grazed her throat. It looked like a dagger against her neck.

'Shall I throw them out? *Madam?*'

She hesitated. 'No, I … no.' Walking briskly over to me, she snatched the articles from my hand. The candle cast dark patches into her eye sockets. 'You won't mention this to Billy.'

Not a request.

'Very good, madam.'

Downstairs, a door slammed. Billy called out a greeting. He was home from the shop.

I went to make my escape. But before I'd taken three steps, Kate's words arrested me.

'I … I … miss her.'

A pause. My chest heaved.

I couldn't contain myself. 'Is it the beating of the workers you'll be missing, madam? Or the starving people to death?'

That's me done for, I thought. Now I'll see if she's her mother's daughter. I darted for the door.

'She was my mother.' The tears in Kate's voice surprised me so much that I turned and stared at her. Her candle juddered beneath her breath. She did look thin, standing there, devoured by sorrow. 'She's my first memory. And no matter how … despicable … she became … I can't undo that.'

'Your *mother*,' I said, leaning on the word, 'killed mine. She threw a blind woman into debtors' gaol and let her rot.'

She hung her head. 'I know.'

'Then you should take my advice and put that lot in the fire. Burn it, like she's burning in hell now.'

'How dare—'

A footstep on the stairs. Someone cleared their throat.

'Excuse me, madam,' said Nell, all innocence. A tray sat in her hands. Steam arose from a cup, so sweet that it was almost foul. 'I've brought you up your cocoa.'

———

Come October, it was working.

When I went in to tidy the bed, Kate was already sitting in her shift on the stool before the dressing table. Reflected in the glass were triumphant collarbones, emerging beneath her skin. Her shoulder blades, like stunted wings, made themselves known through the cotton. My curse was slimming her down to skin and bone.

Billy, fully dressed, made ready to leave for the day.

'When shall I go to the shop with you, Billy?'

'A little while yet, love. Get some rest.' He placed his hand gently upon her head. Her hair looked thin.

I straightened the sheets, keeping my eyes down and taking care to appear absorbed by my chore. The bedclothes retained Billy's scent of cooked oats. There was another smell, sweaty and animal, but I chose not to focus on that.

'All I do is rest! I'll go mad with it.'

'I don't think Mammy's working today. Why not go round and sit with her?'

I folded Kate's nightgown. Dark strands of hair coiled inside her nightcap. There was hair on the pillow, too.

Kate gave one of her grunts. 'I can't. The way she looks at me ...'

'How?'

'Suspicious. And the questions she asks. Did I know it was going on? How long? Had Mother ever hurt my boy? I can't face her, Billy. I can't.'

Billy sighed, removing his hand from Kate's head and placing it on the back of his own neck. 'This is my doing. I should have gone to the police the minute I got out of there. I should have told my parents how it was at Metyard's. It would have spared you all this. It might have spared Miriam ... '

'It's not your fault. You were just a boy.'

'I still knew it was wrong. I should have told my parents what I suffered. But I didn't want them to think ... differently. About me.'

'I was young, too. If the police had come back then, I would have lied for her. I know I would.'

I gave Kate's pillow a hard thump.

True, Billy did share a small portion of the blame for Mim's death. But if he'd told someone what went on at that shop, who would have believed him? There was no evidence, before the body in the coal hole. And wasn't it legal for a mistress to beat her apprentices? I doubt the police would have done anything.

'I'd best be getting on. My father needs me.'

I stooped to pick up Kate's chamber pot. Only a dark trickle swilled inside.

'Lucky you. I wish I was needed. Tell Nell I will take my breakfast up here,' Kate called to me. 'She can bring it on a tray.'

Curtseying, I left the room.

Anger pushed my feet down the stairs. Did Kate really think she was suffering? Sitting about all day, ordering me and Nell around like some kind of lady. I thought of those days I'd spent after her marriage, locked in the captain's room. God above. My corset couldn't kill her fast enough.

I had to pass through the kitchen to reach the privy at the back of the house. Little blue dishes sat on the windowsill, each containing a square of flypaper. There were perhaps two dozen corpses stuck on their backs. One of them twitched.

Nell bent over the sink, scouring pans. Her cheeks were already flushed, hiding her freckles in a blaze of red.

'She wants breakfast upstairs,' I told her.

Nell rolled her eyes. 'Of course she does.'

As I opened the door, a fly drifted up to me, spiralling around Kate's chamber pot.

'Bad luck,' I laughed. 'There isn't much for you, Mr Fly.'

'Isn't there any ... red in it?'

I looked over my shoulder at Nell. 'Red? What do you mean?'

'Well, blood.'

'No.'

She frowned at the soapsuds. 'Don't you think that's odd? We've been here for months. I haven't had to wash a clout once. Have you?'

'You don't think ...' I didn't finish my sentence. The unspoken words clanged around the kitchen, making me totter on the doorstep. I thought of yesterday morning, when Kate had complained of nausea.

'It must be, mustn't it?' She gave the pan a particularly furious scrub. 'I hope Billy doesn't think I'm going to look after his baby, too. Can't you imagine it? A puling brat with Metyard blood in its veins!'

I couldn't answer. Leaving the door swinging open behind me, I stumbled outside on to the mud and reached the privy just before the vomit came.

A baby.

In my mind, every infant looked like Naomi, the child I'd loved and unwittingly killed.

It didn't matter who the mother was. Billy's baby would be a bonny thing, with his sunny face. Innocent.

I retched. The chamber pot sat on the bench, Kate's discoloured urine on the bottom, a reproach to me. Another fly swooped in.

My corset was working. Her hair was falling out, her bones were rising up.

But was it killing Billy's child, too?

45
Ruth

Another few days passed before I gathered the courage to ask her.

We were at the dressing table: she on the stool, me behind, brushing out her hair. How brittle it was in my fingers, like spun sugar. Beneath the *swoosh* of my brush, I heard her breath. She smelt strange; less like lily of the valley, more like … garlic.

'Perhaps we'd better leave your corset off today, madam,' I said. 'Maybe lacing too tight is causing your dizziness and your headaches.'

'No. We'll just fasten it a bit looser.'

Reluctantly, I moved to the press and drew out an old corset of hers, worked in coutil.

'No.' She waved her hand at me. The sapphire ring rattled on her finger. 'The one you made.'

I pulled my corset out by the tips of my fingers. It wasn't pleasant to touch the blue, now. I could feel the death on it.

'I just thought …' I began.

'For goodness' sake! What's the matter?'

'I … I think you're keeping a secret, madam.'

Her jawbone jerked. A world of guilt simmered in the look she returned. 'About?'

'About ... why you haven't bled. Your nausea and
your trips to the privy. I am your maid, madam. I notice
these things.'

A frightening hush fell between us. All I could hear
was my heart, pounding in my throat.

Kate burst into tears.

The sight of it stunned me. The corset dropped to
the floor. I thought I wanted to see her broken, in pain,
but this was horrible. She wasn't a pretty crier. Her face
became a blotchy, shining mess.

'Oh, Ruth? What will I do?'

'*Do*, madam?'

'I don't want it!'

So it was true. I stared at her in blank panic, watching her tears splattering on the dressing table. No sign
of a burgeoning stomach, but that didn't mean the seed
wasn't growing.

I had to protect it.

'I don't want a baby,' she repeated, and only then did
it dawn upon me what she was saying: that I cared more
for Billy's child than she did.

I had a mind to box some sense into her. Any woman
on earth would be proud to carry Billy Rooker's baby.
Although ... Naomi's birth had been terrible, hadn't it?
The way Ma lowed like a cow. Anyone would be scared
by the prospect.

'Look,' I said, as kindly as I could manage. 'I thought
that, before my sister was born. I didn't want her at all.
But in the end, it wasn't so bad. She didn't cry a lot, really.'

'No! It doesn't matter if it's an angel, I don't want ...
any baby. It's not *about* the baby, it's about me. What it
makes me. I cannot ...'

'What?'

'I cannot be a *mother*.'

Her narrow shoulders shook. She sobbed harder than ever. But I was relapsing, reheating all my former scorn. 'Why did you get married, then? Didn't you think this might happen?'

'No, I … I don't know.' Her hands covered her face. 'I just want it to be me and Billy,' she cried.

How could she weep like that? A baby, with Billy's blue eyes! Who wouldn't want it?

I left her to cry it out and began tidying up her food tray. Half of her cocoa lay cold at the bottom of the cup. The milk was curdling, leaving a sediment. Perhaps Nell had left the bottle sitting in the sun for too long.

'Please, Ruth, don't tell Billy. Not yet.'

'It's not my place,' I said, with a sniff. 'But I won't lace you into that corset any more. Not with a baby on the way.'

'You'll do what I tell you to!' She whipped around on the stool. For a moment, she looked just like her mother. Fanatic eyes. The fear of losing control. 'I'm in charge.'

'No you're not. Not of this.'

I stormed out of the room. My hands were trembling. God above. What was I going to do?

No answer presented itself. October passed to November and still there was no happy announcement to the household. I didn't think Kate would be able to hide her secret much longer. But it turns out she was pretty good at concealing things, actually.

The day after I turned sixteen, I was scrubbing the floor in the downstairs hallway, when I was suddenly arrested by the sound of Billy's voice.

'Ruth! Ruth!'

Warmth on my back. I looked up from my brush and the suds to see him bending over me, his hand on my spine. The expression in his eyes was so intense, it seemed to press me into a small space.

'Yes?'

'Will you go and sit with Kate, Ruth? My mother will come and relieve you in a while.'

'What's wrong?' I asked. Too fast. I might as well have the word *guilty* branded on my forehead.

'She's in a bad way. Her gums are bleeding, and the whites of her eyes are all yellow. Maybe it's the jaundice.'

Slowly, I straightened my back and threw the brush into a pail of water. I might wash the flags, but I'd never scrub the guilt off. Those stitches sewn in the past, never to be undone. In my mind, the child Kate carried was a replica of Naomi, except she gazed at the world through Billy's stunning eyes. I was killing her – killing her all over again.

And for what? Kate's pain didn't bring Mim back. It didn't reunite me with Ma. My revenge was hollow. It tasted like gall.

'Are you going for the doctor?'

'Maybe.' He ran a hand through his hair. 'Kate says she doesn't want him to come … '

His face. I could have borne any pain but that. I'd never seen his dear face alive with so much emotion before.

I'd broken his heart.

'You must fetch the doctor,' I blurted out. 'Whatever Kate says, you must go for help at once.' He blinked at me. I took a breath. 'She's with child, Billy.'

I might have smacked him in the stomach with a crowbar.

'I didn't know. I didn't know,' he spluttered, aghast. 'I wouldn't have ... '

No. Neither would I.

'Are you sure, Ruth?'

'She hasn't bled in months.'

'Does Nell know?'

I paused. An odd thing to ask. 'Neither of us *knows* for certain. But if she's not bleeding and she's being sick ...'

He swallowed my words, nodding. His gaze fixed elsewhere.

'Sir?'

'Aye. Right you are.' Patting me on the head, as though I were a favoured dog, he hurried away. The door slammed behind him.

Monster. The word followed me up the stairs. Mrs Metyard in her captain's room, flashing the whip. Me, behind the curtain, sewing, my needle squeaking through the cloth. Both of us, monsters.

Kate lay on top of the coverlet, perspiring, the roots of her hair dark with sweat.

She was wearing the corset.

It blazed brighter than Kate, a mass of peacock eyes watching me. I'd been foolish to think it was a weapon. The corset was me: my bitterness, my pain. My true self, as Pa would say: a killer of unborn children.

'My hands,' she gasped. 'Ruth, they burn.'

Fetching a ewer of water and a cloth, I returned to her side. I dabbed at her forehead and the palms of her hands. She was clammy, not hot at all.

The sapphire ring slipped from her finger and clattered on the floor. I picked it up, set it on the dressing table, where it broke the light streaming in from outside.

'I need to bathe,' she said.

Was that wise? Maybe I should wait for the doctor. But if I ran her a bath, at least I could get her out of the corset straight away ...

'Please, Ruth!'

'I'll go and fetch the water.'

Nell was making breakfast in the kitchen. She stirred a cup slowly, concentrating on the liquid within. Flies hovered, torn between the smell and the deadly allure of the papers.

'She won't want that,' I said. 'She's in a terrible state. A physician's coming.'

Nell let her spoon fall. 'A physician? Really?'

I grimaced. 'I think so. I told Billy about the baby ...'

'You shouldn't have done that.'

'Why?'

She shrugged. 'Kate won't be happy. It wasn't your news to tell.'

'I think we're past that, Nell. Come and help me with this water.'

Between us, we managed to fill the iron tub. The bath was only tepid, so as not to raise Kate's temperature. Three shapes shimmered on the surface of the water: Kate, Nell and me. Broken. Undulating. We might have been three witches around a cauldron.

Nell wiped her forehead with the cuff of her sleeve. 'I've got to get back to the kitchen.'

I didn't want her to leave me. Didn't want to be alone with Kate while her skin was so slick and she babbled nonsensically to herself.

For all the time that I'd known her, I'd imagined Kate's body to be pristine beneath a peacock-blue gown. But now I feared to see under her shift. No breasts pushed out from the white linen; it hung awkwardly from bony shoulders. Where the sweat gathered above her top lip, I noticed a fuzzy down.

'Thank you, Nelly.' As Nell turned for the door, Kate seized her hand and clasped it in a skeletal grip. Her veins were close to the skin, straining.

'*Madam.*' Nell shook her off and strode away.

'Nelly doesn't forgive me, she'll never forgive me,' Kate wailed. 'She doesn't understand.'

It was worse than looking after an infant. 'Never mind about that. Do you want me to help you—' Before I could finish, Kate had swung a scrawny leg over the side of the tub and plunged herself in.

Her hair spread in the water. Her shift swam about her knees, ghostly.

'It hurt less if I did it. I always offered to do it.'

She's hysterical, I thought. A fever in the brain. The ends of her hair were lank and dripping, her teeth had started to chatter. At least that might bring her temperature down.

'Try and sit still, madam. Don't splash about. I'll warm some towels ... '

I might have been speaking Dutch for all the heed she paid. Her glassy eyes peered around, bewildered.

'You forgive me, Ruth? Say you do?'

Hang this, I couldn't watch her unravel into madness. I took a step away from the tub but her wet claw was there, grasping me, tethering me to her.

'I had no choice. Forgive me!'

How could I ever do that? I turned to look at her, shivering, pathetic. White ridges marked the nails that pressed into my arm. The shift plastered itself against her body, revealing the dip of her belly button and the hint of her nipples.

And then I noticed.

'What's that, madam? On your back?'

I pushed her head forwards, so the hair slapped over her face.

Stripes. Diagonal, jagged, some double-scored. Had my corset done this? Surely it couldn't ... I lifted the neckline of her clammy shift away from the skin to see clearly.

Everything moved.

Silvery marks cross-hatched her spine. The uniform we all wore at Metyard's. But Kate had twice as many lines as ever Mim did. Shining, burnt patches too.

She laughed, pitifully. 'I was glad, so glad when Nell came! She'll pick on someone else now, I thought.'

It couldn't be true. But then ...

'Mrs Metyard ... hit you, too?'

The pieces began to slot together, each with a painful click. Kate pushing in front of Mrs Metyard that night, with the poker. The way she'd shoved me down into the coal hole, quickly, before her mother came upstairs. Kate in the captain's room at night, crouching beside Mim.

Not hurting her. Trying to *help*.

'No.' I closed my eyelids but the proof was seared on to the back of them. 'No, I don't believe it.'

'I betrayed Mother.' She squirmed beneath my touch, cold like a fish. 'I'll pay for it now.'

The room spun. I must have caught her fever for I was hot, so very hot. I pressed my damp hands to my temples, trying to hold myself steady. She was mad, it was nonsense, she couldn't have told the police where to find Mim.

'The captain ... You were lucky, Ruth. You never saw ... not in the flesh ...'

The door burst open. Old Mrs Rooker's bosom bounced in, followed by the lady herself, clutching a bottle of Fowler's Solution.

She took one look at us and her eyes seemed to pop. 'Lord bless me, Katie! Get her out of that water!'

I tried, but my hands were shaking. Where could I touch her? She was sure to break.

'I'll do it,' chided Mrs Rooker, taking my place. 'You build up the fire. Go on with you, go!'

Numb, I stumbled from the room to fetch the coal. Billy and Nell stood on the landing in whispered consultation, his hand over his eyes.

My stomach flipped inside out.

What had I done?

46

Dorothea

The prison chapel is a drab, plain room, without the sacred feel of a church. No stained glass, no icons lend their charm. Even the cross on the altar is made of polished walnut rather than gold. Well, you cannot blame them overmuch for that.

I find it a great difficulty to turn my thoughts to God, sitting in such an environment. Everything carries a weary air. Religion institutionalised. There is no spark of the world beyond ours, nothing to lift the spirit from the body.

On Sundays, Papa and I attend St Helen's, a Church of England chapel. It is pleasant in its own manner, a great improvement on this place. Yet my soul yearns for the rare occasions I can slip inside a *proper* church, where there is incense, where I may hear the prayers in Latin and confess my sins to a priest. The opportunity offers itself perhaps only twice in an entire year.

This circumstance alone should be sufficient inducement to leave Oakgate. I cannot be myself, I cannot be the woman I long to be, while I remain under Papa's roof. *His* roof, when it was my mother's house! Soon it will also be *hers*.

'Do not concern yourself with any changes to the household,' Papa says to me on a daily basis. 'If you are patient, I believe you will soon hear something to your advantage.' Then he gives me an odd, knowing smile, and everything behind my ribs seems to crumble.

A tear slides down my cheek and I let it fall, clasping my hands together, as if I might squeeze a sense of God from them. *Grant me the fortitude to bear this trial*, I repeat. Somewhere in the prison, a bolt clangs.

Papa must discover the truth eventually. Sir Thomas sought his permission prior to writing his proposal. Surely he, or perhaps Lady Morton, will reveal that I have already refused the offer of marriage. What shall happen then? Will I be punished like a child? Or will I have already fled my own home to make way for Papa's new wife?

'You will not tell Papa,' I begged Tilda last night. 'Promise me that whatever happens, you shall never tell him about the offer, or about David, or—'

'Miss Dorothea.' The minx was rude enough to interrupt me. 'In all the years I've worked for you, you might be good enough to note one thing: I can keep a secret. Whatever you may think of my hairdressing, or my sewing, you know I can at least do *that*.'

She does have a fair point. But that point was eclipsed when she went on to perplex me with a piece of advice – a servant, advising *me*!

'Mind yourself, miss. I've no complaints about your father; he's always been a fair master. But everyone downstairs knows, he's not a man you want to cross more than once.'

Whatever can the goose mean? I have always been able to turn Papa aside with a smile, a well-placed witticism. I have defied him merrily for years. Yet when Mrs Pearce becomes his wife ... perhaps that shall change. Perhaps those grey eyes will cloud over when they observe me, as they do whenever I mention Mama.

Oh, if only confirmation of David's post would come through! We could then wed and seek out accommodation in London ... But I know in my heart that Mama's house will always be *home* to me. And I shall never rest content in the capital while affairs here wallow in such a state.

I bow my head. My own life is an awful thicket of brambles; how much I should prefer to focus upon Ruth.

In these sober surroundings, I find it even harder to credit her far-fetched claims than usual. Both God and Ruth seem distant from this place. No wonder she struggles to repent, in prison. I should struggle to breathe.

Yet there is sorrow in her story! She speaks of regret as one who has truly felt it. I am at a loss to explain. She *must* have known that Catherine Metyard instigated the arrest. The papers were awash with it. Catherine was the chief witness; it was largely upon her evidence, which was quoted in detail, that the mother was convicted at all! Indeed, there was a moment when it seemed Catherine might stand a trial of her own. Few people could believe she had no involvement in the atrocities committed at Metyard's. It was only the proof of Catherine's own abuse that put a stop to that line of inquiry.

Ruth is purposefully ignoring the facts to suit her own narrative. What does this make her? A liar? A fantasist? I do not know. I do not seem to comprehend the true nature of anyone, nowadays.

A door opens. Startled, I look up to see the chaplain walk in with a book tucked under his arm. He is as nondescript as his chapel: dark, almost-brown hair; regular height; sparely built with plain features. But his smile appears genuine.

'Miss Truelove. I did not think to find you here. I hope I do not interrupt you?'

I sigh, climbing to my feet. 'I was seeking counsel from Our Lord, sir, but you interrupt only His silence.'

He returns my sigh. It is a comfort, a kind of hand-shake we have performed. 'It is difficult for us mortals. We desire responses immediately. But to God, a thou-sand years are as a day ... Do not lose heart. He shall answer you in time.'

'So I trust. Time is running short for me.'

The chaplain seats himself on one of the plain wooden chairs. His smile softens at the edges. 'I am but a poor substitute, Miss Truelove, but if you desire it ... I shall be happy to listen and offer my own advice?'

I hesitate. This is no priest; he cannot absolve me. Yet there are a multitude of thoughts spilling from my brain, and such palpitations in my chest! This man knows God, knows Ruth. He can offer an informed opinion, at the very least.

Inclining my head, I walk towards him and sit in a chair next-door-but-one. My movements echo horribly around the empty room. 'You are most kind. I fear I have forgotten your name?'

'It is Summers.'

'Mr Summers.' I look down at my hands. How differ-ent they are to Ruth's: the lily skin, the clean white crescents of nails. 'Mr Summers, I am rather ashamed to confess that I have been doubting the judgement of my father.'

He releases his breath. 'I see. Ah. Well, I am sure I do not need to remind you of the commandment to honour our parents.'

'No indeed.'

'And yet ... Forgive me, Miss Truelove, for an indeli-cate question. Might I enquire ... Would you kindly tell me your age?'

'It is five and twenty.'

He nods. To my eyes, he appears younger than this himself. 'I have always felt it is a natural progression, for a child to question those around them. It shows the development of the mind, that they are preparing to judge for themselves – as we all must, at some stage. So it may be with you, Miss Truelove. Not a sin, but a sign of maturity. Your mind finds itself ready to rely upon the judgement of a husband, rather than that of a father.'

Heavens, yes. David is ten times the man of Papa. And while I do not like to imagine myself under anyone's *direction*, I will surely do better, be worthier, with a guide such as him? 'Tell me, Mr Summers, do you believe that people can change? Truly change. A criminal to a saint, a good man to a villain?'

He pulls back in his chair slightly. 'Do you consider your father to be changed?'

'No. Not in the least. He is … much as he ever was. This is something beside the point, a matter of my own interest.'

'Well, Miss Truelove, I think you know my answer. Would I be working as a chaplain in a prison if I did not believe that man can reform?'

'No, you would not. But prison, most of all, poses the question to me: at what stage do we cease to be merciful, and become fools? I have been ridden over, roughshod, by those I have shown only kindness to. I always trusted that they would repent. But now … I do not know how I should act.'

He steeples his hands together. He was not anticipating me and my challenges, today. 'All can be forgiven, Miss Truelove. But not all will choose it. God holds out His grace, and we must point towards it, too. Yet some

people will be lost. They will go their own way, there is
no preventing that.'

How useless I feel, how thoroughly impotent. All
my science, all my theology, and this is my reward: the
shape of the skull does not change; the Word of God
is not guaranteed to transform. Each instrument snaps
when I wield it in my hands.

Must I accept this? That some people are born bad,
and will remain bad?

'But what of those that fall from the path, Mr
Summers?' My voice sounds fragile. I am a girl again.
'Those we cannot lead back? What happens to them?'

He looks at me sadly. 'I am afraid it is the same with
God as it is in the prison, Miss Truelove. The wicked
must be punished.'

47

Ruth

Love. Kindness. I'd felt them once, hadn't I? Long ago, in the mists of time, there'd been forgiveness, and a part of me that was tender.

I needed to find it, now.

My needle burrowed through the chintz, searching. Again and again it resurfaced without a catch. Healing. Health. They must be in there somewhere.

Twilight groped its way in through the window of our room. The glass gaped bare, since I'd hauled the curtains down. Only a few lamps glimmered outside, complemented by bobbing scullers upon the river.

How could I have known? She was always so brusque and snippy. The way her nose tilted up, as if she could smell something unpleasant, and that smell was me ... I couldn't think of that now. Only happy, kind, thoughts; gentle stitches.

'Ruth, what are you doing? We need you.' Billy opened the door, startling me. Dark marks sat beneath his brilliant eyes. He'd rolled his sleeves up, revealing tanned, lightly haired arms. 'Kate's very bad.'

'I'll be along in a moment.'

'Mammy wants you to ... Wait, what are you doing? Are they the curtains?'

Tingling shame, throughout my body. How could I explain? 'I'm making a shawl. For Ka— for the mistress.'

'She has shawls, Ruth.'

'She needs – she ...' I shook my head. Useless. There was no time left for excuses. 'Tell me, sir,' I demanded, 'was it really her? Did Kate send the police to Metyard's?'

He stared at me for a moment, as if he'd never seen me before. A sigh left his mouth. Then he ducked his head, came inside and shut the door behind him.

He leant against the panels, as if he no longer had the strength to stand. 'Yes. She did. I never thought I'd live to see that day! But things changed. *She* changed, after Miriam ...'

Whatever I did, I couldn't think of Mim now, couldn't risk her soaking into this shawl. 'You always tried to tell me. You said that Kate wasn't her mother's daughter.'

A bitter gasp of air – it might have been a laugh. 'Did I? I don't know if I believed it. I only wanted ... Ah, but you understand, don't you? You know how good it felt to take something from Mrs Metyard.'

I laid my needle down. Our eyes met, and for an instant I saw him as he must have been, back then: fresh from the Foundling, a gangling, scared boy with plaintive blue eyes.

'Did you ever love her?' I let slip.

'That's not a question for you to ask me!'

I bowed my head. He'd never spoken fiercely to me before. In fact, I don't think I'd heard him angry in all the time I'd known him. 'No, sir. I'm sorry. I should never—'

'No, *I'm* sorry, Ruth. I didn't mean to snap at you. It's just ...' He covered his face with his hands. 'Oh God, it's such a mess.'

He was my master. I should have pretended not to
see his tears. But instead I went to him and wrapped my
arms around his waist, as I'd always longed to do. He
cleaved to me like a child.

'Ruth! Ruth, the things that I've done! I should never
have gone back to that place. I didn't want to! But how
could I leave her alone?'

My pain was so intense that it was almost a pleasure.
Crying burnished his eyes a fiercer blue than ever. I
would never stir a man to desire, to love, but I'd caused
this emotion: I had turned smiling, whistling Billy into
a tortured soul.

If only I could heal him, too.

'What are we going to do?' he cried. 'God, the baby!
If she and the baby die, and the doctor thinks—'

'I won't let them die!' I promised rashly. 'I'll undo it.
I swear to you. I'll find a way to undo it all.'

His wet lashes blinked at me. 'Undo?' he repeated,
uncertainly. 'What do you ...'

Strange, isn't it, how love loosens the tongue? I'd
never said the words aloud before, even to myself. But
standing there with Billy, his tears in my hair, his smell
on my skin, unlocked me. Closing my eyes, I took a
deep breath.

'It's a power, Billy. Kate's corset ... It was my fault. I
did it. I wanted her to suffer.'

'What are you talking about?'

'I thought she hurt Mim!' I wailed. 'I made her ill, I
made the corset to kill her!'

When I opened my eyes, Billy's face spoke of utter
bewilderment. It was as if we'd never met. 'You ... did
what?'

I grabbed my sewing project, waving it at him like
a lunatic. 'Didn't you think it odd that so many of our

customers fell ill? It's in my stitches! Look! I can hurt people, I can make them blind.'

Words flew out and relief streamed in to take their place. Every burden I'd carried alone: Naomi, Pa, Ma – I offered them up to him. With every confession I became lighter. By the time I told him about Mim's fish inside Kate's corset, I thought I might float from the ground.

Billy peered at me from under his lowered brows. The muscles of his face lay absolutely still. I tried to read his expression. It wasn't horror – no, not that. Disbelief. Wariness. A dawning sense of comprehension.

'You aren't well, Ruth. This has all upset you more than you realise.'

'No! It's true. I'll prove it. When this shawl is finished, it will make her better. I just have to—'

He held up a hand. 'Let us understand one another. Are you honestly telling me that you've tried to kill my wife?'

How intently he watched me, breath suspended. In some perverse way, I felt he was willing me to say yes.

I swallowed. 'It's true, sir. I'm so sorry. I never meant to hurt *you* …'

'Good God.'

Without another word, he left the room. The click of the door sliced right through me.

Gone. Gone, never to return.

I hid my aching face inside the shawl and tried to cry.

48

Dorothea

At the prison, I have often heard one inmate inform another that she has 'a maggot in her head'. By this they mean a curious notion or an idea that cannot be displaced. Ladies of my class would call it a freak or a whim, but I find in this instance the common tongue is more articulate. That is precisely what this feels like: a maggot wiggling deeper and deeper, gnawing at my healthy brain matter.

The carriage toils up the hills in the direction of Heatherfield, jerking so wildly that I am obliged to hold on to the leather strap in order to keep my seat. Wind sings past the windows and bristles through the trees. So swiftly do the clouds move that the sun comes in fitful bursts. Perhaps it is not wise to attempt the journey in such uncertain weather. It is most *definitely* unwise to attend the meeting I am jostling towards. But there, you see, I have a maggot in my head. I cannot rest easy until I hear what he has to say.

I must confess, when the second letter arrived from Sir Thomas, I was perturbed beyond words. The very envelope seemed to tremble with disappointment. I believed the missive inside could run along one of only two patterns: either a wail of despair or pages and pages of furious upbraiding. I was mistaken. Instead, Sir Thomas thanked me for my kind words and requested a private interview, if I did not consider it too mortifying to my feelings. He did not wish to embarrass me, he wrote, but he must urge me in the strongest terms to submit to one conversation. That conversation is to take place in the graveyard of Heatherfield parish church.

What am I to make of this? For years I have been arranging assignations with David, but my invention never lit upon a destination so morbid. Certainly, it is a location any two persons may have a right to visit without arousing suspicion, and yet … Perhaps I am grown too sensitive. My talks with Ruth are making me shrink from anything related to death with abhorrence, where I used to find a melancholy fascination.

At length the road levels out before us. Hazarding a glance out of the window, I see a grey stone spire reaching for the clouds, its tip as sharp as one of Ruth's needles.

'We must stop here.' I knock upon the roof and order Graymarsh to slow the carriage. I do not wish for him to see Sir Thomas. If news of this visit were to get back to Papa, I should have no end of difficulties. As the sound of hooves gradually dies away, I turn to Tilda. 'You are to remain in the carriage.'

It is my Mistress of the House voice, the one that brooks no argument, but Tilda has the skull of a person who cannot let any point go uncontested. 'It isn't proper, miss,' she chides. 'Suppose someone saw you, without a chaperone?'

'Saw me, up here? There is nothing but heather for miles.'

'And what if Sir Thomas were to behave … improperly?'

'In a graveyard, beside a church? Upon my word, you have a very low opinion of the gentleman.'

'I only want to protect you, miss.'

This catches me. I have spent so much time marking the signs of stubbornness and vanity in Tilda's skull that I have not dwelt upon her organ for Friendship. Her bonnet hides it at present, but I feel as if I can discern what is written there. The sentiment is manifesting itself not through the head, but in the eyes. Eyes that know something they will not tell, and yet cannot forget.

It is a landslide of feeling I am unprepared for. I conceal it in my brisk voice. 'I do not doubt it, Tilda. You are a good creature. Now come along, do as you are bid and there shall be no quarrels between us. Rest assured that if I need you, I shall scream.'

We have reached a standstill. I open the door myself, not waiting for Graymarsh, and make an undignified exit. The wind is strong here, up in the hills. It pushes me back, tries to prevent me from taking a step towards the church. Head down, I defy it and walk boldly on, but not without misgiving. One could almost imagine it an omen, a sign that I should not proceed.

As I approach, I perceive that Heatherfield Church and its graveyard are tidy, if ancient. The grass is rough but kept short. Dwarf willow creeps in a pleasant mat over the paths. Tombstones jut at a variety of angles, most of them hazed with moss, and the wind makes a gentle lament as it moves between them.

Part of me expects to find Sir Thomas prostrate on a grave, howling with sorrow. I have read too many romances. Of course Sir Thomas is standing quite sensibly beneath the porch of the church, the capes of his great coat flapping in the wind. A top hat is wedged firmly over his hair.

He raises his cane in greeting when he sees me, and begins to walk in my direction. My stomach knots. I

dare not observe him too closely, for shame. Even if I
were to venture a long stare, it would be of no use: the
key to his character, his head, is hidden from me beneath
that top hat.

He opens the creaking little gate that leads into the
graveyard, holding it for me to pass through. I do so
with acute embarrassment. If I had returned a different
answer, he might have met me here with an embrace. We
might have been married in this very church. He must be
conscious of this, too.

He clears his throat. 'It is very good of you to come,
Miss Truelove. I am immensely grateful.'

I wait until I have reached a gravestone, pocked with
black lichen, and can lean upon it for support before I
answer him. 'Your letter expressed urgency, sir.'

'Yes.' He bites his lip. At this moment, it is difficult
to imagine him fervent about any topic. His eyes are
customarily tired and phlegmatic. He walks at a stately
pace. 'There are some words that ... I could not forgive
myself, if I failed to speak them.' He must see my expression, for he adds, 'Do not be alarmed. I am not here to
press my suit or make violent love to you.' He gives a
wry smile. 'I almost wish that I were.'

'I know you are a straightforward man, Sir Thomas.
There is no prevarication about you. Please be so good
as to say these words quickly, so neither of us may find
the interview more distressing than necessary.'

He heaves a sigh. For the first time, his visage grows
troubled, and I find myself obliged to study the tomb-
stone; the worn letters and its patches of white and gold.
I did not believe he truly cared for me. But that sigh ...

'It *will* distress you, Miss Truelove. There is no helping that. The matter has distressed me a great deal, and
you know I am not the sort of fellow to make a fuss

over nothing. But I believe you have a strong constitution and you can take the blow. Should you wish never to see me again after I have spoken ... Well, I daresay I shall survive that.'

His voice rings clear, even through the wind. I regard him quizzically, caught off my guard. These are not the sentiments of a lover. Yet is there not something kind in his words? Something like that gleam in Tilda's eye: a tenderness born of secret knowledge.

Sir Thomas passes his cane into the other hand. 'I do not wish to mortify your maidenly pride, but you are aware – I think you *must* be aware, after that dinner party, Miss Truelove – that I have been under some pressure from my sister to enter the state of matrimony.'

He is right: it does wound my pride, even though I have long suspected it. 'You proposed to me at your sister's bidding?'

'Yes,' he says slowly. 'I came to this part of the country and ingratiated myself with your father, all at her request. But you are not to consider me a weak fool under petticoat government. I would not have complied if I did not possess a certain fondness for you and ... if my sister did not have a compelling reason for her actions.'

I had prepared for dudgeon from him, yet I am the one who is upon my dignity; it is me who speaks with a waspish sting. 'Her reason was the money, I expect? Heatherfield Manor is in need of some repair, perhaps?'

He looks not at me, but at the church; he appears to be asking it for strength. 'You are mistaken, Miss Truelove. If you will be so kind as to recollect, you yourself informed me of your father's plans to remarry long before the engagement was announced. Indeed, it was Mr Truelove's preference of Mrs Pearce that first alerted my sister's attention to your unmarried state. '

He has me there. All the same, my feeling of discomfort lingers. Greed may at least be understood. 'Forgive me for my naivety, sir, but if you do not love me and you do not seek my dowry, I am at a loss for your motive in proposing marriage.'

'My sister and I acted under the same motivation,' he addresses the church, softly. 'We meant to take you under our protection.'

The graveyard has moved and subsided over time; that is why it feels as if the ground is unsteady beneath my feet. The strange, drowning singing in my ears – that must be from the wind. 'Your protection? I do not require guarding. You seem to imply I am in some kind of danger, Sir Thomas.'

'It is my sister's firm belief that you *are* in danger, Miss Truelove. Grave danger.'

'Nonsense. As you can see, I am perfectly well.' I strive for a jovial tone, but my voice sounds peculiar, as if it is originating from somewhere outside of my body.

'Pardon me, you are *not* well. You look as if you would faint. Sit here upon this stone wall.'

I allow Sir Thomas to prop me against the wall, feeling thoroughly foolish. 'I did not break my fast this morning,' I explain. 'I am in need of some refreshment. But as to danger—'

He grips my arm. 'What I have to say, I must say now, and quickly. Be so good as to refrain from interrupting me.' The tone is decided, but not devoid of kindness. 'These things are best completed fast, like the pulling of a tooth.'

I nod, wary.

'You know, perhaps, that my sister and your mother were once intimate friends. You may also be aware that your mother caused a storm of gossip by converting to Roman Catholicism. I am pleased to say the friendship survived the trial. My sister did not desert Mrs Truelove. She would have continued to accompany her to the theatre and invite her for supper parties, if your father had not ... taken his wife out of circulation.' A breath. 'Before she could re-enter society, Mrs Truelove ... Well, as you know, she passed away.'

He has bid me not to interrupt him, but the words pop from me like a cork. 'Papa says it was the onset of her illness: the conversion. He says that she behaved most erratically afterwards, it may have been a fever on the brain ...' I stop, conscious that I am parroting Papa's words, words I have previously scorned.

'You do not subscribe to that diagnosis. You certainly do not believe that Roman Catholicism is a sign of madness.' He presses my hand, squeezes tears from me. 'And neither does my sister.'

I recall that bone face, the way it glared at my papa, and I am thankful for the solid stone wall beneath my thighs. Without it, I feel I might drift out to sea. 'Lady Morton appears to be a woman of very strong opinion. Pray, what exactly *does* she believe?'

'I must be blunt. She believes that your father was ashamed, and made a social pariah by his wife's actions. She is witness to the fact that he argued with her and tried his utmost to control her. But he could not contain the damage and ...' His voice has grown so soft, I must lean in to hear him. 'And he poisoned her.'

'How dare you?' I explode.

He jerks away from me, hands raised. I regret it immediately; without him by my side, the wind is fierce and ready to topple me over. I force myself unsteadily to my feet. The graveyard undulates around me.

'He poisoned her,' Sir Thomas reasserts with a dreadful gravity. 'His friend Dr Armstrong concealed the crime.'

'What nerve—'

'You must hear me! My sister did not report her suspicions ...' He frowns, as if he disagrees with her actions. 'She feared your father's disgrace would blight your future prospects. And she did not truly believe any man would harm his only child. But ... she regrets that now. The circumstances begin to look painfully familiar. Your father cannot control *you*. He cannot marry you off. You stand in the way of his own matrimonial designs. You are causing him embarrassment. Do you fathom my meaning?'

This is lunatic invention – worse than Ruth's fevered tale. My outrage is so strong that I can scarcely draw breath. I estimated Sir Thomas as a good man, a gentleman. He has deceived me.

'Is this my punishment, Sir Thomas?' I spit. 'This gross insult in return for refusing your hand and denting your pride? I could not love you, but I *had* thought better of you.'

He shakes his head sadly. 'I have said my piece. My conscience can demand no more.'

Can he really speak of conscience? When he has invented such falsehoods! And yet ...

There are those bumps, on Papa's head. Signs of cunning and evasion. Tilda has more than once said she would not like to cross him. But that is not the same. It is one thing to be a stern master, quite another to murder one's own wife!

'Truly, you do look unwell. Might I ...' Sir Thomas shifts uncomfortably. 'Would you permit me to walk you to your carriage?'

'No, you may not. You may not write to me, you may not speak to me. You have offended me more than words can express.' I possess some dignity yet. Tossing up my chin, I stalk past him, over the uneven graves, through the gate. My fumbling fingers cannot fasten the latch behind me; I hear the gate banging in the wind as I march down the road. It is all I hear, above the roaring in my ears.

I cannot think. I cannot *allow* myself to think. All I can do is focus on the distance between me and the carriage, willing strength into my tottering feet. I must make it without fainting. I must not let Sir Thomas believe, even for a moment, that I credit his words.

For I do not.

I resolutely do not.

49
Ruth

It was a nice shawl, considering. I tucked it around Kate's scrawny shoulders, where it clung to the sweat on her skin. Even after her bath, she was heavy with that same, garlicky scent I'd detected on her breath.

Candles burnt in the sconces. Mrs Rooker sat in Kate's easy chair, giving directions to Nell. Only I hovered close to the bed, where Kate's misty eyes attempted to focus on me. There was no lustre in them, now.

Male voices murmured behind the closed bedroom door. The doctor had felt her pulse, looked in her mouth and frowned. I imagined him consulting with Billy and Mr Rooker, at a loss to explain my power.

Maybe the doctor would examine *me*, subject me to tests. I didn't care. I thought I'd never care about anything again, so long as the shawl worked.

'I do forgive you,' I whispered, close to Kate's ear on the pillow. 'Sometimes, we all do things that we don't mean.'

Kate gave no sign that she'd heard.

'Why have you stopped bathing her forehead? Can't you see the sweat running into the poor girl's eyes?'

Mrs Rooker's voice sent me scuttling from the bedside to fetch another cloth. Nell had torn up some old sheets and they lay in strips, waiting to absorb Kate's essence. I folded one in my hand, wondering how many materials had touched my skin that day. The bedsheets, my maid's uniform, a facecloth, the curtains … Fabric swam everywhere about me. And wasn't the human body just fabric, too? If I could cut it, why couldn't I stitch it up again?

Bang. We all jumped as one of Kate's arms slammed into the bedpost. She gave a low, tortured moan and then her body went rigid.

Mrs Rooker stood up and crossed herself.

'Help us!' Nell shouted.

As the doctor hurried in, Kate's back arched. An invisible power pulled her stomach up from the bed. It was a hideous sight, unholy, yet I couldn't rip my gaze away. Her hands gnarled by her side, twitching. Skeins of vomit ran from her mouth.

'She's having a convulsion,' the doctor said. 'Make way, there!'

'The shawl,' I whimpered, 'make sure the shawl stays around her shoulders.' But no one paid any heed to me. All eyes were on Kate, thrashing beneath the sheets, writhing in pain.

As if she hadn't suffered enough.

My legs folded, useless beneath me. It hardly seemed to matter now whether I stood or laid down, never to move again.

As a girl, I'd dreamt of embroidering fine gloves, making beautiful things. What had happened? How was it that all I'd managed to create was this: this crucifixion of agony enacted upon the bed?

'Hold her head, she'll bite her tongue!'

She'd sent Billy to find us, that day. Her mother was going to hang, and still she thought about me. Wanted to give me work. She'd saved my corset from the road, because she knew what it meant to me. I couldn't *like* her, but she wasn't a bad person. She didn't deserve to die like this.

'Ruth! Ruth, come and help!'

I had no strength to rise. The stenches wove about me like snares: garlic, body odour, sour vomit.

'Billy! Someone fetch our Billy.'

All at once, Kate fell slack. I could hear something rattling in her chest, like a pebble in a jar. Mrs Rooker screamed.

They made an eerie strange tableau around the bed: the physician, with his fingers at Kate's neck; Mrs Rooker, her hands raised to her cheeks. Nell stood back slightly, stunned, a soiled cloth clutched at her chest.

There was a moment with no movement, no sound.

'She's gone.' The doctor bowed his head.

Who was it keening, like an animal in the jaws of a trap? Someone hysterical, far away. They were beating the floor, crying out, 'I killed her, oh God, I killed her!' in a voice that couldn't be consoled.

Boots pounded into the room. Too late. Billy and his father ran over to the bed, recoiling from the mess splayed there.

'I am truly sorry, Mr Rooker. I did everything within my power,' the doctor said.

I, too, had done everything I could. My influence was the stronger, it seemed.

I thought Billy would bend to kiss Kate's forehead, touch her hand. But he was speaking – or at least, his lips were moving. I heard nothing. I was underwater, caught, at last, in my own vicious riptide.

One by one, the faces around the bed turned in my direction. They seemed to ripple and break. Noses, brows, gaping mouths. In each one I saw Kate, staring back.

There was a bubble, my ears popped.

'I'm going to fetch the police,' old Mr Rooker said.

50

Dorothea

Ruth once told me that she had lost the capacity to shed tears, but she is crying now. Fat drops slide down her cheeks as fast as rain. If I did not know better, I would take her for a lost child.

Yet no child can invent a tale like this. These are not the hands of a child that slumber, clasped in the lap of her serge prison gown. Do not crocodiles weep, to lure in their prey?

Papa's engagement and Sir Thomas's accusations have made me short of temper. Ruth's sniffles, which would usually arouse my sympathy, serve only to irritate my nerves. I rise from the creaking, uneven chair and begin to pace her compact cell, as if I myself am the prisoner.

'Your sins are heavy enough, Ruth. Why do you insist upon adding dishonesty to their number?'

She covers the wreck of her face with her hands. Is this repentance, at long last? Or perhaps it is a screen. Perhaps she is laughing at me, behind her fingers.

'The time for your fairy tales is over. You stand trial tomorrow. Tomorrow!' How small this room is. Walking does no good at all, it only makes me feel more hemmed in. 'Why will you not save yourself? You cannot lie to God! Admit, now, what you have done, before it is too late.'

'I have, I have!' she wails.

An unpleasant noise escapes my throat, a sound half-way between a laugh and a groan. 'Oh yes! Murder with a magical corset. Will you truly stand in the dock, tomorrow, and swear to this deranged fantasy?'

'I can't testify at my own trial, miss.'

Her words annoy me all the more, because I should know this. 'It is just as well. You would perjure yourself, alongside all your other transgressions.'

A sob bends her forwards. I am confronted with the mass of her black curls, cloaking all marks of the crania beneath. For a moment, I quite forget myself. My hands grip her hair, roam over her skull without seeking her permission.

Bone. Inflexible, immovable beneath my fingertips, as if the matter of the brain could not shape it at all. 'You do not have the skull of a madwoman! Or a liar, or even a murderer! What *are* you?'

My own voice echoes back at me from the lime-washed walls. I have been shouting. Ashamed and short of breath, I retake my chair. Ruth remains in the same position, tucked in on herself.

I cannot endure this. Not any longer. I have sorrows of my own.

'Why don't you believe me?' Ruth gasps. 'Billy believed me. He saw what I'd done and ...' Her breath hitches. 'He hates me for it. I wish he didn't hate me.'

'You have killed his wife!' My tone is harsher than I intend it. 'And what is more, you are making a mock-ery of the fact! Pretending you are so powerful, beyond medicine, killing without a trace. Well there *were* traces, Ruth. I expect you have never heard of the Marsh test. And for all you pretend to know about the inside of the human body, you are ignorant of its workings. Your mistress was not pregnant! The autopsy showed no signs of a child. She had only lost so much weight that her body ceased to menstruate!'

Her hands drop from her face, fast as a curtain. Red blotches linger on her cheeks, but the expression in her eyes has changed. It is so eager, so *genuine*, that it knocks the breath from me.

Hope.

'I didn't kill Billy's baby?'

'No. He did not have a baby.'

More tears fall, but they drip past a watery smile. 'Oh, thank God! Thank *God*!' She is almost laughing. But then she collects herself. 'Poor Kate. If only she'd known. Her last days might have been easier for her, in the mind. She thought the same as me. And so did Nell. We didn't realise ... '

And as she trails off, it comes to me like an epiphany: bright light, shining into the hidden corners, revealing the deeds of darkness. The scales fall from my eyes.

She does not know.

I think I may choke. There is no joy, as in biblical revelations; this knowledge is painful, too searing to hold. All these visits, and I never suspected. I worked on the assumption that she knew how Kate had died.

Footsteps outside, the slide of the bolt, a key grinding in a lock. Too soon.

'Ruth ...' I begin. With her background and education, of course she would not have arranged the pieces into their proper shape. But me! What is my excuse?

'Miss Truelove, I am afraid I must ask you to leave.' Matron looms in the doorway, keys glinting at her waist. 'Butterham has her trial tomorrow. Her lawyer is here.'

'I must speak to him.' Even as I rise to my feet, I hear the mounting hysteria in my words. 'I must ...'

What can I possibly say? What evidence do I have to present him with? There is not sufficient time to prepare a case, I have frittered it all away pursuing my scientific theories – and even they have proved to be false.

Matron places her hand upon my arm, steers me towards the door. 'I think it will be best if we leave the learned man to deal with his client alone, don't you? They do not have much time together.'

I see it now like an hourglass, the sand spilling. 'Ruth!' I call desperately. 'Did you tell this story to your advocate? The chaplain?' If I deciphered the clues, perhaps they might, also.

But Ruth shakes her shorn head. 'I only trusted you.'

I am distraught, I want to grip at the doorframe with my nails like one of the rabid prisoners and refuse to leave, but the door clangs behind me.

'Ruth!' I shout. 'Ruth, I believe you!'

I do not know if she has heard me. I am marched, as if in custody myself, down the halls and away from her.

———

'Dora? Are you listening?' I snap my eyes up from my plate of eggs and see Papa, fork suspended halfway to his mouth, intent upon me. 'I bid you to remain at home. You appear most unwell.'

I feel it. Nausea and giddiness are my constant companions. I have neglected my health, in the tumult of these past weeks. *That* is why my stomach cramps, why I do not wish to eat, why even my coffee tastes strange of late.

It must be. I will not countenance any other possibilities.

I lace my fingers around the cup and stare into its dark depths, rather than Papa's face. The similarities

I detect between his countenance and mine repel me. 'Not in the least. One of my women stands her trial today,' I say, as casually as I can manage. 'I am simply nervous for her.'

'That is all?'

It is *not* all. Already Mrs Pearce hovers like a spectre at our breakfast table, shoving aside the quiet, gentle spirit of Mama. But I nod, attempt another sip of my coffee. Was it always this bitter?

Sir Thomas's worried visage obtrudes itself into my memory. I slam the door upon it.

Papa is evidently thinking of Sir Thomas too. 'You have not received any post? Something distressing, or … interesting?'

I feel his grey eyes probing, cool as a steel scalpel. Subtlety was never his strength. 'No, I do not believe I have. I must work on my correspondence tomorrow, I owe Fanny a letter.'

He chews, meditatively. Swallows. 'I thought,' he says, spearing another piece of ham, 'that I saw something arrive from Heatherfield, the other day.'

I dab my mouth with a napkin, concealing its tremor from him. 'Goodness me, no. Lady Morton does not correspond with me, Papa. I do not believe I am quite elegant enough for her.'

'Then I must have been mistaken.'

'Yes.'

'For you must know I could not tolerate any neglect towards that family. Not now our name is finally return-ing to its proper dignity. I have worked tirelessly to cultivate an acquaintance with Sir Thomas, and should anything happen to offend him … I do not believe I could abide such embarrassment, Dora. Neither could dear Mrs Pearce.'

I push back from the table. It is difficult to muster the strength to stand. 'Will you excuse me, Papa? I must prepare for this trial.'

He harrumphs. 'Not in your present state. Your hands are shaking. I forbid it.'

'I really must attend, for the sake of this woman. She is friendless.'

Still watching me, he pulls his napkin from his lap. 'Well, then. I must accompany you, I suppose, and ensure you conduct yourself correctly.'

I can devise no excuse. If it is a case of going with Papa, or not going at all, my choice is clear. I must hear the evidence, I must either confirm or quash my fears.

'I am not certain the nature of the trial will be pleasant to you,' I warn him. 'You may become uneasy.'

Without meaning to, I have made him laugh. 'If you can withstand it, Dora, as a young lady, I certainly can. Do you view me as your silly old papa, tender in his age? I have far more backbone than you give me credit for.'

He is correct. Perhaps, in my filial partiality, I have not given him credit for nearly enough.

51

Dorothea

The courthouse is already heaving by the time we arrive. Graymarsh is forced to set us down a good three hundred yards from the doors, while he contends with the line of stationary, cursing cab drivers. I am glad of Papa's arm to steady me through the crush of people and horses that swarm about the streets. Clearly, news of Ruth's infamy has spread far and wide. A poisoner: a murderer of the blackest dye.

Policemen surround the entrance, keeping order. Amongst the impassive faces, squashed square by their tall hats, is the one I am always watching for. David's eyes meet mine. I manage to stifle my reaction, save for the slight tightening of my grip upon Papa's coat. However, my father's gaze is sharp.

'Do you know that young man?' he barks.

'Which man, sir?'

'That young constable who stares at you so intently.'

'I did not – oh! He does look somewhat familiar. Perhaps I have walked past him at the prison.' I toss my head, as if policemen stare at me every day of the week.

Papa does not cease watching David until the doors obscure him from sight.

Our place is in the public gallery, with the other spectators. Hot, stinking air fills my lungs, the mixture of a
thousand breaths. Papa attains us a position as near to
the front as his influence can command. One or two men
note the quality of his clothes and give way, but others
remain truculent. I peer over the side of the gallery,
down upon the proceedings, my head swimming. We are
late. They have begun.

I have missed the indictment and the opening state-
ments. The Crown are calling their first witness for the
prosecution: William Rooker, I saw his name at the top
of the list. Craning my neck for a better view, I discern a
man rising from his seat. It is always a curious sensation,
beholding a person after you have allowed a picture of
them to form in your mind. Billy is at once a little less
handsome and a mite tidier than I anticipated. That girl
sitting beside him must be Nell; I recognise her hair
from Ruth's description.

The pair look at one another, as if they are about to
jump from a great height. Then Billy makes his way
towards the stand.

As I track his progress, I catch my first glimpse of
Ruth. She looks tiny, stricken. How much has she heard,
before my arrival? From the state of her, I would wager
the prosecution mentioned the cause of death in their
opening speech. What thoughts must have crossed her
mind at that juncture? What agonies are chasing through
it, now?

My heart breaks for the dark, lovesick eyes that
follow Billy. He does not even incline his head in her
direction.

He is sworn in. A sleek man in robes and a wig rises
to question him.

'Mr Rooker, I appreciate that this line of inquiry may prove painful to you. Before we begin, I wish to assure you that you have our deepest sympathies.'

Billy mutters his thanks. He is still dressed in mourning, although the black jacket is a touch shiny at the seams. Were you to paint a picture of a heartbroken, working man, this would be it.

'As we have already heard, a great quantity of arsenic was found in the body of your late wife. However, to successfully prosecute this case, we have not only to prove that arsenic was the cause of death, but how it was obtained and administered. To begin with, can you think of any reason that your wife may have ingested this poison herself?'

'None whatever.'

'You believe, then, that it was administered to her?'

'It must have been,' Billy says.

The advocate flicks through his notes. 'Our medical professionals are of the opinion – as the gentlemen of the jury shall hear – that the late Mrs Rooker consumed small amounts of the substance over a long period of time. Towards the end of her life, the dose increased considerably, causing the symptoms we have previously detailed. Can you offer any explanation as to how the poison had been present for so long?'

Papa's arm twitches beneath mine. I did not tell him that it was a case of poison. Nor did I warn him of the similarities between Kate's symptoms and my mother's.

'Goodness, Dora, this is horrible. How can—' He is shushed by those around us.

'I don't know,' Billy answers. 'There's a bit of it in most things, isn't there? She had a skin tonic … something with benzoin and elderflower. And then … my mother gave her a drop of Fowler's Solution.

A physician has since told me you can find arsenic in that.'

'And what quantity of the solution did your mother give to the late Mrs Rooker?'

'Only two drops. It was over the last … hours of her life.' He leans forward to grip the bars, as if the memory bends him in two. 'That's all. I watched her dispense it myself.'

The lawyer refers to the bottle of Fowler's Solution, now in the court's possession, and the very small amount missing.

'Would it seem reasonable to you, Mr Rooker, to deduce that the arsenic must have been administered by food or drink?'

'Yes, I suppose that's reasonable.'

'And will you tell us if you have any suspicion yourself, as to who might have sullied the late Mrs Rooker's victuals?'

We all stretch to catch his answer. Billy still has his arms braced against the bars. The whole court hears him wet his lips and take a breath. 'It's my belief that it was … the defendant. Ruth Butterham.'

Gasps and shouts from the spectators. How can it be that they were not expecting this? Have they not heard the ballads? The only one with a right to surprise, Ruth herself, simply closes her eyes and looks as if she has taken a bullet.

When order returns, the lawyer follows up his inquiry. 'Your belief is based upon the defendant's statement of confession which we heard earlier today: that she did, wilfully and with intent, murder Catherine Maria Rooker?'

Billy shakes his head. 'No. It's because the day Kate died, Ruth told me, told me with her own lips, that she was trying to kill my wife.'

More commotion. Over it, the lawyer raises his voice. 'And why should she wish to do that?'

'She never liked Kate. She blamed her for what Kate's mother did to her. That was ... Mrs Metyard,' he exhales on the name, shuddering. 'She was a killer.'

No doubt they will battle it out, in the hours to come; reveal how Ruth was found that day, what she suffered at Mrs Metyard's hands. Will it sway the jury? I do not know, but I am glad the trial has tended down this path. If Billy had cited jealousy as a motive, if he had turned for a moment to see how Ruth regards him ... But perhaps the jury can see it, even now.

I miss the first questions of cross-examination, as Papa is urging me to leave, saying I look unwell. By the time I return my attention, Ruth's advocate, an elderly, doddering man appointed by the court, is in mid flow. He cannot hope to exonerate her, only lighten her sentence. What has she told him?

He asks if the late Mrs Rooker was in the habit of taking a cup of cocoa, and Billy agrees that she was.

'And, Mr Rooker, who would fetch that drink for your wife?'

'It would have been ... Ruth. Ruth was my wife's personal maid. She would be the one to bring her break-fast and attend to those things.'

If you were not acquainted with Ruth, as I am, you would take the expression on her face for a scowl. But I see the utter blankness of confusion, a feeling that seems to pass to her lawyer.

'And ... there was not anyone else who could have tampered with the drink? There was another woman working in your household at the time, I believe; an Eleanor Swanscombe.'

'Nelly could never have done such a thing.'

'And what convinces you of that?'

The blue eyes that turn upon Ruth's advocate are ice cold. 'I have known her from a child. She is as a sister to me. I would trust her with my life.'

This is a grand introduction to Eleanor Swanscombe, who takes the stand next. The diminutive, rather wiry figure does not correspond with Billy's words; dressed in a grey gown that has seen better days and a pair of mittens without the fingertips. Yet to do her credit, she is not afraid. She folds her arms, as if it is an inconvenience to be present, and gazes about her. Unlike Billy, she does not avoid Ruth's eyes, but stares resolutely at the dock. Unashamed of her betrayal.

I might have written the prosecution's questions with my own hand; they are exactly as I expected them to be. After establishing that Nell entered Metyard's as a girl and knew both Mr Rooker and the late Mrs Rooker as if they were family, the lawyer is careful to mention her kindness to Ruth, her visits at the hospital.

'And what did you consider to be the character of the defendant?'

Nell turns to assess Ruth. 'She was ... an unfortunate young girl. An orphan. It mixed her up, I think, the loss. She was always very jealous and fierce in her moods. At times, I thought she'd do herself a mischief.'

'Did she at any time express animosity towards the victim?'

'She did.'

'And yet she urged you to join her in working for Mrs Rooker?'

'Yes.'

'Did that not seem odd? The defendant's eagerness to work for a woman she disliked?'

'Very odd.'

Succinct, cool. As Ruth described in her story, a strange deadness of tone. As if nothing remains in this world that can surprise or shock Nell.

The prosecution asks if Ruth ever went shopping for groceries, was ever left in the kitchen unsupervised. Nell confirms both. Repeats Billy's assertion that Ruth mixed and carried the cocoa to Mrs Rooker's lips.

'And was there anything about the kitchen that may have been used for this criminal purpose? Rat poison, or the like?'

'This is highly unsuitable for you to hear.' Papa's whisper blares hot, his moustache scratching against my ear. 'You are my daughter, it is my duty to—'

I am focusing so intently upon Nell's pinched lips that I do not distinguish the remnant of his tirade.

'There were … I suppose …' She shifts her feet. 'We had a fly problem. There were always plenty of flypapers in the kitchen.'

'Could you tell me whose responsibility it was to purchase and hang these flypapers?'

'Ruth's.'

I cannot help it. 'Nell, you lying little slut!'

Papa baulks at my side, but no one else has heard my hissed words.

'Come, Dora. I have seen enough.'

No doubt he has. No doubt it is all sounding most familiar.

'One moment more, Papa.'

Nell has served her turn; she is permitted to quit the stand. She unfolds her arms, pulls the shawl up around her shoulders before she steps down. And then I descry it.

A minute, blue flash from beneath the mitten. It lasts for the briefest of moments; few people would even mark it. Her left hand.

Her ring finger.

Everything pulls together, as neatly as one of Ruth's stitches. I see two youths from the Foundling, stood shivering, hand in hand, outside Metyard's dress shop. I see a maid and her master in hurried conversation on the landing of the house in Water Mews.

Not like brother and sister.

Lovers.

My head begins to twirl. Billy is not the duped innocent that I supposed him. He did not purchase that ring with Kate in mind; she was merely its custodian until the true owner could take possession. When he told Ruth he could not leave *her* alone at the shop, he was not speaking of Kate. He was referring to Nell; it was ever Nell. They were in cohorts from the very commencement.

He must have given her the money to stay in the lodging house. Informed her where to locate him in the square on the hanging day. And Nell was weaving her own deceptions, placing Ruth in a position to take the blame for her …

The giddiness that started my morning has intensified; I view the world as one trapped under warped glass. Distantly, the local grocer answers questions.

He has seen both Nell and Ruth in the shop. Never serves himself, has a boy to do it. He starts to explain that there are three-quarters of a grain of arsenic in each flypaper, and these can be extracted by soaking the paper in water.

Papa pulls at my arm. 'Make way, there,' he calls. 'My daughter requires air, she is faint.'

It might be my spinning vision, but it is Papa's face that looks pale to me. He has the demeanour of a man caught in a transgression.

'… a very dangerous substance,' the lawyer is saying.

'Yes, and that's why I make my boys keep a record of the people who purchase it. They have to take down the date, the customer's name and address.'

The judge is referred to the evidence in his possession.

Men tut as they step aside to let us pass, loath to miss an instant. Already, two plump old women have filled our vacated space. Truly, I am ill, yet I do not wish to leave. Who does Ruth have, if not me? There will not be a single soul left in the courthouse to pity her.

The voices come faintly now. 'Can you tell us how many times Eleanor Swanscombe's name appears in that ledger of yours, Mr Nasby?'

'None.'

'And the name of Ruth Butterham?'

I do not hear the answer. Papa hurries me from the public gallery, into the blinding light of day.

His arm shakes under my hand. I smell the fug of his perspiration, creeping through his shirt and jacket.

'That was terrible, Dora!' he rages at me. 'What in the world would possess you to attend a trial of such an ugly nature?'

Judging by the drips of sweat falling from his hatband, I believe that he already knows.

52

Dorothea

They keep the wretches condemned to death in the cells beneath the courthouse. These are not bright and clean like the ones in New Oakgate Prison; they are chambers of crumbling brick and rusted iron. A rat scurries past my foot as I walk with David, causing me to flinch and raise the hem of my skirt.

'Don't worry. He won't hurt you. It's the people here you need to be afraid of.' His voice carries the weight of fatigue. It is not merely the low light that has altered his mien. He stoops his shoulders, shelters his hands inside his pockets. Something has disturbed him.

I do not believe my heart has accommodation for further sorrow; it throbs so painfully on behalf of Ruth. But then the poor dear does look so very dismal. I must offer him some succour.

'Has something unpleasant occurred, David? You appear out of spirits.' He regards me quizzically. 'I do not mean to imply that one should be joyfully animated in our present surroundings, but ...'

'It's London,' he replies heavily. 'My services have been declined.'

It is as if he has shifted a load on to my back. I stagger, am forced to take his arm. 'Oh. Oh, I see.'

'I wasn't going to say anything until you'd spoken with your friend,' he apologises. 'I know you have sorrow enough already'

Indeed I do. But there must be a solution, a way forward for us, if I could only think ... Yet I cannot. These debilitating feelings of giddiness and nausea are getting the better of me. I am losing Ruth. I must forgo all hope of London. Why, that means I shall be at home for the dreaded wedding. A social embarrassment to Papa. Forced to 'play step-daughter' after all ...

I will not allow myself to consider that at present. The time to shed tears shall come later, in private. For now I must sustain Ruth, sustain poor David ... 'I am extremely sorry. It is a blow to us both, my dear.' I apply pressure to his arm with what I hope is a mixture of sympathy and encouragement. 'Especially considering how worthy you are for the position. Did they not give you a reason why?'

He shakes his head. 'It's a rum do. Something has felt ... off kilter. Just this week. The sergeant's watching me more closely than usual. I can't think why he should.'

Is it foolish that I suspect my father of making enquiries, trying to ascertain just what the look that passed between us at the trial concealed?

To own the truth, I find every act of Papa suspicious of late. That maggot in my head ... Rather than taking the carriage to visit Ruth one last time, I actually waited until Papa was out of the house and *walked*, until I could find a cab.

Despite my intention not to give any credence to Sir Thomas, I am behaving as if I believe every one of his words. As if I expect, at any moment, to be poisoned.

'At least you cannot run into trouble for this,' I reassure David. 'Given my connections to the prison, it is natural that I should visit.'

But there is nothing truly natural about this underground warren with the damp floors and ingrained sense of despair. One woman, dirty and missing teeth, clangs at the bars. The rest cower or lie supine, drained, waiting for Death to take them. He is hovering, just out of sight. You can smell him.

Ruth kneels at the corner of her cell, in prayer. I have never seen her in this attitude, or looking so pale.

'I'll come back for you in fifteen minutes,' David says, unlocking the door and administering a secret squeeze to my fingers.

She must hear me come inside, but she waits until she has finished her supplications before opening her eyes and turning her head in my direction. Poor child, she is like a whipped dog.

'Miss! I'm so glad you've come.'

Reserve is at an end between us. For the first time, we approach each other and embrace. Her arms are still strong, around my waist, but already she has taken on the scent of mould and decay.

'You knew, didn't you?' she says sheepishly. 'All along. About the poison?'

'Of course I did. I thought that you knew, too! If only I had explained, if only I could have helped you!'

She blows out her breath. 'I was a dunderhead. A regular dupe. I just kept telling the police I killed her, and didn't bother going into the *how*. I never let them question me properly, or talked to my lawyer the way I should. Because ...' She trails off, gazing somewhere over my shoulder. There is a pause. Then, it is as if she is looking at the world through a new pair of eyes. 'I didn't do it.'

'They must have planned it for years, the pair of them. They always intended to kill Catherine and take her mother's money for their own. Each time he visited the shop and made her cocoa ... You were simply an excuse too good to pass over.' Pain wedges in my throat. 'But they need not have blamed you! From the way you spoke of your mistress at the end, she was depressed in her spirits and full of a strange remorse over her part in her mother's death. Why could they not have claimed suicide?'

I remember the way Ruth watched Billy at the trial. Nell might be wicked, but she is not a stupid woman, nor blind. Perhaps she has had enough of rivals for Billy's affection.

'No,' Ruth says, grasping my hands. 'You don't understand. *I didn't do it!*' A smile breaks over her face. I stare at her, confused. 'The corset was powerless. All that hate and it didn't touch Kate at all, only the poison did.'

'What are you trying to say, dear?'

She bursts into tears, but the smile only grows wider. She is almost pretty, with that smile. 'I never had a power in my sewing, did I? Naomi ... Pa ... It wasn't my fault. None of it was my fault.'

Had I given her the key to her cell and a hundred pounds, she could scarcely look happier. The strain of the past few days must have made her hysterical.

'And yet they are going to hang you all the same. Poor child. Here.' Disentangling my hand from her, I reach into my reticule. 'The constable you just saw is my friend, he did not search me. I have brought you a gift.' The needle winks gold, a tiny drip of sunlight in this dank place. 'Forgive any association with your former work; it is the smallest article I could smuggle. This needle belonged to my mother. Her life was also cut tragically short. I hoped it might comfort you. To have it with you ... at the end.'

Ruth takes it from me solemnly. The gold warms beneath the grip of her fingers. 'Thank you, miss. It will help. Not that I'm as afraid, now.' She looks up from the needle, hopeful. 'I can be saved, can't I? I'm not a killer. I can go to God, and my ma.'

Tears prick my eyes. This is all I ever wanted for her: the chance of salvation. I do not understand why there is a bitter taste in my mouth. 'But are you not angry? I should be furious! Billy and Nell used you; they murdered Kate, and they have got away scot-free!'

She sobers a little, at this. Then she shrugs. 'Once, I would have hated them. Not now. Since I've been speaking to you and the chaplain, I feel ... sorry for them.'

'You cannot! Do you not wish for revenge?'

'I must forgive them, mustn't I? That's the only way I'll get to Heaven. I wish there was something I could give Billy, something I could make him, to show I don't hold a grudge.'

Pondering for a moment, I produce my pocket handkerchief. 'It is clean,' I tell her. 'Although what you will do for thread I cannot ...'

I do not finish my sentence, for she fairly snatches the article from my hand and crosses her legs to sit on the floor of her cell. One by one, she plucks strands of dark hair from her head and slots them through the eye of the needle.

What a strange girl she is. How I shall miss her.

'What are you going to work?'

'An initial in the corner,' she says, 'like Ma's handkerchief had. I'm going to do an R. R for Ruth, R for Rooker. That's both of us together, at peace.'

Billy. So much eagerness to complete this task for him. Not a word of forgiving Nell, being at peace with Nell, who sticks in my mind as the main culprit.

This claws through me more painfully, I believe, than all the rest: she still loves him. The man who sold her to the gallows to protect Nell. I do not want him to have a handkerchief made with her tenderness.

'Do you wish me to attend?' I ask quietly. 'Tomorrow?'

'No, miss. I'd spare you that. It's a horrible sight for you and it's ten to one whether I even set eyes upon you in the crowd. I'll have this needle and I'll know that you're praying for me.'

'Indeed I will be.' These busy, active hands. It does not seem possible that they can hang her. All the spark and wit in Ruth, snuffed out. 'Try not to be afraid, my dear. I know what you saw at Mrs Metyard's execution was … unpleasant, yet these things often look worse than they truly are. You must take courage. Be brave and know that a far better home awaits you.' Even to my own ears it sounds trite, but I can furnish nothing better. What *does* one say at such a pass?

Her fingers do not cease in their motion, but I can tell from the set of her lips that she is picturing it, that day. 'Mrs Metyard's was pretty bad. Especially as she didn't have the hood. To fight for breath like that, feel it leaving you … But it won't last for long, will it? I'll be dead fairly quick. Sometimes, if you jump as the door goes, the rope breaks your neck, just like that.'

She mentioned to me once that her parents used a falsely jovial tone to speak to her, and I think I hear its echo now, in her voice. She may have hope in God, but she is still nervous, pretending a bravery she does not feel.

The black R takes form beneath my gaze, squeezing through and around the white weave of my handkerchief. It is a skilful hand they will stop tomorrow at noon. Out of mere hair it has made this bold letter. A clever device, although I cannot say I like it. Worked in this material, it reminds me of mourning brooches, dead birds.

'You will give it to Billy?' she pleads, placing the finished piece into my hand. I am glad to be wearing my gloves, not to have direct contact with the morbid item. 'Find his house on Water Mews? It's just by the river, the door's green.'

I tuck the little parcel into my reticule, keen to have it out of my grasp. 'I will certainly deliver it, Ruth.'

'And make sure he knows it's from me?'

'I will arrange everything.'

David is coming back. For once, I am not glad to hear his familiar tread. The sound seems to pull Ruth away, each step a bit farther. I stare into her brown eyes with the stubby lashes, set too far apart in her head, for the last time. Her inscrutable skull will take its secrets to the grave with her.

But what about mine?

'God bless you, Ruth. Do not be afraid.'

She grips my glove in her sweaty palm. Tight, as if I could save her from the jaws of death. 'Thank you, miss. For everything.'

The door whines open.

'It's time, Dotty.'

I will not sob. Not until I reach home and may cry, deep into my pillow. I embrace Ruth again, stumble out on to David's waiting arm.

The door closes, the shadows of the bars fall into the cell.

She is so youthful. Dark of complexion, ungainly in stance. Nothing akin to the blonde beauty that was once my mother. Yet as I look back over my shoulder at the figure hunched in her iron cage, I see a similarity between the two.

Frightened eyes, attempting to brave the stare of death. Lithe bodies, summoned, before their time.

I see two women who trusted in the wrong man.

Two women, betrayed.

———

Warily, Wilkie hops to the open door of his cage. He perches on the edge, surveying his surroundings. This is his custom: always check, before taking flight. In this, a mere bird proves himself wiser than the majority of humankind.

The coast is clear. Wilkie jumps, spreads his wings.

I find it helpful to have him flutter about my bedroom as I stare at my reticule, sprawled before me on the desk. Although I am stationary, my thoughts are flying with him, exploring every corner, stretching themselves out.

In the end, it has all come down to this: what do I believe?

Do I put my faith in phrenology? Accept that I cannot escape the contours of my skull, reflected in the dressing-table mirror? For the bumps are still there, despite all my efforts, and the man who was to be my better half has not redeemed me.

Or perhaps I should trust the chaplain's words. The blessed mercy that says *all may be forgiven.* Ruth, for her part, seems to have embraced them. Yet did not the chaplain also tell me that *the wicked must be punished?* I cannot puzzle out which is more important: forgiveness, or justice. I cannot have both.

Two yellow feathers fall from Wilkie's tail. I watch them drift to the floor. They might be my choice, laid out in allegory.

Once, I would not have hesitated. But it seems to me that I have absorbed Ruth, along with her tale; I hear her voice, beside my own. Not the pitiful whine from yesterday, in the condemned cells; it is the strong, measured cadence of hate inside my ear.

There, again: what do I believe? That the circle of death surrounding Ruth was all mere coincidence? Every death has a rational explanation but, strange as it sounds, I cannot dismiss the notion that there *is* something unearthly about that girl. A power science cannot explain.

I made her speak of hanging, did I not, while she worked at the handkerchief? Suppose she does not forgive Billy Rooker after all? This creation of cotton and hair does not resemble a gift in my eyes. It is a memento mori.

I take a sheet of brown paper from inside my desk and tip the handkerchief out of my reticule, into the centre of it. The musk of the condemned cells mingles with bergamot oil, rising in wisps of confused scent. Careful not to sully the fabric with my touch, I wrap the handkerchief up, securing it in a parcel with string. Although it is covered, I can still see that R etched on to the back of my eyelids. Raven black.

My hands are trembling. White lines mark the pinks of my fingernails. Time has elapsed since the trial, but nausea is still crouched in my stomach, stirring up trouble, waiting to pounce. Perhaps it is the strain of the last few weeks taking its toll upon my body. Or an infection, picked up from my visits to the poor and unfortunate.

Perhaps I am going the way of my mother.

With a clatter of claws, Wilkie perches on the desk beside me. His inky eyes are fathomless. 'And you, sir?' I ask him. 'What is your opinion?'

Of course, he does not answer, but something inside of me does. I am no fool. I have lied to myself for long enough. Deep down, I have always known what I believe. What I must do.

I must deliver the handkerchief.

The clock strikes eleven when I arrive, giddy, at his door. Nothing but silence lies within. Nervously, I clutch the package in one hand and raise the other to knock. My strong *rap* suggests a confidence I do not feel.

What shall I say? Will the words come to my aid? Maybe I cannot see it through – but I must, I *must*, for her.

I wait. It is a few moments before my heart stops pounding in my ears, affording me the opportunity to listen for approaching footsteps or handles being turned. There is nothing.

Perhaps he did not hear. I knock again, louder this time.

The hush is so profound, it is almost painful.

To tell the truth, I am relieved. Everything will be much easier without having to face him. Scribbling a note with his name at the top, I wedge it beneath the string on the package and leave it at the foot of the door. It is quite secure; there is no wind to blow it about or snatch the note away. Another person may steal it, I suppose, but that is a risk I shall have to take.

By the time I am back in the safety of my own room, Wilkie has voluntarily re-entered his cage. I shut the door upon him, but I am the one that feels restless, trapped. Time moves by with the speed of a slug.

These will be Ruth's last moments upon earth. The seconds that pass so slowly for me shall fly all too quick for her. Or perhaps she does not mind if they race along, towards noon. Perhaps she only longs for it all to be over.

Downstairs, Papa returns to the house. I hear him speak to the footman, hand over his gloves and hat. He has been visiting Mrs Pearce. His steps stride towards his library – once, he would have come straight upstairs to see me, but these days I do not expect it.

Just fifteen minutes to go.

Did Billy and Nell venture out to watch poor Ruth die? I should have thought of that possibility. They will not be in the house at Water Mews but in the square, jostling for the best view of the scaffold. Wicked poisoners, the most cowardly of all murderers, watching the punishment that should have been their own.

The clock chimes. Noon.

I fall to my knees, clasp my hands and pray. I pray with a ferocity I never felt before, picturing her poor, dying face. Four bells. Five. Ruth on the end of a rope, gagging. Seven bells.

The image in my mind is achingly clear. Between the chimes I can practically hear her, choking for air.

No.

I hear *him*.

As I rise to my feet, I catch a glimpse of my reflection in the mirror and it is smiling. At last I have placed my faith in the correct quarter. Ruth.

Ruth always told me the truth.

I take the combs from my hair. The bumps above my ears, the centre of Murder, are more pronounced than ever. No need to hide or deny them any longer. My destiny is finally played out.

I open my door.

Servants rush through the corridors. Tilda stands at the head of the stairs, wringing her hands.

'What is it?' I ask. 'Is Papa unwell?'

She bursts into tears.

Leisurely, I descend the steps, follow the footmen to the library. They do not notice me in their haste.

'A physician!' Granger calls. 'Run for a physician.'

Papa is slumped in his chair. They have pulled him back from the desk, tilted his head up, tried to loosen his cravat and collar. Useless. Red burn marks circle his neck. Blood vessels have burst beneath his skin and in his eyes; he is a curious shade of grey-blue.

'Good heavens!' I cry. 'However can this be? He looks as if he were hanged!'

On the desk, the brown paper parcel lies open. Ruth's handkerchief is still clutched in his rigid hand. A corner flaps over his fingers; I see it in flashes as the servants bustle around him.

Woven in black hair, the letter R.

Acknowledgements

I have been blessed with a wonderful team to help me create *The Corset*: my agent, Juliet Mushens; editors Alison Hennessey and Marigold Atkey, not forgetting their lovely assistants Callum Kenny and Lilidh Kendrick; David Mann in design; Janet Aspey in marketing and Philippa Cotton in publicity; plus a raft of hardworking copyeditors, proof-readers and behind-the-scenes magicians at Bloomsbury Raven. Thank you all, none of this would be possible without you.

On the personal front, a huge round of applause to my family and friends for supporting me through another year of author neurosis, in particular my husband Kevin, who always rescues me from the coal hole. Special thanks go to Louise Denyer for naming Wilkie the canary in a suitably Victorian manner.

I would like to give a mention to Jennifer Rosbrugh, whose online historical sewing class provided me with the theoretical knowledge of how to make a corded corset, even though I wasn't brave enough to try the practical side! Also to Alison Matthews David for including a wealth of useful information in her wonderful book *Fashion Victims*, including the real life inspiration for what happened to Rosalind Oldacre.

Dorothea's particular brand of phrenology is based on *The Self-Instructor in Phrenology and Physiology* by O.S. and L.N. Fowler, with elements of *Vaught's Practical Character Reader.* An excellent overview of the subject can be found at http://www.historyofphrenology.org.uk/

Finally, I would ask you to spare a thought for thirteen-year-old milliner's apprentice Ann Nailor, whose real death in 1758 at the hands of a mother and daughter both named Sarah Metyard inspired Miriam's story. Details of her case are on record in the Proceedings of the Old Bailey.

A Note on the Author

Laura Purcell is a former bookseller. She lives in Colchester with her husband and guinea pigs. Her first novel for Bloomsbury, *The Silent Companions*, was a Radio 2 Book Club pick and Goldsboro Book of the Month.

laurapurcell.com

@spookypurcell

A Note on the Type

The text of this book is set in Linotype Stempel Garamond, a version of Garamond adapted and first used by the Stempel foundry in 1924. It is one of several versions of Garamond based on the designs of Claude Garamond. It is thought that Garamond based his font on Bembo, cut in 1495 by Francesco Griffo in collaboration with the Italian printer Aldus Manutius. Garamond types were first used in books printed in Paris around 1532. Many of the present-day versions of this type are based on the *Typi Academiae* of Jean Jannon cut in Sedan in 1615.

Claude Garamond was born in Paris in 1480. He learned how to cut type from his father and by the age of fifteen he was able to fashion steel punches the size of a pica with great precision. At the age of sixty he was commissioned by King Francis I to design a Greek alphabet, and for this he was given the honourable title of royal type founder. He died in 1561.